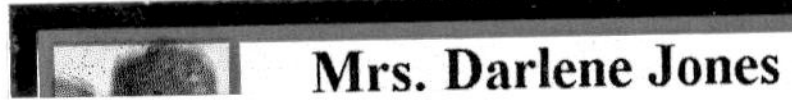
Mrs. Darlene Jones

MW01166300

The McNaughton Rule

Enjoy!

Mary Dieter and Tim McClure

AuthorHouse™
1663 Liberty Drive
Bloomington, IN 47403
www.authorhouse.com
Phone: 1-800-839-8640

First published by AuthorHouse 8/12/2009

ISBN: 978-1-4490-1447-6 (e)
ISBN: 978-1-4490-1446-9 (sc)

Printed in the United States of America
Bloomington, Indiana

This book is printed on acid-free paper.

For our angel, Amelia

CHAPTER 1

"Thirty-four, thirty-eight: multiple ten-zeroes at 3540 North Ellison."

Despite the static of his radio, Jack McNaughton, car number 3438, caught that he was needed – apparently desperately – at Indianapolis's latest crime scene. He swallowed hard: multiple homicides, bad enough. But quite unexpected in such a nice, middle-class neighborhood on the city's near north side. The one-and-a-half-story houses were about fifty years old and generally populated by blue-collar working families that pulled down a decent, if not extravagant, wage. He dodged the visor that shielded his eyes from the bright mid-April sun to look for house numbers, then spotted two police cruisers about a block ahead. He pulled his black, unmarked Ford up to the curb, carelessly scraping tires against concrete while his mind focused on what lay ahead. He glanced back to be sure that another fast-moving cop car wouldn't take his door off, then hopped out of the car into the sunlight, pulling on his jacket and straightening its collar. He broke into a jog up the broken concrete walk, an obstacle course of jagged chunks, and dodged a pastel plastic tricycle that had been left, tipped over, just off the edge.

He was greeted with the retching sound of somebody vomiting. He saw the uniform, bent over and tossing his lunch all over the front yard. When the black-haired beat cop straightened up and turned back around, his face was ashen, his eyes red. Jack realized the guy had been crying.

"Sergeant McNaughton," another uniform said from the front porch. His voice had a slight quiver to it. It was Jimmy Davis, a young cop with about three years on the department. His face was contorted into a grimace. "We've got six dead – all *kids.* Looks like they've been beaten. We don't know how old or what sex yet. Uh, you can't really tell. But they're young."

Davis's somber voice betrayed his distress. McNaughton's heart sank; the worst part of being a cop was when the victim was a child. But *six* of them? And *beaten*? He tentatively entered the front door, followed by the young officer. McNaughton wiped his feet on the dingy floor mat and stepped further into the hardwood-floored foyer.

Davis, who had managed to keep his lunch down, slipped past McNaughton and waved his hand to signal the sergeant to follow. To the left of the foyer, on the south side of the house, was the living room, darkened from the bright sun by drawn curtains. To the right was an equally dark staircase lined with textured wallpaper that was yellowed and peeling at the corners. The two officers mounted the hardwood steps, which were lined up the middle with an ancient avocado green runner. They reached a landing, and Jack startled when he caught his own stark image in the big, dusty mirror on the wall. Beneath it was a single, enormous, smeared handprint that appeared to be made of dried blood. It was illuminated eerily by a sunbeam that pierced through some unseen window, causing lazily floating dust particles to sparkle like brilliant jewels. Jack's sense of apprehension grew heavier with each step.

Davis topped the stairs and slowly walked straight ahead into a darkened room. What little light seeped in from the outside came from an easterly window in the room. McNaughton followed, stepping over the threshold to see a large dormitory-like bedroom converted from storage space. The walls were straight for four feet or so off the floor, then bent at a forty-five-degree angle to follow the roof line. Jack noticed a stuffed bear lying on the floor. It was identical to one Angelica had, with the bright green satin ribbon tied around its neck, except that it was streaked with what appeared to be blood.

Four twin beds were lined against the long wall. Plump down comforters were pulled up, preventing the occupants from being seen from the doorway. Jack moved closer, and blinked in disbelief.

In each bed lay a small, motionless body, dressed in blood-covered pajamas. The once-white pillows now were soaked in blood, and the tiny heads that had snuggled into them twelve hours earlier had been shattered. McNaughton turned away and gagged; his stomach churned, but he willed himself not to vomit. He had seen a lot during ten years in homicide, but this was the worst he had ever seen. He took a deep breath to fortify himself and turned back for another look. With the steely professionalism required of a homicide detective, McNaughton took in the long, matted hair on one victim and spied patches of matching pink-flowered pajamas on two others. All girls, he surmised. It was impossible to say, but a couple of them had to be near Angelica's age – four. One was clearly much younger; the bottoms of her pajamas bulged out from the underlying diaper. McNaughton looked at the yellow walls, which appeared as if some half-crazed Pollack imitator had splashed deep red paint in a frenzied moment of artistic inspiration. Some inspiration, McNaughton thought. Somebody was inspired to beat the brains out of four little girls.

Davis tapped McNaughton on the upper arm and, without saying a word, gestured with his head to indicate that the detective sergeant should follow. Jack swallowed hard and did so. They crossed the hallway, bypassing what looked like the master bedroom in the southwest corner of the house, with a tidy double bed perfectly made with a white nubby Washington-style bedspread. A small sewing room was next to it, on the west side of the house and directly across from the landing. They headed for the last bedroom, in the northwest corner. Two more twin beds with two more tiny victims. This was the boys' room, decorated with the smiling faces of basketball stars. McNaughton briefly wondered what the boys' smiles might have been like. Between the beds was the corpse of a dog, a little mutt that had met the same fate as its former playmates. The men turned, walked out of the room and headed down the stairs to the living room.

"We got a call from a woman, the kids' mother, who asked us to come and check on her kids," Davis said. "She said that she was away on business and that her husband called her at her hotel and said that he had killed the kids and that he was going to go kill himself too. We found this family photo on the mantle in the living room," he said, passing a ten-by-thirteen framed photo to McNaughton. "We think it's pretty recent, because the kids' ages seem to fit. It gives us an idea what everybody in the family looks like – or used to."

McNaughton studied the children, taking in their beauty and innocence and momentarily allowing himself to think about his Angel. But he pushed his personal life from his mind, just as all cops must do under such circumstances, and his gaze became transfixed on their father, a behemoth whose ham-sized hands were around the scrawny shoulders of two of his offspring. His face was smooth and his cheeks were so puffy that they reduced his eyes to slits. He smiled broadly, revealing a gap between his front teeth, which were stained, McNaughton figured, by years of drinking coffee and perhaps smoking cigarettes. He looked like the proud patriarch of his brood, six children who likely were born in the space of just eight or nine years. Behind him stood a woman – the worried wife and mother, of course. She was much smaller than him, almost absurdly so. They looked like a circus mismatch. Her hand rested tentatively on her husband's shoulder, as if she weren't sure she wanted it there; her smile seemed forced. Was this photo of an allegedly happy family taken to throw people off the scent of an unhappy marriage? Or was he just imagining the look of discomfort in her eyes? Perhaps something had just happened to cause a rift – but what could possibly have gone so wrong for a father to kill his own flesh and blood?

McNaughton's eyes returned to the children. They resembled one another; there was no sign that any of them had a different parent. So the trouble likely had started in the last few years, sometime after the last baby, who appeared to be about two, had been conceived. The children's smiles were radiant; was that, Jack wondered, because they were genuinely happy, unaware of their parents' troubles, or were they merely resilient, as children were wont to be? His thoughts were interrupted by the uniformed cop who had puked up his guts. He seemed to have recovered physically, but his face was grim and his eyes were squinted in pain. He bore the stale odor of vomit.

"Sergeant McNaughton, there's a call for you," he said, his voice barely audible. For a moment, Jack wondered why the call hadn't come in on his cell. But he turned and saw the receiver off the phone on a telephone table, and he reached to pick it up. The voice was a woman's; she was frantic. "How are my children?" she screeched. "This is Barbara Peterson. How are my children?"

"Mrs. Peterson," Jack began, "this is Sergeant McNaughton of Metro Police. Is there anyone there with you?"

"No. Please. Just tell me: How are my babies?"

"Mrs. Peterson, I think it might be best if I come to you. Where are you?"

"No. Tell me. *Please.*"

He thought for a moment, and then began. "I'm very sorry to tell you, ma'am, but . . ." His voice trailed off as he heard the woman at the other end of the line break down in deep, guttural sobs.

"No, no, no, no!" she moaned. "Not my babies. Not my babies." She paused a moment, sobbing heavily, then catching her breath.

"Is he dead? Is *he* dead?" she screamed.

"Your husband, ma'am? We don't know," McNaughton said. "Do you have any idea where he might have gone?"

"That *coward!*" she screamed. "That's *just* like him! Hurting the children but chickening out before he ended his own miserable life!" She was crying uncontrollably now, but Jack needed to know more.

"Mrs. Peterson, we're concerned that your husband may have, uh, hurt himself." She interrupted him.

"We could only hope! But he's a *coward*, I told you," she shouted. "Why couldn't he have killed *himself* – or even *me* – but let the children be?"

"Mrs. Peterson," Jack tried again, "where might we find your husband? And *why* do you think he would have done this?"

She took a deep breath, audible even over the crackly telephone line. "First tell me the truth," she said. "Did he smother them? He used to hold the pillow over their heads when they were sleeping, telling me that's what he was going to do if I didn't do what he wanted. Did he smother them?"

"Ah, no, ma'am," he said.

"Well, *what* then?" she begged. "Surely he didn't . . ."

"The coroner will have to rule on this, ma'am, but it appears that they were bludgeoned."

Mrs. Peterson started screaming, and then the phone went dead.

There was far more work than just one detective could perform – the young uniforms couldn't do much to help – so McNaughton called downtown homicide. None of his squad members picked up – everybody must been out on cases – so he zeroed out and asked the operator to patch him through to Lieutenant Doyle C. Stumbo, his immediate supervisor at downtown homicide and a royal pain in the ass.

"Do you really need somebody? We're really short-handed," Stumbo drawled. He kept sucking on the toothpick that was ever-present in his mouth. The phone line seemed to amplify the smacking.

"For God's sake, Doyle, I've got *six dead kids,*" McNaughton said angrily. "I need you to track down some of my people and get them out here." This was *so* typical, he thought. If Stumbo can make it difficult, he will. And what the hell was the city paying cops to do – sit at desks and file reports, or investigate homicides? He should have been used to it by now, but Stumbo always had the ability to make him crazy.

"Well, it's gonna cost me a lot of overtime," Stumbo said, "but if you can't handle this alone, I guess I'll have to send somebody."

McNaughton bit his tongue. The asshole. Naturally he'd try to make it seem as if Jack were incompetent. The truth was that Stumbo couldn't stand that Jack was good at his job – much better than Stumbo was at his – and they both knew that McNaughton was the likely successor when their mutual boss retired in another year. The situation had rendered a once-cordial relationship into jealousy and professional friction. McNaughton lamented that two people who had gotten along, despite their differences, when they were beat cops could barely be in one room together anymore.

McNaughton, ever the professional, shook off the exchange. It suddenly occurred to him that the father might want to harm his wife – finish off what he had started – before killing himself, so he hustled back into the house. Davis, who had just completed Jack's first assignment – to call in evidence technicians, a photographer and the coroner's office – was just hanging up his cell phone.

"Jimmy, did Mrs. Peterson say where she was calling from?" McNaughton's voice was tense; all of a sudden, the focus had shifted from solving six homicides to possibly preventing one.

"We know she's in Chicago, sarge," Davis said, "but we don't know where she's staying. They don't have caller ID."

"Look around – start with the desk but look anywhere else that seems logical – to find something that would show the name of her company. A pay stub or something. And call them to find out where we can find her," McNaughton said. "As soon as you get any ideas, let me know. We've got to get a hold of her."

McNaughton went back to the telephone and punched in star-six-nine, hoping it would ring back the number from which Mrs. Peterson had called. It was picked up after the second ring.

"Stumbo."

"Doyle." McNaughton's voice was sullen.

"Now what do you want, McNaughton?" He always stretched out Jack's surname.

"Nothing, Doyle. I used star-six-nine to dial back. Why'd you call here – the Peterson house?"

"I was looking for you."

"We just spoke. And besides, why didn't you call me on my cell?"

"Well, obviously it was before we talked. You hadn't called, so I went looking for you. All I got was those people's answering machine. You know, I've talked to you before about improving your communications."

McNaughton refused to take it on. "I've been available by radio or cell phone all morning, Doyle." His voice barely concealed his contempt.

"Well, whaddya want?"

"Never mind." McNaughton hung up the phone before Stumbo could give him any more grief. In the few moments since Mrs. Peterson's call, Stumbo had managed to wipe out Mrs. Peterson's number. Jack knew it wasn't fair to hold him responsible for that; it was just an unfortunate coincidence. But Stumbo couldn't be bothered to use the radio, and he considered cell phones too modern to understand, so it was hard for McNaughton not to blame him.

It occurred to McNaughton that Peterson wouldn't have stopped to get his wallet before heading out the door, so Jack dashed upstairs to the master bedroom. He found a worn black leather billfold atop the clutter in the top drawer of the bureau. John Pius Peterson was six-foot-five and two hundred sixty pounds, according to his driver's license. It had been renewed two years earlier; he could be even bigger now. It would take someone of that enormous size to have inflicted so much damage on the kids, McNaughton thought.

Back downstairs, McNaughton used his cell phone to call dispatch to provide a preliminary description based on the driver's license: White male, DOB 4-24-64. Peterson was about to turn forty. Brown over brown. Dispatch transferred him to Ident, which ran Peterson's license plate number, providing McNaughton with a description of the family's vehicles but, more important, a Social Security number and his criminal history. Peterson had a couple of old drunk-and-disorderly convictions and an arrest a couple years earlier for assault that was subsequently dismissed – nothing that would suggest that things could go so horribly wrong.

Both of the Petersons' cars – a blue 1996 Chevrolet minivan and a black 2000 Volkswagen Jetta – were registered in the husband's name, so only his Social Security number appeared on the paperwork. He asked Ident to try to come up with the wife's Social Security number by doing some cross-checking. He wanted to see if she had a criminal history too.

"Davis? Any luck on a pay stub yet?" McNaughton knew the Social Security number would be on that.

"Not yet, sarge. These people aren't exactly meticulous in their filing system."

Jack would have bet that Mrs. Peterson would be driving the Jetta, a small compact, in Chicago and that Peterson would fit better in the van. Neither car was in the driveway; he dashed out back to check the detached garage, but saw only yard equipment and toys through its filthy, web-covered window. He walked back to the house as he called dispatch again to update the description, and he mentioned that Peterson could be driving either of the vehicles. He finished the conversation and looked up to see Mitch Simons and Kit Alvear, two of his best detectives, walking hesitantly through the front door. The uniform who had lost his lunch had written down their names and badge numbers and noted the time they arrived, as McNaughton had ordered. Jack was pleasantly surprised that Stumbo hadn't tried to sabotage him by sending some of the less competent detectives.

"Geez, how'd I luck into getting you two?" McNaughton asked. "Where's Allen?"

"That's exactly what Jumbo Stumbo wanted to know," Simons said. "He acted kind of pissed when I told him that Allen was at the dentist and wasn't due in 'til this afternoon. So he sent us."

It wasn't that Chris Allen was so bad; he was just *so* green. And McNaughton didn't feel like breaking in some rookie detective on a multiple homicide, even if there didn't seem to be much of a mystery as to who the perpetrator was. McNaughton didn't want *anything* to go wrong on this case; he wanted this sick bastard to be put away for a long, long time. Simons and Alvear had fifteen years of homicide work between them, and McNaughton rarely had to tell them to do anything. They respected his experience and conviction rate enough, however, to bounce ideas off of him and ask his advice, especially when they hit dead ends. Simons, a good-looking guy on whom a long line of division secretaries and not a few female cops had developed crushes, was thirty-two, self-possessed and cocky. Alvear, a year older, had been toughened by having to fight the bureaucracy, as well as sexism, on her way to the homicide division. Her appearance – petite and feminine – belied her experiences, and she wouldn't take shit off of anybody, including Simons, who had learned years earlier that she was not taken by his charms. Simons, for his part, had claimed that it was his obligation to hit on her, lest she get her feelings hurt. That explanation alone was a constant source of banter between the two, but it was always good-natured. The fact was Alvear and Simons were a great team – always cooperative, ever capable of anticipating the other's thoughts and actions. McNaughton was thrilled when, shortly after his promotion, they were assigned to his command, but he didn't let Stumbo know the extent of his delight.

Simons and Alvear had seen just about everything, but Jack warned them to brace themselves anyway. Alvear did not have children of her own, but she was passionate about her seven nieces and nephews. Cases with kids particularly got to her. Simons, on the other hand, found humor in everything. "This seems to be a little extreme just to get out of babysitting duty," he said irreverently. Alvear slugged him in the solar plexus.

"Ow," he howled, unhurt.

"Shut up, or I'll really hit you next time," Alvear said. "This is serious, you asshole." Her tone told him she was in no mood for goofing around, and he heeded the command.

They followed as McNaughton, leading them upstairs to view the crime scene, briefed them on what apparently had occurred. They went to the girls' room first. The blood drained from both of their faces as they viewed the carnage. Alvear got mad, and even Simons was rendered silent.

"Good God! This is insane! What the hell could have provoked this?" she asked.

"That's what we've gotta find out," Simons said, his usual jocularity drained by the sight.

McNaughton divided up the duties: Kit and Mitch should go talk to the neighbors to find out what they might have seen or heard. That might provide some insight into the parents' relationship with each other and with the kids. McNaughton had little reason to doubt Mrs. Peterson's accusations that her husband had killed the children, and he couldn't believe that a mother could ever commit such a sickening crime, but he wanted to be thorough. The person who did this, he thought, *cannot* get away with it because of some oversight or technicality.

The evidence technicians and a department photographer had arrived in a crime-scene van while McNaughton was talking with his detectives, and Davis pointed them to the crime scene. Jack took a moment away from his detectives to draw their attention to the handprint on the staircase wall; even the greenest rookie wouldn't miss the rest of the evidence upstairs. Harry Hiroshima, a deputy coroner who was a trained forensic pathologist, arrived shortly thereafter. He was a compact man of Asian descent who wore thick, large-framed spectacles that made him look studious; the appearance fit his top-notch ability. McNaughton was glad to see that the elected coroner, a self-important pediatrician who had persuaded the voters that his medical training somehow made him equipped for the job, wasn't tagging along. Not yet, anyway. Jack knew that his tolerance for a politician's grandstanding would be in short supply today.

Alvear squinted in the sun as she knocked on a few doors, but she didn't have much luck. She found just one neighbor home – an elderly woman who lived two doors down – and the woman could barely hear Kit's questions, much less anything from behind her neighbor's closed doors. Alvear stopped back in at 3540.

"Jack, I'm going across the street to find Mitch, unless there's something else you need from me first."

Before he could answer, Davis bounded into the room. "Sarge, I've got a pay stub. She works for Pendleton Manufacturing."

"Great, Jimmy. Thanks," McNaughton said. Then he turned to Alvear. "Kit, call Pendleton and find out where Mrs. Peterson is. See if you can get her on the line, and keep her there. Jimmy here will stand by to call the local police – I don't know if she's in Chicago P.D.'s jurisdiction or one of the suburbs' – to get somebody over there with her. She may need medical attention for shock. Jimmy, you call Ident with her Social Security number and see what kind of a criminal history they've got on her."

Alvear began making calls. Davis called Ident and found out that Mrs. Peterson had no criminal history. That didn't entirely put her in the clear, but she wasn't a very good suspect to begin with.

By now, reporters from every media outlet in the city had gathered in the warm sun outside the dank bungalow, and Jack knew that, as senior officer on the scene, he couldn't put them off any longer. It was getting too close to the noon news program, and he knew that he was in for an earful from the television reporters if they didn't have something to go with. A couple of the stations had equipment capable of handling a live remote shot, but the others would have to get something on tape and then return to their studios. Jack didn't want them making something up to appease their bosses, so he ventured outside, and the frantic pack rushed up the sidewalk toward him, microphones outstretched and cameras perched on their operators' shoulders.

Unlike a lot of his colleagues, Jack wasn't immediately put off by this. He had been married to a reporter for nine years now, and Renee had told him how much she and her colleagues hate to work in packs, but sometimes – when the news is big enough – there's no avoiding it. Everything on this story – and it *was* a big one – was emanating from one place, the Peterson house, and from one source, McNaughton. He had known several of the reporters from previous homicide scenes, and he knew they weren't as obnoxious as the TV dramas made them seem. "Jack, what the hell is going on?" asked Myra Spricker, a colleague of Renee's at the Sun. Myra, who wore her thick, red hair in long, cascading waves that drove men wild, knew Jack from newspaper parties as well as murder scenes, and she was Jack's favorite cop-shop reporter – indeed, next to Renee, his favorite reporter, period.

Jack ran down the gruesome facts for them, and then answered questions. It was just too early in the investigation, he told them, to be of much help. Alvear was still trying to run Mrs. Peterson down by phone. Without her help, they didn't even have the kids' names and dates of birth. With so much else to do, McNaughton didn't want to waste precious investigative time searching for school documents or birth certificates that would provide such basic information. But he told the sad news that there were six little victims, as well as the family dog, that the parents were not at home and neither could be located.

"Do you have a suspect?" a television reporter shouted belligerently.

"I wouldn't characterize anybody as a suspect yet," McNaughton said. "We have to talk with the parents first and try to get this straight in our own minds."

"Sergeant, did the mother or the father do it – or did they work together?" another asked. "Or is there a crazed serial killer on the loose?"

"I'm not being coy with you," Jack said. "We *do* know that we have to talk with the parents, and as soon as we have anything solid, I'll be back out here to tell you about it. OK? Meanwhile, let's not incite the public with wild speculation."

McNaughton was careful to not repeat the reporter's words about a serial killer. Videotape could be edited to make it sound as if that were a possibility – and the last thing he needed was a panicked public. Privately, McNaughton considered the father the suspect, and he was directing the investigation with that in mind. But it wasn't official yet, and he couldn't yet say publicly that the police were working on the assumption that the father had done it. If the father knew he was the suspect, he might think he had nothing to lose – and he might go after his wife or flee the area or take his own life. For that matter, he might take it out on strangers, and Jack didn't want any more of a bloodbath than had already occurred.

Within the hour, Stumbo witnessed Jack's impromptu news conference on the noon news. One station cut away from Jack to catch a young uniformed officer dabbing his teary eyes; that infuriated Stumbo, who made a mental note to reprimand the officer for appearing weak and to write a memo ordering police officers not to cry. He was further agitated when he saw the interview McNaughton gave the newsies. It was clear that he wasn't handling this properly, Stumbo thought, so he'd better get out there and take charge of the scene. Stumbo wouldn't admit it to himself, but he couldn't stand McNaughton getting so much attention. He was the homicide unit's commander, so he figured he ought to be getting all that air time. Wouldn't his mother be thrilled? So the glacier pushed himself up from his lopsided, broken-down chair and waddled out to his car – a brand new, hot red Mustang that should have been assigned to an undercover cop but that Stumbo managed to bully out of the garage manager. He squeezed behind the steering wheel and stretched his arm to its fullest extent; he could merely touch, but not grasp, the steering wheel, so far back had he pushed the seat to accommodate his girth. He pushed the air-conditioning control to its highest position and pulled out of the parking lot. Stumbo wasn't sure how to get to North Ellison Street, but it was a nice afternoon for a drive, and he didn't mind making a few wrong turns.

Then it occurred to him that Jack might be talking to the newsies again. He radioed to dispatch, where a patient dispatcher gave him directions to the scene three times. Stumbo had always had trouble listening. When he finally arrived, he used his hands to lift his left leg out of the car and then lumbered around to pull the right one out too. He grabbed on to the frame to pull himself upright and then glanced about sheepishly to make sure that no one had witnessed that humiliating spectacle. Nobody cared. The reporters were talking among themselves, sipping the iced tea that the hard-of-hearing neighbor, Mrs. Parsons, had brought out to them on this unseasonably warm afternoon after she realized, from watching the noon news, that something was happening in her neighborhood. She hadn't even heard the early sirens and she hadn't put two and two together from Kit's visit. A few of the reporters tried to interview her by shouting questions, and she scolded them for being rude. She hadn't known the family well but, for TV reporters, any talking head was better than none.

Stumbo began to push his way past the pack, and then thought better of it."Uh, excuse me, folks," he said officiously. "I am Lieutenant Doyle C. Stumbo, commander of the downtown homicide division. If you'll just give me a few minutes to get the scene under control, I will come back out here and answer all of your questions."

"Lieutenant, lieutenant," a bubble-headed blonde from WMAT called out. "Can't you give us just a little something?" Her voice was flirtatious, causing the more veteran print reporters to roll their eyes. Stumbo was thrilled; he'd hooked one.

"As I said, I am here to take control of this scene. That is my first duty. But I know I have a duty to you folks and to the public at large, so I will return shortly with," he said, his face blossoming into a goofy smile and his eyes squinting, "the scoop, as you all say." He beamed broadly, proud of his cleverness, then turned his back, ignoring the flirtatious woman's further pleading, and labored up the front steps – hoping no one would notice that he had to breathe hard to do so.

Jack was hanging up the phone when he looked up and saw the mountain moving toward him. He closed his eyes slowly and took a deep breath. "Oh shit," Jack muttered quietly. "Just what I need."

"Uh, Jack," Stumbo's dull voice intoned, "I saw you on the television and thought you might need some help with them newsies."

"That's OK, Doyle. Everything's under control. They understand that I've given them all I can right now and that we've got some stuff to do before we can give them any more." Jack was in no mood to deal with Doyle. "You can go back to the office now. " He recognized a moment too late that his voice may have sounded too eager.

"Thanks for making me feel so welcome," Stumbo said, chuckling at his bitter little slam. "I thought that someone with some rank ought to handle this matter. I'm not sure that you can think straight enough to handle this investigation and talk to the newsies. You didn't look so hot on the television."

"I think I'm capable of giving reporters information about a case I'm working, Doyle," Jack said. He was barely able to mask his exasperation. "But fine – you talk to the reporters. Just don't screw up my investigation."

"I hardly think it's necessary to get huffy," Stumbo said huffily. "We're all on the same side, Jack."

McNaughton couldn't stand it when Stumbo got self-righteous. But he had neither the time nor the inclination to argue with him. He watched in silence as Stumbo tried to interrupt Alvear's phone calls to ask her about the case, but she dismissed him off with a wave of her hand and a look of disdain.

She pressed down the "end" button and began punching in another number, but Stumbo wouldn't let her get away that quickly. "Detective Alvear," he said lazily, his voice like the lowing of cows, "I want you to brief me on this case so I can tell the newsies what's going on."

"Lieutenant, I've barely begun my work," she said. "Jack – uh, Sergeant McNaughton – has been here the longest, other than the uniforms, so you'll have to get the lowdown from him." She knew that Stumbo, too dull to be interested in important matters, was a stickler for protocol. As a detective, she was to refer to her superiors by their ranks, not their first names.

Frustrated but undaunted, Stumbo lumbered over to Davis and to the uniform who had lost his lunch. He wasn't about to give McNaughton the satisfaction of briefing him – even if Jack had been willing to give him the time. The uniforms told him what they could, but since the detectives' arrival, their roles had been reduced to standing sentry at the front door, a task that, under the horrific circumstances, suited them just fine.

"Well, if nobody can tell me anything, I'll just gather my own information," Stumbo drawled, to nobody in particular. He stuck his toothpick back into his mouth and began what would be a long journey up the stairs for a man of his heft. He took a rest on the landing, leaning over and bracing himself with one hand on the banister, the other on his gigantic knee. He panted, trying to catch his breath after his huge exertion. Still breathing hard, but self-consciously aware that somebody might see him in that condition, he gulped another breath and began the rest of the journey.

McNaughton, who had gone upstairs to check on the evidence technicians, saw him coming. "Doyle, I wish you'd stay downstairs. We've got enough people up here as is; I don't want to risk messing up any evidence."

Stumbo knew better than to insist that Jack calls him "Lieutenant." They'd known each other too long. "Now, Jack, don't you think I've been a police officer long enough to know not to get in the way of an investigation?"

Jack didn't say what he was thinking; he figured it'd just get him in trouble. "Doyle, we just have to be real careful. There is not a square inch in either of the kids' bedrooms that doesn't have to be gone over for evidence; just the presence of the first uniforms on the scene may have disturbed something. *Please* don't disturb anything else."

"For God's sake, Jack. I think I'm a better cop than that."

But Stumbo had never even been a detective, and certainly hadn't handled any homicide investigations. He had gone from being a traffic cop to the commander of the downtown division of homicide detectives through a screw-up that occurred when the old Indianapolis Police Department merged with the Marion County Police to form the Metropolitan-Marion Police Department. The mistake was eventually caught, but by then it would have been an administrative nightmare to try to remove Stumbo from his position. That, and the powers that be feared he would file a lawsuit. So they wimped out and left him to plague the lives of every homicide detective in the downtown division – that is, every detective good enough and strong enough and ambitious enough to seek a transfer to the most active homicide division, where the deaths were gory and confounding and plentiful. It was well known that those who wanted an easier time of it would generally transfer to the outlying divisions, where the killings were less frequent and less mystifying. Everybody waited for the day when a lieutenant's job would open up in one of those four spots; at least if they transferred Stumbo there, he could do less damage. But when a spot did finally open, he refused to put in for it. "This is the premier spot for a homicide commander," he told McNaughton at the time. "Why would I want to transfer out?"

Alvear went to the bottom of the staircase to shout to McNaughton. "Jack, I think we've found her." McNaughton started down the stairs, but turned first to Stumbo. "Doyle, it's pretty gruesome in there. Maybe you should skip it."

"Now Jack, just what do you think I am? Some kind of a *woman*?" It was the ultimate insult from Stumbo, who knew nothing of women, except what he had seen in his porn magazines. He thought they were weak and couldn't handle police work, particularly homicide. They did much better as secretaries, he figured, although he wasn't so sure that they ought to be exposed to the more sordid details of homicide and vice cases.

But it was useless for McNaughton to object to Doyle's staunch political beliefs, even when there was so much evidence to the contrary right in front of him. Alvear was one of the best detectives Jack had ever known. Renee liked to say that, if courageous men had big balls, then women like Kit must have huge ovaries.

Jack ignored Doyle's commentary. "OK, then," he said, noticing that Stumbo was breathing hard from the journey upstairs. He couldn't resist a subtle dig: "Then take a deep breath and prepare yourself."

McNaughton turned to go downstairs, denying Stumbo the opportunity to respond. Stumbo waddled into the boys' bedroom and bumped smack into one of the evidence technicians, who had been crouching down, dabbing at a blood stain with a wet cotton ball to retrieve the sample from the wall. The technician lost his balance, and the evidence was lost. "What the fuck are you. . ," he began, turning to see who had run into him. He stopped short when he saw it was Stumbo. "Uh, lieutenant. Uh, excuse me, sir." The technician was livid, but he bit his tongue. The last thing he needed was to be brought up on insubordination charges by this goof.

Stumbo also had lost his balance, and caught himself on the foot of the bed. His face was less than four feet from that of the victim, a boy of about six. Doyle leaned over, grabbed his throat and vomited up the two quarter-pounders and extra-large order of fries that he had had for lunch, dropping his sputum directly on the dog's corpse.

"Uh, somebody'd better clean that up," he said, mustering all the authority he could in a futile attempt to regain his dignity. He turned, without looking at the other bed and without going into the girls' bedroom, and went back downstairs.

"Who the fuck is supposed to pick that up?" the other evidence technician said.

"I don't know," the first one said. "Leave it to the friggin' brass. They can never stomach anything. You'd think they were never cops."

Doyle Stumbo *had* been a cop – a pretty good street cop at that. He hadn't always been this way. McNaughton could remember a trimmer, happier Doyle, who for years was content patrolling the dank streets of the near north side where the houses were set so close that the new Stumbo could no longer squeeze between them. With that southern lilt in his voice, his good-ol'-boy knack for bullshit and the toothpick forever dangling out of the left side of his mouth, Stumbo had a way with the people on his beat – even the black kids who hung out on street corners and shouted epithets at most passing cop cars. He'd park his cruiser and drink coffee and eat crullers with them, rarely hassling them and usually paying. But the brass, concerned that Stumbo didn't write as many tickets as some of his colleagues, decided to take him off the streets. Trouble was, the only place to put him was in a traffic sergeant's job, so Stumbo was rewarded for his low productivity with a promotion. Then, when the two departments merged, there were too many traffic sergeants. Attempts to sort things out resulted in Stumbo accidentally being assigned to homicide and bumped up to lieutenant. The promotion caused enormous dissension in the ranks, especially among homicide sergeants who should have had a shot at it, but the brass – grateful that Stumbo had not caused them trouble – used the urgency of the merger as justification of that and other bad decisions. Stumbo was petrified to be in charge of veteran investigators, but he hoped that the wild current of activity in the squad room every day would be strong enough to drag him along – and that no one would notice.

McNaughton understood this, and some small part of him felt sympathy for Stumbo, but he was the only one. The younger guys saw a fat, stale slug of a man who would not tell them what he wanted, but would rave when they failed to fulfill his wishes. They mocked Stumbo's inability to make crucial decisions, his bombastic, buffoonish behavior and his pretentious pronouncements. They also sensed Stumbo's discomfort with his job, but they attributed both his indecision and his discomfort to stupidity and laziness, not the fear that McNaughton saw in him. On one of his squad's occasional outings at the Willow Glen Bowl, McNaughton tried to appeal to his people to at least show some respect. "DC-10 don't deserve any," Simons grumbled.

That's what they called him: DC-10. His size, Simons said, rivaled that of an airliner, and he had the cruel misfortune of sharing initials with one that was common in the 1970s and '80s. Jumbo Stumbo. And how could McNaughton disagree? He had watched as Stumbo nervously ate his way from one hundred seventy to three hundred fifty pounds, transforming a pleasant, amiable – if unambitious – fellow into an embittered, uncouth lump. And there was no sign that the food fest would abate any time soon. Food was DC's comfort and his solace; he mistakenly thought eating was the one area of his life that he could control, but his ever-expanding waistline was proof of that delusion. He appreciated that food didn't talk back – not unless you counted the explosive belches that Stumbo unabashedly let erupt in the middle of most any conversation. But even they were preferable to the volcanic farts he'd let blow without warning, sending gasping cops flying of out of the stationhouse in all directions.

Stumbo regained his composure and made his way down the steps. Even that was strenuous for him. It was a while until the next newscast, so Doyle figured he'd have some time to calm down. He started puttering around the living room, running his fingers over the fireplace mantle and the desk. Not a very good housekeeper, he thought of Mrs. Peterson as he peered at dusty fingers. He picked up several books off the shelves and fingered through them. One in particular caught his eye, and he glanced around to see if anybody was looking. Jack had gone back upstairs; Alvear was sitting at the kitchen table with her back to him, talking on the phone. Stumbo slipped the thick volume under his jacket, pinning it under his arm.

CHAPTER 2

Uniformed partners Randy Harding and Alex Shoemaker found John Pius Peterson sitting at the polished bar of Jake's, a blue-collar lounge in Butler-Tarkington, a quaint neighborhood near Butler University where Booth Tarkington had been reared. They had seen the blue minivan, license plate 49 T 6005, parked on the street outside the tavern, and they entered cautiously, unsure of what they would confront. But Peterson was docile as a sleepy kitten when the uniforms approached him and told him they wanted him to come downtown for questioning.

He had been drinking club sodas with a twist of lime. Nothing stronger. The bartender, Luke Linley, said that was Peterson's usual. He rarely drank alcohol, only when a companion pushed him into it. Linley, a short guy who showed off his bulging biceps by rolling the sleeves of his skin-tight t-shirt, said that Peterson had been there since shortly after noon. He could tell that something was eating Peterson, but the customer had little to say. Just some routine bitching about his wife, Linley said. Nothing out of the ordinary.

If McNaughton had known that Peterson frequented Jake's, he would have sent uniforms there immediately – before doing virtually anything else. Jack knew that people, particularly those in trouble, gravitate to what they know. The familiar provides comfort, even for somebody that you might expect would try to get away. But the cops knew nothing about Jake's until the uniforms happened upon Peterson's van parked outside. It happened about the same time that Alvear finally connected with Barbara Peterson, who suggested that the police might find her husband there.

He was not under arrest; there wasn't enough evidence for that yet. But the uniforms asked him to come with them to downtown homicide, and he slipped unsteadily off his bar stool, never saying a word. He just nodded his lowered head slowly when they asked him if he was John Peterson. They took him by the arms – Harding on the left, Shoemaker on the right – and led the giant into the April sun. He hung his head and squinted his eyes to avoid its intensity as they took him to their cruiser, where they helped him get into the back seat. One placed his hand on Peterson's head and nudged it downward so that he wouldn't strike it against the top of the car. He said nothing for the ten-minute ride to homicide, instead staring through glazed eyes at the passing scenery – houses, stoplights, garbage trucks, kids on bikes. The cops exchanged quizzical glances: If he hadn't had any booze, was it the experience that dazed him so? But they made no attempt to find out. McNaughton had given strict orders to the many units looking for Peterson: Do not try to engage him in conversation. If he says something before he's Mirandized, we may have trouble – and we *don't* want to mess this one up.

Despite losing the sample that was ruined when Stumbo collided with him, Dooley, the evidence technician, found gradually smaller amounts of blood trailing from each bedroom, as might be expected, and going down the steps to the first floor, and then through the house to the kitchen. There was none in the master bedroom; the perpetrator did not disturb its pristine condition. But the trail of trace amounts continued into the basement, and it was there that Jack made the discovery that would greatly enhance his case: Blood-soaked clothing – clearly belonging to someone the size of Peterson – and a blood-covered rubber mallet matted with hair, its wooden handle broken jaggedly in two. McNaughton made a mental note to get a search warrant – or at least permission to search from Mrs. Peterson – to ensure that the evidence would not be excluded at trial.

The basement – dark and muggy from what had been a typically wet Indianapolis spring – was fairly primitive, except for the corner that had been fixed up as a laundry. The stench of mildew was strong. Off to one side, someone had taken advantage of the close proximity of the water pipes, and had added a shower stall and a toilet. A few drops of water lay on the shower floor and the soap bar was wet, but the walls were dry. McNaughton thought that that suggested that someone had taken a shower several hours earlier. Later, he made sure the photographers took pictures and video of the stall and that the technicians checked it for blood and, sure enough, they found trace amounts.

So John Pius Peterson had savagely beaten his children to death, and then he calmly walked to the basement where he cleaned up as if he were getting ready for a social occasion.

Once the minute evidence had been gathered, the technicians began the gruesome task of gathering up the bed clothing, and now Peterson's clothes, in several large, extra-thick paper bags made to carry wet evidence. The technicians would worry later about drying them out in a low-humidity room. Observant veteran reporters waiting in the afternoon sun, and videographers with their cameras rolling, knew what was being carried out in the many bags and placed in the police mobile lab, and it turned even Myra Spricker's stomach.

What the reporters didn't know is that Jack had the murder weapon. The jagged break suggested to him that the blows had been so fierce that even this tool couldn't withstand the force. But what Jack couldn't figure is why Peterson would be so cavalier about leaving his clothing and, even more significant, his weapon in plain sight. As soon as he learned that the uniforms had brought Peterson in for questioning, he headed downtown to get the suspect's explanation.

He had already assigned Alvear to talk with Barbara Peterson, who was being flown back to Indianapolis in her company's plane. The company president, Bernie Pendleton, himself the father of four children, had authorized that the Lear jet be flown to Midway Airport on Chicago's south side to pick her up, and Alvear asked if she could hitch a ride. Mrs. Peterson had been staying in Arlington Heights, a northwestern suburb, and the cops there offered to ferry her to Midway. Officer Paul Mason warned Alvear that Mrs. Peterson might be descending into shock, but that she had refused medical treatment in Illinois, insisting that she had to get back to Indianapolis for her children's sake.

So Alvear didn't know what to expect – whether she'd get any information out of Mrs. Peterson on the flight or whether she would just hold her hand. But it was a gamble worth taking. It wasn't costing the department anything – always the topmost consideration for the brass – and it would give Alvear some time to talk with her before the television camera lights set her off.

The Lear jet arrived at Midway shortly after three p.m., beating the Arlington Heights cruiser there. An airport security crew took Alvear and Pendleton Inc.'s company nurse, Paula Zimmerman, to security headquarters. Rain has recently passed through the Chicago area, and the sun was considering making an appearance through brightening clouds. Mrs. Peterson arrived at the concrete-block building about fifteen minutes later, emerging from the back seat of the unmarked police cruiser with Mason's help.

She was smartly dressed in a navy blue, double-breasted coat dress with small shoulder pads and long sleeves. She wore navy pumps to match. Her short, light brown, wavy hair looked as if it had been properly coiffed sometime today, but she clearly had run a nervous hand through it many times since. Her head was down, but Alvear could see that her once-perfect face makeup was streaked by track marks from tears. She had managed to dab away most of the mascara that had run, but there was a small black smudge under her left eye. Her eyes were reddened and sad; Alvear wondered if she would ever brighten again.

"Mrs. Peterson, I'm Detective Kit Alvear of the Metro-Marion police," she began self-consciously, extending her hand. "I'm very sorry for your loss."

Mrs. Peterson slowly raised her head and peered at Kit, as if she were trying to figure this cop out. She took the detectives hand and squeezed lightly. "Thank you," she whispered. "I want to go see my babies now."

The nurse took Mrs. Peterson's trench coat from Officer Mason and put it around her shoulders, then placed her arm there. Kit and the airport security officer got her luggage, and they walked slowly back to the security officer's cruiser. No one spoke during the brief ride back to the jet; Nurse Zimmerman gently rubbed Mrs. Peterson's hand.

They climbed the steps to get back onto the plane, and Mrs. Peterson soon signaled that it might be OK to talk. "It was really nice of Mr. Pendleton to send the plane," she said. "I dreaded having to drive the three-and-a-half hours back home."

"Don't worry about your car, Mrs. Peterson," Alvear said. "We'll make sure it's returned pronto." She felt stupid suggesting that this woman, who had just lost her six children, might actually be worrying about a car. But it was a way to open the conversation, and if Kit could just ease her mind in some small way, perhaps Mrs. Peterson would begin to trust her.

"Thank you," she whispered again. "Where's my husband?"

"The last I heard, just before we left Indianapolis, was that he was headed downtown for some questioning," Alvear said. "He's not injured," she added, unsure if Mrs. Peterson would care.

"That's good," she said. Alvear thought for a moment that Mrs. Peterson might be feeling some sympathy. "Because I want that bastard healthy so he can hang."

It was an abrupt change from her mannerly, sophisticated demeanor – but an understandable one. It opened the flood gates.

"He was always – I mean *always* – accusing me of having an affair," she began. "With my clients, with my co-workers, for God's sake – with *Mr. Pendleton!*" Alvear, who had spoken by phone with Pendleton, didn't realize until much later – when she met the courtly old gentleman for whom the company was named – how silly that was.

"When I volunteered at church, he accused me of going there to meet my lover. He even accused me of sleeping with Father Renault," she said. "I have never – *never* – cheated on my husband in our eleven years of marriage, not even when things got *really* bad. I wasn't brought up that way.

"But he kept telling me that, if I didn't quit it, he'd kill the kids. How can you quit something you haven't done? And how do you prove something has never happened? He just went crazy."

"Mrs. Peterson," Kit interrupted, "if you thought your husband was crazy, why'd you leave the kids in his care?"

"I never thought it would come to this," she said. "He *loves* them. Loved," she said, gulping. She breathed deeply, then continued with a faltering voice. "He was the best father you could imagine. He had some trouble with the modern definition – you know, like when he'd have to handle the bedtime chores or take care of the kids when I was gone on a business trip. But he lived for those kids.

"Besides, what choice did I have? We have to have something to live on, and I've got a good job. Good pay and benefits, which is no small consideration when you've got a bunch of kids. John hasn't worked in more than a year. He could have, even in this economy; he's certainly talented enough. But he always had an excuse why he shouldn't go out and look."

"What work does your husband do?" Alvear asked.

"He's a computer whiz," she said. "He can program them, fix them, do anything with them. To me, they're nothing more than a fancy typewriter. I mean, I have to use them at work – I carry my laptop with me all the time – but typing in orders is about all I can do with them. But John is a genius with them. He's just not particularly driven."

She was talking more animatedly now, almost as if she had forgotten what had happened. Kit worried that she might go into shock, especially when she got back to Indianapolis and couldn't go back to North Ellison Street.

Kit decided to broach the unspoken topic. "Is your husband capable of hurting the kids?" she asked gingerly.

"I guess so," Mrs. Peterson answered, and she began to whimper. "Oh, God, why didn't I *see* that? I *never* thought . . . "

Her voice trailed off, and she was crying quietly now. Alvear decided to push anyway.

"Mrs. Peterson, what could have driven your husband to do something like this?"

"All I can think of," she answered, "is that he must have gone crazy."

Stumbo strutted around the bungalow like the man in charge – or at least, like a man who thought he ought to be. He *was* the highest-ranking officer on the scene, and Jack had left for downtown, so there were no pretenders present to usurp his authority. A man utterly lacking in self-confidence, he convinced himself that he could tackle the world that day – to say nothing of that motley crew of newsies who, in his mind, were so lazy that they had nothing better to do that hang out here. So Stumbo swaggered outside and announced that he would hold a news conference in five minutes.

The reporters were less than thrilled. For most of the media outlets, they were the B team, sent to the scene just in case, while the lead reporters worked the story. As if that weren't insult enough, they were stuck outside in the unseasonably hot sun. One male reporter who wore pancake face makeup patted at it carefully with a handkerchief, dismayed that his perspiration might cause it to run before he did his standup. And now, as if this makeup problem wasn't enough, this dufus wants to hold a news conference? As Jack dashed down the sidewalk an hour earlier, he had told the lead reporters that he or a public information officer would be available at downtown homicide at four-thirty p.m., just in time for their five o'clock broadcasts, so nobody could figure why this guy was calling a news conference here for four.

"Ladies and gentlemen, I am here to answer your inquiries," Stumbo said, trying to sound important.

"Officer . . ." the made-up reporter began.

"It's *Lieutenant*. Stumbo," the fat man said. "Lieutenant Doyle C. Stumbo. S-t-u-m-b-o. Commander of the downtown homicide division. Did everybody get that?"

There was general grumbling. Reporters want to find out if somebody has something to say before they go to the trouble of writing down their ID.

"Lieutenant, have you arrested the father?"

"Yes, we have," Stumbo said, incorrectly.

"What are the charges?" the bubblehead asked.

"Six counts of murder," Stumbo said, without knowing. He didn't care if he was right, as long as he got on TV.

"How did the kids die?" asked a grungy male reporter with a ponytail. Must be a newspaper geek.

"It appears as if they were beaten," Stumbo said. He had miraculously gotten one answer right, no small feat considering that, after taking one brief glimpse at one of the corpses, he had gone on an involuntary weight-loss plan. But he had overheard the evidence technicians talking about the number of blows that it must have taken to inflict the damage, so he did not go to the news conference totally unprepared.

Not that that would have mattered to Stumbo, who had skated so many times in the past. His luck never ran out, it seemed; he was sure he would never be caught.

Fortunately, the lead reporters were gathering downtown as Stumbo spoke, waiting for Jack or a public affairs officer to give them the lowdown. It was PAO Pat Houston who faced the anxious media types, and he had little more to tell them than Jack had related hours earlier.

"The children's father, John Pius Peterson, is on his way here for questioning, but he has not been arrested or charged," Houston said. "Their mother, Barbara Peterson, is on her way back from a business trip to Chicago. We'll talk to her as soon as she arrives.

"Detective Sergeant Jack McNaughton is the lead investigator on the case, and he'll normally be your contact. But Sergeant McNaughton is tied up right now, so he couldn't come out. We wanted to make sure you guys had something for your early broadcasts."

"Pat," Myra Spricker started, "do you have IDs on the kids yet?"

"Yeah, we do. Mrs. Peterson provided those for us right away. You ready?"

Reporters readied their notebooks and pens, and Houston consulted his notes. "Mary Elizabeth, DOB four-twenty-ninety-four. By the way, all of these are common spellings unless I indicate otherwise, OK? Matthew – that's with two Ts – Mark, DOB six-thirteen-ninety-five. John Peter, DOB eleven-twelve-ninety-seven. Sarah-with-an-H Ruth, DOB one-sixteen-ninety-nine. Claire-with-an-I-and-an-E Marie, three-twenty-two-oh-one. Teresa-no-H Ann-no-E, DOB three-fourteen-oh-two." There was no fluctuation in his voice, as if he had practiced reciting the horrifying list, and practiced some more. He could have been reading a basketball roster.

Myra was not religious, but she recognized Biblical names when she heard them. "Are these people some kind of religious fanatics?" she asked Houston.

"Not that we know of," he said. "Just good Catholics."

Some good Catholics, Myra thought. Reproduce like rabbits, and then kill them off.

As soon as McNaughton learned that the uniforms had found Peterson, he wrapped up at North Ellison Street – leaving the rest of the work in the technicians' hands – and headed back to the stationhouse. He was concerned that Peterson had been in a bar; if he were intoxicated, he couldn't be questioned until he sobered up. That might not be until tomorrow, and McNaughton did not want to wait. What was worse was, even with the bloodied clothing and the weapon, Jack wasn't sure a judge would agree he had probable cause for an arrest. So he didn't know how he could hold Peterson, and once the father sobered up, perhaps he'd rethink his situation and flee. Jack mulled the problem as he nervously fiddled around his desk and paced the empty, second-floor squad room. He spied a photo of Renee on his desk, and decided he'd better let her know that it might be a late night.

"Indianapolis Sun. Renee Somers," she answered the phone, using the no-nonsense tone that she also used when she answered the phone – *and* when Jack frustrated her or Angel had pushed her limits.

"Hi. It's me." He sounded wistful.

"Oh, hi, honey. How're you doing?" Her voice immediately softened. She had heard about the homicides and Myra had told her that Jack was the lead detective. Renee knew how it bothered Jack when kids were killed; she also had figured that she wouldn't be seeing much of him that evening. But she was glad for the call.

"I'll be a while. I'm working the Peterson case," he said.

"I know. It's *awful.* It makes me want to go hug Angel."

"Me too," he said. "But I won't be able to for a while. Will you tell her that Daddy loves her and that I'll kiss her tonight when I get home?"

"Sure. Any idea what time?"

"None. Sorry."

"That's OK. Any idea if we're going to get something for tomorrow morning's paper?"

"I think so. Peterson, the father, is on his way down here right now. I told Myra and the others that I'd give them something yet tonight, and I think I can still do that."

"Good. We'd like to have something fresh for the morning, since it's been all over TV all day. Saw you, in fact, on the five o'clock. You looked good. Sounded good too. I saw Stumbo on the five-thirty, that buffoon. He made an ass out of himself, of course. Do you realize that he said Peterson had been charged?"

"Oh, God! He hasn't been!" Jack said. "I don't believe . . . " His voice trailed off; he decided he wasn't going to take it on. "I'm glad you thought I did OK. You know how I hate cameras. That interview was done this morning, not all that long after I got there. I gotta tell you, it wasn't easy. I haven't done one this bad in a long time. Maybe ever."

"I know, honey," she said soothingly. "I'm really sorry you've got to see those kids that way. And don't worry about Stumbo; everybody knows that he was talking out his ass, and I'm sure they'll drop him from the six o'clock."

"God, I hope so."

Renee hesitated, as if she had to screw up the courage to ask. "Jack? Did the father do it?"

"I think so."

They both paused. "Honey, I've got to go so I can get Angel from day care before they're ready to wring my neck. Love you. Be careful," she said.

"I will. Love you too. And give her a kiss for me."

They hung up. Jack knew that what he told Renee went no farther; for the eleven-plus years they'd been together, they had an understanding that their conversations were off the record. It was the only way their relationship could exist, and the only way they could trust each other in other, more important ways.

He was fiddling with some paper clips on his desk, too anxious to delve into meaningful work, when he heard the rustle of people coming up the stairs. A uniform that Jack didn't recognize led the entourage. But when John Pius Peterson stepped onto the landing, Jack knew exactly at whom he was looking.

Peterson looked much like he had in the family photograph. But the smile was gone, so his eyes were fuller, his cheeks flatter. He had the typical pallor of an office-bound – or in his case, a house-bound – person. His hair was a thick brown brush, cut in an outdated crew cut and sticking straight up. He was a bear of a man – somewhat overweight but mostly just *big*. His hands, with their thick fingers casually curved in, looked like paws and his arms hung at his sides. His feet, wearing thick, black, industrial-type protective shoes, were huge. He wore navy blue work pants, a matching shirt and a white T-shirt underneath – clothing that rang a bell with Jack. Peterson wore no belt and no jewelry, almost as if he had prepared himself to be put into jail.

Jack walked over quickly and thrust out his hand. "Mr. Peterson," he said, "I'm Detective Sergeant Jack McNaughton. I'd like to talk with you about your children."

"Yes, I'd like to do that," Peterson said in a deep, sullen voice. He ignored Jack's extended hand. "I think I should call my lawyer first, though."

"That's fine, Mr. Peterson. Here's a telephone." Jack led him to the nearest desk and pointed to the land line. "Dial nine to get out."

"Can I use a phone book?" Peterson asked. Jack nodded, and grabbed one off the next desk and handed it to him.

While Peterson flipped quickly through the pages and punched in a number, Jack signaled to the uniforms who had brought him in to wait a moment. He wanted to ask them if they had told him that his children were dead. Otherwise, how would he know – unless he had done it?

Peterson spoke into the phone. "May I please speak to Knofel? Tell him this is John Peterson. It's an emergency."

Knofel. With a novel name like that, McNaughton knew that Peterson's lawyer must be Knofel Fortner, a decent criminal lawyer that McNaughton had faced several times before, and had usually beaten. Fortner did right by his clients – he protected their rights by watching what they said and objecting at the right time during trials, but he was nothing spectacular and certainly not flashy in the courtroom. Jack knew that Peterson could have gotten a much worse lawyer, and he was sort of relieved to know that somebody with some knowledge of criminal law would be coming in. A lot of suspects – at least those who didn't make a habit of being arrested – called their tax or divorce lawyers.

Jack had backed away to give Peterson some privacy. The conversation was short; Peterson gently placed the receiver in its cradle and turned toward McNaughton.

"We know each other from church. St. Mary's," Peterson said. "We're both in the Knights of Columbus."

"I'm Catholic too, but I've never joined the Knights," Jack said. "Is Knofel coming down?"

"Yeah. He said he'd be here in ten minutes."

Peterson must have told Fortner the gravity of the situation to get him down here that quickly. "Would you like some coffee while you wait?"

"Yes, please," Peterson said softly. "Black."

Jack went to the dilapidated coffee maker and poured a couple of cups. He wasn't sure how long it had been sitting on the hot plate; he hoped that it would at least resemble coffee, but it looked fairly thick. He gestured with his head to get Peterson to follow him into the interrogation/conference room. It was devoid of character. Off-white walls; no pictures; no books. One end of a small, rectangular wooden table was shoved against the short wall; two wooden chairs were on each long side and another was at the open end. Straight-backed with no arms and no pads, they were not unlike the kind the nuns used in Jack's elementary school. A telephone and a thin section of the newspaper rested on the table. A tall, cheaply made end table was against the opposite wall. Next to it were four more chairs, two across from two. A conversation pit of sorts.

Jack placed one cup on the table and pulled out the chair at the end for Peterson. "Have a seat, Mr. Peterson. There's the sports page, if you want it. I'll be outside at my desk, and I'll bring Mr. Fortner in when he arrives."

"OK," Peterson said. He picked up the steaming coffee and tentatively took a small sip. He looked down at the table and made no move toward the paper.

Jack left and closed the door. He summoned the uniforms over. "Guys, when you found Peterson, what *exactly* did you say to him?"

The red-haired officer, whose name plate identified him as Randy Harding, spoke. "I identified myself and Officer Shoemaker here and said that we wanted to take him to the stationhouse to discuss his children."

"Are you absolutely sure that's how you put it? That you didn't say that we wanted to discuss the *deaths* of his children?"

They both thought for a minute. "No, Sergeant," Harding said. "I'm sure I just said 'discuss your children.'"

Shoemaker nodded. "That's right, sir."

"And he didn't ask for details – like, what specifically do you want to discuss?"

"No, sir," Shoemaker answered.

"What was his demeanor?" Jack asked.

Harding answered: "He seemed very calm, Sergeant. Almost catatonic. He didn't really say anything, except something about the Lord being mad at everybody."

"No," said Shoemaker. "It was a quote from the Bible, from Isaiah. I remember it from Sunday school: 'For the Lord is enraged against all the nations, and furious against all their hoards; he has doomed them, has given them over for slaughter.'"

"Peterson said that in the car?" McNaughton asked. Both nodded. "OK, thanks, guys. Good work. Could you write me a short report with that in it, Shoemaker? It could be important." Shoemaker nodded and started searching in his jacket for his notebook.

As the uniforms turned to leave, Jack resumed his pacing, stopping only to sip the putrid coffee. He began to stew over the fact that Peterson apparently knew his kids were dead, but he stayed so calm, even quoting the Bible. And what the hell was he doing, sitting in a bar, unless he was guilty as sin? If it had been another perpetrator – a stranger, say – Peterson would have been dead too, because certainly he wouldn't have left six young children home alone. Besides, strangers don't overkill; that happens only in crimes of passion. Jack's mind was reeling when Fortner burst into the squad room.

"McNaughton. Where's Mr. Peterson?" He was out of breath, and Jack wasn't sure if it was because of his haste in getting there or his anxiety over the situation.

"Hi, Knofel. Mr. Peterson is in the conference room, waiting for you. This way."

Fortner followed Jack like a puppy follows its new owner – right on the heels. "Jack, have you charged Mr. Peterson with anything?

"No, Knofel. We want to talk with him about the deaths of his children. Did he tell you that?"

"Well, certainly," Fortner said. "But is he a suspect?"

"Yes. His wife has implicated him, and we have evidence to suggest he did it."

"OK," Fortner said, sighing heavily and combing his thin hair with his fingers.

Jack led him to the room, opened the door and let him in. Peterson looked up from the table; it seemed he hadn't moved. "Let me know when you're ready," Jack said as he closed the door.

The flight had been rough, thanks to the worsening weather as the plane moved southeast. Chicago had sent its rain to Indianapolis. Alvear, who had flown commercial airliners all over the place, was unpleasantly surprised to find that small jets made her queasy. The trip wasn't made any easier, either, when she recalled that, just a few years earlier, two of these small planes collided over the south side of Indianapolis and burst into flames. Five civic leaders, as well as both pilots, were killed. And that was on a bright, sunny day. So she smiled wanly when the Lear landed bumpily at Mount Comfort Airport on the far east side of town. The place was virtually deserted. The Pendleton pilot chose Mount Comfort because it was easier to get clearance for landing than the Indianapolis International Airport on the west side, which – naturally – had airliners and other private planes competing for landing rights. But Kit was glad for another reason: Just in case any reporters got word that Mrs. Peterson was coming in from out of town, it was less likely that any of them would think to camp out here. And while Alvear had learned tolerance for the press from Jack, this moment was difficult enough without intruders.

Barbara Peterson stepped warily off the plane, as if she were stepping onto thin ice. What must she be thinking? Kit wondered. But the truth was, Barbara Peterson's mind was blank. It had shut down, some sort of defense mechanism that clicked in when the pain became overwhelming. She was operating by rote now, just going through the motions. If Barbara began to internalize what had happened to her children, she might go as nuts as her husband had – but permanently.

The pilot had radioed ahead, as Kit had requested, so Mitch Simons knew where to pick them up. Kit and Nurse Zimmerman, a plain woman dressed in a traditional uniform and a pink sweater, again took Mrs. Peterson by both arms and guided her toward the back seat of the navy blue unmarked cruiser. Mitch had placed his removable flashing red light atop the sedan; it was an audacious move that smacked all too much of television cop shows, but he didn't want to mess with traffic in case Mrs. Peterson needed fast transport to the hospital. Mitch was surprised at her calm demeanor, but he realized that she might be in shock – if not by the medical definition, then at least by the emotional one. It was pretty unlikely that he was going to have to rush anywhere, but he decided to take advantage of the luxury of the flashing light anyway – how often did a real-life detective get the excuse to do this? All three women scrunched into the back seat, which reeked of the French fries Mitch had finished just before he arrived at the airport, and after Kit helped Mrs. Peterson find the left end of her seat belt, Mitch took off.

Just as Simons was merging the nondescript cruiser onto rain-covered Interstate 70, a cocky Stumbo was wedging his body behind the wheel of his Mustang. He planned to return to the stationhouse and make a grand and triumphant entrance in front of his appreciative underlings. He was feeling good; he had held those damned nosy newsies at bay. But they would have to be so appreciative that he gave them their stories that surely his name would be high up in the newspaper articles and his face would be displayed prominently on the TV programs. With any luck, he would get back to the stationhouse before the six o'clock news started, and he could flip from station to station and see which one displayed him most prominently. Darn; there was no way to get home in time to program his DVR to record himself.

He picked up his cellular phone and punched in seven numbers. "Mother? It's Doyle. I'm in the car. Can you hear me?"

"Well, yes, dear. Sort of. Where are you? Timbuktu?" his mother drawled on the other end. "What is it?"

"Mother, I want you to set your DVR to record the TV news at six. I think channel thirteen should be the best. I'm liable to headline the news."

"Why, sweetheart, that's fantastic. I'm so proud of you."

"Gotta go, mother. I'm in traffic and it sets a bad example for police officers to talk on their cell phones while driving."

"Yes, dear. Be careful. Bye!"

She was always so cheerful and so supportive. It was good that someone was. Doyle needed all the support he could get.

A few minutes later, after he had made a couple of wrong turns, he somehow found the stationhouse and turned into the lot. After extricating his physique from the front seat, he attempted a confident swagger – as best as a three-hundred-fifty-pounder *can* swagger – as he walked across the lot and mounted the four steps leading into the stationhouse. The uniform at the front desk nodded and greeted him unenthusiastically: "G' afternoon, lieutenant." Stumbo slowly negotiated the steps to the homicide division and took a quick look about. Surely there was someone here to whom he could brag about his press conference prowess. But the place was virtually empty. "Shee-it," Stumbo mumbled under his breath. His bragging would have to wait.

But then he saw McNaughton, leaning against the wall and looking anxious. "Jack, come 'ere. You gotta see my press conference."

Stumbo was gaping about, looking for the remote control that always seemed to disappear. He finally found it on Simons's desk and pressed thirteen. Jack's face filled up the screen. Stumbo's eyes bugged out, but he quickly flipped to channel eight. McNaughton again! He pressed six. Goddammit! It was McNaughton on all three stations. And then, to add insult to injury, Pat Houston came on channel six. That goddamn flack!

"Jack, what the hell were you doing? I was the senior officer at the scene."

"Doyle, I have no control over what the TV stations put on the air. And I don't have time to argue now. Mr. Peterson is in the conference room, talking with his lawyer, and I think they're going to agree to let me interview him. Let's talk about it later."

"Goddammit, Jack, I want to talk about this *now*!" he bellowed. "You are to leave the press interviews to *me*!"

"Doyle, those interviews were done this morning, before you even came to the scene. Pat Houston handled things this afternoon. I didn't even know you were having a news conference." He was getting agitated now. "I wish you had told me before you did that. Among other things, you shouldn't have said that Peterson has been charged. He hasn't been."

Stumbo's mouth dropped open. He was about to defend himself when the conference room's door opened.

"Jack?" Knofel Fortner said. "We're ready to talk to you."

McNaughton glared at Stumbo with a look of disgust and turned away, hurrying over to the conference room. He went inside and closed the door.

"Let's sit over here, Mr. Peterson. It's more comfortable." Jack directed Peterson and his lawyer to the chairs across the room. Peterson looked at Fortner as if to get his approval; he didn't quite understand why he should move from the table at which he had been sitting. But Fortner nodded almost imperceptibly, and the two of them moved to the chairs to which Jack pointed, their backs to the room's only door. McNaughton sat directly opposite Peterson. The end table was to Jack's left, Peterson's right. On it was a box of tissues, a pitcher of water and some plastic cups and a digital recorder with a power microphone.

The chairs, straight-backed and armless but with thin pads across the back and on the seat, were only slightly more comfortable than the wooden numbers at the table. But Jack was less interested in comfort than in removing the table – an obstacle, a protective barrier – between him and Peterson.

"Mr. Peterson," he began, "have you decided to talk with me?"

"Yes," Peterson said.

"Our discussion will be recorded. I'm turning on the recorder now." Jack pushed the "record" buttons and spoke toward the microphone. "This is Detective Sergeant Jack McNaughton of the Metro-Marion Police Department. Today's date is April thirteen. This interview is in reference to the homicides of the six Peterson children. With me are John Pius Peterson, the children's father, and Knofel Fortner, his attorney. Please identify yourselves for the record."

"I am Knofel Fortner, attorney at law with the firm of Williams Fortner and Stephenson." Fortner nodded to Peterson to speak.

"Um, I'm John Peterson. John Pius Peterson." He looked quizzically at Fortner, wondering what else he should say. Fortner nodded that he had done fine.

Jack spoke again. "You understand that you're not under arrest, correct?"

"Yes."

"As a formality, however, I'd like to tell you about your Miranda rights under the Constitution. 'You have the right to remain silent. Anything you say can and will be used against you in a court of law. You have the right to talk to an attorney and to have him with you during questioning if you wish. If you decide to start answering questions now, you have the right to stop answering at any time until you speak to an attorney.'

"Now, obviously, you already have your attorney present. Can I assume you have discussed your rights?" Jack looked from Peterson to Fortner and back again. Both of them nodded, and Fortner answered aloud: "Yes, we have."

"All right, then, let's start," Jack said. "First, for the record, Mr. Peterson, I want you to tell me if you've had any alcoholic beverages today."

"No. I was drinking club soda at Jake's. I haven't had a drink in, oh, a few days, I think."

"OK. Then I want to focus your attention on yesterday, about twenty-four hours ago. Late afternoon and evening. Can you please tell me what you were doing at that time?

"Well, I made dinner for me and the kids. My wife was gone on – well, she said – on a business trip to Chicago. We had spaghetti and garlic bread. And chocolate cake."

"Mr. Peterson, you say that your wife *said* she was on a business trip. Do you have any reason to doubt her?"

Peterson paused, as if he were considering the ramifications of his answer. "Well, no. Of course not. You must have misunderstood. She was in Chicago on business."

Jack made a mental note of it. Peterson doubts his wife, but he doesn't want to admit it.

"Go on, please, with your description of the evening."

"Well, the kids needed baths. You know, cleanliness is next to godliness. Lizzie – that's the oldest one – always helps me. She got Claire and the baby, Teresa, and started running their bath. Little Sarah Ruth – she's five – was running around, not cooperating. The boys, Mattie and Petey, were putting the dishes in the dishwasher until their turn for a bath. After all the little ones were done, Lizzie went last. Then I put the children to bed, and I headed to bed myself.

"It was just a normal evening," he said. Then he began to whimper. "Until *he* came."

CHAPTER 3

Peterson began to weep, his huge body heaving as he sobbed. "I'm sorry," he said. "I'm sorry." He shook his head back and forth, then took a few deep breaths to get himself under control.

Jack wanted to get Peterson's focused, and move him away from that emotional state, so he immediately began his questioning.

"Who is '*he*,' Mr. Peterson?"

"That awful man who hurt my children." Peterson's head hung low, his enormous shoulders slumped. He stared at the floor that separated him from McNaughton, and breathed so deeply that his shoulders slowly rose and fell.

"What's his name?" Jack asked.

"I don't know. I wish I did."

"Mr. Peterson," McNaughton said, "why don't you tell me what you *do* know about your children's deaths? Start at the time you all went to bed."

Peterson's head did not move, but his eyes lifted to look at Jack as he posed the question. Then the big man looked down again, as if transfixed by something invisible on the floor.

"Well, I kissed the kids good night and tucked them into bed. The girls sleep in one room – we fixed up that big room for them when Claire was born three years ago – and the boys sleep across the hall." He paused to lick his lips. "I always say good night to the boys first. They wanted to read last night, but I let them all watch a rerun of "I Love Lucy" and it was past their bedtime. So it was lights out. They grumbled, but after saying their prayers – I suggested they ask Jesus for some help in developing respect for their elders – they went to sleep. Then I went into the girls' room. Lizzie was putting Teresa down since *Mommy was out.*"

The last three words resonated with anger. She was "out," McNaughton noted. Not working. Not out of town on business. Just "out."

"Uh, I kissed Sarah first – her bed is farthest from the door – then Claire, then Teresa and then Lizzie, whose bed is right there when you walk in. Teresa asked for Mommy, but I said she'd just have to get along without her because Mommy had more important things to do than to put her babies to bed.

"Oh, yes. Before I tucked them in and kissed them, the girls all knelt down next to their beds and said their prayers."

"What did they pray for?" Jack asked.

"I suggested that they pray for their mother."

"Why? Was she ill? Did she have some sort of problem?" McNaughton queried, attempting to draw Peterson out.

Peterson again raised his eyes to look directly into Jack's eyes as he answered, telling McNaughton that he really believed this: "Because my wife was going down the wrong path," he said. "She had lost sight of The Way. She had abandoned her relationship with Jesus Christ."

Peterson's gaze drifted away, and his eyes glazed over. "'This is the way of the adulteress: she eats, and wipes her mouth, and says, 'I have done no wrong.'"

Jack recognized the formal language, if not the passage itself, to come from the Bible. Despite twelve years of parochial school, Jack, like most Catholics, wasn't very familiar with specific Bible verses, particularly those from the Old Testament. It was the moral of the stories that counted. He noticed that Peterson's demeanor changed when he recited the quote, that his otherwise dull tone became emphatic.

Jack was curious about the meaning behind the quotation, but he had more pressing matters at hand. So he moved on. "OK, Mr. Peterson. Let's go back to last night. After you kissed Lizzie good night, what happened?"

"Well, I left the door ajar – the girls like it that way – and I went into my room. It's right next door. I changed into my pajamas," he said, glancing at Jack and then veering his eyes to the right, "and went to bed."

The blood-soaked garments that Jack had found in the basement were street clothing – a navy work shirt and matching pants, much like those Peterson was wearing now. If he had changed into pajamas, why would he have changed back to street clothes before doing the deed?

But more important, Jack noticed Peterson avert the detective's gaze by shifting his eyes to the right. McNaughton drew on his criminal psychological training, in which he learned about a long-held theory that a person who does that while speaking is lying. Based on the fact that the right side of the body is controlled by the left side of the brain, the creative side, the theory holds that someone who looks to his right is creating an answer rather than reciting a fact drawn from his memory.

"Sometimes I read when I go to bed, but I was pretty tired last night," Peterson continued. "So it was lights out for me around ten or so."

"Did you speak to your wife by phone?" Jack asked.

"Oh, yeah. I forgot that *she* called. Of course, she waited until the children were in bed. Wouldn't you think a mother would want to speak to her children?"

Jack noticed that Peterson's apparent sadness about his children turned to barely contained anger when he spoke of his wife. His body language spoke too: He straightened up when she was mentioned, slumped again when he spoke of the children.

Jack decided to allow Peterson to digress, even encourage him to. He leaned forward and lightly touched Peterson's knee, employing a standard questioning strategy designed to convey intimacy, in hope that Peterson would confide in him.

"I'll bet that was tough to live with," Jack said sympathetically. "I'll bet you were really feeling overwhelmed, having to take care of six kids. Maybe even a little betrayed."

"I sure was," Peterson said, looking directly at Jack again. "I just couldn't believe how she would treat us. She didn't deserve to be a mother."

Fortner, realizing his client was establishing a motive, butted in. "Sergeant McNaughton, I must object. I think we're getting far afield. Can we talk about the night in question, please?"

"Mr. Fortner," Jack began, addressing the attorney formally for benefit of the recorder, "please remember that your client is not under arrest and that this is not a deposition." Knofel shot him a look of incredulity – they both were good enough at this serious game to respect the other's role – but remained silent. Jack continued: "But yes, let's get back to last night." He was thinking, too, that Peterson had revealed a possible motive. "What happened next, Mr. Peterson?"

"Well," Peterson said, "I must have fallen asleep pretty quickly – a deep sleep, because I was dreaming. I heard a noise, but it took a minute for me to wake up. I thought it was part of my dream. But then I heard it again, and I got up to investigate.

"I went to the stairs, but I couldn't see or hear anything. So I went downstairs and looked around the living room and out the front windows, and then I went into the kitchen. I thought I heard something in the basement, so I opened the basement door – it's next to the refrigerator – but didn't hear anything. I turned on the stair light and went downstairs, but there was nothing. Then I thought I heard something back in the living room, so I went back upstairs. That's when I saw him. He was going upstairs with something in his hand."

"You say you don't know who he was, Mr. Peterson," Jack said. "But what did he look like?"

"He was big, about my size. He was dressed in dark clothing. I couldn't tell you anything specific. His hair was short."

Peterson paused. Jack jumped in: "Sounds like he looked a lot like you, Mr. Peterson. Could you see his face?"

"Well," Peterson said, gazing into Jack's eyes, "I couldn't see him very well – he didn't look at me – but you're right. He looked a little like me."

"And what was in his hand, Mr. Peterson?"

"It looked like some kind of a rubber mallet," he answered.

"Do you have such a mallet?"

"Oh, dear Lord. You don't suppose he used one of *my* tools to hurt my children?"

"I don't know, Mr. Peterson," Jack said. He had an instant flash of anger, recalling that Stumbo had said publicly that the children had been bludgeoned. If he hadn't opened his big mouth, nobody but the cops and the perpetrator would have known that, but now, Peterson's possible knowledge of the bludgeoning was meaningless. "Why don't you tell me?"

"Well, I just don't know. It was too dark to tell for sure."

"Did you say anything to him or try to stop him in any way?"

"I screamed and screamed at him," Peterson said, "but it was if he couldn't – or wouldn't – hear me. He didn't stop."

Peterson's enormous arms were wrapped tightly across his chest, almost as if he were hugging himself. He sobbed again, and his chest heaved. He continued in that manner for several minutes, and Jack let him go. He wanted to watch Peterson, see how he was reacting. Was this a mourning father or a remorseful killer? And if it were the latter, was he sorry for having killed the children, or for having been caught?

A good investigator keeps an open mind, even in the face of a fairly obvious scenario. So Jack was determined not to prejudge Peterson, not to assume his guilt. Maybe there *was* somebody else. But the story was getting weird. The intruder – and there were no signs of forced entry – didn't hear him scream?

Peterson calmed down. "Could I have a drink of water, please?" he asked. Jack nodded, and Peterson leaned over, poured a cup and gulped half of it. Jack continued: "Mr. Peterson, you said the man was going up the stairs, ignoring – or not hearing – you. What happened then?"

"I followed him, but it was hard. He was moving so slowly, almost like he was in slow motion, but I still couldn't catch up with him. My legs felt so *heavy*. He always seemed to be four or five steps ahead of me, no matter how hard I tried to catch him.

"He went up the stairs and paused for a moment on the landing. Then he went right for the girls' room, as if he was on a mission. I kept yelling at him to stop, but he didn't pay any attention to me. He pushed the girls' door open and it bounced off the wall, but it didn't make any sound. At least I don't remember hearing it, and the girls didn't wake up. Lizzie was lying there looking so pretty. I love to watch the kids when they sleep; no matter how bad a day we've had, they look like little angels lying there. I remember she was lying on her back, with her dolly in her right arm and her left arm flung up over her head. And then I saw him lift his right arm over his head and it came crashing down on *Lizzie's head! He hit her! And he kept hitting her – over and over!"*

Peterson sat motionless, but his eyes darted across the floor. His face was distraught. Neither Jack nor Knofel moved. The only sound was the ticking of the clock on the wall. Then Peterson continued: "Blood spurted everywhere. It was flying in slow motion all over the walls. All that hitting made just an awful noise, but the first one was the worst. I told him to stop but he wouldn't. He just kept hitting her. She didn't look pretty anymore.

"He finally stopped and I told him to get out. That was enough. I mean, even the Lord stopped after striking down the firstborn. But he didn't even look at me. He just walked around the end of Lizzie's bed and walked toward the baby's bed. She was lying on her left side, and her thumb was in her mouth. She just started sleeping in a big-girl bed a few weeks ago. And then he went and ruined it for her! He started hitting her too! And he hit her and hit her and hit her. I don't know why he had to hit her so many times. She's just so little.

"Then he walked around the end of her bed and came up on the right side of Claire's. He swung his arm way up in the air and came down on the top of her head. She was lying on her tummy. He hit her just once, and that made Sarah, who was in the last bed, stir. So he left Claire's bed and went to Sarah's and started hitting her. Her bed is pushed up against the wall, and the wall just got covered in blood. He acted real mad that she had stirred. He acted like he was mad at her, and you know, she, she was pretty naughty yesterday. He hit her the hardest, I think. Then, when he was finished, he just turned around and started hitting Claire again. I don't think he would have had to. I think she had already passed from the first time."

Peterson's dull voice trailed off for a moment. He licked his lips again. A rivulet of mucus ran out of one nostril and stopped just above his lip.

"He was breathing hard by now. He was about worn out. I wanted him to stop, but he wouldn't. I wanted him to quit and just go away, but his work wasn't done. So he went out of the girls' room and crossed the hall. He didn't even look in my wife's and my room; I guess he figured that of course she wouldn't be home. He headed for the boys' room. I tried to reason with him. Hadn't he done enough? Hadn't he proved his point? Wasn't she punished enough? But he ignored me. I guess he figured that the girls weren't lesson enough. I guess he wanted to make sure that she didn't have anybody left.

His eyes glazed over again: "'Thus says the Lord: I am going to break down what I have built, and pluck up what I have planted – that is, the whole land. And you, do you seek great things for yourself? Do not seek them; for I am going to bring disaster upon all flesh, says the Lord; but I will give you your life as a prize of war in every place to which you may go.'

"Then he went into the boys' room, and Sammy – that's our dog – was sleeping at the foot of Mattie's bed. Like always. Sammy woke up and wagged his tail but he stretched out his little neck to sniff and I guess he figured that the dog would give him trouble so he whacked him twice. Then he went to Mattie's bed and started hitting him. The same routine."

Except for the Bible quotations, Peterson's recitation began to sound as if it *were* routine, as if he were just rattling off some catechism lesson that he had memorized but not taken to heart. The longer he spoke, the duller his voice became.

"This time, the blood splattered all over the boys' sports stuff. They'd be mad. They aren't very good about picking up their toys, but they always take such good care of that stuff. They really like

Jalen Rose, and they'd be so disappointed that their picture of him got messed up. Then he turned around and hit Petey once, and the mallet's handle broke. The top of it flew back toward the door. That made him angry. He dropped the handle and he leaned over and he could hear Petey was still breathing – sputtering, really – and he put his hands around Petey's neck and squeezed. He just kept squeezing and squeezing until Petey stopped that awful noise. Then he turned around toward the door and he lifted his head and he looked at me.

"And it was me."

His voice registered no excitement; his tone was matter of fact. He had just told about witnessing *himself* beating his children into the next life, and it was as if he were discussing what to make for dinner.

Then he got that faraway look again, and he spoke with a vengeance: "'O daughter Babylon, you devastator! Happy shall they be who pay you back what you have done to us! Happy shall they be who take your little ones and dash them against the rock!'"

He stopped just long enough to take a long gulp of water, and his voice went dull again. "I looked at his hand – *my* hand. Deuteronomy says 'Show no pity: life for life, eye for eye, tooth for tooth, hand for hand, foot for foot.' So I went downstairs into the basement and I found my circular saw, and I cut off my right arm, the one that had done it. That made my clothes bloody, so I took them off and took a shower in the basement stall. And then I went upstairs and went to bed."

Peterson stopped. McNaughton allowed himself to take his eyes off of the father for the first time in many minutes, and he glanced at Fortner, whose mouth hung open. Knofel felt Jack's gaze, and he shook off his shock and closed his mouth. Neither spoke for what seemed like a long time.

Jack finally broke the silence. "Mr. Peterson, your kids were lying dead or near dead and you went to bed. You didn't call nine-one-one or the neighbors or anybody, right? And the next morning, you got up and went to Jake's. How could you do that?"

"There was nothing I could do for them," he said. "He had made my children angels, and they had gone to a better place."

"He made them angels? Does that mean he did them a favor by killing them?" Jack felt the anger welling up inside, and modulated his voice to disguise it.

"Well, I don't know," Peterson answered. "They're in heaven, I know. And I know that's much better than being on earth. But I miss them. I miss them."

They sat in silence again for a few moments. McNaughton rose from his chair. He didn't see much point in going on now. "Mr. Fortner, I'd like to see you outside."

Knofel looked relieved to be getting away. "OK," he said quietly.

They left the conference room, leaving Peterson slumped in his chair, staring at the floor. "Knofel," Jack said, "I don't think it would be productive to continue any longer tonight. And after hearing that, I have no choice but to charge him."

"I know, Jack. Good God."

"Go on back in, Knofel. I have to talk with my lieutenant, and I'll be back in a moment."

Knofel gingerly opened the door and slipped back inside the conference room. Jack felt sorry for him; he wouldn't want to be in his shoes just now. But he also knew what must be going on in Knofel's mind: This guy needs a psychiatric examination in the worst way. Jack went to find Stumbo, who was sitting in his office, pouting that his fifteen minutes of fame hadn't materialized.

He was none too happy with Jack, either. How dare an underling read him off like that? He ought to be more deferential.

When he spotted Jack coming through his door, he jumped on him. "Jack, I'm serious about handling these press conferences from now on. And your attitude . . .," he began, but McNaughton interrupted him.

"Doyle, let's talk about that later," he said calmly. "I've just gotten a confession from Peterson; I'm going to charge him and take him down to lock up."

"So I wasn't wrong, was I?" Stumbo said. "By the time the papers come out in the morning, he'll be charged with murder."

"No, Doyle, you weren't wrong," Jack said, trying to hide his exasperation. He sighed. "Just premature. At any rate, I wanted you to know what was happening."

"Well, thank you, Sergeant McNaughton. I'm glad you've seen fit to inform your superior about your actions." The words sagged from sarcasm. "You know, Jack, you need to work on your communication skills."

"Doyle, can we save it?" He answered his own question by doing an about face and starting to leave. "Oh, yeah, Doyle, I want Pat Houston to tell the media that Peterson has been charged. Or I can do it, if that's preferable. You got any problem with that?"

"Uh, well, uh . . ." It was classic Stumbo. He couldn't decide, even something this simple. "Will you excuse me a minute, Jack?"

McNaughton nodded and stepped outside the office, closing the door behind him. He knew the routine. Stumbo swung his swivel chair around, and faced the wall. Though his back was to the window, Jack could see that he picked up the phone to make a call. After a moment, Stumbo's head nodded a few times, as if he were listening to instructions. He placed the receiver down, turned around and came out.

He approached Jack, planted his feet two feet apart and stiffened his knees. He placed his hands on his hips and adopted an attitude.

"Have Houston do it. That's what we pay him for," Stumbo said, with as much authority as he could muster.

Under other circumstances, McNaughton could have been amused by the theatrics. No matter what Doyle did, he would never convince Jack that he was in control. They both knew it, of course, but Jack decided long ago not to discuss the matter, and Doyle gratefully acquiesced. Tonight, it didn't even cross McNaughton's tired mind. His only thought was that he was sorry that he'd have to call Pat back out, but he wanted to wrap up an ungodly long and weird day's work and go home.

Jack went back to the conference room, knocked twice and opened the door.

"Mr. Peterson, I'm placing you under arrest for the murders of your six children. You've already been read your rights; now I'm going to take you to lock up where you'll be processed – fingerprinted and photographed. You'll be spending tonight there; you'll see a judge in the morning for your initial hearing, where a preliminary plea will be entered for you and the judge will set bond. If you make it, you can go home. If not, you'll be transferred to the county jail. Do you understand?"

"'Pray for us as well,'" Peterson said, "'that God will open to us a door for the word, that we may declare the mystery of Christ, for which I am in prison, so that I may reveal it clearly, as I should.'"

He fell silent, and stared at the floor.

Jack returned to the squad room from taking Peterson to lock up. He had a few things to wrap up before heading home. He moved laboriously; it had been a long day anyway, and that interview – one of the weirdest and most emotionally draining ones he had ever conducted – took it out of him. And he was eager to get home, sneak into Angelica's room and kiss his little doll good night.

John Pius Peterson had been right about one thing: Children do look like angels when they sleep. Jack had thought the same thing many times when he watched his Angelica late at night.

"Jack." It was Alvear. Jack didn't know if he was pleased or sorry to see her. They had a lot to do to wrap this case up, but he *really* wanted to do it tomorrow.

"Mrs. Peterson is here. In the conference room. She's holding up pretty well, but she keeps insisting that she wants to see her babies. I told her I didn't know if that's possible."

"Not now," he answered. "They're in the morgue for autopsies, and I'd say, by now" – he glanced at his watch – "at least one's been completed and another is underway. Maybe more, if the county sprung for the overtime to bring an extra pathologist in. Besides, I don't think she's ever going to want to look at those children. Better that she remembers how they used to look. I don't think the best funeral director in the city – hell, not the best reconstructive surgeon in the country – could make those kids look like they used to. Nobody's that good."

They both shuddered at the memory of what they had seen in those bedrooms twelve hours earlier. It a sight neither would be able to forget for a long time, if ever. "I'll tell her," Alvear said, turning toward the conference room.

McNaughton sighed, unhappy with what he was about to say. “Kit, I really think we need to interview her tonight, and it probably would be best if we did it together. OK?”

“Oh, good. I didn’t want to do it alone. Let’s go.”

“You go on in. I’ve got to call Pat Houston and make sure he gets the information about Peterson being charged out to the media.”

Jack had promised the reporters, and he wanted to make sure he didn’t let any of them down, especially Myra Spricker. For one thing, Renee would be furious if her paper didn’t have the latest information in tomorrow morning’s story. For another, Jack agreed with his wife that the cops needed to put out as much information as they could, especially on such a heinous case. It would put people’s minds at ease if they learned that, as horrible as the crime was, it was a domestic dispute, not the work of some crazed serial killer preying on strangers.

He caught Houston right out of the shower, and asked if it would be a problem for him to get a hold of the reporters. Pat, who had one of the most positive attitudes McNaughton had ever witnessed, immediately dismissed any hardship and asked for the details. Pat, of course, had a list of all the reporters and their phone numbers – work, home and cells – with him at all times, and he had taken home the messages left by out-of-town reporters who called because of the sensational aspects of the crime. He set about calling each of them as soon as he hung up with McNaughton.

Kit bit her fingernails as she waited for Jack to get off the phone. She had lucked out that Stumbo had stalked off in a huff sometime while Jack was taking Peterson to be processed, so that was one less problem to deal with. It was bad enough that Kit had to tell Mrs. Peterson, a woman whom she had come to like, that she may never see her children again. She knocked on the conference room door and opened it carefully, so as not to bump Mrs. Peterson if she were walking around. Sure enough, she was standing to one side, as if she might have been pacing. "I'm just too riled up to sit down," she said, almost apologetically.

"That's OK, Mrs. Peterson. I want you to meet Sergeant Jack McNaughton. He's the lead investigator on your case, and an all-around good guy."

Mrs. Peterson managed a slight smile. Jack was startled to see her holding up so well, not just in demeanor but in appearance. They shook hands. "I'm sorry to meet you under these circumstances," Jack said. These moments were so awkward, no matter how many he had endured. He used his standard line, the one he had worked on to try to make survivors feel like *somebody* was on their side. "We'll do everything we can to make you comfortable, and we'll do even more to make sure whoever did this to your children is brought to justice."

"Sergeant McNaughton, there's no question *who* did this to my children, or why. The only question is whether you'll do your job well enough to make sure that he fries. Have you charged the bastard yet?"

Jack hoped that his shock didn't register on his face. God, she was cold. He didn't know how she was even functioning – he suspected he couldn't if the situation were reversed – and here she had already set her sights on the death penalty.

"Why don't you sit here, Mrs. Peterson?" he said, directing her to the same chair her husband had occupied a short while ago. Kit sat next to her, where Fortner had been, and Jack sat opposite them, in his usual seat.

Mrs. Peterson's eyes locked onto Jack's as he began to speak.

"We charged your husband with six counts of murder earlier this evening. He's probably being processed now – fingerprints and photograph taken, his valuables locked up and the like – and he'll spend the night in our lockup.

"He'll be making his initial appearance tomorrow morning. They're usually held at nine-thirty or ten o'clock. If you want to be there, we'll make sure somebody calls you early to let you know the time, and Kit" – he looked at her to make sure she agreed and she nodded – "will pick you up at your hotel."

"Yes, I want to be there," Mrs. Peterson said.

"We'll also make arrangements for you to get into your home tomorrow so that you can get some clothing and other things that you'll need, OK?"

She nodded. "Thank you, sergeant. Now when can I see my children?"

"Mrs. Peterson," Jack said sympathetically, "as Kit probably told you, the coroner automatically orders autopsies for any homicide – that is, any death for which the causes aren't natural. We need the information for trial. Your children are being autopsied by a very competent forensic pathologist now, and we'll have the preliminary results sometime tomorrow. The bodies will be released to the funeral home of your choice – Kit, let's make sure we get that information from Mrs. Peterson later – and then you'll have to talk with the funeral director to see if it'll be possible for you to view the bodies."

She said nothing. Her head lowered, her shoulders slumped and she looked at the floor. "OK," she whispered.

McNaughton paused a moment. "I know that it's been a horrendous day, Mrs. Peterson, but we'd like to talk with you a bit, if you think you're up to it."

"I'd like that," she said quietly. It wasn't so long ago that her husband answered McNaughton's question in much the same way. "If I keep talking about the children, they seem more alive."

"OK, then. I'm going to record our conversation." He pushed the recorder buttons. "This is Detective Sergeant Jack McNaughton of the Metro-Marion Police Department. Today's date is April thirteen. This interview is in reference to the Peterson homicides. With me are Barbara Peterson, the children's mother, and Detective Kit Alvear of the downtown homicide division. Will you both please identify yourselves for the record?"

"I'm Kit Alvear of downtown homicide."

Mrs. Peterson took a deep breath. "I'm Barbara Peterson. My six beautiful children were murdered," she said bitterly. "By an animal."

"OK, Mrs. Peterson. We're here to establish who did kill your children," Jack said. "First, please tell us when you left for Chicago and what you were doing there."

"I left yesterday – uh, yes, yesterday morning. This day has been so nightmarish, I'm having trouble keeping track of anything."

"That's OK, Mrs. Peterson," Kit said, patting her arm. "Just tell us as best as you can remember."

"Well, I went to Chicago on business. I'm a sales representative with Pendleton Manufacturing, and I do some traveling – usually just one-day trips in the vicinity. Within easy driving distance. John has never liked my traveling – and I'm not particularly thrilled to be away from the children – but it's a good living. We need the money; he hasn't worked in months."

"Did anything happen before you left that might precipitate a violent reaction by your husband?" McNaughton asked.

"Nothing more than usual. We *always* fought when I was getting ready to leave. John is very old-fashioned, and he thinks my place is in the home. That's a nice romantic notion from the past, but it just doesn't work anymore. Not with six kids, not in this economy and especially not when your husband doesn't work.

"My husband also is convinced that I'm having an affair. I'm not; I never have and never would. I take my wedding vows seriously. But you cannot reason with him. John lives in another world, actually. For the last couple of months, he's been reading the Bible incessantly and has insisted that our family ought to follow it literally. He knows more verses than our priest does. In fact, Father Renault has told John that Catholics don't take the Bible literally, but rather use its stories as lessons we can apply to our lives.

"That always makes John mad. Of course, one reason he gets mad at Father Renault is that he's convinced that's who I'm having the affair with. He told me that he wanted to take Father's clerical collar – John called it his 'blasphemous collar' – and wring Father's neck with it! It's *insane*. I'm not having an affair with my priest; my relationship with him begins and ends at Mass. But, because of his ridiculous suspicions – as well as his growing discontent with the Catholic Church – John has threatened to leave it. That probably wouldn't be a bad idea. Lord knows his beliefs are more fundamentalist. He had such a strict upbringing. He was even named for Pope Pius, who died just a few years before he was born, because his parents preferred him to the more progressive pope who replaced him – John the twenty-third. He just takes it too far now. Mass became an important family time for us – John loved to show off his trophy family – and I think that's why he hasn't left the church. Doing so would break up that weekly tradition.

"Yes, we had words before I left, but we always had words. About my travelling. About my alleged affair. It is so depressing to leave on that note, but John makes sure that's the mood whenever I'm on my way out of town. I guess he wants to make me feel guilty, and it works."

Alvear joined in. "Mrs. Peterson, if nothing out of the ordinary happened, do you have any idea why your husband would do something like this?"

"Well, nothing out of the ordinary happened *before* I left. But when I called last night, he went off half-cocked. Screamed at me for calling too late to talk to the kids. He accused me of being too busy with my boyfriend to have time for the children. He said that he'd show me. If I didn't have time for the children, then I didn't deserve to have them. I asked him what he meant by that, and he said he was going to kill them.

"I didn't believe him. He's made the same threats before, usually as they lie sleeping. He'd go into one room or the other and hold a pillow over one of the kids' faces and say, 'See how easy it would be? No muss, no fuss.' It was so cold. It used to terrify me, but it became so frequent that I started to believe he was just trying to control me. I never dreamed . . ."

Her voice broke. McNaughton knew her stoic demeanor couldn't last forever. She put her face into her hands and wept mournfully. Her body shook from the sobs.

Jack and Kit looked at each other and decided, without words, to let her go. Jack leaned over and turned off the recorder. "Mrs. Peterson, we'll give you a few minutes. Is there anything I can get you?" he asked.

"No, thank you," she managed to say through the tears.

Kit and Jack left the conference room for a few minutes. They left the door ajar, and went back when her sobbing subsided. Kit brought a cup of the awful coffee with her.

"Here you go," she said, handing it to Mrs. Peterson. "It's not good, but it's hot."

"Thank you," she whispered. "I'm sorry about that."

"Don't worry about it," Jack said. He had followed Kit into the room. "We know you've been through a lot today, and we're sorry we're putting you through more. It won't be much longer."

"That's OK," she said. "I want to talk about this. I want you to have everything you need to make sure he rots in prison or, better yet, hangs. Isn't that how we put such monsters to death?"

Jack had to try again not to show surprise. The language and the tone seemed so incongruous, coming from such a seemingly refined woman. But then, he didn't suppose there were rules on how to behave after your husband beats your children to death.

"Uh, no, ma'am," Jack said. "Indiana's method of execution is lethal injection. But it's way too early to talk about that. It'll be up to the prosecutor to decide if he'll even seek the death penalty."

"I can't imagine a more deserving person," she said coldly, her eyes fixed on his.

McNaughton was uncomfortable discussing the death penalty with a perpetrator's wife, and he decided to change the subject. "Mrs. Peterson," he said as he picked up several heavy-walled paper bags from beneath his chair. "I wish I didn't have to ask you to do this, but I need you to look at some clothing to see if it belongs to your husband. I'll warn you in advance that it's stained with blood. A lot of it."

She gulped. "OK. Whatever it takes." She subtly shifted her body, as if steeling herself.

He put the bags on the floor between his legs and pulled out a work shirt. Mrs. Peterson gasped. Although the blood had darkened as it dried, it could still be easily seen against the stiffened navy blue. "That's his shirt," she said.

"How do you know, Mrs. Peterson?" Jack asked.

"I bought it for him. And I've washed it a hundred times. Let me see the tag. It should have an eighteen-inch neck or so."

Jack looked at the tag and showed it to Mrs. Peterson. Neck: Seventeen and a half inches.

He repeated the routine, pulling from another bag a pair of pants that Mrs. Peterson likewise identified as her husband's and predicted a forty-six-inch waist and a thirty-eight-inch inseam. The tag revealed them to be forty-six by thirty-eight.

McNaughton did not see the point in showing Mrs. Peterson the undershirt, which was especially gruesome. The blood was particularly stark against the white V-shaped space of the undershirt that apparently showed under Peterson's open shirt collar.

"John favors work clothing, even though he works – or used to work – in an office. When he still had a job, he wore white shirts and ties, and he still wears those to Mass, but that's about it."

"Mrs. Peterson," Kit asked, "where did your husband last work?"

"He wrote programs for CompuTech, but he got fired from there a year ago last month."

"Why?" McNaughton asked, making a mental note to have Simons check that out.

"John has trouble getting along with people. He was always proselytizing, making people feel uncomfortable and inadequate. I don't think it was any one incident, just one thing after another until they couldn't handle him anymore. He didn't seem too disturbed about being fired, and he hasn't made much effort to find another job since then. He keeps saying that *somebody* ought to stay home with the children and, of course, the implication is it ought to be me. But I like my job, and it pays well. Thank God I had it when he lost his."

"Mrs. Peterson, let's get back to yesterday," Jack said. Because she had calmed down, he decided he might be able to get a little more information from her. "Did you have any more contact with your husband after that phone call, the one in which he made his threats?"

"Not last night. Not until this morning. He called me at my hotel and told me that he had killed the children."

"He called and told you *that*?" Alvear was incredulous. "What exactly did he say?"

Peterson thought for a moment. "This is hard; I wasn't exactly thinking straight after that call," she said.

"It's OK; take your time," Kit said. "Did he actually say he killed the children?"

"I think he said he had made sure that I had nothing left in this world, that he had taken away everything that I cared about. He said he did the same thing to me that I had done to him. And I asked him what he was talking about, and he said that he killed the children. I didn't believe him at first. I said that wasn't very funny. And then he got sickening, and asked me if I could imagine what the children looked like without faces.

"You know, he's right." Her voice was mournful, but she didn't cry. "He *has* robbed me of everything I care about in this world – my children, a happy family life, peace and tranquility and privacy. I can't even think about what my life is going to be like. I'm not sure I want to live it, except I know I want to make sure he never, *never*, gets out of prison.

"I know it sounds horrible when I say I hope he gets the death penalty. The truth is, it doesn't matter. There is no punishment sufficient for him in this life. I've never been sure if there was a hell, despite what the Church teaches us. I couldn't imagine the God that I love being so vindictive as to send someone to eternal damnation. But in the last few hours, I've started to change my mind. Nothing *but* an eternity in hell would be sufficient for my husband." She paused and then continued, her voice subdued:

"Then again, I'm not sure what I believe in anymore. How could God even allow this to happen?"

Jack was glad he was asking, not answering, questions. That one was unanswerable; he knew, because he had asked it himself so many times. Especially when the victims were children. An all-knowing God? A merciful God? A God who loves children? Then why?

"I wish I could give you an answer, Mrs. Peterson," McNaughton said. "Maybe we can call your priest for you."

"No. I don't want to talk to anybody who will try to persuade me that this was God's will. That's what everybody always says when something awful happens. 'It was God's will.' Or 'God doesn't give us anything that we can't handle.' How the hell does He know? How do *I* know? Can anybody handle having their children killed?"

She paused again. "Are we finished?"

"Yeah," Jack said. "I think that's enough for tonight. Kit, have hotel arrangements been made for Mrs. Peterson?"

"Yes," Alvear answered. "We have a room reserved at the Omni, and a couple of uniforms are waiting downstairs to take her. Mrs. Peterson, you have my home phone and of course you know you can call nine-one-one if you need anything. I also want to give you another number." She handed Mrs. Peterson a business card; it belonged to Dr. Eric Skelton, a psychologist. "Dr. Skelton is on call for our department. Call him if he can help you."

"Thank you," she said.

"OK, Mrs. Peterson, I'll show you out." Kit motioned for her to go ahead, and then pointed at the stairs. Alvear turned and called. "I'll be right back, Jack."

"Good night, Sergeant," Mrs. Peterson said quietly as she stepped away.

"Good night, Mrs. Peterson," Jack said. "Thank you for your help."

McNaughton started his pacing again. It was beginning to come together in his mind: A jealous husband. Insanely jealous, or jealously insane? Was the jealousy justified? He would get Alvear or Simons to check that out. Not that his wife having an affair – or fifty of them – would justify what he did to those kids. But while it's not legally necessary to establish a motive to win a conviction, Jack knew that jurors like to know why somebody commits a heinous crime. And they'd really be searching for answers in this case.

If adultery weren't the answer, what was? What could provoke somebody to go this far? The cops would have to find some reason for him going off like this, lest a jury decide that he was crazy and let him off. Meeting the legal definition of insanity wasn't easy; the burden was on the defense to show he didn't know the difference between right and wrong. But juries – even the most conscientious ones – often had trouble with the concept. Obviously, you've got to be nuts to kill your kids – but nuts in a layperson's terms. The real question was: Was he legally insane?

Jack wondered if Mrs. Peterson's apparent hatred for her husband was longstanding or a result of his deeds of twenty-four hours ago. No matter which, he wondered what kind of a witness she'd make if she maintained that cool exterior. Would anybody believe that she loved her kids? Would some goof on the jury decide that she deserved this? But then he recalled the first emotional phone conversation he had had with her.

Kit stepped onto the landing as if her legs hurt. It had been quite a day for her too. "Well, what do you think, Jack?" she asked.

"I think we've got a problem," he answered. "I interviewed Peterson right before you got back, and it was the all-time weirdest interview I've ever conducted. I think he's angling for an insanity defense, and his wife could blow that right out of the water – except for the spousal privilege."

"I'm not sure I follow you."

"Well, the phone call that Peterson made to his wife this morning shows how cold-hearted – and premeditated – his actions were. Her story alone could convict him – maybe even get him the death penalty. At the very least, she could show that he didn't act in the heat of passion – you know, what he'd have to show to get off with a conviction for manslaughter instead of murder. But Peterson can invoke the spousal privilege, which basically says she can't testify against him, unless he gives permission. Obviously, he's not going to give her that permission."

"Oh, shit," Alvear said. "Surely we can find somebody who heard him make threats or witnessed his bad relationship with his wife."

"God, I hope so. But I don't know, Kit. It worries me. I've seen some people literally get away with murder, all because they can convince some naïve juror that they must have been nuts to do what they did. We can pull the phone records and show that he telephoned his wife this morning, which ought to raise some questions in the jurors' minds, but we can't answer the questions for them. And maybe Mrs. Peterson can testify that the clothing belongs to her husband, but I don't think that fact's going to be disputed. I mean, if he pleads 'not guilty by reason of insanity,' he admits he did it but claims he wasn't responsible."

"Why do you figure he's going for insanity?" Alvear asked.

"Well, among other things, he said that he cut off his own arm with a circular saw."

"OK – I'm convinced," she said, her voice incredulous. "That's sick."

"I know. What I'd like to know is, if his crazy mind could conjure that up, why didn't he just *imagine* beating the brains out of his kids – instead of really doing it?"

"Because he didn't want to just imagine that, Jack. That wouldn't have accomplished his goal of breaking his wife's heart."

CHAPTER 4

McNaughton gingerly turned the key in the lock, doing his best to ensure the cat didn't escape and that he didn't startle Renee. They rarely waited up for each other; they had learned long ago that, with the unpredictable schedules they both had, it didn't make much sense. Not with a four-year-old in the house, anyway. Neither was a morning person, and at least *one* of them had to be lucid enough the next morning to ensure that Angel got breakfast and was decently dressed for day care. But this night Renee and Belle Starr, the aging, white-and-grey short-hair cat that she brought to the marriage, were curled up together on the green floral couch in the family room. Renee was reading a John Irving novel and stroking Belle, who purred contently and snuggled under a multi-colored afghan Jack's mother had crocheted years earlier. One dim bulb lit the house when he tiptoed in.

She craned her neck to greet him. "Hi, love," she whispered sweetly. Angelica was long asleep; talking wouldn't waken her now. But the lights were low, as was the mood, and it seemed appropriate to keep her voice that way too.

"I'm so sorry you had to go through that," she said sympathetically.

"Thanks, babe," he answered. "You didn't have to wait up."

"I wanted to, Jack. I made my world-famous peasant soup. Want a bowl?"

"That would be great."

Renee moved the cat from her lap and rose from the couch to go into the kitchen, an extension of the family room separated only by the breakfast table. On the way, she stopped to kiss Jack on the mouth. Belle watched with a cocked head, incredulous that she had been summarily dismissed. Then she wound herself into an oval and nudged her nose beneath her paw, apparently to block out the light. Renee, arriving in the kitchen, took a filled soup bowl out of the refrigerator and carefully put it into the microwave, wrinkling her nose in frustration when she spilled a bit anyway. As she punched the buttons, she turned to Jack.

"How about a glass of wine?"

"I could really use it," he said. "You too?"

She nodded. He hadn't sat down yet, so he retrieved two wine glasses from the cupboard above the tiny wet bar in the family room and headed toward the refrigerator. She had already gotten out an opened bottle of zinfandel, pulled out the cork and handed the bottle to him.

He poured two glasses fuller than they do in restaurants and set them on the table. "I feel really grimy; I want to get out of these clothes," he said, turning to leave the room. He slowly mounted the stairs, careful to keep his footfalls from landing too loudly. He went to the master bedroom, and doffed his khakis and forest-green golf shirt in favor of an old navy-blue MMPD t-shirt and grey gym shorts. Then he went to Angelica's room and, barefoot, slipped in quietly to watch his angel sleep.

He stood there a few moments, gazing at her smooth, peaceful face – the slightly pink cheeks, the pursed red lips, the long, delicate eyelashes that framed those lovely eyes. He brushed back wisps of brown hair from her face. It was damp from perspiration – too many blankets, he noted – so he pulled one back to the bottom of the bed. He thought about the horror beneath the blankets at the Peterson house and shivered. But he pushed the thought away as quickly as it had arrived, and marveled at his daughter's beauty, her innocence. He didn't allow himself to even consider how he would feel if anything bad ever happened to her. It was beyond comprehension. And to think a father actually did *that* to his precious children.

Jack leaned to kiss Angel's smooth cheek. "Daddy loves you more than you know," he whispered. She stirred, stretching and throwing an arm over her favorite toy – a stuffed manatee – and Jack tiptoed from the room and down the steps.

Renee had removed the bowl from the microwave after the buzzer sounded, wiped up the spillage, fetched a spoon and placed it with the soup bowl on a placemat at Jack's regular place at the table. She sliced a thick slab of sour dough from a dwindling loaf, and set it on a plate. Then she sat in her regular spot beside him, hoisted one foot up onto the chair so that her knee could serve as a resting spot for her elbow. She grasped her wine glass and waited for him to return.

She had worked a lot of big stories, and she knew that adrenalin had kept him going for the last eighteen hours. It was still pumping, and would be for another hour. Then he'd crash – fatigue from both the number of hours of work and the emotional intensity of them.

She knew, perhaps more than he did, that he needed her here to listen. She sipped her wine as Jack returned to the kitchen, but said nothing. Jack would talk when he was ready.

"It feels good to be out of those clothes," he said. He sat at the table, scooped a spoonful of the hearty vegetable soup, blew on it and tasted it. "Mmm. This is good," he said between sips. He had never been good at small talk, nor had she. They preferred silence to banalities – had since the day they met eleven years earlier – because they had always felt so comfortable with each other.

He dunked the bread into the soup, took a bite and spoke: "It was unreal." He said it so matter-of-factly, so out-of-the-blue. Almost as if he were answering a question that Renee had been reluctant to pose. "I cannot think of anything I've ever witnessed that is worse than what I saw today.

"I mean, how *could* he do it? I look at Angel, and I think how it hurts me when she stubs her toe. How could he?"

"I wish I knew, babe," Renee said.

"You know, he kept quoting the Bible, and according to his wife, he's some kind of religious fanatic. A Catholic, by the way."

"Oh, really?"

"Yeah. I just don't get it. How could somebody who believes so fervently do something like that? But what gets me even more, babe, is, how could *God* let it happen? I remember wondering about that when we lost the baby. Why would God take a baby away from two people – three, really, because Angel lost the chance to be a big sister – who wanted her so much? I've never figured that out. It doesn't jibe with everything else I've been taught about God. But as bad as that was for us, this goes so far beyond."

"Yeah," Renee said, nodding her head slowly. "As horrible as we felt after the miscarriage, it's hard to equate that with this. I mean, we didn't know that baby, no matter how much we wanted her. These children were living, breathing people who'd been in his life for years. I wish I could give you an answer, Jack, but I'm as baffled as you."

Again they sat in silence for several moments, sipping their wine. Jack finished his soup and pushed the empty bowl toward the middle of the table. It served as a signal to the cat, who jumped onto his lap and rubbed her face against his arm, encouraging a stroke.

Renee spoke first. "Do you have a motive yet?"

"We think he did it to get revenge on his wife for an affair. But we don't think she was even having one. It's so unbelievable. You know, there've been plenty of times that Angel has made me crazy."

"Me, too," she interrupted, her voice empathetic.

"And at those moments, I could relate to people who hit their kids. I mean, it doesn't seem so remote, but something inside me stops me. Sense. Maturity. Compassion. *Something*. But even at the worst of those moments, I cannot, for the life of me, fathom being angry with *you* and taking it out on *her*. And in such an extreme way.

"If there is a God, how could He let it happen?"

Renee had no answer for him. But they sat there for a long time, as he recounted his day – the horrifying sights, the shocking Peterson interview, the devastating look on Mrs. Peterson's face. The story was new, but the scene was familiar. Jack and Renee had always talked this way. It had started on their first date when they talked for hours over a dinner of Greek chicken and inexpensive white wine. In retrospect, they both admitted that, even that first evening, they knew they had met a soul mate. That feeling continued over the years, even in the days when Renee didn't think she could take another minute of the demanding role of cop's wife.

In the early days, the similarities in their work provided fascinating fodder for dinner conversation. They marveled at how much police work was like newspaper reporting. Both of them sought out facts and details. Both liked minutia. Both wanted to get to the bottom of things, and both had to sort through a lot of garbage to do that. Both wanted to do the right thing, to do what they could to right a wrong. Jack's successes resulted in an arrest, Renee's, in a good story.

She used to work the police beat, so she loved hearing about Jack's cases, as well as the gossip about his colleagues, many of whom she had known from her days in the cop shop. But after a while, the stories about the department reminded her all too much of the beat she had eventually won – politics. She felt strongly that politics were appropriate in the Statehouse, but not in the stationhouse. Before long, Renee came to loath the characters whose antics had undermined Jack's idealism and had rendered him a sullen, disillusioned man.

Indeed, Jack wasn't the same person that she had met outside an old clapboard house all those years ago. She was the cop-shop reporter then, sent to cover the shooting deaths of three black men and grumbling all the way because she heard about the triple ten-zero on the police scanner just minutes before she was due to get off work. She had even had to cancel a date that she had with an interesting guy she had met through her best friend Marilyn, the newspaper's controller. Renee was irritated that such a last-minute cancellation would give him the impression that she hadn't really wanted to go out, when, in fact, she had.

Jack was still a beat cop, the first one on the scene of what appeared to be the work of a hit man. (Later, the cops would piece it together: The victims, all small-time drug dealers, hadn't made good on an aging debt, so their supplier got his revenge.) McNaughton followed procedure and called in the homicide dicks, who worked the case, but they asked him to field questions from the growing mass of newsies. A couple of the television stations had sent reporters – in their endless competition to be the most sensational, this was right up their alley – as did the two big newspapers, a neighborhood weekly, two radio stations and the wire service. It wasn't every day that three guys got killed, execution-style, in Indianapolis. So Jack held court with the reporters just outside the yellow plastic police line, and when he set eyes on Renee, it was all over for him.

Her dark brown hair was waist length, full and straight. She parted it on the right side, and combed it back to reveal high, defined cheekbones accentuated with big gold hoop earrings. Her hazel eyes were huge and piercing; Jack felt as if she looked right through him as he spoke. She hung on his words, keeping those luscious eyes on him except to glance down occasionally at her notebook, on which she was scrawling the most atrocious chicken scratch he had seen this side of a doctor's office. How on earth would she be able to decipher that? he wondered. Then again, within moments of knowing this incredible, inquisitive, exquisite woman, he was sure that she could figure out anything in the world. Including an instant way to his heart.

She felt the immediate attraction too, but they were both too professional to let that get in the way of their work. She hung around after the impromptu press conference was over; newspaper reporters always need more details than the broadcast people. She was about to start her routine grilling – cops were notoriously tight-lipped – but he was unusually solicitous. "Is there anything else you need to know?" he asked her. In all her years on the beat, he was probably the first cop who had ever graciously offered her information. So she peppered him with questions: Were they all killed with the same weapon? How many perps? Where were the wounds? Were the victims bound? What kind of rap sheets did they have?

His cooperation showed in her story the next morning. Nobody else had nearly as much information, including the bigger Indianapolis Star. A scoop over the Star was particularly gratifying for Sun reporters, who had adopted the bygone slogan of a car rental company – "we try harder" – and generally proved it. Even the managing editor, a skinny, staid fellow who wore skinny bow ties and rarely had anything good to say about anybody, sent a note congratulating her tenacity in ferreting out the specifics. The note, a rare occurrence in any newsroom, was gratifying, but

Renee couldn't get that blue-eyed cop off of her mind; he was *so* nice. She picked up the phone and did something she had never done before, or since: She called him to thank him for the help.

That's not something reporters do. They thank a source as the interview concludes; that's that. If a reporter does more, the source wonders what's up. But Renee knew that Officer McNaughton didn't often deal with the press, so she figured he wouldn't doubt her sincerity. And she really wanted to talk to him.

"Hi, this is Renee Somers from the Sun," she said with as much spirit as she could muster over her nervousness. She looked at her own hand quivering as she fidgeted with her pen. "I just wanted to thank you for all your help last night. It really made for a good story." She doodled on the desk pad in front of her.

He stammered. She had caught him off-guard, just as his shift was scheduled to start. "Oh, oh, yeah. Well, you're welcome. You ask good questions. A *lot* of questions," he said. "I saw the story this morning; you really handled it well. Got it all right, too." He wondered immediately if he had put his foot in his mouth; was it OK to compliment a reporter? He wondered why she was calling; he had told her everything he could the previous night – everything he'd been authorized to say, and probably a bit more. And he didn't know anything else.

"You'll have to talk with Detective Thompson at downtown homicide for more information," he offered. "I'm out of the picture now. Back to chasing robbers."

She chuckled at the feeble attempt at humor. "Oh, yeah, I know," she said. She had already talked to Thompson that day, and the information he had given her, combined with the reactions from scared neighbors, gave her a good follow. Thompson, a gruff fifty-five-year-old veteran who was inches away from retirement, had been a good source of Renee's for years. Knowing that she wasn't married, he had taken it upon himself to try to set her up with a few cops, but she had steadfastly resisted. Renee had promised herself, as well as a few female colleagues, that she would never date a cop. They were invariably obnoxiously flirtatious, even the married ones. Some were even crudely grabby and offensive. Most of them were too macho for her taste, and many were morbid, daring her on a regular basis to go to the morgue to witness an autopsy.

Thompson had noticed the long conversation Renee had had with McNaughton outside the clapboard house the previous night, and he made sure to mention to her that Jack wasn't married. She groaned; Thompson would have wondered what was up if she hadn't. But she was secretly pleased to have that information, and decided then and there to act on it.

What, after all, did she have to lose? She had already missed the date that Marilyn set up and, come to think of it, what had she seen in that guy? Wasn't he just a pencil pusher? McNaughton was different. He had remarkable eyes – round, blue and expressive – and brown hair so sun-bleached that he surely had been blond as a child. He was about five-foot-nine and one hundred seventy-five pounds; his arms and thighs were tight from working out, but he wasn't musclebound like some bodybuilder. Better yet, his brain didn't seem to be musclebound. She had never before been attracted to light-haired, blue-eyed or muscular men. But she also had not been attracted to cops. The same could not be fairly said of her again.

"So, I'd like to take you out to lunch to show my appreciation. My boss, who's such a jerk that he usually acknowledges that we lowly reporters exist only long enough to yell at us, actually sent me a note saying he liked the story. I grant you, that made me wonder for a moment if I had done something wrong," she joked, with an uncharacteristically girlish giggle, "but I know it was a good story. And I owe that to you."

Jack couldn't believe it. As attracted as he was to her, he never could have imagined dating somebody who worked for the Sun. He had grown up with it in his home every day. His parents read it cover to cover, and discussed stories over dinner. Jack was impressed the first time he had met a reporter, and now one – one very beautiful one – was asking him to lunch.

"Well, I'm usually asleep at noon time, what with this goofy shift. But I get a dinner break – if you could see your way clear to having dinner instead."

"Sure. That'd be great," she said. "How 'bout Friday night – eight or so?"

"That sounds good," he said. "What's your address?"

She lived on the near north side, not all that far from him. He was off on Friday – but he didn't mention that to her. If the date went well, it could go on for more than an hour, he figured. If it didn't, he could beg off early, saying he had to get back to the stationhouse to get back into uniform and back out on the street.

But the evening went better than either could have imagined. They held hands over dinner; he politely asked her in the elevator if he could kiss her; she invited him upstairs to her apartment for a night cap, where he was thoroughly investigated by Belle. They talked until the early morning hours, and when they finally parted, it was with reluctance and an assurance that they would see each other again.

Two years later, they were married. Since then, Renee had seen Jack through more nights like this than either could remember.

Jack sipped the last of his wine. "As if this weren't enough, Doyle was at it again."

"Oh, God. What now?" Renee asked. She proffered her glass as he reached to pour more wine into it. He added some to his depleted glass as well. The alcohol and the conversation were working; he could feel his body relaxing, the tenseness leaving his shoulders and neck.

"Well, you saw him on TV, right?" She nodded. "I think he was angry that he didn't make the six o'clock. But things had moved so fast, and Doyle wasn't really up on what was happening.

"Then tonight, he started in on me about communication and my attitude and that stuff. Not much, really. It was just that I didn't have the stamina to listen to that bullshit again."

By his regular standards, Stumbo *was* rather subdued this evening. There were times when he would go on a rampage, raging at anyone who got in his way but especially at anyone who forced him to make a decision. But Jack had learned over the years how to deal with Doyle, and he could generally tolerate his massive incompetence, often working around him. What he could not tolerate was the pervasive laziness that afflicted much of the department's brass. It was easier for them to accept the status quo than to try something new, easier to do things the way they had always been done than to consider what might be a better way. Jack virtually begged the brass to send some of his detectives to seminars where they'd learn the latest innovative investigative techniques; instead, their idea of good training was taking a first-aid class and target shooting once a month. What made that all the more troubling was that, no matter how important the investigation the detective was working, he or she had to drop everything to attend those classes. McNaughton feared the day when evidence was lost or a suspect got away because one of his people was learning, for the umpteenth time, how to perform CPR.

But his disgruntlement went deeper than that. He had grown weary of a city administration that cared more about the bottom line than about good police work. He was tired of a promotional system that rewarded incompetence, because it was easier for the top guys to keep their thumbs down on their underlings if the underlings were dolts. He was frustrated by the brass's insistence that cops blindly adhere to an interminable chain of command, no matter how small the issue.

It had been a gradual awakening for someone who had always wanted to be a cop. The desire was nearly as old as Jack was; he had dressed up as a policeman for two Halloweens before he started kindergarten. His drive was reinforced in the third grade, when a lieutenant from what was then the Indianapolis Police Department came to Jack's elementary school on career day to explain what he did. Some of the other kids were more tantalized by the priest who brought unconsecrated, but real, Communion hosts and a bejeweled gold chalice when he visited. (As far as Jack knew, though, none of them had made good on those third-grade pledges to go into the priesthood. They had proven in high school that they didn't have the knack for celibacy.) Despite the influences of his mother, who attended seven-fifteen a.m. Mass nearly every day, Jack was more interested in temporal concerns even then. The shiny gold badge and buttons on the lieutenant's crisp dress blues had first caught Jack's Wedgewood blue eyes, and for years afterward, police work put a sparkle in them. Throughout high school and into college, he longed to be a police officer, even scrupulously avoiding all the campus parties where pot was smoked, and in his early years on the department he refused to allow anything to cause him to become jaded about the job. One guy called him Pollyanna; McNaughton didn't care.

He came on in mid-1989, straight out of Indiana University's criminal justice program, where he had earned a B+ average. Ever the perfectionist, he stewed for years that he could have done better, if only he had tried harder. Since that day in third grade, he had dreamed of getting on the Indianapolis department. But when there was no recruit class in 1988 – the result of city budget cuts – McNaughton worried mightily that there wouldn't be a recruit class after his graduation either. By 1989, though, city officials couldn't schedule a recruit school fast enough. There had been a rash of armed robberies in some of the city's better neighborhoods, some that ended in shootings, and city council members were taking a lot of heat from their constituents to beef up the police force. The newspapers had a field day criticizing the city for failing to bring in more recruits the year before, so intimidating the mayor that he immediately ordered a new recruit class. Years later, when the department had a spate of police-action shootings – some of them questionable – Jack thought that the newspapers weren't aggressive enough in pointing out that new cops weren't getting any training beyond the basics – again, the result of budget cuts. McNaughton would defend to the end a fellow cop who justifiably shot somebody in the line of duty; he hoped he'd never have to experience the devastation that he had seen in the eyes of some of his colleagues who had done it. But he was deeply bothered by the questionable shootings, many of which seemed to be more the result of the overwhelming fear inexperienced officers felt than any real threat to their well-being. He was convinced that, if the city weren't so cheap and would train these people, some of the shootings would never have happened. But what disturbed him the most was the other kind of police shootings, in which McNaughton was sure that the cop had a cowboy complex. With those kinds of guys, that big gun was a second dick, and using it, Jack feared, gave them the same thrill as using the real one. Enough of them bragged about it, anyway.

McNaughton didn't know much about those kinds of cops in the early days. All that came later, after his light brown hair had turned the corner toward grey, when he worked homicide and sometimes had to wallow in their mess. For his first four years on the department, he drove a marked cruiser on patrol around one of the city's worst neighborhoods. He saw plenty of dead bodies, but they usually were the result of some stupid feud between two scumbags who had been drinking too much. He also worked a lot of domestic disputes in those days; it was always so frustrating when the woman – eye blackened, mouth bleeding – would refuse to press charges against her man. For a long time, Jack didn't understand, but a counselor who worked at the shelter for abused women finally convinced him that the women feared being alone and maybe destitute more than they feared the physical abuse. She explained to him that abusers undermine the women's self-confidence, making the victims all the more reluctant to leave. He did not give up, often spending more time trying to persuade the victim that she could make it on her own than he did writing his report. And when he got a rare victory, he silently wore it like a badge of honor that he had persuaded a woman to leave behind a man who professed his love all the while he was beating the hell out of her.

Even with those minor moral victories, McNaughton eventually decided that he was not cut out for such work. There were too many defeats, too many women who went back to their assailants despite his best efforts. And Jack liked to win. So after two years of sleepless nights filled with wondering where he should go with his life, McNaughton decided that he'd prefer working in an area where he'd likely win a higher percentage of his cases. He put in for a promotion to become a detective in homicide.

It was grim work, to be sure. But McNaughton had a curious mind that refused to turn off even when he desperately needed sleep. The brass thought he had deftly handled the minor investigations that a beat cop does, or so they said, and he had the college degree that few beat cops but most detectives had. So McNaughton got the job and was assigned to the downtown homicide bureau.

"At least the victims I deal with now can't back out of filing charges," he told Renee then, only half kidding.

In recent years, he made no secret of his burgeoning disenchantment with the department, and that caused considerable consternation. Captain Ryan, his and Stumbo's superior, had fretted over how to shut Jack up without provoking a big stink, and he had finally hatched a plan: Discipline Jack until he was silenced. So in the last twenty months or so, McNaughton had gotten in trouble twice. One time, he had an I-number drawn on him – that is, he became the subject of an internal investigation – and was eventually given a letter of reprimand for authorizing his detectives to work excessive overtime, thus costing the department money. Ryan himself had told Jack to do whatever it took to solve the case at hand – the second rape and murder in as many weeks of a downtown businesswoman walking in a high-rise parking garage – because the mayor was taking a lot of heat over it. But "whatever it takes" didn't include working more than forty hours that week.

When McNaughton's performance was reviewed a few months later, Stumbo and Ryan blasted him for every misstep, most of them imaginary, that they could dream up. They accused him of being too friendly with the troops – even, they charged, stooping so low as to attend the bachelor party of one of his detectives. They considered such fraternization with the troops to be unhealthy. They accused him of being a weak supervisor who failed to keep close enough tabs on his people. His detectives, for their part, loved Jack for trusting them enough to make their own decisions in the field. The brass also accused McNaughton of failing to communicate well and failing to follow the chain of command. They cited an instance when Jack allegedly had not gotten authorization to pay an informant who eventually helped crack a seemingly unsolvable case. He *had* run the matter by Stumbo, who failed to bring the issue up with Ryan, but it was McNaughton who was disciplined. Ryan rather liked having the suck-up Stumbo below him, and did not want to jeopardize that cozy situation.

The reprimand and bad review served their purpose. McNaughton realized he couldn't win, and he didn't want to jeopardize a stellar career. So he shut up.

Renee could see, though, how it ate at his gut. He was constantly chewing Tums tablets, and he brooded about the deterioration of the department. She tried to reason with him; after all, his job was to solve murders and oversee detectives who did so, and he was among the best. It was not his job, she would say, to run the department, so he needed to let go of it.

She listened sympathetically tonight, knowing instinctively that he needed unconditional support after working the Peterson case. Other times, though, she thought he needed a kick in the butt, and Renee was never reluctant to give it to him. On a recent Sunday morning, Stumbo, who had no life outside the office, called to ask Jack a few questions about a case; he had been reviewing reports. The "minute or two" call turned into a thirty-five-minute invasion of the limited time Renee and Jack considered theirs, when they sipped steaming lattes, ate onion bagels with cream cheese and lox and lingered at the breakfast table with the Sunday Sun, the Star and sometimes, for a treat, the New York Times. She generally shrugged off such calls; it would be hypocritical for her to do otherwise because she got plenty of calls at home from her office too. But calls to Jack had been more frequent of late, and too often they were inconsequential matters that easily could have waited for regular office hours.

Jack was particularly congenial on the phone that morning – something that irritated Renee all the more. After the lengthy conversation, he hung up the phone and went back to the sports page. Renee glared at him, hoping he'd feel the heat of her eyes and look up. Nothing. She fumed.

"Why don't you tell that fat fucker to leave you alone on your day off ?" Her voice was furious, but she kept the volume down; Angel was still in bed.

"For God's sake, Renee. He's my boss. How the hell am I supposed to do that?" He knew that she was right – that the stupid calls during off-hours were coming all too often – but he couldn't acknowledge that. He didn't wait for her to answer. "Get off my case!"

"Damn you, Jack!" Renee was livid. "How many times have they screwed you with bad reviews and I-numbers and letters of reprimands and lousy pay and hassles out the wazoo? They said in your review that you're mediocre. They put it in writing! So be mediocre! Quit trying to be supercop! Why not live up to what they wrote about you? You don't owe them anything more!

"You put more energy into that damn job than into your family," she continued, building up steam as she went. "You care more about it than you do about Angel and me! You treat that asshole Stumbo like he's some great guy, but you blast the shit out of your daughter and me if we fail to read your mind and do exactly what you think we ought to do! Snap out of it, Jack. Face reality!"

Without giving him a moment to respond – and to deny the allegations about where his priorities lay – she got up and shoved her chair under the table. She stomped up the stairs and headed for the shower. So much for a relaxing Sunday morning.

The mood was considerably different this night, as the clock ticked past midnight Wednesday and into the early Thursday morning hours. "Honey," Jack said, "I really appreciate you waiting up for me and making the soup and listening to me, but you'd better go to bed. You've got to get up early. I'll be in in a little bit, OK?"

She had to agree; she was exhausted, and she had an early interview that she couldn't miss if she hoped to get her weekly column written. "You'll be OK, honey?" He nodded, and she rose to kiss him on his earthy-smelling hair. He lifted his head, and they kissed. "Good night, sweetie," she said sleepily.

"'Night, babe."

She left, and Jack went into the den. He ran his eyes over the crowded book shelf, looking past the dozens of dog-eared paperbacks and old college texts and the few special hardbacks that they had splurged on. There it was: the Bible. It was pristine. The fake-leather cover was unscratched; the binding was stiff. He pulled it out and plopped on the couch. Belle Starr promptly leapt up and lay beside him.

He could remember Peterson mentioning only one specific book – Deuteronomy – so he flipped through until he came to it. Rubbing Belle's neck with one hand, he paged through with the other, looking to see if he could find the quote. He read a few here and there, but couldn't find anything that sounded familiar. So he paged through the rest of the Book, reading an occasional verse. "The inhabitants of the land will become pricks in your eyes and thorns in your sides," he read from Numbers. His mouth turned up into a smirk; what an appropriate verse for a cop, he thought.

He read until his eyes couldn't focus any longer, and he fell asleep with the cat beside him and the open Bible across his chest.

CHAPTER 5

Despite his horrendous Wednesday, Jack had little trouble getting up Thursday morning for Peterson's initial hearing. One reason was the ache in his neck, born of too many hours of sleeping upright, chin on his chest, on the couch. He had awakened himself abruptly with a snort around five a.m. and headed to bed, but it was too late for his neck. The other reason was his desire to see how Peterson would behave in court.

McNaughton was pleased when he saw the judge who had been assigned to the Peterson case under the county's blind selection process: Superior Court Judge Laura Linden, whose pixieish appearance belied her reputation for being a hanging judge. Linden didn't take guff off anybody, and she dished out maximum sentences when she thought they were deserved without a moment of reluctance. What McNaughton liked best about her was her abiding sense of justice. If she thought someone was being railroaded or that the prosecution didn't have its ducks in a row, she was equally hard on the state. McNaughton felt that her demanding behavior made him a better cop and made the prosecution do a better job preparing and presenting its case. And he believed that was what it was all about. He did not fear Linden's wrath today, because he felt confident that his case against Peterson was rock solid already, after a single day of investigation. The prosecution had assured him that, by the time trial rolled around, Peterson might as well substitute a noose for his neck tie.

"The Marion Superior Court, state of Indiana. The honorable Judge Laura Linden presiding," the bailiff bellowed. "All rise."

Linden swooped in, her black robe billowing behind her. "In the matter of the state of Indiana versus John Pius Peterson," she said. "Gentlemen, are we ready?"

"We are, your honor." It was Terrence Bennett, the county prosecutor himself, making a rare appearance in court. He was a tall man of average build who wore his medium-brown hair cut short. His hairline had receded so much that it was even with his ears, making it appear as if he were wearing a toupee that had slipped back on his head. He seemed to be perpetually drowsy, the result of droopy eyelids that stayed at half-mast over his brown eyes. Bennett usually left courtroom duties – especially initial hearings – to his deputies, which was fine by Jack, since Bennett had considerably less courtroom experience than several of the assistants who had made a career out of prosecuting. Bennett was all right – not too bad for a politician – but his most grating personality trait was showing today: His insatiable desire to see his name in the newspaper. He was sure that the many media outlets that had covered the sensational story yesterday would be back for more, and they didn't disappoint him.

To his right was Paul Santini, a short, wiry guy with short-cropped, tightly curled black hair, who would have been dwarfed had he stood next to the defendant. McNaughton was particularly pleased to see Santini; they had worked together many times before, and Paul, a fourteen-year prosecutor, was among the best in Bennett's office. His assignment to the case was testament to Bennett's political acumen. He couldn't afford to lose this case, so even if he put in appearances, it would be Paul who was quietly directing the prosecution's efforts when the media weren't looking.

"The defense is ready, your honor," Fortner said. McNaughton thought that Knofel looked exhausted; perhaps the specter of defending somebody who had committed such a heinous crime had kept him up last night. Knofel had three kids of his own, two little girls and a boy, and McNaughton suspected that Fortner may have done just what Jack had – paid a late-night visit to their bedrooms to drink in their angelic faces.

"Mr. Peterson," Linden said, "you have been charged with *six counts of murder*. As I am required by the law to do, I am now entering a plea of not guilty for you. Your trial is set for . . ." She looked down at her calendar and flipped the pages. "July eighteen." She paused. "Mr. Fortner, I understand you have a motion regarding bond?"

"Yes, your honor. Mr. Peterson has always been an upstanding citizen, a valued member of the community, a church-going, God-fearing man. Until he lost his job – through no fault of his own – he had been gainfully employed since his graduation from college and, indeed, had worked part-time to put himself through school." Jack couldn't believe the tack Knofel was taking; he half expected Fortner to claim next that this good, upstanding husband and father should be released so he could attend his children's funerals.

"The defense asks that you set bond as low as possible; in fact, were you to see your way clear to allowing Mr. Peterson to be released on his own recognizance, we are sure that you would not be sorry."

You can't blame him for giving it his best shot, Jack thought. Clearly, Fortner knew it was unlikely the judge would release somebody charged with six murders on his own recognizance. He also knew that Peterson had no money and it was unlikely Mrs. Peterson would be willing to bond him out.

"Your honor." Bennett was indignant; the showman was at work. "This man has been charged with *six counts of murder*. The state maintains that he has beaten *his own children to death*. We ask the court to hold him without bond. There is no amount of money that would keep Mr. Peterson in this jurisdiction; he has too much to lose by staying."

"Mr. Fortner, I'm inclined to agree with Mr. Bennett. Mr. Peterson has been charged with very serious offenses. We're going to hold him without bond."

Fortner was neither surprised nor dismayed. "Uh, your honor?"

"Yes, Mr. Fortner?"

"For the record, I want to inform the court that we plan to file a motion immediately that Mr. Peterson will plead not guilty by reason of temporary insanity. We also ask that the court order psychiatric tests to determine whether Mr. Peterson is able to stand trial."

"Yes, I think that's a good idea, Mr. Fortner. So ordered. Is there anything else, gentlemen?"

"No, your honor," Bennett and Fortner said in unison. And that was that.

Jack sat in the middle of the courtroom, staring into space. Not guilty by reason of insanity. Of course, Peterson had been setting up that defense in their interview the night before. This was no surprise. But it hurt to hear the words enunciated in court. All Jack could think was "not again."

"Knofel," Jack whispered to the defense attorney as they walked toward the back of the courtroom. "When can I get a copy of your motion?"

"It's nothing much, Jack. Just notice of our intent. I've arranged for Mr. Peterson to be interviewed by a psychiatrist this afternoon. After that, we'll file an affidavit regarding Mr. Peterson's specific condition."

That struck Jack as strange; they were filing a motion regarding the insanity plea *before* Peterson was examined? But Peterson couldn't plead anything but insanity, unless he was willing to take the rap and plead guilty. He had sat there and admitted, in detail and on tape, how he had bludgeoned his children. Finding a psychiatrist who would agree that he was nuts was merely a formality. It was a wonder what payment of an hourly rate could accomplish.

The courtroom announcement proved, too, that Knofel's political savvy rivaled Bennett's. He knew the initial hearing, little more than a formality in Indiana at which a judge automatically enters a not-guilty plea for the defendant, would nevertheless be heavily covered by the media interested in getting their first look at Peterson. He didn't want to leave the reporters and the public with an image of some monstrous guy who beat the brains out of his children, but rather that of a sad, desperate man who didn't know what he was doing. Announcing his plans to plead insanity would, Fortner thoughtfully wagered, breed sympathy instead of contempt.

"Sergeant, we've got a ten-zero and a suspect with a gun in Mars Hill." Joe Stutz, one of the newer members of McNaughton's squad, hadn't yet been assigned a partner, and Jack didn't want to assign him and the rookie, Chris Allen, to work together – not, at least, until they each had a little more time on. So McNaughton often worked with Stutz. The blond-haired, blue-eyed kid – tall and well-built with a ready smile and an eagerness to please (except when Jack implored him to stop calling him "Sergeant") – looked excited.

"Let's go," Jack answered, grabbing his nine-millimeter Sig Sauer from his desk drawer and his jacket from the back of his chair.

The lovely, unseasonable weather of the previous day had faded into a gloomy, grey day in which the mist persisted, but stubbornly refused to evolve into rain. It was typical Indiana weather: beautiful one day, putrid the next.

Joe took few precautions for the wet pavement as he drove to the Mars Hill neighborhood, an incongruous rural enclave of poor eastern Kentucky immigrants on the far southwest side of the state's most metropolitan city. When Kentuckians looking for work migrated there in the 1940s and '50s, Stumbo's family was among them. Doyle loved to talk about his hillbilly roots, laying the accent and the attitude on as thick as the coal dust that lined his father and his grandfather's lungs before they left the hollows of Appalachia – his father, by migration; his grandfather, by death.

Mars Hill was a respite from the coal mines, but not poverty. It was a small, unkempt neighborhood with tall weeds, pitted roads and emaciated, wild dogs that roamed the streets in a city with a mayor who focused on the business district to the detriment of the neighborhoods.

Joe pulled his dark green LTD up to a uniformed officer, the first cop on the scene, who had positioned himself to ensure that no one left the house where the shooting had been reported. "What's happening?" Stutz asked, and the uniform – squinting to keep the mist out of his eyes – briefed him and McNaughton about the single shotgun blast that had been reported by a neighbor.

Gun blasts were not uncommon in Mars Hill; target and varmint shooting was sport here. But it was the middle of the afternoon, and the neighbor reported the shot coming from inside the house, not out back.

Neighbors peered from behind drawn curtains as Joe parked the car. Only one man, a massively wrinkled skinny fellow, had ventured outside, and he looked as if nothing – not a gun blast nor the foul weather nor, for that matter, a tornado – would have budged him from the rickety front-porch rocking chair in which he was spending the afternoon. He wore a red-plaid flannel shirt – much too heavy, even on the cool spring day – and sipped a Pabst Blue Ribbon. His house was across the street and down two from the one in question. "It's that one," he croaked as they emerged from the car; he used a long, crooked forefinger to point at the tiny frame structure. Its sky blue paint was peeling; what was left was filthy from years of neglect.

"He's crazy, I tell ya," the old man called, his voice heavy with smoke. "Crazy as a goddamn loon."

McNaughton nodded his acknowledgement and then addressed his partner. "Joe, you take the front; I'll take the back." Both men instinctively reached across their chests and under their jackets to withdraw their handguns from their shoulder holsters. Stutz bounded up the front stoop and slipped to the side of the door; McNaughton slid down a broken concrete walk along the side of the house toward the back. He glanced in the living room windows as he scooted past. It was sparsely furnished, but for one unusual feature – a long gun, either a rifle or a shotgun, leaned in every corner of every room. So the guy's crazy, Jack thought, and he has an arsenal.

McNaughton ran further back, toward the overgrown back yard. The rain had greened everything up, and tall lavender-colored clovers waving in the breeze made it look almost pretty. But the ridiculously tall grass and the rusted power lawn mower, which apparently lay where it had broken down, ruined the idyllic picture. The next window, smudged as it was, gave him a good view of the kitchen. At the table sat an old woman with stringy, greasy, grey hair and wearing a dirty pink house smock. Her multiple chins lay on her chest; her breasts sagged to her waist; her eyes were closed. One hand lay in her lap; the other still grasped a half-empty whiskey bottle. Passed out, McNaughton figured.

Hands cupped around his gun, elbows locked and his finger ready near the trigger, McNaughton slipped from the kitchen window, past the dirty siding, and took a quick peek into the next window. It was a bedroom, and he realized that that was the extent of the house. In one corner lay a conspicuously stained bare mattress and an overturned crate that served as a nightstand. In the middle of the hardwood floor was a long-haired man's body, dressed in jeans and a T-shirt. He lay on his back in a massive pool of blood, his dead eyes staring blankly at the ceiling. Over him stood another man, dressed similarly and swaying unsteadily. His eyes were droopy, and he took a clumsy step backward and caught himself before stumbling. The guy's drunk, Jack thought. But the good news was that his skinny arms hung at his side and his calloused hands were empty; he obviously had laid down the weapon he had just used.

Jack scrambled back toward the kitchen. His heart was beating harder now; the adrenalin kick that was inevitable – and so necessary in this line of work – had started. At times like this, his senses seemed to sharpen: His ears tuned out peripheral noise, but he could hear the woman's snorting even with the door closed. His eyes darted about. McNaughton caught the eye of the uniform, poked at his own chest and then at the house. The signal was clear; he was going in. He hoped that the backup that had been ordered would arrive soon.

McNaughton carefully turned the knob on the back door and stepped in as quietly as he could. He knew that Stutz would stay at his post outside the house until he was signaled to enter; McNaughton's squad was the best-trained in homicide, and they sensed one another's movements so well that he sometimes wondered if they could read one another's minds. The kitchen reeked of rancid oil; the odor emanated from a fry pan filled with a half-inch of used oil that sat on a burner. Unscraped dishes had been shoved haphazardly in the sink; a half-eaten banana – the mushy flesh blackened and seeping from days of exposure – lay on the counter, a fly on it enjoying a midday meal.

He felt the mud-tracked linoleum give way as he stepped cautiously along the wall. He crunched something – a stale piece of cereal, perhaps – and thought that it had created a horrible racket, but it was only his own sensitivity to it. It occurred to him that virtually every house that he had been in in Mars Hill had a hound dog roaming about; where the hell was this guy's mutt? Ready to take a bite out of his butt? But he neither heard nor saw any sign of a dog; the water bowl on the floor was so small, it clearly was used by the huge yellow tom cat that had watched his movements from a fence post out back. Holding his gun in his right hand, he nudged the woman with his left. Nothing but a head bob; she was out cold. He slipped with his back against the wall to the bedroom and peered through the door.

"Who shot that man?" Jack said abruptly, loudly, authoritatively.

"Well, I did," the man answered, his voice oozing booziness.

McNaughton grabbed the man's left wrist and whipped it behind his back. "Joe! In here," he shouted. Stutz burst through the front door and bounded for the bedroom, running so quickly that Jack envisioned him blasting through the back wall of the house. McNaughton pushed the perp to the floor, an easy task given the man's blood-alcohol content. "You're under arrest," he said flatly as he holstered his weapon, grabbed his handcuffs and slipped one on the perp's wrist.

Joe grabbed the man's other hand and pulled it behind his back, making it easier for McNaughton to cuff him. Then Stutz leaned down, planning to feel for a pulse in the prone man's neck, but changing his mind when he saw the open, glazed-over eyes of death staring straight up.

McNaughton spoke first. "Joe, there's an old woman in the kitchen – she's out cold – but you'd better sweep the rest of the house," he said. "And then call for an ambulance."

"Uh, sarge? I think the guy's dead," Joe said sheepishly, as if McNaughton couldn't figure it out.

"I know, Joe. I want the ambulance for her. I don't want anything happening to her on our watch. And besides, if she sobers up at the hospital – in the secured ward – we have a better chance of talking to her before she leaves town or gets shit-faced again."

"Oh, yes, sir, sergeant," Stutz said. Jack smiled slyly, thinking "there he goes again."

They were on their way back to lockup when the perp, Lester Trueblood – whose traditional Kentucky name they had learned from the expired driver's license in his wallet – announced that he had to use the facilities. "Hold it," Jack told him curtly. He didn't mean it literally, of course, but Trueblood wiggled about, crossing his legs this way and that in an apparent effort to do just that. His hands, still cuffed behind his back, were unavailable.

"I'm going to fuckin' piss my pants and all over your fuckin' car if you don't fuckin' stop right now," he said, and then added – under his breath, he thought – "Fuckin' pigs."

Stutz looked to Jack for approval, and McNaughton nodded. They hadn't gotten far out of Mars Hill, so the area was still somewhat rural and there was a convenient fence row that would have to suffice. Jack winced from the rain as he got out of the car and helped Trueblood to step out without hitting his head. "Take these fuckin' cuffs off me," he slurred. "How the fuck am I supposed to fuckin' piss?"

McNaughton wasn't about to take the cuffs off of this guy, but he was less than thrilled about the alternative: Assisting Mr. Trueblood's effort to relieve himself. It was bad enough reaching into the slimeball's pocket to retrieve his wallet, and reaching into his fly was unthinkable. Stutz caught Jack eyeing him. "Sarge, I don't think so," he said in answer to a question not yet posed. Jack was about to pull rank and insist that Joe do it anyway when Trueblood, still swaying from his date with Jack Daniels, tumbled headlong into the ditch that ran along the fence row. He landed in the multi-floral rose hedge that covered the barbed-wire fence. Jack could see the widening wet spot on Trueblood's lap and a smile of relief break out on the drunk's face.

Neither admitted it, but both McNaughton and Stutz were privately pleased that they didn't have to deal with Trueblood's natural needs. Bad enough that they had to hitch him up by the armpits and guide him back into the cruiser. Thank God for vinyl seats.

With traffic, it took nearly fifteen minutes to reach the lockup, and Trueblood continued his vulgar diatribe about cops the entire time. After ten minutes, Joe had had it. "Shut *up!*" he screamed into the rear-view mirror. "I don't want to hear one more goddamn curse word!"

Jack stifled a chuckle by turning his head toward the window and covering his mouth with his hand. Joe, typically calm and reserved, didn't realize what he had said.

"Joe, just ignore him," McNaughton said. "It's just the booze talking."

"Sarge, I just get so tired of listening to these scumbags' bullshit."

"I know. But sometimes you just have to let things roll off your back."

By the time they had deposited Lester Trueblood with lockup, it was quitting time, and McNaughton was glad that he would be getting out of the office on time.

"McNaughton, get in here," Stumbo bellowed from behind his desk. McNaughton couldn't believe it. Here he had a chance to pick up his daughter from day care, and Stumbo was going to blow it.

"Doyle, I'm on my way to pick up Angel," he said as he entered Stumbo's disheveled office. "Can we talk in the morning?"

"As usual, Jack, you have failed to tell me what transpired today. No calls from the scene. No report on my desk. No verbal report." Jack resisted the urge to tell him he surely meant "oral;" that common error was one of McNaughton's pet peeves. But it was the least of Doyle's linguistic sins. His stilted language was his attempt to sound authoritative, but it instead made him sound pitiful. He was even known to use the computer's thesaurus while talking to superiors on the phone so that he would seem smart. It was one of the few computer skills he had mastered. Jack almost felt sorry that Stumbo had such a need to be important, but right now his emotions were reserved for his daughter.

"Well, the Trueblood case was no big deal," McNaughton said. Actually, some people might have deemed Jack a hero for the way he had handled the case in such a low-key, uneventful manner. But Jack never fancied himself a hero; in his mind, he was merely doing his job.

"I want a complete report on my desk by eight a.m.," Stumbo said. It was an unreasonable request, and he knew it, but Doyle reveled in forcing people to do unreasonable things. It made him feel powerful and decisive, but everyone but Stumbo himself knew that he was incapable of making real decisions, and thus wielded no real power.

Consequently, it was no use arguing with him when he had made one of those arbitrary pronouncements; you could never win. The fiercer you fought – especially if you had a logical argument – the more Stumbo dug in. Jack occasionally fell into the trap and took it on, something that invariably brought Renee's disapproval, but he didn't want to waste time tonight. Renee wouldn't like it that he'd have to leave the house at six-forty-five to get a routine report done, but she'd like it even less if he had to do it after arriving home late too.

"OK, Doyle. See you tomorrow." He turned quickly, refusing Stumbo the opportunity to continue the argument. Doyle's mouth fell open, but Jack moved away so quickly that he couldn't hear if Stumbo said anything more.

McNaughton's escape gave him the happy opportunity to pick Angelica up from her day-care center, always a gratifying experience. Aware that it was about the time for Mommy or Daddy to pick her up, Angel would occasionally glance up from her task – be it finger-painting or listening to a story or swinging sky-high on the playground – to keep a watch out. Jack knew that, when she spotted him, she would literally drop what she was doing and dash over as fast as she could dodge the other kids. She'd throw herself into his arms and he would swoop her up and swing her around and she would release her smile only long enough to kiss him. And for a split second, Jack could forget people like John Pius Peterson and Lester Trueblood and Doyle Stumbo.

Angel followed the script perfectly this day, letting out a squeal of "Daddy!" when she spotted him, and scrambled over. Jack could feel his love for her well up into his chest, and he held her little body tightly against him for a minute, shutting out the din of a dozen preschoolers who had reached the arsenic hour, the time when their caregivers joked that they wanted either to ingest arsenic – or administer it.

"C'mon. You want to call Mommy and go out to eat?" he asked her excitedly.

"Yeah! Let's go see the belly dancer!"

"OK. Sounds good to me."

Angel had been taken by the belly dancer who performed at Theo's, the family's favorite Greek restaurant, where the elderly owner usually gave Angelica a free rice pudding – whether she had eaten her meal or not. They called Renee from cell – Angel loved doing it – and she promised to meet them there in twenty minutes.

The dolmades and gyros were especially good that night. Or maybe it was just that they hadn't had such a relaxing evening in a while. Jack and Renee held hands across the table for a while and Angelica even cooperated, eating her Greek spaghetti fairly well without constantly being asked, quietly enjoying the belly dancer and thanking the owner without prompting when he brought her her treat.

It was past Angel's bedtime when they got home, but Jack, ever the sucker for his little girl's smile, agreed to read one book anyway. They climbed onto her twin bed, and he read "Amelia Bedelia" to her. He loved to listen to the natural giggle that came up from her belly when she was amused by the main character's literal interpretation of clichés. He finished the book, and she turned over and clasped Flower, her doll, close to her. Jack leaned to kiss her and then climbed out, pulled up the covers and hoisted the railing that ensured that his active four-year-old didn't fall out of bed.

"I love you, Daddy," she said sleepily as he slipped out the door.

"I love you too, sweetheart," he answered.

Both he and Renee were tired too, so they skipped TV and headed straight to bed, where they read a few pages in their books before turning out the lights. Belle Starr curled between their pillows, and they fell asleep to her rumbling purr.

Orval Crumpacker was a good family man who wanted to take his wife and their four children on decent vacations, but the salary he earned as town marshal in the tiny Southern Indiana hamlet of French Lick didn't allow for extravagant ones. Since Christmas, he and his wife Karen planned to take the kids to Lake Shafer, north of Indianapolis, for a long weekend in the spring. They kept it a secret until one week before they planned to go, and the kids were thrilled when their parents told them of the surprise.

So nobody grumbled when Karen jostled them awake at four a.m. and herded them into the gassed up black-and-white patrol car. One of the few perks of the job was that the town board allowed Orval to use the car on in-state trips, but he and Karen found it to be a dubious benefit. All too often, he felt compelled to stop to help a stranded motorist or to handle some other police work – even out of his jurisdiction – because people expected somebody in a black-and-white to do so. But it saved wear and tear on the family's own car, a nine-year-old Chevy station wagon that they had bought used eight years earlier, which may have been incapable of making the trip anyway.

Karen figured the kids could get washed up and dressed when they arrived at the lake, so she left them in their pajamas. Orval climbed behind the wheel, Karen balanced the coffee mugs and they were off. The kids were unusually quiet – still not awake – and Karen secretly wished they'd all nod off so that she and her husband could have a rare hour or so of uninterrupted conversation. It didn't happen quite like that; there was no time when all four were asleep at once. But the drive was fairly uneventful anyway; at least nobody was fighting. About three hours into it, just after the car had passed the Indianapolis metropolitan area, seven-year-old Jennifer announced that she had to go to the bathroom. "Why didn't you tell me ten minutes ago, when there were places to stop?" her dad asked.

"'Cause I didn't have to go then," Jenny said, as if the answer was so obvious that the question shouldn't have been posed.

"Well, can you hold it a few minutes? I think I saw a sign a couple of miles back that said we were coming to a rest stop."

"OK, Daddy. But hurry."

If it had been one of the boys, Orval would have pulled onto the shoulder, unloaded his son and told him to relieve himself then and there. But there was no way his fastidious Jennifer would even consider doing that, and Orval had to admit that he couldn't blame her; it just wasn't so easy for a girl. So he pushed his foot onto the gas pedal a little harder and headed for the rest stop north of Lebanon.

The sun hadn't yet peered over the horizon when they arrived. Karen got out to take Jenny to the washroom. Orval glanced into the back seat of the car; the other three children were asleep. That gave him the opportunity to get out a stretch his legs; three hours behind the wheel were enough to ignite that familiar cramp in his back. So he unfolded his lanky legs, ducked his head and emerged stiffly from the patrol car. He wore his brown polyester uniform pants and a white V-necked undershirt. He closed the door quietly, so he didn't wake the kids, and he began strolling the rest park's parking lot, stretching awkwardly and groaning as he went.

He looked back, and Karen and Jenny still hadn't emerged from the restroom, so Orval kept walking. A lone car was parked at the end of the lot, away from all the others and too long of a jaunt for the motorist if he had had any urgent need for the facilities. Crumpacker wondered what that large pink object was in the back seat, so he moved closer. Still unable to make it out, he walked up to the back door window and peered in.

Orval gasped and took a step backwards. He cleared his throat, took a deep breath and stepped forward for another look. Lying across the back seat were two naked bodies, their arms and legs intertwined. The one on top – a woman – was lying on her stomach, and her face was buried into the other body's shoulder and covered by mussed, straw-colored hair. Beneath her lay a man, his face turned away from the woman and her hair, his mouth open, his eyes closed. His left arm had fallen off the seat and hung limply, suspended in midair.

"Oh, my God!" Orval said. "Oh, my *God*!"

He turned and began to run toward the patrol car. He arrived, breathing hard from the unusual physical exertion, and threw open the front door. He grabbed his microphone and pulled the cord taut so that he could speak into it from outside the car; his kids didn't need to hear this.

"French Lick Car one to the Metro-Marion Police Department," he said, his voice quivering. Despite his agitation, he had had the presence of mind to use Indiana Law Enforcement Emergency Network, a radio system that allowed all law enforcement agencies in the state to communicate with one another during a crisis.

"Go ahead French Lick one," a disinterested woman dispatcher intoned lazily.

"I'm at the rest park just north of the city," he barked between deep breaths, "and I've got two ten-zeroes in a car here."

It was as if two ten-zeroes – dead bodies – were an everyday occurrence to her. Perhaps they were. "If you're at a rest park north of Indianapolis, you're in the Boone County Sheriff's Department's jurisdiction," the radio operator, still distant, said.

"Clear," Crumpacker said. He stopped to collect his thoughts and to calm himself. Before he could call for the Boone County sheriff, that agency's dispatcher addressed him: "French Lick one, this is Boone County," she was considerably more interested in his call. "I overheard your radio traffic. I will notify state police and I've already got a sheriff's deputy en route. Please advise: What is the vehicle's license plate number?"

A flash of embarrassment overtook Crumpacker when he realized that he had forgotten to take note of that important fact. "One moment please, Boone County," he said as flatly as he could, but the quiver was still there.

Crumpacker jogged closer to the car, grabbed a pen from his pants pocket and wrote the number on his palm. He ran back to the car and picked up the radio. "Boone County, it's forty-nine P five-six-five-five."

"OK, French Lick. We're on the way."

He collapsed, exhausted, into the front seat and waited. He wasn't sure what to do, but it was fortunate he had not left the radio. A few moments later, it crackled: "French Lick one, this is Boone County. Do you copy?"

"French Lick one," he said.

"Let's double check that number, French Lick one. Can you read it back to me?"

He looked at his left palm again and read it back: "Forty-nine P-like-Paul five-six-five-five," he said, enunciating each number as clearly as he could.

The dispatcher came back on, and she was even more sober than before. "French Lick one, for your information, the vehicle is registered to the Metro-Marion Police. We're in the process of getting an ID on who it's registered to."

Crumpacker's mouth dropped open. Good *God*, he thought. We've got a dead cop. Or two.

Karen and Jenny had returned from the rest room by then, and Orval hustled them into the car. He mulled what to do, and signaled his wife to get back out. He filled her in – her mouth dropped open too – but they agreed that it wasn't a good idea to alarm the children. Orval paced outside the car: What to do? What to do? All four kids were awake by then, and he got an idea: He could get his eleven-year-old son, their second oldest, to help him rope off the area around the car to keep onlookers from closing in. Orval, who thought it proper to protect women from such sordid things, didn't even contemplate asking Rebecca, his thirteen-year-old daughter, to participate in such a grisly task.

He rifled through the car trunk and came up with a roll of yellow plastic crime-scene tape and motioned for Ernie to come with him. He left it to Karen to explain to the others, including five-year-old Crystal, what was going on; she told them that Daddy thought the car had been involved in a crime and was helping the local police, and she left it at that. The girls were satisfied with the explanation; they were more interested in discussing what they would do once they got to the lake.

Orval gaped about, trying to figure out what he could attach the tape to and forgetting about Ernie for a moment. He had not thought about how curious an eleven-year-old boy can be, and certainly had not considered the allure of what lay inside the car. Naked bodies. A naked woman. A naked woman's athletically sculpted buttocks.

Like his dad and mom before him, Ernie's mouth fell open and his eyes bulged.

"Ernie! Knock it off and get away from there!" his father scolded. They fixed one end of the crime scene tape to the handicapped-parking sign, wrapped it around the vehicle, tied it to the right rear bumper and pulled it around the car to a seedling planted just off the car's left front. Crumpacker finished the perimeter by returning to the parking sign.

"OK! Scoot!" he said to Ernie, who took one more quick glance before he dashed away from the car.

A Boone County deputy's beige sedan raced into the rest park, and pulled toward Crumpacker, who was waving his arms above his head to draw the officer's attention. The sun had peeked out by then, casting a pink light across the parking lot. The radio squawked with traffic; word that a fellow cop might be down had every officer within miles converging on the rest stop. A state trooper pulled his white cruiser in next. "Metro-Marion is on the way," he said breathlessly, "but we don't have an ID on this guy yet. Have you checked the car doors yet?" Crumpacker shook his head, so the trooper tried them. Locked.

"Wait a second," the deputy said. "I've got a Slim Jim."

He retrieved a flat, ruler-like metal straight edge that police and crooks use to quickly open locked car doors. He slipped it between the window and the rubber gasket, fished around for a moment and heard the lock pop. He opened the door, and the male corpse stirred.

"What the *fuck?*" Mitch Simons bellowed as he fumbled for something to cover himself and his lover, who promptly let out a screech of her own.

CHAPTER 6

By the time the last sheriff's deputy arrived at the Lebanon rest park, twelve officers from four agencies – Metro-Marion, Boone County, the state police and Lebanon city – had already converged on the alleged crime scene. Some of the cops weren't due to start their shifts for another hour or more, but they rushed out – sirens screaming, tires squealing – when they thought one of their brethren had been killed. The news media, which monitor police radios, were going bonkers, sending reporters and film crews to the scene, as well as to Mayor Horace Arnold's house, where his honor was holding an impromptu news conference to express his dismay, as well as his condolences, to the family of the as-yet-unidentified fallen hero.

Like a character out of a movie, Arnold moved his flattened hands up and down in front of him, patting the air to calm the crowd – which consisted of several thoroughly unriled reporters. Dead cop or not, it *was* seven a.m., and reporters, even those who worked the early shift, tended not to get riled over much of anything. But Arnold knew his gesturing made for good TV – made it appear he was in control. And he liked that, not unlike Doyle Stumbo. In fact, it had struck Renee a long time ago that the two of them could be brothers, if not because of their appearances – Arnold was not nearly so hefty – then because of their pompous behavior.

"People, people," Arnold began. "We don't know the details yet, but we do have a situation here. It appears that at least one of our men in blue has been slain. We are still learning the facts, but we are extremely distressed, and we express our sincere sympathy to the officer's family, whoever they are. They don't know who they are yet, either."

Arnold had no idea that reporters' eyes were rolling over his awkward statement; he was merely interested in getting his ubiquitous face on television again. An election was coming up in a little more than a year, and a bereaved mayor was a compelling political image. A skinny, bespectacled man, the quintessential nerd, the likes of whom regularly surrounded the mayor, interrupted Arnold's soliloquy to whisper something in his honor's ear.

Arnold's sympathetic countenance folded into a deep frown as he listened. He wrinkled his bulbous nose, turned his face into his aide's and, with just an inch or so between their noses, angrily mouthed the word "*What?*"

The aide whispered something else. The mayor pulled on his lapels, as if the classic politician's gesture would help him regain his composure. He cleared his throat. "This news conference is over," he said abruptly. "We'll talk with you again when we have more information."

Even as reporters shouted to try to get him to answer more questions, Arnold turned about face and marched back into his house. The door closed, and Arnold promptly started screaming at the aide, who had had the misfortune of telling the mayor that he had jumped the gun – that the dead man in blue was, in fact, a living man in nothing at all.

"I'm not going to talk to them again! Tell them I'm in a meeting if they call!" the mayor, who fancied himself a man of his word, bellowed.

"Your honor, you said . . ."

"I don't care what I said. They're going to get surly when they find out what really happened. You know how *reporters* are. Always trying to dig dirt. They're going to start poking around, trying to find out how something like this could happen, and *I'm* not going to be the one who has to explain. Can you *imagine* how bad that would make me look?"

"Your honor . . ."

"Shut up, Wilkins. *You* talk to them. You think *you're* so smart, interrupting my press conference with news like that? Just when I was starting to sound really good? *You* tell them!"

Arnold never did have much compassion for the messenger. Feeling burned, Wilkins was reluctant to play the same role with a bunch of reporters, but he felt compelled to call a news conference of his own. He procrastinated until shortly before noon, when the reporters, ravenous for news after a morning of evasiveness, had him for lunch.

Back at the rest park, the relief that the responding cops felt that a fellow officer was not dead gave way, for some of them, to peevish irritation that they had rushed out of bed for nothing. Even more of them found the situation humorous. They milled about, lingering over soda pops they had gotten out of the rusty machine and leering at Simons's girlfriend as she struggled in the cramped back seat to pull her t-shirt over her large breasts. An impromptu competition raged as they vied to offer the best cracks about the situation; no doubt this would be fodder for jokes for days and legend for years.

Simons, known for his unflappability – even in the midst of a police shootout – was ranting furiously as he awkwardly lifted his buttocks up to pull on his jeans, intentionally bypassing his thinning red Jockey shorts. He nearly elbowed his mortified girlfriend in the face as she struggled to pull on her jeans. Mitch didn't even wait for her to accomplish that before he bounded from the car and she angrily pulled the door shut in a hopeless effort to regain her privacy. "Who the *hell* is responsible for this bullshit?" he screamed. "So you all think this is so funny? I'm off-duty, and this is none of your goddamn business. Get the fuck outta here!"

His anger provoked them all the more. "Hey, Simons," Deputy Sheriff Leon Johnson, who was built like a tank, drawled. "We knew you were a stiff, but this is taking it a little far!"

"And to think that the rumor was that he *couldn't* get stiff!" state Trooper Dan Worth chided loudly.

"Well," a bespectacled deputy sheriff joined in, "I had heard that he had trouble getting girls, but he's got to be really hard up to go for a dead one!"

"He's got a lot of practice," a skinny Lebanon cop offered. "Word is that his steady girl is a model at Macy's – a mannequin!"

"No – you've got that all wrong," Worth shouted. "She's inflatable!"

"Now guys, guys," a Marion-Metro patrolman with graying temples said, "have a little sympathy for my colleague. He's such a lousy lay that he puts 'em to sleep – or bores 'em to death!"

They continued with their juvenile jokes, guffawing at themselves and infuriating Simons, who leaned on his car and pouted until a contrite Orval Crumpacker approached.

"Officer? I'm Orval Crumpacker of the French Lick Police Department and I'm afraid I'm responsible for this mishap." He hung his head deeply. "I'm sorry that I embarrassed you."

Crumpacker knew that, if he had just looked closer, he probably could have seen them breathing – maybe even have heard Mitch snoring. And if he had thought about it, before the ruckus began there had been *three* "lifeless" bodies in the back seat of *his* car – his sleeping children – and that was certainly innocent enough. But the nudity had startled him – he had never seen two people like that in the movies, much less in person – and his deep born-again religious convictions prevented him from peering too closely at the exposed bodies. Besides, he had never worked a homicide; French Lick was not nearly as exciting as its name.

Simons was ready to sneer, but stopped himself. "That's OK, Crumpacker. You just did what you thought you should do. It's these assholes who are pissing me off." The words shocked Crumpacker, but he was relieved by Simons's subdued statement. Little did he know that this was an unusually controlled response from the volatile detective, whose legendary quick temper was tolerated by the brass because he was so exemplary at the job.

This, however, would not be well-received. Simons had gotten into similar trouble before, and his superior at the time had threatened his job. Mitch, then a uniform cop, had visited his then-girlfriend immediately after his shift ended, stopping only long enough to pick up a bottle of cheap blush wine, but not to change clothes. It was early in their relationship, when their skin still tingled at the mere thought of each other's touch, and his rotating shift, the brainchild of some sadistic commander who thought that, by golly, it had been done to him so he could do it to them, had kept them apart for too long. So the conversation lasted only long enough for them each to finish half a glass of the cloyingly sweet wine, and Mitch and the woman started undressing each other in the living room. With the room strewn with a trail of blue polyester and blue denim, they retreated to her bedroom and were too involved to hear when the front door of the apartment swung open. It was the woman's husband, from whom she was separated and who, Mitch would have thought, shouldn't have a key to the apartment to which his estranged wife had moved. But the couple had been working on a reconciliation, and the man, a bouquet of pink carnations in hand, had come to surprise his wife. He could hear the muffled sounds of lovemaking in the bedroom and angrily contemplated bursting through the door, but he abandoned the plan in favor of a more diabolical one: He scooped up Mitch's uniform, underwear and equipment, including his service gun, and drove to the closest police stationhouse. There, he deposited the assorted clothing and equipment in a mound on the front desk. "This is what your goddamn cops are doing on duty – screwing other men's wives!" he yelled at the desk officer. "Tell him to keep his goddamn hands off of my wife!"

Mitch's badge was on his shirt, his wallet in his pants, so it took all of thirty seconds to identify the wayward cop. He *was* off-duty, so he wasn't in trouble for messing around on the department's time. But the brass quickly deemed his activities "conduct unbecoming an officer." When a cop did anything that struck the brass as off-key but there was no specific policy against it, it got put into that catch-all category. That infuriated Simons, who had to arrange for a friend to retrieve some fresh clothes from his apartment so he could even leave his girlfriend's place. He wondered how could his off-duty sexual activities be unbecoming an officer. Weren't cops supposed to have sex lives?

Apparently not – at least not with married women whose love-sick estranged husbands might burst into their apartments. Mitch drew a two-day suspension without pay, a penalty considerably stricter than some guys had drawn for considerably more serious, on-duty infractions – some even that jeopardized other officers' lives. Simons thought about appealing, but decided that Indiana's conservatism had dictated that such a harsh punishment be levied for a sex-related infraction and that it likely would stick. Mitch had always liked Hoosiers for their hard-working, salt-of-the earth lifestyles, but he had little appreciation for the prudishness that the relatively few but politically powerful religious conservatives had managed to impose on the rest of Indiana, giving Hoosiers an unfair national reputation for being a bunch of rubes.

After the suspension, Simons vowed to clean up his act by forswearing married women, even separated ones, and by keeping his private and professional lives entirely separate. And he had been behaving as well as anybody could expect of Mitch Simons. Until now.

It was past ten o'clock, more than two hours since McNaughton's report on the Trueblood case was due on Stumbo's desk. The hulk hadn't erupted yet; he had been on the phone all morning, asking his superiors what he should do about Mitch Simons. Stumbo wasn't terribly bright, but he could fake it enough to make it sound as if he were seeking their advice and fulfilling his sacred responsibility of communicating with them. The brass valued nothing so much as communication, not because it fostered better police work but because the top of the top-heavy Metro-Marion department loved to micro-manage. So the mutually masturbatory phone calls were satisfying for all participants: The indecisive Stumbo got somebody to make a decision for him; the brass got to meddle in a matter that should have been handled in the squad room.

Meanwhile, McNaughton got his first chance to talk privately to Simons. "Geez, Mitch, didn't you learn the last time?" His voice betrayed his exasperation. It was not that he thought that Mitch's crimes were so heinous, but that he knew the brass' reaction, starting with Stumbo's, would be dramatically out of proportion to the incident. Jack secretly worried that they might try to fire Mitch over this one, and he didn't want that to happen to his friend and talented colleague. There was no predicting Stumbo. In the old days, he would have been laughing right along with the others; these days, he would have to exercise his authority. Jack thought that appropriate to the extent that the brass can't play buddies and overlook missteps by the ranks. But he feared that

Stumbo's overwhelming hunger for power would cause him to come down unnecessarily hard on Simons.

"Jack, what's so wrong with what I did?" Mitch demanded. "I was off-duty, and last time I looked, we didn't have any rules against screwing – although I wouldn't put it past the jerks who make the rules."

"Mitch, you know as well as I do that this doesn't look good – you screwing around in an unmarked car, and in a public place where some Baptist guy from Southern Indiana and his kids are going to see you. And especially because of all the press that this is going to get. You know what they're going to call it: conduct unbecoming. The best thing you can do is own up to the situation, apologize and hope that your contrition will be enough so they let you off easy."

"Let me off easy! I didn't *do* anything wrong, goddamn it!" Jack could see that Mitch wasn't ready to be contrite, so they'd just have to wait to see how the brass reacted. He suggested that Mitch get out of the stationhouse for a while, so Simons tagged along with Alvear, who was talking with some acquaintances of the Peterson family. They were trying to find out if anybody knew anything about the dynamics of the family and whether there was any credence to Peterson's belief that his wife was having an affair. But before they were a third of the way down the list of people they planned to talk to, they got a sinking feeling that, despite Peterson's membership in the Knights of Columbus and his church, *nobody* knew the Petersons very well.

With Simons gone and Stumbo still busy deciding, McNaughton used the relative peace to work on the Trueblood case report, which had been delayed by the hubbub over Simons. He had Stutz out in the field, wrapping up the loose ends of the straightforward case – a good one for the enthusiastic kid to handle. The phone rang.

"Jack, it's Knofel. You asked for a copy of my motion, so I wanted to let you know that I'll be filing it right after lunch. My client was examined by a psychiatrist yesterday afternoon, after the initial hearing. Do you want me to fax over a copy of the motion and the affidavit?"

"That's OK, Knofel. Kit's on the street; I'll have her swing by court and pick up a copy. Thanks for letting me know." He didn't want to tell Fortner that the department's antiquated facsimile machine produced almost illegible documents. He paused, then added, with a light-hearted lilt: "So I take it your client's insane?" Jack knew that the psychiatrist's finding was a given; Fortner wouldn't be filing the affidavit if he hadn't yet found a psychiatrist who agreed with the defense of choice.

"Of course he's insane, Jack," Knofel said soberly, without a hint of sarcasm. "How the hell could somebody sane do what he did?"

"Well, Knofel, he's sick, all right," McNaughton, turning serious, said. "But he's not legally insane, and we're going to show that at trial."

"We'll see, Jack. We'll see."

"McNaughton." It was Stumbo, waddling out of his office. It was a change for him; he usually summoned McNaughton to stand before his highness. "The captain – uh, I mean I'm suspending Simons for five days without pay and he is warned: 'Do it again, and you're out of here, buddy.'"

"That's awfully harsh, Doyle. *Five* days for conduct unbecoming? C'mon. The guy over on east side didn't get five days for getting drunk, threatening his wife and waving his gun around a crowded bar."

"Jack, Simons was fucking in his police car. Lord knows what condition it's in now. He may have cost the taxpayers money. And he certainly caused our department a lot of embarrassment."

That, of course, was the bottom line. At most, Simons's escapade occupied less than an hour of several cops' time – nothing more than they might have spent over coffee and a donut somewhere. Certainly there was no damage to the police cruiser, which Simons was allowed to use off-duty; even Mitch's enthusiastic and athletic lovemaking wasn't likely to break a spring in the car seat or hurt the shocks. But Jack wasn't sure that Doyle was experienced enough to understand that and, after all, he was looking at the situation from the perspective of a three-hundred-pounder. Simons *did* embarrass the brass and the mayor, and it was a wonder that they were allowing him to keep his job.

Jack briefly considered arguing with Doyle; there were times when Stumbo was so insecure in a decision that he had anguished over that he could be backed down. But McNaughton knew that Captain Ryan had decided this one for him, and on such occasions Stumbo was as immovable as the mountain he resembled – and as apt to explode over such a confrontation as a volcano. "OK, Doyle. I disagree – I think this is way too harsh – but I know you outrank me and have the final say."

That pleased Stumbo, who had previously seemed nervous. He had Jack just where he had always wanted him, and he allowed a closed-mouth smile to break on his lips. "That's right, McNaughton. I do. You can let Simons know that his suspension starts tomorrow."

"You want *me* to suspend Mitch? No way. Do your own dirty work," Jack said, bordering on insubordination, but sure that Doyle was too weak to call him on it. He paused, picturing that scene. "On second thought, Doyle, never mind. I think it's best if Mitch hears this from me."

"Well, thank you so much for agreeing with your *superior*, Jack," Stumbo said sarcastically. "Get Simons in here, and get it over with." He rotated and padded away.

Jack began to brood over how he would break the news to Simons, and how he would handle Mitch's ensuing tirade. He knew that Simons was no saint. He and Mitch were vastly different; Simons was a womanizer who frequented strip joints and had little desire to ever get married. But as long as his behavior didn't affect his job, Jack didn't care about it – or think that it was anybody's business but Mitch's. It had, unfortunately, become Jack's business this time. He had little time to mull the situation, however; he looked up to see Alvear and Simons top the stairs and head for Jack's desk.

Kit, having lost interest in Simons's exploits hours earlier, started yakking even before she reached McNaughton. "We talked to the priest and he confirms that Mrs. Peterson told him that her husband suspected they were having an affair," she said. "And he says it's absolutely not true. I believe him; he's one of those sincere types."

Alvear had already wondered why, given the priest's demeanor, Peterson would suspect something sordid was going on. But that was for the defense to explain; it was her job to show that his alleged suspicions were groundless and that he killed his children in cold blood.

"Good work, guys." McNaughton said. "Kit, Knofel called and said that he filed his motion on Peterson. He's already been examined by the shrink. Will you go over to the courthouse and get a copy? Please."

"Sure. I'm eager to see that. C'mon, Mitch."

"No, uh... Mitch, I want to talk to you," Jack said, then turning back to Kit: "Run over there without him, OK?"

Alvear looked wary; if her partner was about to be disciplined, she would quickly regain interest in the morning's episode. "Jack?" her voice implored him, but McNaughton knew he owed it to Mitch to inform him before he answered Alvear's unasked question.

McNaughton pinched his lips and shook his head conservatively. Kit, her eyebrows raised and her forehead furrowed, flashed a look of sympathy at Mitch, who smiled back wanly.

"Don't worry, kiddo," he said. "I won't let the assholes get me down."

She squeezed his well-muscled forearm and forced a return smile, then dejectedly walked away. She was still within earshot when Mitch sat down in the grey chair next to Jack's desk and turned to McNaughton. "How long?" he demanded.

"Five days. I'm sorry, Mitch. I told Stumbo that was way too long, but you know how he gets when you challenge him."

"*Five days!* The *asshole!* That goddamn drunk Farrington over on east side got only four days for threatening his wife with his weapon. I don't *believe* this. I could *kill* that fat fucker! Where is that son of a bitch? I'll kick the shit out of him right now!" Simons stood up and violently swung his arm, knocking some papers off McNaughton's desk. Jack sighed and watched them float to the floor. Reprimanding Mitch for his renowned temper would not be a good idea just now.

"Take it easy, Mitch. I agree that five days is ridiculous, but it's not worth getting fired over. *He's* not worth getting fired over."

"I don't know, Jack." He was calmer now. He plopped back into the cheap chair and slouched low. "That fat fucker has been a pain in the ass for years. He'll be the death of me yet." Simons paused; Jack peered at him in sympathy but said nothing.

"I'm getting out of here," Mitch said, standing. "You can start my five days right *now*."

"We'll sign you out at quitting time, Mitch," McNaughton answered. "The suspension will start tomorrow and we'll count the weekend. That'll get you back to work faster, but you'll still get docked for five days."

"OK, Jack." He sounded resigned. "I'll talk to you next week." He picked up his jacket, which he had flung across McNaughton's desk, and started toward the door. Then he made an abrupt about-face and headed toward Stumbo's office.

Jack started to warn him off, then stopped. Simons is an adult, he thought; if he wants to get himself fired, that's his business.

But Mitch stepped into Stumbo's office calmly, and gently closed the door behind him. Jack watched the action as if it were a silent movie. Mitch gestured animatedly, pointing his finger at Stumbo.

"Oh, God," McNaughton mumbled, turning his attention to his paperwork.

Simons leveled his voice so that he couldn't be heard outside the office. "Payback's a bitch, asshole," he said steadily. Stumbo sat motionless, stunned by the assault. "You're going down."

He turned on his heel and headed out. "Simons," Stumbo started, but he stopped when it was apparent that Simons had no intention of listening.

McNaughton, who heard only Stumbo's attempt to summon Mitch back, planted his elbows on his desk, wove his fingers together and rested his forehead on his hands. He shut his eyes and pondered for a few moments, but the noise of some detectives from another squad returning from a murder scene snapped him out of it. He opened his eyes and peered at his desk calendar setting squarely in front of him.

April fifteen. Oh God, he thought, groaning aloud. It was tax day, and he hadn't even begun filling out the forms. Renee had warned him not to take it on; it would be so much easier – and well worth the expense – to get an accountant recommended by her friend Marilyn to do it. He had insisted he could get it done.

Renee would not be pleased.

Kit was reading the affidavit and scowling as she walked into the squad room. Her honey-toned skin was folded into deep furrows across her brow, and her black, shoulder-blade-length hair was in disarray, as if she had repeatedly run a nervous hand through it. She had somehow picked up Joe Stutz, who was bounding behind her like an eager puppy. As usual, Alvear started talking to Jack before she was halfway to his desk.

"I don't believe this shit, Jack. This shrink," she said, poking the affidavit as if it were the psychiatrist himself, "says that Peterson was suffering from 'dissociative reaction.' That he has two personalities, and that the one who did the killing was unaware of his other personality." She nearly spat the words, clipping them off abruptly.

"Listen to this." She read from the document, her voice sarcastic and sing-songy. "'Mr. Peterson suffers from dissociative reaction, a psychoneurotic disorder that manifests itself in one of several ways. In Mr. Peterson's case, it manifests itself through multiple personality. Usually, the patient alternates between personalities, but Mr. Peterson exhibits a condition known as co-consciousness. That is, he felt that his conventional self watched as his second, aberrant personality – without any knowledge of the conventional self's presence – committed the acts from which this criminal case arose.'

"Can you believe that? 'Acts from which this case arose!' Good God, he slaughtered his kids! And now he's saying he's not responsible!" Kit was livid, and she wouldn't be calmed.

"And then Knofel says in the affidavit that Peterson's disorder renders him not guilty by reason of insanity. The case, he says, passes the M'Naghten test – whatever the hell that is. That he was unable to discern right from wrong."

Even Alvear's disgust couldn't dampen Joe Stutz's enthusiasm. "I think that's what John Hinckley cited when he was acquitted for shooting President Reagan and James Brady," he said. "The jury said he didn't know right from wrong, and so he couldn't be held responsible – even though he shot them in front of the whole world. You know, I just saw something about the M'Naghten Rule in the book I have for my criminal-law class." Joe was pursuing his bachelor's degree, not a requirement to be on the department but an asset if he were to seek further promotions. "Wait a second; I've got the book over here."

He jogged over to his neat work station, pulled a thick black volume from a drawer and began flipping through the pages as he shoved the drawer closed with a knee. Under different circumstances, McNaughton would have been amused that Joe was so orderly that even his school books were filed away. But his mind now was on the M'Naghten Rule. The definition that Joe would find came as no surprise to Jack.

In a moment, Stutz had found the reference in the index, and leafed to the proper page.

"Yup; just as I remembered. The M'Naghten Rule has to do with differentiating between right and wrong." Joe's eyes scanned the text. "It says here that it resulted from the case of Daniel M'Naghten in the 1840s. He tried to assassinate the prime minister of England, but he accidentally shot the prime minister's secretary to death instead. M'Naghten was found not guilty by reason of insanity because he didn't know the difference between right and wrong when he committed the act. Even though that case provided the name, it says here that the concept that somebody isn't responsible if he can't tell the difference between right and wrong dates back at least to the sixteenth century."

Joe looked up from the text, and peered at McNaughton. "It's funny, Jack. The name is so similar to yours."

It wasn't so funny to Jack. Even if he hadn't immediately noticed the similarity years earlier, when he was taking criminal law for his undergraduate degree, his classmates wouldn't have let him miss it. Little did they or he know then how often, in the ensuing years, he would be haunted by the M'Naghten Rule. The first time was soon after McNaughton was promoted to homicide. He had arrested David Snook, an average-looking, bespectacled plumber who lived in a tidy rented trailer on the near south side, for strangling his girlfriend. Snook was the one who called the cops, and then he sat there on his garish, crushed-velvet floral couch, with the corpse sprawled on the floor – it was the *only* thing on his immaculate floor – just a few feet away.

Snook was amazingly matter-of-fact about it all, never exhibiting any remorse for what he had done or fear for what might happen to him. Jack surmised that the guy was a sociopath, that he showed no remorse because he felt none. While he appeared crazy as a loon, being a sociopath was different from being legally insane. Theoretically, for a defendant to be found legally insane, he had to show that he didn't know the difference between right and wrong – and even the weirdest wackos usually were sufficiently aware that they were violating society's sense of what is proper conduct that they would try to hide their aberrant behavior. But that was theory, and the defense attorney convinced the jurors that, to behave so nonchalantly shortly after squeezing the life out of his girlfriend, his client had to be insane, and they acquitted him. After forty-seven days of a court-ordered stay in a mental hospital, he was deemed mentally fit, and Jack had wondered over the years how many women had dared to date David Snook – and what their fate had been.

Some years later, McNaughton and Simons encountered Donnie Crawford, who gave new meaning to the term "over my dead body." Crawford was a something of a nomad, a homeless man who preferred to travel the Hoosier highways rather than frequent the underpinnings of a bridge, a habit of many of the homeless in Indianapolis. One cool Friday evening in September, Crawford was thumbing a ride along U.S. 31 just south of Kokomo when Patricia Swearingen, a pert, twenty-six-year-old divorcee with short brown hair and a ready smile, drove by. Swearingen, who worked as a checkout clerk at the local Wal-Mart, was feeling good; she had just been given a twelve-cents-an-hour raise, and she was on her way to visit her friend Maria Parsons in Indianapolis, where they planned to go out dancing. Her good feelings turned into good will and, ignoring all of her mother's admonitions over all of those years, she stopped to give the hitchhiker – Donnie – a ride. She told him she could take him as far as the northern leg of Interstate 465, the bustling beltway around Indianapolis; she planned to continue south on U.S. 31, which became Meridian Street, to go to Maria's place in Broad Ripple, a trendy, bohemian neighborhood on the city's north side. While she wasn't terribly bright, she had enough sense not to take him too close to Maria's one-bedroom flat, and she cautiously avoided telling him much about her life. She stayed on 31 as it snuck under the beltway, then pulled into an abandoned gas station at the northwest corner of 96th Street, where she informed him that this was the end of the line. He pleaded with her to let him come to her friend's apartment, where, he promised, he would show them both a good time. His coarse language failed to seduce Swearingen, who became angry at his lewd suggestions, and she told him harshly: "I'd rather be dead than have sex with you."

Donnie took her at her word, sweeping a thick-bladed hunting knife from inside his battered leather jacket – a bomber type that looked as if it dated to World War II – and stabbing her repeatedly in the chest and neck. He gaped around nervously, wondering if he had been seen by anyone passing by on the busy four-lane or stopping for a shake at the McDonald's across 96th Street. Feeling comfortable that he had not been spotted, Crawford shoved her compact body into the cramped back seat of her maroon Ford Escort and began driving, making several turns until he found his way to the darkened parking lot of a huge Lutheran Church. Safely away from the main drag, he pulled over the car and pulled out his penis, and he found Patricia had become remarkably co-operative. By the time a traffic cop stopped the car four days later for a broken tail light and noticed the putrid stench, Donnie and Patricia had visited the parking lots of the Indiana University law school and Crown Hill Cemetery, and they had parked on the circle around the Soldiers' and Sailors' Monument that marked the center of downtown. And, by his own count, Donnie had had sex with Swearingen's corpse about twenty times. Between the episodes, he kept her body in an Army sleeping bag, one of his few possessions.

Of course Donnie Crawford was crazy, Jack would tell anybody who would ask. But he knew what he did was wrong – otherwise, why would he have hidden his actions? So he was not legally insane. Still, a jury couldn't get past the mental image of him screwing a corpse, and Donnie was found not guilty by reason of insanity.

CHAPTER 7

Joe Stutz took it upon himself to research the M'Naghten Rule. That, Jack was learning, was Joe's way. As his open, honest face would suggest, Stutz was always enthusiastic, always eager to tackle any project, any case. That's why he was already a detective. He had been an exemplary street cop, always going beyond expectations and requirements, and word got to McNaughton that this was an up and comer, in what Jack considered to be the best sense of the term. He called Stutz in and talked to him about the homicide division, suggesting that Joe take the promotions exam and select homicide as one of his choices for assignment. Joe had misgivings; he didn't know if it was realistic to expect that someone with only two years on the department would get such a plum assignment. And he wondered if he could handle the emotional burdens of homicide. But after lengthy discussions with Jack, first over coffee and later over a beer, Joe took McNaughton's suggestion. He scored third-highest among all the test-takers, bolstering his chances of getting the assignment of his choosing. Now, two years had passed since he won a post in homicide and was assigned to McNaughton's squad, which was down several detectives. The vacancies had occurred for the best of reasons, even if Stumbo didn't want to acknowledge it. People kept getting promoted out of McNaughton's squad; he was so good at bringing the best out of his people that those who sought promotions generally got them. In the six months before Stutz was assigned to homicide, Frank Basker had moved up to supervise his own narcotics squad, Martha Morrison was named squad sergeant in sex crimes and Bill Warner went into central command to become Pat Houston's assistant in public information. The turnover made Jack's job more difficult, and to this day, his squad was still down two, but he didn't want to hold good people back. Yet he was quietly grateful for Alvear and Simons, both of whom swore that they would retire from Jack's homicide squad after they had their twenty on.

So here was Joe Stutz, who was too young to make such a promise but whose short-term future looked bright. Jack had already told Renee how well Joe was coming along.

He was a big, lanky, blond-headed kid with rosy cheeks and an easy smile, which made him look even younger than his twenty-five years. He had wanted to be a cop since high school, where he had been the star quarterback. He married his high school sweetheart, Anna, shortly after graduation. His sights were so firmly set on the Marion-Metro Police Department that he turned down several college scholarship offers from some decent schools looking to beef up their football programs, not realizing at the time that a college degree would be valuable both in the department and in life. So he worked construction to bide his time from his graduation until his twenty-first birthday, when he reached the required age to join the department. And of course, he excelled at that too, and the added benefit was the toned muscles that solidified his application for the force. Joe and Anna, who was a surgical nurse, had a year-old daughter named Grace on whom Stutz doted unabashedly. It was her birth that prompted him to go to college after all, determined that he would give her the best life and the best example that he could.

He had persuaded Anna that it was for the best for her and Grace, as well as for him, if he were to move to homicide. It was much safer to be cleaning up the aftermath of somebody's violent act than to approach darkened cars in which a driver could just as easily be reaching for a semi-automatic handgun as his driver's license. It was true that homicide detectives had to arrest perpetrators whom they had reason to believe had blown somebody away. But, no matter what impression the television cop shows made, few perps gave the arresting officers any trouble, and those who did had to face an army of well-trained, heavily armed and armored cops who were ready for virtually anything. It was the same argument that Jack had used on Renee years earlier, when he made the move to homicide. When he had a good recruit like Stutz on the line, McNaughton was more than happy to provide him or her with a way to persuade the spouse that homicide was a good choice.

Then there was Chris Allen, who didn't seem to be catching on to anything. He was eager, in a puppy-dog way, and he meant well, but he lacked the innate ability that Jack saw in every good detective with whom he had worked. They just *knew* how to conduct an investigation. Training helped, to be sure, especially when there were new laws or updated equipment or innovative techniques. But Chris, for all his good intentions, should have been capable of taking the lead on an investigation by now, eight months into his tenure in homicide. There was no question that he was book-smart – brilliant, in fact. He had a remarkably high grade-point average in college and scored tops in the promotional exam, assuring that he got his first choice of assignment: Homicide. But he had led a sheltered life in Bloomington with two IU philosophy professors for parents, and Allen lacked the street smarts that were essential in a good cop. Jack worked with him as best he could, but there wasn't a lot of time for hand-holding. All homicide squad sergeants were supposed to have six people in their command. McNaughton had four. It *should* have been easier; he had just four people to supervise, four cops' case reports to review. But the big shots at command didn't care if McNaughton had one detective or a full complement of six; homicide cases were assigned on an alternating basis to each squad and, consequently, his squad was assigned just as many as the others in the downtown division. With Simons and Alvear's expertise, the situation wouldn't have been overly burdensome, but it had dragged on too long. The pressure was too much, and McNaughton made appeals, as often as he thought politically wise, in the name of his overworked people. But Stumbo would usually throw the requests back in his face.

"Well, Jack, I thought your people were so competent. Can't they handle the work?" Stumbo would drawl sarcastically, his toothpick stuck to his thick bottom lip with a dot of dried spittle. "You know, your squad isn't the only thing on your superiors' minds. We have more pressing things to worry about."

"Doyle, I just think we're putting too much pressure on our people. Homicide is tough enough, in the best of circumstances; you're asking my people to deal with about a third more cases than the average homicide dick has. And you've got to remember, Stutz has just two *years* on, and Allen is as green as they come."

"Well, now, Jack, you're downright legendary in your supervisory skills. And I thought that master's degree of yours would be worth something. Didn't those eggheads teach you how to get the most out of your underlings?"

"Doyle, you know that my people give a hundred ten percent *every day.* That can go on for only so long. All the supervisory skills in the world will not alleviate sheer fatigue."

It was just another fight in a long line of them, another loss for McNaughton. Still, he remained sure that he would prevail someday on this one; he had to. McNaughton was *not* one to tilt at windmills; he judiciously decided to take on fights only if he had a reasonable chance of winning. It was his way of staying sane.

"Jack." The voice on the phone sounded breathless, almost desperate. It was Nola Donnelly, a sergeant in enforcement, and it was unusual for her to be calling him at home, especially at nine-thirty p.m. "You're not going to believe it."

"What now?" McNaughton groaned. He wasn't sure that he wanted to hear.

"The city-county council just turned down our raise," Donnelly said dejectedly. "I can't believe it."

"Nola, I told you not to expect it," he said. He knew that she had gotten her hopes up despite his warning. But he realized that expecting her to do otherwise might be expecting too much. So many of the cops took politicians at their word, but Jack had the benefit of Renee's experience in such matters. She had gotten pretty adept at reading the political tea leaves, and as a result he was getting better at it too. As much as McNaughton had hoped that Renee would be wrong when she told him the city-county council would never approve a raise, he knew that she was probably right. It would make the fourth year in a row that Mayor Arnold had balanced the city's budget on the cops' backs.

"The handwriting's been on the wall since the council president said he thought the mayor ought to institute the raises by executive order," he reminded Donnelly. "You know that Arnold has said repeatedly that he supports raises, but only if the council approves them. Seems to me they did a good job of covering each others' asses."

"I know," Donnelly said, despondent. "I just thought . . ." Her voice trailed off, and McNaughton waited a moment to see if she'd continue. When she did not, he responded.

"Nola, when are you going to understand that these bastards don't *care* if you've got to work a second job to make ends meet? They can talk a good game about how much they want to stop crime, but that doesn't translate into more money for us. As far as they're concerned, a rookie in a uniform is just as good – maybe better – than a fifteen-year veteran. He's cheaper, that's for sure."

Donnelly had been on the department for fourteen years. She was a single mother, left with her nine-year-old son and seven-year-old daughter after her husband informed her on a memorable Mother's Day that he wanted a divorce so that he could marry one of the numerous bimbos he had been doinking while Nola worked the second shift and thought he was watching the kids. To make matters worse, he quit paying child support two weeks after the judge's order was issued, and nobody in officialdom seemed to care if Nola's kids got the money or not.

Had she not won a promotion to sergeant, her pay would have been so low that she would have qualified for food stamps. Even with the small increase the promotion brought, her finances were so tight that for the past two years she had left the kids with her mother for four nights a week and worked the seven p.m. to two a.m. shift behind the bullet-proof glass at a self-serve gas station.

"Jack, what the hell am I going to do? To be honest, I'm thinking about leaving the department. My mom says I can make more at the plant where she works, and they might be hiring again soon."

"I'd hate to see you go, Nola, but you've got to do what's best for your family." What else could he say? McNaughton had long ago quit trying to persuade people to stay. His own loyalty had been shaken by his evolving realization that the city's cops were political pawns – well-dressed symbols of the mayor's pledge to get tough on crime and handy fall guys for city-county council members who needed someone to blame for the rising crime rate.

A sense of duty and loyalty go only so far when you realize it's all one way, and it rang false for Jack to appeal to his colleagues' guts.

So Nola Donnelly would become yet another veteran cop who'd have to leave before she'd reached her twenty years, at which time she could have retired. And the Metro-Marion police would remain the lowest-paid big-city cops in America.

Mitch had changed when he returned from the suspension. It was particularly noticeable to McNaughton, who had been unsuccessful in reaching Mitch during the five days. Simons had not returned his boss' calls, and he was unusually subdued when he came back to work. The confident strut was gone from his walk. Jack pulled Kit aside to ask if she knew what was going on, and Alvear merely shrugged. McNaughton sensed she knew something, but Kit apparently was reluctant to talk for fear that she would betray her partner and close friend. Jack was close to the members of his squad, but in these kinds of situations, the gulf between detectives and supervisor was painfully wide. McNaughton tried to let it go, thinking that it was natural for Simons to be low-key for a while, feeling as if his ears had been pinned back. And he continued to do his usual good job. But by the second week in May, after enduring three weeks of the cold shoulder, McNaughton decided he had to act. He called Simons into the conference room where so many accused had been interrogated, and did his best to interrogate without accusing.

"Mitch, you avoided my calls while you were on suspension and you've been distant ever since returning. I want to help you, but I don't know how. What's going on?" McNaughton asked.

Simons sat with his legs wide apart. He leaned forward and rested his elbows on his muscular thighs. He folded, then unfolded his hands, played with his ring, examined his fingernails – anything to avoid Jack's intense gaze. Then Mitch looked up and met McNaughton's eyes.

"Jack, I want you to know that this has nothing to do with you. You've always been good to me. But I've had it. That fat ass Stumbo has gone too far this time. He's going to get his."

Simons took a deep breath. "I've been talking to Frank Basker about transferring to narcotics as soon as he has an opening on his squad. You know, Frank and I got to be pretty good friends when he was here, and he said he'd love to have me on his squad."

"I know Stumbo's been tough on you, Mitch. But think about what you're saying. Do you realize how *dangerous* narcotics can be? Good God, why the hell would you want to get into that when you're really not that far away from retirement?"

"Jack, I've got nine years 'til retirement and I'm not gonna do 'em under DC-10." Mitch's Chicago accent was coming through; it always did when he got emotional. "And you know, Frank says that narcotics isn't any more dangerous than homicide. Shit, I've been in two shootouts since coming over here. How can it be any worse working with the dopers? Besides, after I do a little time on the streets, maybe I can get a promotion to sergeant over there. I know I'll *never* get promoted around here, not as long as asshole Jumbo Stumbo is around. And how the hell are you ever going to get rid of him? *Nobody* wants him. He's never going to leave 'cause nobody's ever going to let him into their division. Everybody knows how he got promoted, Jack. Nothing stays secret for long around here, and this has got to be the world's worst-kept secret. I figure they're never going to demote him either – that'd be admitting a mistake – so I imagine that he'll go on being lieutenant in homicide until – shit! – until we're all dead! Geez. He'll probably be the death of *all* of us." He paused for a moment, but Jack kept quiet. "I never told you this, and I trust that Kit kept her mouth shut, but at my last physical, the doc said I'd better be watching my blood pressure. I have *never* had blood-pressure problems and I'm way too young to be starting them already, but you know as well as I do that that asshole drives everybody up a wall. Jack, I'll be damned if he's going to give me a heart attack. I made up my mind while I was off that I would be getting out of here as soon as I could. I admit I've been avoiding you, because I didn't want to tell you." He paused. "I didn't want to let you down."

Mitch finished his soliloquy. Such a diatribe was out of character. So was any professed desire for a promotion; Simons had always said that he'd *never* leave the streets, not even to become a sergeant, who would split his time between street supervision and desk work. Not only had Mitch and Kit always claimed that they'd retire from Jack's squad, they also promised to stay partners permanently. It was their shared dream to be remembered as the most successful homicide partnership in the department's history. Jack didn't know what to say; what do you say to somebody who has been driven from his dream?

"Is there anything I can say that will make a difference?" McNaughton asked. His voice implored Simons to give him some chance to change Mitch's mind.

"Sorry, Jack. There's nothing you or anybody can say. Believe me, Kit has tried. Hell, *I've* tried to talk myself out of it. But it's too late. It's just a matter of time; Frank said he expects one of his people will be getting promoted in the next round, and then I'll put in for a lateral. I expect the big shots will be more than happy to transfer the troublemaker out of their favorite division. They probably will be hoping that I'll get shot by some crazed doper, and then their troubles will be over."

"That's not funny, Mitch." Jack knew a narcotics officer who had been shot in the line of duty; they had been in recruit school together. The narc now sat in a wheelchair, paralyzed below the waist.

A moment of silence passed, and then Mitch spoke, his demeanor changed markedly. He clearly felt better for having fessed up. "You playing ball tonight?"

"Yeah, I guess so," a dejected Jack said. "You?"

"Oh, yeah. Wouldn't miss it. Kit and a few of the other guys can't make it, though, and at last count we're going to have only seven people. Do you know anybody you can bring?"

"Not offhand," Jack said. "I'll think about it, though."

"OK. See you at seven?"

"Yeah."

His shift had ended, and Jack was in the locker room, changing into his favorite grey sweats, when Stumbo waddled in, bumping into the puke-green bench set before the row of dented lockers. He sent it reeling, and did nothing to upright it. "Where're you going, Jack?" he queried.

It was a question dreaded by anybody who participated in the weekly basketball game put together by a bunch of people in homicide; nobody wanted Stumbo to play. Having a lieutenant around was bad enough, but having *this* lieutenant around was much worse. God forbid that anybody say anything against the department, for fear that he'd report it back to the higher ups, post haste. And he was miserable on the court – slow, lumbering, uncoordinated and intent on hogging the ball. He'd move in what appeared to be slow motion toward the basket, act as if he was going to jump for a layup, and fail to get more than three inches off of the floor. And invariably, he'd miss.

"Uh, playing ball," McNaughton mumbled. He kept fiddling in his locker, doing nothing but hoping that he'd appear too busy to be bothered. It didn't work.

"Gee, Jack, I'd like to play. Can you use another warm body?" He laughed at his statement, never considering that this was the last body that anybody would warm to.

"Yeah, sure, Doyle. Why don't you meet me over at the gym?"

"Well, hold on there, Jack. I can be ready in a jiffy. Why don't you just wait a minute and I'll go over with you?"

McNaughton nodded. He righted the bench and sat down. It would be a long wait while Stumbo, jabbering all the while, peeled off his polyester street clothes and squeezed his heft into his one-size-too-small gym shorts, about which he fooled only himself.

When he was finally dressed, Stumbo padded after Jack into the parking lot. The drizzle that had persisted all day, creating a damp coldness that permeated every layer of clothing, shone on the blacktop. Jack turned up the collar of his jacket in an unsuccessful attempt to fend off the mist. He succeeded in persuading Stumbo that they should drive separately, since they lived in opposite directions from the gym, and McNaughton sighed heavily at the thought that he might get a few moments respite from Stumbo's obnoxious banter. Try as he might, though, McNaughton couldn't lose Stumbo on the way, and Stumbo's snazzy red Mustang pulled into the parking lot immediately after Jack's boring black Ford.

"Golly, Jack," Stumbo shouted from his car as he began to extricate himself. McNaughton was trapped; he had no choice now but to wait for him. "Were you trying to lose me?"

Stumbo laughed, as if Jack couldn't possibly have wanted to do that. "Of course not, Doyle. I just knew that we were going to be late if we didn't get a move on."

They were late anyway, and when they entered the gym – a smelly, dilapidated facility previously used for elementary school games but taken over by the department a decade earlier – the other players, all men tonight, were jocularly bantering as they passed two basketballs around and took practice. They looked like tall versions of the grade-schoolers who used to play here; they were slower and stiffer, to be sure, but the excitement their momentary freedom from responsibility brought rivaled any enthusiasm a fifth-grader might muster. The stench of sweat, intensified by the damp weather, permeated the peeling walls of the old building, never to be removed no matter how much painting or cleaning was done – and there was seldom much of either. McNaughton almost liked the putrid odor, which took him back to his grade-school basketball games. All that was needed was the smell of popcorn to recreate the experience.

Somebody noticed Stumbo walking behind Jack, and signaled to the others. The din stopped abruptly. Jack knew they were cursing him under their breath.

Mitch was there; so were Joe Stutz and Chris Allen. The other team – three guys from a neighboring homicide squad – had just three players, so at least they'd get stuck with Stumbo. McNaughton could feel the glares of everybody except Joe, who didn't much like Stumbo, but was too gentle a soul to hate anybody. Then again, Joe had not yet incurred Stumbo's wrath.

They divided the teams and got immediately to the task at hand. Most of the people who played had families who were frequently neglected in favor of the job. But their spouses had unanimously decided that it was good for them to work off steam, as well as to keep in shape, and there were few objections as long as the games didn't go much past nine p.m. They played full court, which was challenging but not overly taxing for most of the players.

Simons appeared to be in perfect shape, but Jack couldn't help but let his mind return to Mitch's confession about his blood pressure. McNaughton knew all about Simons's regimen – daily exercising and weight-lifting had kept Mitch the specimen and ladies' man he fancied himself – but Jack found himself watching Mitch especially closely this evening. God forbid that anything happen to him.

Simons was single and had the time to devote to his physique. He also had the desire. He was intensely interested in women, and they were equally enamored of him, with his longish, wavy hair the color of late autumn corn stalks and eyes the shade of mid-summer magnolia leaves. He had chiseled features, including high cheek bones that suggested he might have Native American blood in him some generations back. He had broad shoulders and chest, slim hips and a tight rear, and they were put together in a way that pleased women but did not resemble comical bodybuilders' physiques. Jack never seemed capable of recognizing when another man was good-looking, but Renee assured him that Mitch was extremely attractive. Trouble was, Mitch knew it too.

But his cockiness also had a charm to it, and over the years Renee had learned to love Mitch, almost as if he were Jack's younger brother. She also loved to be a matchmaker, and had suggested years earlier that Kit take him under consideration, but Alvear quickly set her straight. There was the perfect man out there somewhere for Kit – and both Jack and Renee knew she deserved him – but Mitch, she assured them, was not the one. On the other hand, Kit thought that Mitch was about as perfect a professional partner as she could hope for, and he felt the same about her.

Stutz was hot tonight, hitting virtually every shot he took and prompting Simons to dub him "Studs." Joe even sunk two three-pointers, feats that brought a roar of approval and a flurry of high-fives from everybody on the court. Everybody, that is, except the dour Stumbo, who resented anyone with athletic ability. For that matter, Stumbo resented anyone with any ability that he lacked, which meant that he resented virtually everyone. Simons was having a decent game too; while he couldn't match his much younger teammate's prowess, he was successfully driving to the basket and pulled off a couple of nice layups. McNaughton, an average athlete, was having an average game, passing off the ball more than shooting it but reveling in the moment when he spied the opportunity to break away and race down the court to complete a reverse layup.

Stumbo, meanwhile, got the ball more often than his ability would dictate, only because everybody felt obligated to give it to him. You don't skunk the lieutenant. Once he got hold of it, he would hog it, awkwardly dribbling about, and traveling plenty, until he got to his favorite spot – six feet from the basket, on the right, front side – and then he'd shoot. And miss.

Partly because the opposition got stuck with Stumbo, but mostly because of Stutz's hot streak, McNaughton's team was up 45-37 when Joe rebounded the ball just under the basket and broke into long, swift strides toward the other end of the floor. Nobody could catch the youngest, most athletic person on the court. And everybody was getting tired. Stumbo was particularly dogging it in his half-hearted pursuit of the charging opponent. At half-court, Stumbo stopped – not that anybody noticed – and gasped for air. His usually pink and pudgy face turned pallid and drawn; his eyes bugged out, overcoming the folds of fat. He grabbed his throat, and the mountain collapsed in a heap.

The thud alerted everybody whose back had been turned. McNaughton did not even pause; he dashed to Stumbo and dropped hard to his knees, automatically reaching to Doyle's neck to feel for a pulse. His fingers palpated the saggy, sweaty jowls, and he found no beat. As he stretched across Stumbo's enormous chest, he wondered how any heart massage would penetrate all those layers of fat, and everybody here was too exhausted to offer the kind of vigorous stimulation that would undoubtedly be necessary. "Mitch, you do the mouth-to. . .," he started to say, automatically calling on his most experienced detective. But he was interrupted when Simons and Jim Barton, a veteran detective from the other squad – having exchanged brief but knowing glances – reached under McNaughton's armpits and scooped him up and away from the whale-sized hulk. "Guys, somebody call nine-one-one," McNaughton said excitedly. "Do CPR!"

They were all paralyzed. "Let nature take its course," Simons said quietly, spookily.

They stared, all seven of them, at the sprawled body, its giant chest rising from the gym floor like an Indian burial ground rises from the Southern Indiana plain. Stumbo was sweating so profusely that rivulets meandered down his face and dripped into pools on the floor. McNaughton briefly struggled against the men's grips but then stopped, resignedly accepting that they were not about to loosen their holds of his arms and shoulders. The eerie silence was broken only by the players' heavy breathing.

Stutz gaped about around helplessly, distraught but unsure what to do. He shifted his weight from one foot to the other, and wrestled with a conscience that urged him to act. Allen and the others just stared blankly, unbelievingly, at Stumbo. How many times they had wished him dead, even called for his eternal damnation – and now at least the first wish seemed to be happening. It was too good to be true, but it was also petrifying. Several excruciating moments passed.

"OK," Simons said somberly. "Somebody call nine-one-one."

His paralysis lifted by Simons's words, Stutz spun around and ran to his cell phone, laying on a folding chair in the corner of the gym. Would the ambulance come in time? Did they want it to? Everyone there knew that the elementary school was about as far from the ambulance garage as you could get, so it would take some time before the medics would arrive. Perhaps nature will have smiled on them by then, Simons thought.

It was not to be. Stumbo's flabby, fatty, diseased heart roared back with a vengeance – indeed, as if taking its revenge on Simons and the others who thought this might finally get him out of their lives. The medics, aware that manual heart massage wouldn't be effective on a man of Stumbo's girth, turned to the defibrillator, and they had only to hit him once for Stumbo to register a strong heart beat. Simons could have sworn the blips sent out by the medics' equipment were laughing at them all.

The technicians got Stumbo stabilized, and then set off to transport him to the hospital. There were just two of them, and after two tries they realized they could not lift the collapsible stretcher so that its legs would unfold and lock beneath it. They asked for help, and McNaughton and Stutz helped them heave Stumbo so that he could be rolled to the waiting ambulance.

Stutz was in a panic. "I've heard that you can still hear when you're unconscious," he said quietly, nervously. "What if Jumbo *heard* us? What if he heard us?" His voice became a panicky whisper that was out of character for the usually open and ebullient young man.

"Don't worry about it, Studs," Simons said nonchalantly. He could feel the heat of McNaughton's glare, but was unmoved.

"Hey," he said, turning to Jack and responding to the unspoken accusation. "Stumbo is the one who let his body go to hell, and he's the one who chose to play ball tonight. Who are we to interfere with fate?"

The sarcasm in Mitch's voice was too much. "Mitch, what happened here tonight was *wrong*. Doyle could've died, for God's sake. I know that he's an asshole, but we're talking about the life of a fellow cop. It's not up to you – or any of us – to play God."

"You're right, Jack," Simons responded. "And if you ask me, you messing with CPR and wanting to call the paramedics – that was playing God. I think we should have let nature take its course. Let God follow through with what he started."

McNaughton did not answer. Barton, Simons's partner in crime, hung his head deeply. He wandered over to McNaughton as Jack started toward the broken-down bleachers. "Uh, Jack, I'm sorry for my part in this mess. I, I don't know what came over me. I guess I was just pissed at what DC had done to Mitch, and got caught up in the moment."

"Yeah, sure," McNaughton said unconvincingly. He reached the bleachers, and pulled his sweatshirt and pants over his damp playing clothes. He picked up the old towel that Renee had given him and drew it around his neck like his Aunt Agnes used to wear her flat-headed fur fox stole. Then he headed for the door and home.

Renee greeted him with a smile, expecting the same in return. He always felt good after a basketball game – invigorated and spent and horny and romantic – a jumble of emotions wrought by the physicality of the exercise. But not tonight. "Hi, babe," he said soberly. Renee knew instantly that something was wrong; she could always tell, sometimes before Jack even realized it.

The cat rubbed against his leg, but he ignored it.

"What's the matter?" she queried, her voice reflecting her concern. He told her about Stumbo's heart attack – a story that caused her jaw to drop and, in the moment that her defenses also did, gave her a fleeting moment of satisfaction. She quickly recovered her senses and asked with genuine concern about Doyle's prognosis. The medics, Jack said, thought that he'd be OK.

He told her the story, about how he knew that heart massage and mouth-to-mouth resuscitation likely wouldn't have accomplished much when all those layers of fat had to be penetrated, all those years of eating donuts had to be overcome. "But it bugs the shit out of me that nobody *tried,"* McNaughton said, the distress evident in his voice. "I mean, they even stopped me from trying. These guys are sworn to help other people, and yet they let Doyle lie there dying. I still don't believe what I just saw."

"Not everybody has as strict a code of ethics as you have, Jack," Renee said. "Haven't you figured that out yet? What would you do if you found some guy you had been chasing, somebody you planned to charge with the most heinous murder of – oh, I don't know, a nun or something – and this guy was lying there, gasping for breath? Would you do mouth-to-mouth? I bet you would. But you're the only person that I know who would. Including me."

Jack thought for a moment. "I don't know what I'd do. Don't make me out to be such a hero," he said. "Besides, this isn't the same thing. Doyle's a colleague. He's a cop – used to be a pretty good one, too. I cannot understand how Mitch and Joe and everybody else could just overlook that. And I've got to be honest with you. I'm thinking about bringing them up on charges."

Renee did not speak for a few moments. She studied him, her dark brown eyes darting back and forth as she looked into his. Finally she spoke: "Jack, are you sure you want to do that? I mean, I doubt those guys had any evil intent. They were probably just caught up in the moment."

Jack interrupted. "That's exactly how Barton described it. But *Renee*."

She seized the conversation back. "Think about it, Jack. They were physically exhausted and probably mentally spent. They had had a long day at work, and then finally got to let their hair down during the game. They probably couldn't believe their eyes when Stumbo collapsed. It had to be surrealistic – especially for Mitch. Hell, he probably felt like he was watching the answer to his prayers."

"It's not funny," Jack said.

"I don't mean to imply that it is," she responded. "I'm dead serious. I doubt that Mitch or anybody else literally wants Stumbo dead. But when they viewed the scene through their mental fatigue, it probably seemed like an attractive twist of fate – for a few moments, anyhow."

He gazed at her, but did not speak. He finally took a sip of the zin that Renee had waiting for him when he arrived home, then rose and went to the bathroom to shower. It was the last time that the heart-attack episode was ever mentioned in Jack's presence. From that moment on, it had never happened.

Stumbo was hospitalized for just four days, after which the doctor ordered three weeks of bed rest. It was the most peaceful period in the downtown homicide division that anybody could remember. Mitch began to wonder privately whether he should have put in for the transfer, but then he'd return to reality – that Stumbo would be coming back – and felt a sense of relief that his time in homicide was short. The transfer was quickly approved, and as the day on which it would become official – June one – approached, Alvear was inconsolable that the person whom she had expected to be her career-long partner was leaving the squad.

Her dismay was manifested through anger, causing the usually amiable Alvear to snap at anybody who looked her way. She was of Hispanic heritage, and Simons always kidded her – ignorant of the ethnic slur – that that ensured a fiery temper. Alvear had always been able to keep her temper in check – until now. Jack was relieved that Stumbo was out of the office; he surely would have blown Kit's mood out of proportion, accusing her of having an attitude problem or worse. But just as someone who has lost a loved one must adjust, Kit slowly came to terms with Mitch's decision to depart. Her good nature gradually returned, and she forgave Simons, deciding that their friendship would endure even if their partnership could not.

Mitch joined Basker's narcotics squad as scheduled, on the first of the month. While the work remained grim, his demeanor changed markedly. There were still plenty of bureaucratic hurdles that needed to be cleared and sometimes it seemed that the bigwigs were even more nervous about drugs than homicides. But his supervisors were eminently more tolerable than those he left, save Jack. And the freedom of a narc – who, granted, had to write plenty of reports to document what becomes of confiscated drugs – suited Simons.

"I have to admit I miss you guys," he told Jack in a rare show of emotion. They were talking on the phone about two weeks after Mitch had left homicide, when Stumbo had been back on the job for a little more than a week. "But I'm *so* glad to be away from that fuckhead Stumbo."

"I know. I don't blame you. Stumbo's heart attack seemed to kill off what little heart he had. He's a bigger asshole than ever, if that's possible, so it's just as well that you're gone." McNaughton was going out on a limb, speaking derogatorily of a supervisor to a lower-ranking officer, but he knew he could trust Mitch. "I'm sorry to lose you, but I know you'll be happier."

"I'm in a happier place, huh?" Simons said, chuckling.

"Well, yeah. But do me a favor," Jack said. "Watch your back."

"Jack," Simons said. "I think my back's a helluvalot safer now that Stumbo isn't just waiting to stab me in it."

Chapter 8

By the time John Pius Peterson's trial rolled around that brisk November, having gone through the typical delays since it was originally scheduled for July, Mayor Arnold had announced his plans to seek re-election the next year; Lester Trueblood's case had been continued for the umpteenth time; and Mitch was content over at narcotics. Ronald Reagan had died; George W. Bush was re-elected president; and Martha Stewart had gone to prison. McNaughton, having exhausted every extension the government would allow, had finally filed his income taxes. It pained him to write a check for eight hundred fifty-two dollars in taxes and interest. Stumbo had returned to relatively good health, although his doctor termed him "morbidly obese" and ordered him to lose a hundred pounds. It was an impossible task, as everyone but Doyle realized, but it made his mood even more foul than usual.

The weekly basketball games continued, and there was yet to be a mention of the Stumbo incident. And despite his perpetual scowl, Stumbo never gave any indication that he had heard any of the ominous conversation while unconscious. So Stutz's fear had been assuaged.

The late summer and early autumn months had not been without their turmoil. There were enough deaths to keep everybody in downtown homicide so busy that McNaughton feared mistakes would be made. It didn't help that Mayor Arnold was convinced that the rise in crime would hurt his re-election chances, causing him to pressure the chief, who in turn leaned on homicide. The summer months had been unusually hot, even by Indianapolis standards, and tempers flared as the flat plains of Central Indiana baked. Shootings, stabbings, strangulations happened day in, day out. A thirty-three-year-old man shot his own nine-year-old stepson dead to get hold of the cocaine the boy had been dealing. An angst-filled teenager turned homicidal, shooting his Sunday-school-teacher adoptive parents with a double-barreled shotgun. At least two women stabbed their boyfriends to death, each saying she acted in response to continual abuse. It was plausible in one case, less so in the other. By November, it appeared that this was the year that Indianapolis would experience a record number of homicides, a dubious achievement that had not been approached for several years.

But no case held Jack's attention like the Peterson homicides. He had placed the Peterson family photograph on his desk, and he was haunted by the beautiful faces that beamed out from it. He kept wondering what he had missed that would secure a conviction. Terry Bennett, the prosecutor, and Paul Santini, his experienced deputy, felt good about their case and repeatedly assured McNaughton that it was not only winnable, but as close to a sure thing as they had tried in a while. They had Peterson's confession, his blood-covered clothing, the bloody, broken rubber mallet and several witnesses who could testify about the Petersons' deteriorating marriage. "This isn't an O.J. Simpson case," Bennett told Jack. "Peterson is no celebrity, and he's anything but sympathetic. There's enough physical evidence for two cases, and his confession makes the case rock solid."

Santini, who had more courtroom experience and was less prone to grandiose statements, was more circumspect. "I think we're in good shape, Jack," he said. "But I won't complain if you come up with more evidence – another witness who knew about their marital problems or something concrete to point to motive.

Just don't worry; I don't want the jury to sense your discomfort." McNaughton always worried, and even the slightest possibility that a guy who had slaughtered his six kids might get off petrified him. But he kept his fears to himself. Or so he thought; Renee could always tell.

"Jack, you're in good shape," she echoed to him the evening before jury selection was to begin. "You've covered every angle, right?" He nodded and she continued, counting on her fingers for emphasis. "You've got a ton of physical evidence. You've got a confession, for goodness' sake. I know juries can be flaky, but I can't imagine that anybody'd vote to acquit this guy."

"Yeah, but he's really convincing. I mean, I know he's faking. He knew full well what he was doing when he killed those kids. But he gets that glazed-over look and his nose starts running when he talks about it. It's so bizarre. I just wish to hell that I could figure out some way to *prove* to the jurors that he was faking the symptoms – that somehow he figured out how nutcases act and put on a good show. But we've been through every inch of that house; we've gone to the central library to see if he'd checked out any reference books from anywhere in the nine-county radius; we've checked his credit card for book purchases; we've checked his computers – and nothing."

He went to the dishwasher and retrieved two water-streaked wine glasses and wiped them down, then turned to the refrigerator, from which he pulled out the half-empty bottle of zinfandel. He stopped at the kitchen island to pour some in each glass and brought them to the table, where he offered one to Renee. She mumbled "thanks" and he continued: "To make things worse, I read the other day that a university study found that juries tend to sympathize with parents who kill their kids. Can you imagine? As horrendous as it is, jurors apparently can empathize. So they let them off easy – you know, find 'em guilty of manslaughter or even involuntary manslaughter."

"Well, Jack," Renee said, "who among us hasn't said we could kill our kids?"

Jack fell asleep, more quickly and deeply than he had thought possible. He had feared it would be a sleepless night in which he would endlessly review the case in his mind; he had done that plenty of times before. But the fatigue of preparing for trial and the stress associated with such an important case combined to become a powerful sedative.

Vivid dreams came fast. He couldn't remember most of them the next morning, but he couldn't shake one particularly disturbing one. In it, McNaughton found himself roaming a deserted city street lined with dingy, darkened buildings, tall and ominous as they created an eerie canopy over him. The light of a full moon cast an unusual sheen on the wet pavement. He walked casually, gaping about as if he had never been in this place. Then he came upon a set of stairs leading from street level down to what appeared to be a nightclub. He did not know where he was, but he was drawn inside. It was so dark that he could not see, so he felt his way about the blackened room until he found an empty chair. There was a familiar, sickeningly sweet smell, but he couldn't place what it was. Just then, spotlights blinked on, lighting a stage. Standing in the middle was a huge, hulking figure: John Pius Peterson. Several musicians – a guitarist, an organist and a drummer – were behind him. Peterson wore a white clown uniform with huge red buttons and outsized shoe like the main character in *Pagliacci*, an opera about a jealous husband. The costume was spattered with blood, just as it would have been had he been wearing it when he bludgeoned his babies. Peterson grasped a cordless microphone in one hand and raised it to his lips. He began to sing the Patsy Cline classic, "Crazy."

Crazy. I'm crazy from being without you.

Crazy. I'm .....

He finished the song and took a deep bow as dim house lights came up just enough for Jack to see the others in the audience. Each person – and there were hundreds – had only a bloody mass of pulp where his or her face had been. Jack, horrified but moving in the slow motion of the dream world, shifted uncomfortably in his seat, moving his feet and feeling the slight resistance of something sticky clinging to the bottom. In a flash, he realized what he had smelled. He looked at the floor, and saw that it was a sea of blood. He looked at his hands in horror; they too had been stained by Peterson's actions. And then he looked back to the stage, where Peterson, peering down at Jack, opened his huge smile into a series of hysterical guffaws.

Jack awoke abruptly and sat up.

He dozed on and off after that, unable to fall back into deep sleep. So he arose early, took a long, vigorous walk on the tread mill and left home long before he had planned. Renee suggested that he not wake up Angel, who had gotten to bed later than usual the previous evening. It killed him not to say goodbye in the morning, but he knew that his little girl would be over-tired and cranky if she didn't sleep a while more. He thought about the great weekend they had had, and a smile broke on his lips. The three of them had trekked to the Children's Museum, Angel's favorite place, and ate dinner out at Muldoon's, an old favorite of Jack and Renee's B.B. – before baby – which only recently had added a family-dining area that allowed them to return. With those happy thoughts in mind, he couldn't resist sneaking into Angelica's room before he left, kissing her cherubic face, smelling her sweet breath and mouthing "I love you, sweetheart," before tiptoeing out and gently closing the door. It was a moment that would sustain him that day, when the talk would be about six dead babies.

The late fall winds that cut across the flat plains of Indiana and get whipped up in the Indianapolis skyscrapers slapped Jack awake as he headed south toward the City-County Building, which housed most city offices, the bulk of the police department, and thirty-three municipal, criminal and superior courts. It was tall and boxy and ugly and typical of the Neoclassical buildings constructed in the late 1960s after the federal Omnibus Crime Control Act indirectly made money available for such boondoggles. The act, intended to spur widespread reforms in the criminal-justice system, was urgently passed by Congress after the outbreak of race riots and a surge in violent crime in the country. But instead of putting more cops on the streets, many cities, including Indianapolis, used its money to construct shrines to the city fathers at the time. It did prove helpful years later, however, when the city and the county merged their police departments. The county had long ago outgrown the ornate Second Empire-style courthouse on Washington Street, and it was razed, much to the dismay of preservationists, when the city made room for its new partner in crime-fighting.

The City-County Building, as some unimaginative flunky had dubbed it, was of course built of Bedford limestone, the plentiful, strong rock mined from the quarries of Southwestern Indiana. As a young boy, Jack's great-grandfather often snuck away from his house on sultry summer days to do the forbidden – go swimming in the crystal clear but deathly deep water that had filled the abandoned quarries. He had lived to tell about it; not all such daredevils were as lucky. All Hoosiers loved to tell how limestone was the marvelously strong, if plain, grey material used in the Empire State Building, as if connection with that once world's-tallest-building somehow made Indiana limestone more worthy.

The twenty-eight-story, vertical rectangle was kitty-corner across Alabama Street from the vacant lot where Market Square Arena, the last venue Elvis Presley performed before his death, once stood. While the main door to the City-County Building was on Market Street, across from the struggling, dilapidated City Market, many visitors entered the building through a revolving glass door on the Alabama Street side. A desk sergeant sat in a high, glass-enclosed box above the fray, directing the swarm of high-priced attorneys, bewildered traffic violators and low-life types who passed through his doors to wherever they wanted – or had – to be. The process had been slowed in recent years, since metal detectors were installed several feet inside, causing backups that sometimes extended out the door. The entryway perpetually stank. Jack finally realized it was the odor of rotting garbage and, considering some of the people who frequented the place, he thought it not inappropriate.

What *did* seem inappropriate, however, was that this bustling, stinky place was the awkward location the city leaders had chosen for its memorial to police officers killed in the line of duty. Surely, Jack thought, they could have found a more solemn, worthy place, away from the noise and the stench. Apparently not; the navy blue tri-fold screen, bearing photos of each dead officer in uniform, stood directly behind the sergeant's high-rise, in the thick of the comings and goings.

He didn't come here much, although many of his colleagues reported here. Downtown homicide was located in its own stationhouse about a mile north in a building by itself, having outgrown the paltry space once allotted it here. The unit's growth mirrored the increase in homicides, and a graph showing the increase in personnel was virtually identical to one showing the increase in violent deaths in the county – although there was the inevitable time lag while politicians waited to see if the public would scream about the crime rate before they would act.

The courtroom where the Peterson trial would be held was on the second floor of the judicial wing. Jack glanced toward the elevators, where at least a dozen people waited, and decided to make the trip up the stairs despite lugging a box of his files, copies of what he had provided to the prosecutors. He knew that things could be lost, and he didn't want to leave anything to chance. McNaughton entered the courtroom through the judge's office, nodding a subdued hello to the secretaries and bailiffs. "He's not his usual friendly self," a fifty-ish, bleached blonde secretary commented about McNaughton to her black-haired colleague. "Trial's starting," the other responded, nodding knowingly. "He's nervous."

McNaughton shoved his file box under the long prosecution table and took his seat at the far left end. Santini would sit beside him, and then Bennett. Jack pulled out one manila folder and started studying its contents, taking one last opportunity to figure out what he might have missed.

The next two days or so would be spent selecting a jury, an inexact science in which both sides do their best to hone down a pool of people to a panel of twelve, plus two alternates, who would most likely agree with their take on the case. The prosecution would be looking for law-and-order types and maybe some parents – maybe even older ones, who had already gone through the tribulations of raising kids, and did it without hurting them. Jack doubted that Fortner would be looking for any particular type of person – just any individual in the jury pool who, for one reason or another, seemed to be sympathetic to his client's situation.

"Earth to Jack. Earth to Jack. Come in Jack." It was Santini. McNaughton squinted up at him and briefly wondered how he could be so light-hearted.

"Hey, Paul, what's new?" McNaughton said grimly.

"Nothin' but my underwear," Santini said.

"I'm glad to see you're improving your wardrobe," he said without humor. Before Santini could respond, Jack felt the familiar vibration of his cell phone on his hip, where he wore the device on his belt. He reached down, pulled the device from its holster and read the caller's name and number. He pressed a button that would send the call to voice mail. Then he sighed, pinched his lips and blinked twice. It was Stumbo.

"What's the matter, Jack? Your stocks go down?" Santini asked.

"Worse," Jack said. "Stumbo's calling me."

"That asshole's back to work already?"

"Afraid so. For quite a while, actually. You can't keep a good man down, you know."

"Why in the hell didn't he just take disability? He could milk that for two years, get eighty percent of his salary tax-free and then retire at full pension. And he could have given you all a break."

"Oh, sure. That's exactly what Stumbo longs to do. In case you haven't noticed, Paul, Stumbo doesn't have a life. The only way we're going to be able to get rid of him is to carry him out of the office on a stretcher."

McNaughton stood up, muttered a quiet "excuse me" and headed for the hallway to return the call. He punched in the office number and waited, watching as some obviously confused people wandered the hall, peering at each doorway in an attempt to figure out where they were. Potential jurors, he was sure. The criminals always knew their way around.

The phone rang once, then again. "Downtown homicide. Carla," the voice on the other end said.

"Carla, hi. It's me." His favorite secretary would recognize his voice. "Stumbo called."

"Hi, Jack," Carla said. "How're you doing?"

"I'm OK, thanks. Do you know what he wants?"

"No. I didn't even know he called you. But he's awful gleeful. Somebody must be in trouble. You know how he loves it when he gets to give somebody a load of shit."

"Yeah. I guess I'm the one who's going to get the load today. Lucky me."

"Hold on a minute. I'll get him."

After making Jack wait the obligatory three minutes listening to obnoxious on-hold music, Stumbo came on the line. "Jack?" he drawled, his accent particularly thick today.

"Yeah, Doyle. You called?"

"Yes, I did. Uh, you need to be informed that a Mr. Lester Trueblood has filed a complaint against you and Stutz charging you two with brutality. Let's see, it says here that you two beat him up when he was arrested and that you refused to allow him to relieve himself, causing him what this here complaint calls 'deep emotional distress and possible physical damage.' Count three says that you shoved him into a ditch. Shit, Jack, haven't you two learned how to deal with a prisoner?"

McNaughton could hear Stumbo sucking on a toothpick "Well, thanks for the vote of confidence, Doyle," Jack said, the slightest hint of sarcasm in his voice. But he stayed cool. "Just because the complaint says those things doesn't mean it's true. In fact, it's ludicrous. Do you have any interest in my version of the story?"

"I don't think so, Jack," Stumbo said. "We're drawing an I-number on you."

"An I-number!" Jack began to get excited now. "Doyle, that guy was so shit-faced that he couldn't stand up. Yes, I pushed him to the floor to cuff him – as the SOPs say I'm supposed to – and, yes, he fell into a ditch when Joe and I stopped to let him take a leak. But that's as far as it went. We did *not* hurt him!"

He realized that he was soundly plaintive, and he knew it wouldn't do any good anyway. "Just get it over with quickly," he said firmly. "I don't want this hanging over my head, especially over the holidays."

"Do you know where Stutz is? I've got to inform him too," Stumbo said.

"No, Doyle. In case you forgot, I'm in the middle of a capital murder trial. Remember John Pius Peterson?"

"Very funny, McNaughton. I just thought you might be a good enough supervisor to know what your people are doing."

"He's working his cases, Doyle. If he doesn't come into the squad room, call him. I've gotta go." He hung up before Stumbo could say another word.

McNaughton was chagrined about the I-number; those kinds of things could continue interminably, hanging over one's head like a guillotine blade. He worried, too, that an internal investigation would demoralize Stutz, maybe even harm his career. They both had heard all too much about cops who'd been railroaded, even in situations as transparent as this one. Jack knew he'd have to reassure the kid that they'd be exonerated – who in the hell would believe that scumbag Lester Trueblood? But he could feel the acid churning in his stomach, and he wondered how convincing he'd sound when he tried to do it. After all, he'd seen what happened to those other cops too.

He reached into his pants' pocket for his extra-strength Tums, and popped two in his mouth, then strode to the nearby men's room. As he shoved open the door, he nearly knocked defense counsel to the floor.

"Gee, Jack, I know you'll be gunning for me in the courtroom, but in the washroom too?" Fortner said.

"Sorry, Knofel," McNaughton said. "See you in court."

Fortner, curious about Jack's curtness, shrugged inconspicuously and left, and Jack headed to the urinal. After relieving himself, he washed his hands, patted some cold water on his face and ran his damp hands through his hair. Then he straightened his tie and returned to the courtroom.

Bennett and Santini were standing at the prosecutor's table, flipping through questionnaires the prospective jurors had filled out. Santini noticed Jack's flushed face and leaned close.

"Jack, what's wrong?" he asked with a note of worry in his voice. But the bailiff's arrival precluded an answer. In as deep and as authoritative a voice as the sixty-eight-year-old Ford factory retiree could muster, he announced: "All rise. Superior Court One of Marion County, Indiana, is now is session. The honorable Judge Laura Linden presiding."

Judge Laura Linden floated in, moving more quickly than imaginable for someone of her tiny size. She was a sight to behold. She had broad, square shoulders that she pushed back with great dignity and, when juxtaposed to her five feet of height, made her look as wide as she was tall. Emerging from beneath her black robe, custom-made to fit her short stature, were size five feet, perpetually clad in classic black pumps. At sixty-two, she had a mass of salt-and-pepper hair swept back from a full cherubic face and sparkling sapphire eyes that belied her age. But that was hardly the only contradiction about Laura Linden. She was the mother of four daughters, the grandmother of nine, and her usual demeanor befitted that role. She was eminently polite and eternally patient. But she had no tolerance for nonsense or dishonesty in her courtroom, and she had been known to find an attorney or two in contempt, ordering them to jail to ponder their misdeed. The judge, widely respected for her fairness and impartiality, was equally renowned for her penchant for sternly lecturing newly convicted defendants, even reducing a few to tears, and then giving them the maximum sentence. "Grown men cry from the Linden eye," cops would say. Others dubbed the petite grandmother "Grambo," a play on the tough Rambo character that Sylvester Stallone had portrayed in the movies.

But Linden's high spirits and enthusiasm for the law were in evidence more often than her toughness. When the youngest of her girls was a sophomore in high school, Linden, then age forty-seven, started law school. She loved it, and finished at the top of her class. She practiced law for five years before the governor appointed her to fill a judicial vacancy, and she subsequently won election to the bench. Later, she would joke that going to law school and serving as a judge were cinches compared to raising four daughters.

"Be seated," Linden intoned in her soft voice. "Gentlemen," she said, turning to the all-male cast of lawyers, "are there any matters to be considered before we bring the jury pool into the courtroom?"

"Your honor, the prosecution is ready to proceed with *voir dire,*" Bennett said ingratiatingly.

Fortner leaned over and whispered something to Peterson. The huge hulk of a man wore a old, conservative grey suit made of inexpensive polyester, a white shirt and a dated, striped grey tie that wasn't long enough to cover his middle. His meaty hands were folded in front of him on the table. He sat impassively, and seemed oblivious to what Knofel had told him.

"Your honor, if it pleases the court," Fortner began. "Mr. Peterson would like for the court to take judicial notice of the brief that we have previously filed with regard to the insanity defense. If it pleases the court further, we would request a hearing on Mr. Peterson's competency to stand trial and to aid in his own defense."

"Mr. Bennett?" the judge said, turning to the prosecution.

Bennett looked perturbed. "Your honor, Mr. Fortner made no reference to such a hearing in our pre-trial conference," he said. "If we proceed with that, it will cause a great inconvenience to the ladies and gentlemen who reported for jury duty today. In addition, he had ample time to prepare everyone for a competency hearing, but today is the first we've heard of this. While, as a matter of course, our witness, Dr. Friedmann, examined Mr. Peterson as to his competency to stand trial, she is not prepared to testify about that today. We would strenuously oppose such a hearing."

Linden turned back to Knofel. "Mr. Fortner, do you have any new information for this court that wasn't contained in your pleading on the insanity issue?"

"No, your honor," he said. "Mr. Peterson merely wanted his psychiatrist, Dr. Rosterman, to be heard on the competency issue in court and we had hoped to cross-examine the state's witness on this issue."

"OK, Mr. Fortner. Thank you very much," Linden said in a voice that indicated it was time for Fortner to sit down. "I tend to agree with Mr. Bennett. Some prior notice about a competency hearing would have been appropriate. We're going to be disrupting our jurors' lives enough – uh, Mr. Bennett, didn't you inform the court that this trial may take more than a week?"

"Yes, your honor," Bennett replied.

"Well," Linden continued, "I don't want to make this any more difficult than absolutely necessary for these people who are trying to do their civic duty. We have your pleading on the subject, complete with psychiatric evaluations. We also have the state's response with its psychiatrist's observations." She was talking with her hands, ticking off the items she listed on her fingers. "I don't suppose it would surprise anybody that their opinions are widely divergent. I expect that we'd hear the same if a hearing were held on the matter. So we'll proceed with jury selection. I'll monitor Mr. Peterson's demeanor and his reaction to the events before the court, and I'll keep in mind his alleged mental condition. If I find that he demonstrates that he does not understand what is happening or is incapable of aiding in his defense, I'll reconsider a competency hearing. And I expect that you'll inform the court if he should have any substantive change in demeanor. For now, we'll proceed with the thought in mind that the jurors will determine the truth of the issues before them."

"But, your honor," Fortner began.

"Mr. Fortner, are you familiar with *Ake v. Oklahoma?*" Linden asked sternly.

"Yes, your honor," he answered.

"Well, then, you know that it is the opinion of the Supreme Court that juries are the primary fact finders on the insanity issue. It is for them to resolve differences of opinion within the psychiatric profession. Let's proceed and give the jury the opportunity to do its job, OK?" It was rhetorical question; she did not wait for Fortner to respond. "Now, is there anything else?

"No, your honor," Fortner said.

"No, ma'am," Bennett replied.

"Then, bailiff, let's bring in the first group for questioning."

Bennett, mindful that the public would seek vengeance for such a horrific crime, had filed a motion indicating that he intended to seek the death penalty against Peterson if the defendant were convicted. In Indiana, a death-penalty trial had two phases – first, the ordinary trial in which the jury decided if a defendant were guilty or not, and then a mini-trial in which the state had to prove, again beyond a reasonable doubt, that at least one aggravating circumstance existed during commission of the crime, thereby warranting the death penalty. The legislature had spelled out fourteen such circumstances, including multiple murders and the murder of a person under age twelve. With the Peterson crime meeting not one but two aggravating circumstances, Bennett felt as confident about the sentencing as he did of a conviction. But McNaughton was leery. Even though they are instructed that the death penalty is not mandatory in case of conviction, jurors sometimes feared that a vote to convict was an automatic vote to condemn. And, as heinous as the crime was and as much as he thought Peterson a worthy candidate for the death penalty, Jack thought it better not to seek it, lest sympathy creep into jurors' minds. Perhaps there'll be a lingering doubt – not a reasonable doubt, but a lingering one, he thought – that would make somebody reluctant to impose the death penalty. And the same somebody might therefore deny the jury of the unanimous vote it would need to convict.

But it was not his decision. He weighed in with his concerns, but Bennett had the final say. Because the death penalty was an issue, *voir dire*, a French term that meant "to see, to tell" – and the pronunciation of which was invariably badly mangled by American lawyers – included numerous questions about capital punishment.

"Good morning, ladies and gentlemen," Bennett intoned after the first group of potential jurors had filed into the jury box. There were fourteen chairs – twelve for the people who would make up the jury and two for alternates, who would be asked to listen to the entire trial, but who then would be denied the opportunity to participate in deliberations or vote on the verdict unless an original juror was dismissed for some reason.

Bennett, a tall, lean man who favored expensive Italian suits despite their drain on his meager public salary, paced casually in front of the jury box during his questioning, stopping only when he directed a question to a specific person. Then he'd lean on the railing at the front of the jury box, oozing sincerity and sobriety. His arms were crossed against his chest with his hands placed just so, so the panel could see the huge Notre Dame class ring he wore on his right ring finger.

"I'm Terrence Bennett, prosecutor for Marion County." He gestured toward the prosecution's table and continued: "Sitting in the middle of that table is my associate, Paul Santini, who will examine some of the witnesses you will see if you become a member of the jury. Next to him is Detective Sergeant Jack McNaughton of the Metro-Marion police, the lead investigator in this case. Now, you've been asked to do your civic duty by sitting on a jury in the case of *State v. Peterson*, in which John Pius Peterson, the gentleman sitting over there," he said, pointing, "is accused of bludgeoning his six children to death. I'm sure most of you have read something about this case in the newspapers or seen something on TV. And that's OK; that doesn't automatically mean that you'll be dismissed from the jury. What both sides will be asking of you is that you listen to all of the evidence and, at the end of the trial, make as sound a decision, following Judge Linden's instructions, as you're capable of making.

"Now, I won't pretend that we're not asking you to participate in something very profound. Mr. Peterson's life is at stake. And so is justice. While we do not expect you to take such a responsibility lightly, the state will endeavor to make this decision as easy as possible for you. We will meet our charge – and that is to prove to you, beyond a reasonable doubt, that Mr. Peterson took a rubber mallet and methodically beat each of his children, and even the family dog, until they were dead. We believe the evidence is so overwhelming that you will be able to render a guilty verdict without reservations."

Fortner, perched on the edge of his chair, was getting restless, irritated that Bennett was making more of an opening argument than an introduction to potential jurors. He silently looked to Judge Linden for relief, but Linden kept her steady gaze on the panel. So he held his tongue, hoping that the prosecutor would quickly get to the point.

Bennett continued: "Now, Mr. Fortner, the gentleman sitting next to Mr. Peterson, will try to convince you that Mr. Peterson was insane when he committed these acts. Uh, Mrs. Stein," Bennett said, smoothly plucking the name of potential juror in seat number eight from his memory, "it might seem that someone would have to be crazy to commit such heinous acts, wouldn't you agree?"

The bespectacled woman of about fifty with dyed brown hair nervously looked about the courtroom, as if she were seeking advice on what to do. Finding none, she nodded sheepishly. "You'll have to answer aloud, for the record," Bennett said soothingly, gesturing toward the court clerk. "Uh, yes, I would say so," the woman responded.

"But Mrs. Stein, let's say that Judge Linden instructed you that, under the law, the only way Mr. Peterson could be excused for committing these crimes was if he were unable to tell right from wrong. Could you follow the law?"

"Well, yes, I imagine so."

"OK. And if the state proved to you that Mr. Peterson knew that what he was doing was wrong – even if it seems like a crazy act – could you find him guilty?"

"Well, yes, I think I could."

It continued like that for nearly two hours, with Bennett addressing seven or eight questions to each individual. Some were perfunctory: Had they ever been victims of a crime? Did they know any of the principals in the case? Had they formed an opinion about the case? But Bennett was more interested in the potential jurors' opinions about the insanity defense and the death penalty.

Finally, Bennett said, "That's all I have, your honor," and Linden called for a five-minute break. When she said five minutes, she did not mean six. And then it was Fortner's turn.

"Good morning, ladies and gentlemen," he said, standing at a rostrum that he had turned to face the jury box. "I'm Knofel Fortner. I'm counsel for Mr. Peterson, the defendant in this case." Knofel looked over toward Peterson, who had been coached to acknowledge the panel when he was introduced. He barely lifted his chin from his chest, and did not move his eyes.

"The first thing I must tell you is that Mr. Peterson has pleaded not guilty by reason of insanity. By making that pleading, Mr. Peterson admits to committing the acts for which he is on trial."

There was a rustling in the jury box. Two of the potential jurors' eyebrows rose visibly; another's mouth dropped slightly open.

"I realize that's surprising to you," Fortner continued. "But in our system of justice, just because Mr. Peterson physically committed an act does not mean that he is guilty of breaking the law. It doesn't mean that he's *responsible*.

"What we – Mr. Bennett and Mr. Santini *and* I – are looking for in this case is justice. No one is sorrier or more distraught or more remorseful that the Peterson children are dead than their father, John Pius Peterson. He wishes he could give you an explanation; he wishes he could explain all this to *himself*. But he can't. Mr. Peterson can't explain what happened, because he was experiencing a psychological episode, a phenomenon known as 'dissociative reaction,' at the time of the events. Mr. Peterson's physical body committed the acts; this we acknowledge. But his mind did not. His mind could not. He had no understanding of right or wrong at the moment he picked up that rubber mallet.

"You'll hear all this – in more scientific terms and with more explanation – from a psychiatrist who has examined Mr. Peterson at great length. He will tell you that Mr. Peterson had no idea what was happening at the time, and thus could not possibly have distinguished right and wrong. And that's the crux of this case. The law says that we can't be held responsible for something if we do not appreciate that it is wrong. Mr. Pelletier, do you understand that?"

Pelletier, bald but for a dark fringe above the ears, nodded and then, remembering Bennett's admonition about speaking for the record, answered aloud, "yes."

"And, sir," Fortner continued, "if the defense showed you that Mr. Peterson could not distinguish right from wrong, could you vote to acquit him – that is, find him not guilty?"

"Well, I'm not sure about that," Pelletier answered. "I mean, he killed his own kids and all."

"Mr. Pelletier, do you consider yourself a law-abiding citizen?"

"Why, of course, I do." He was almost indignant.

"Then, sir, would you agree to follow the law if you became a juror?"

"Well, yes, of course," he answered.

"Then, sir, would you not agree that, if you believed Mr. Peterson could not distinguish right from wrong, you would have to follow the law and vote to acquit?"

"I guess so," he said, plainly unconvinced.

Pelletier didn't make it on the jury; Fortner struck his name from the roster. Peterson didn't need anybody who couldn't at least consider seeing it his way.

By the time Judge Linden called it a day, nine jurors had been tentatively seated. It would take the better part of the next day to seat three more jurors and two alternates, so Linden, intent on having the opening statements made before the end of the day, called for court to convene at an unusually early eight a.m.

Bennett, Santini and McNaughton learned that it had started to drizzle when they left the courthouse to retreat to the Legal Beagle, the bar where courthouse regulars congregated. There, they would discuss what had transpired and plan how they would proceed the next morning.

"I can't believe what a great group we've got!" Bennett said. "I mean, we've got conviction in the bag."

Jack frowned. "Terry, let's not get ahead of ourselves. Knofel's good, and you just can't predict juries these days."

"God, Jack, if I were as negative about everything as you are, I'd just sign myself into the loony bin. Lighten up. We're in great shape."

There he goes again, Jack thought. Great shape. We'll see.

"Guys," McNaughton said as he sucked down the last swallow of his beer, "I'm out of here. I've got to get home to my girls."

Renee had had a long day at work too, and she figured Jack would be no more in the mood to cook than she was – even if all it meant was opening a box of macaroni and cheese. By the time Jack pulled in the drive, she had already ordered their regular – alfredo vegetarian pizza – and had poured a couple of beers to accompany it. He wrestled with Angel for the twenty minutes or so before the doorbell rang. As usual, Angelica scooted for the door and insisted on handing the delivery boy with dripping hair his three-dollar tip.

The pizza was unusually tasty and loaded with fresh vegetables, making Renee happy and Angel growl, but it was Jack who picked at his meal. He could not focus on food.

After they ate, Renee took Angel to her room for a story and bedtime while Jack deposited the paper plates and napkins in the garbage and the glasses in the sink. Then he checked his voice mail and listened to Stumbo's irritating voice whine about scheduling a meeting on the Trueblood I-number. He made a conscious decision that even Stumbo would not bother him tonight, and he did not mention the matter to Renee.

There also were four messages from Sniffy Smith, a long-time informant of Jack's. It was late, and Sniffy probably would be out at the bars, where it would be impossible to hold a phone conversation. So Jack decided to wait until the morning to return the calls.

"Let's go up to bed and read," Renee said as she entered the family room, fresh from cuddling Angel. McNaughton, who readily agreed to get horizontal, didn't feel much like regurgitating all that had happened that day, but he did allow that the jurors seemed OK.

"I think they're fine," he told her. "About as good as can be expected. But I still think we're worried about everything around the edges and forgetting the core of the case. Sort of like a paramedic who's worried about an ingrown toenail while the patient is choking to death."

Chapter 9

McNaughton decided to make a quick trip to the squad room before heading over to court. It wasn't out of the way, and he wanted to check his voice mail again, as well as messages and mail he was sure was piling up on his desk. The early start of court made it harder to get there, but at least he'd avoid a rush of people, including – and most important – Stumbo.

There were two more messages from Sniffy Smith on Jack's voice mail. Smith, whose given name was Walter, had been a CI – a confidential informant – for Jack for years, almost since McNaughton was assigned to homicide. Jack was relatively sure that Sniffy also worked as a CI for some drug investigators, but they never discussed it. Neither he nor Sniffy could remember any longer how they had met, but Sniffy had provided Jack with a lot of good information over the years. It was usually correct, or almost so, and invariably useful. The guy clearly had a lot of connections, a good memory and a sense of what would be valuable to police, even the less obvious stuff. Jack had mentioned to Renee that Sniffy was smart and savvy enough to have been successful on the other side of the law. But there was the problem of his nasty cocaine habit. Jack had regularly nagged Sniffy to quit, and when he realized that his pleas were akin to talking to the wall, he resignedly insisted only that Smith stay far away when he was using. On occasion, Sniffy even professed a desire to quit, but when a physician deemed his deviated septum (the acquired deformity that had earned Smith his nickname) to be so deteriorated that it was inoperable, it seemed that Sniffy had resigned himself to cocaine as a way of life. It no longer made McNaughton uncomfortable. In an ideal world, the cops wouldn't have to rely on junkies to get information, but then, in an ideal world, there wouldn't be any need for the info. Jack had come to terms with it: Sniffy's information had put away several criminals – including a couple of murderers – whose actions were considerably more heinous. Situational ethics? Jack pleaded guilty. But he found it easy to rationalize when he heard judges order sentences that put some disgusting crooks away for life.

He didn't plan to be in the office long, but Jack chanced it that Sniffy would be in a position to take a call. Most likely, he'd get him out of bed. McNaughton punched in Smith's phone number, fiddling with the mail while he waited for Sniffy to pick up.

"Jackie," came the almost-whispered greeting, following by a quick sniff. "Where the hell you been, man?"

"It's a long story, Sniff. How're you?"

"Good, Jackie, good." Another sniff. "I got something hot for you, buddy. We gotta talk. Soon."

Jack, still flipping through unopened envelopes, noticed one from the department. He split it with a letter opener and found it to be written notification that he was the subject of an internal investigation – the Trueblood case. It was all the impetus he would need to propel him out the door.

"Well, I've got to be in court in less than an hour. How quickly can you meet me at the Mickey D's at Sixteenth and Tibbs?"

"I just got up, man. But I think I can be there in ten minutes."

"Great. See you in ten."

The rest of the work would have to wait. McNaughton grabbed his sports jacket from the back of his chair – his overcoat was, characteristically, left in the back seat of his sedan even though it was raining – and dashed down the stairs.

"Jack." It was the desk sergeant whose job sometimes seemed to be a scumbag-infested, crisis-oriented perversion of receptionist work. "That I-number on you is bullshit. Absolute bullshit."

McNaughton wondered for a moment how word had gotten out so quickly, but he let it slide. "Thanks, Nick," he said as he pushed through the glass door.

The rain had continued throughout the night and into the morning, so Jack jogged to his squad car. He drove to the McDonalds at Sixteenth and Tibbs to await Sniffy, ordering two large black coffees before he sat in a corner booth. Sniffy rode up on his dilapidated bicycle a few minutes later and jogged in. He brushed rain off his water-proof windbreaker and shook his head, spraying water like a dog, before waving to Jack. McNaughton held up a steaming cup to signal Sniffy that he didn't need to buy coffee.

"Jackie," Sniffy said, elongating the word as he slipped into the booth, sniffing. "Shit, man. You didn't tell me it was raining when you called. Long time, no see, man."

"I know, Sniff," McNaughton replied, sliding the coffee across the table. "I was wondering if you'd forgotten me."

"No way, Jackie. Ain't no way." Smith was about thirty-five and painfully thin. He had long, bony fingers and an equally long, bony neck, making his head seem too large for his body. He wore his dark brown hair slicked back into a short ponytail; his left ear sported a small hoop earring. The windbreaker hid several tattoos, including a heart inscribed with the illegible name of a long-forgotten love and a skull with a dagger and a red rose through the eye socket. His skin was unusually tanned for this time of year, but McNaughton knew that Sniffy had family in

Florida, where he may have picked up his color. He was perpetually tan, it seemed, and Jack didn't know if the wrinkles Sniffy sported on his face were prematurely brought on by the sun, the cocaine or both.

"Didn't you say you just got up, Sniff? Do you want something to eat? I'll buy."

"Oh, thanks, Jackie," he said, pausing to sip the hot coffee, "but I'm not hungry." Sniffy never was, Jack thought. Cocaine, the diet wonder drug.

"Jackie, I really hate to ask, but I'm a little short. Do you think I can get something for my information?"

"You know how stingy the department is, Sniffy, but I'll make sure you're taken care of if the info is good."

"Oh, it is, man." He sniffed. "I was at work at the club a couple nights ago, and this guy I know, Baden Baden, comes up to me and says he needs my services."

"Baden Baden. As in Baden & McAllister?" Jack was referring to a local law firm that handled defense work, nothing major and mostly for low-life clients that the firm got by advertising on the slimiest of the daytime talk shows. Baden, only mildly more refined than his clients, had been named after Baden-Baden, the 1877 winner of the Kentucky Derby; the horse's owner was a close friend of the lawyer's great-grandfather. It was the sleek and swift thoroughbred's misfortune to have a namesake of such dubious distinction.

"Yeah. That's the one," Sniffy said. "He says he has a client who has a problem, and he needs somebody to 'remedy' it. That was the word he used. 'Remedy.'"

"OK. Did he go into details?"

"Not really, man. He just asks if I know anybody who could handle a real major job. Says he has a client who's worried about the competition and will pay big money if it's done right. So I say, well, what about me? I could use the cash. And what's so major that I can't do it? He says it's not the kinda stuff I'm into. I say, so try me. He says, no, Sniffy. You're a real good connection for blow – oh, Jackie, pretend you didn't hear that. Then he says you don't have experience in the stuff I need. So I start to get hinky that he's talking about some pretty heavy shit. And he's right – I don't want none of that heavy shit."

"Sniffy," Jack said, "what are you trying to say?"

"Jackie, I think he's wantin' to *kill* somebody. I mean, I don't want you throwin' this back in my face someday, but there's not a whole lot of shit I won't do. I mean, a man's gotta make a living. But man, I won't kill nobody; I never did kill nobody and I don't want to go to hell for nobody, Jackie. So I'm thinkin' he wants to off somebody. He says he thought maybe I know somebody who could handle something major and, if I did, there'd be something in it for me if I found somebody."

"What'd you tell him, Sniff?"

"I said I'd have to get back to him, man. I mean, I couldn't think of nobody right then, and I didn't know if I wanted to get mixed up in that shit anyway."

"Good thinking. How well do you know Baden?"

"Pretty good, man. That's why I called you, Jackie. I think I can read him pretty good, and it just sounded kinda fishy to me."

"Yeah, I agree. But why'd he come to you, Sniffy, if he didn't think you'd handle it yourself? I mean, I wouldn't think he'd want too many people to know what's going on. And I'm sure he wouldn't talk to anybody unless he's absolutely sure he can trust 'em."

"He was pretty drunk, man. And Baden and I have – how should I put it? A *relationship*."

"Defended you on a coke charge, right?" Jack asked matter-of-factly.

"Yeah, something like that, man. But it was a long time ago."

"Yeah, yeah, Sniffy. I know. You're clean now," he said sarcastically. "Sounds like you and Baden have a mutually beneficial relationship – you scratch his back and he'll scratch yours, huh?"

"We've done a few lines together," Sniffy said. "And I used to help him out on that shit. But lately, I've just been getting him some clients, so he feels like he owes me."

McNaughton knew what Smith was talking about. Sniffy worked on and off as a bouncer – as if anyone would be intimidated by the scrawny guy – at a strip joint called The Fantasy Club. And the women there would occasionally get carried away with their role-playing, and find themselves in a bit of trouble with the authorities.

"Sniff, I'm not sure this is enough to go on. I mean, you and I both know what this sounds like, but it might not be enough."

"I know, Jackie, but I feel *real* strong about this. I know somebody's going to get hurt."

"I tell you what, Sniffy. You and I are going to put down a call to Baden. I want to make sure it wasn't the liquor and the cola talking the other night. All you have to do is talk to him about your conversation at the club – you know, stuff like, was he serious and what kind of work does he need done and how soon and how much will it pay. You can tell him that you've got somebody in mind, but you need more information before you contact him. And if we get enough, with just me listening in, then I'll get authorization for a body transmitter, and we'll wire you up for a visit to his office, OK?"

"Not gonna work, bud. He won't talk to me on the phone; he's told me that a lot of times. Besides, Baden's used to me just dropping in. He's usually just sitting there twiddling his thumbs."

"Well, Sniff, I'd rather hear it for myself first. Let's just give it a try. If he says anything at all incriminating, it'll make it easier for me to get the OK for the transmitter. Let's go out to my car, and we'll call him."

They each clutched a coffee cup and headed out to Jack's car. There, he had Sniffy use his own cell phone to call Baden Baden's office.

"Will it alarm him if you use the speaker?" Jack asked.

"No, I don't think so," Sniffy said as the call went through. "He's used to that."

"Baden & McAllister," a receptionist said.

"Let me talk to Baden," Sniffy said. "It's Sniffy."

"One moment, please." A moment passed.

"Sniffy, my man," the lawyer said with a drawl.

"Double B. Man, we gotta talk. I think I got somebody for you."

"Sniffy, I'm not sure what you're talking about."

"B, you know. The shit we talked about the other night at the club. I think I got somebody but you gotta tell me more before I ask him. Like, what's the job and what's it pay?"

"Sniffy, you know I don't like to discuss business over the telephone. Delicate matters demand personal meetings. As I mentioned to you, a client of mine would like to engage your services as a liaison. You'll be compensated. Call it a finder's fee. Why don't you come in this afternoon and we'll discuss the transaction?"

Smith looked at McNaughton quizzically as if to say "what do I do?" McNaughton nodded.

"OK, my bro. I'll be there about four this afternoon."

"See you then," Baden said, and hung up.

Sniffy turned to Jack. "Did I do good?"

"Yeah, Sniffy, you did good. I'm glad you put the meeting off until late this afternoon. That'll give me time to get the OK on the transmitter and wire you up. I'll call you a little later to finalize the plans."

Smith's face broke into a ragged smile, revealing ghastly teeth. He was proud of himself.

McNaughton took his wallet out of this back pocket and extricated thirty dollars. "Thanks, Sniffy. Your info was good." He handed a twenty and a ten to Sniffy. "Don't put it up your nose," he said, knowing full well exactly where it was going.

"Course not, Jackie. No way, man."

Jack's adrenalin was pumping as he headed back to his car. He looked at his watch and realized that court was due to start in fifteen minutes. He called the prosecutor's office and reached Santini. Between the rhythmic thump of the rain and the back-beat of the windshield wipers, it was hard to hear the other end of the line.

"Paul, I've got something hot going on here. It won't take long, but I'll be late for court this morning. Do you see any problem in that?"

"No, Jack. I think we should be OK. But remember, we have only five more jurors to pick. I think the first nine'll stick, don't you?"

"What was that last thing you said?"

"I think the first nine jurors will stick. What about you?"

"Yeah – if you're satisfied with them. Knofel seemed happy enough with them."

"Yeah, he did. OK – promise me you'll be in by the afternoon session."

"No problem," he shouted over the rain. "I'm sure I'll be there even sooner."

McNaughton had nearly reached the stationhouse by the time he and Santini signed off. His curiosity had been piqued by Sniffy's tale and, while Baden had been cryptic, he said enough to suggest that something heavy *was* in the works. But McNaughton's level of excitement was tempered with his knowledge of what he was about to face: The king naysayer, Doyle Stumbo, who seemed to think it was his role in life to be as negative as possible. Jack appreciated that a good supervisor should be a skeptic – someone who can look objectively at a set of facts and raise issues that the investigating officer, caught up in the moment, may overlook. McNaughton tried to do that for his people. But Stumbo's motives did not seem to be solid police work, just the negativism for which he was known. As he turned onto Senate Avenue, Jack could picture the scene he was about to face: Doyle, asking him to wait outside even thought he clearly had nothing of importance going on. Shifting papers from the right side of his desk to the left, just to make it look as if he was doing something. Asking inane questions that had nothing to do with the matter at hand. And giving his typical knee-jerk response – no – unless Jack could think of something to short-circuit it.

It was so frustrating to have to go through such machinations just to do one's job, and it was all the more so for Jack because it was a job he loved. Or used to. When someone close would ask how things were going, McNaughton found himself musing that he still loved the work but hated the job. Internal politics and bureaucratic hassles had made it nigh impossible to focus on the real task of solving crimes. The brass were concerned with making themselves look good – whether by racking up good statistics or meeting arbitrary deadlines – but not necessarily by solving cases. Consequently, they often put up barriers that made it difficult for the front-line officers to do the job.

So it was with considerably dampened enthusiasm that Jack, holding an old newspaper over his head to guard against the drizzle, mounted the steps of the stationhouse. He thought about how remarkably satisfying it was for a homicide detective to solve a crime – and how it would be that much more satisfying to solve it *before* the intended victim had to die. That doesn't happen very often, but this might be one of those rare occasions, Jack thought.

"Mornin', sergeant," the uniform at the desk mumbled. Nick must have taken a break. "Good morning, Lansing," Jack responded as he doffed his jacket and shook off the excess water. He took the stairs to homicide two at a time and tossed his jacket on his desk as he hurriedly passed it, making his way to Stumbo's office. There Doyle sat, aimlessly hooking one paper clip onto another.

"Doyle," Jack said as he stepped inside the open door. Stumbo hastily covered the paper clips with one beefy hand as he opened the front middle drawer of his desk with the other. He slid the clips inside and looked sheepishly at Jack.

"It'd be nice if you knocked, McNaughton," Stumbo said sarcastically. Jack sensed Doyle was in a surly mood, and he didn't want to alienate him, so he responded with a quick, "Sorry, Doyle. I'm in a hurry. I've got court this morning."

"Well, I was going to say," Stumbo drawled. He shifted a pile of papers from the right side of his desk to the left, and then folded his hands in front of him. He looked up at Jack. "Don't you think you should be at the courthouse?"

"Yeah. I'm on my way in just a bit. Santini knows I'll be a little late, and they're just finishing up *voir dire*. Anyway, Doyle," he continued, "I've got a CI with some pretty good information on a local attorney. Baden Baden. Ever hear of him?" He did not wait for a response. "Sounds like he could be looking to do a hit on somebody. I had the snitch put down a call to the guy just a little while ago, and I heard enough to convince me that something heavy was in the works. So I want to wire him up for a meeting late this afternoon, when they're supposed to finalize the details on the plan. I need you to OK use of a body transmitter. So can I go ahead?"

"Uh, Jack, I don't think so," Stumbo said. His eyes returned to the papers in front of him, as if that would be his last word.

"Whaddyamean?"

"I *mean*," Stumbo said, his voice dripping sarcasm, "that I'm not going to be authorizing the illegal use of a body transmitter."

"Doyle, there's nothing illegal about this. Believe me, if the meeting doesn't pan out, I'll nip it right then. But I've worked with this CI quite a bit, and he's generally right on."

"I do not care if he is 'generally right on,' Jack," Stumbo continued condescendingly. "He's not 'right on' this time. God, McNaughton, you've been a cop almost as long as me and you still don't know shit about the law, do you? For your information, we can't act on anything Mr. Baden Baden told your snitch."

"Why? What are you getting at?"

'McNaughton, haven't you ever heard of attorney-client privilege? You ought to know by now that the things attorneys say can't be used against them because of attorney-client privilege."

"No, no, no, no, no, Doyle," Jack said exasperatedly. "Attorney-client privilege applies only when the client is under suspicion of committing a crime, not the attorney. Only the client can invoke it."

"No, no, no, yourself, Jack. You need to brush up on the law, especially if you plan to be taking the promotions exam one of these days. I've been doing a bit of studying myself."

Jack ignored the last remark. "Are you telling me that *anything* an attorney says to anybody is privileged? If one walked up to me and confessed to thirty killings, I couldn't use it against him?"

"I didn't say that, McNaughton. But why would an attorney be talking to some low-life scumbag like one of your snitches unless he was representing him? Admit it: Your snitch is the attorney's client, right?"

"He has been, but that's moot. It has nothing to do with this situation. The lawyer is not currently representing my CI and, even if he were, the information has nothing to do with anything my CI has done. And the privilege would be my CI's to invoke. *He* can insist the attorney not talk to anybody about anything he's told him – not the other way around."

"Jack, I have made my decision and explained it to you. Is there something about it you don't understand?"

"Yes, Doyle. I don't understand how you can be so frigging stupid."

"Would you care to repeat that, Sergeant McNaughton?"

"No, Doyle. I'm sorry. Please reconsider. This could be a matter of life and death."

"I said 'no' and I meant 'no,' McNaughton. I consider this conversation over."

Jack turned on his heels and left Stumbo's office, leaving the door open behind him.

Jack tamped down his anger so that he could call Sniffy on the way to court. "Sniffy, something's come up," he lied, trying to avoid the humiliation of admitting his boss denied his request for a transmitter. "I'm not gonna be able to get with you to wire you up before your four o'clock with Baden."

"Shit, Jackie. What am I supposed to do?"

"Go ahead with the meeting, Sniffy. See what he has to say. Ask him a lot of questions, but don't give him any names. If he bites, we may send an undercover cop in as the hit man. Call me immediately after you're off the phone, so we can discuss it. I'll be in court this afternoon, but I'll keep my phone on 'vibrate' so I won't miss you. If I don't answer immediately, sit tight. I'll leave the courtroom and call you right back."

"Geez, I don't know, Jackie. If this shit is as heavy as I think it is, I'd feel a lot better with you listening in."

"I know, Sniffy. Me too. But I just can't make it happen. Let's go ahead and see what we get, OK?"

"Oh, OK," Smith said dejectedly. "I'll call you later."

"Thanks, Sniffy," McNaughton said. "I'll make sure you're taken care of."

"Yeah, bye."

McNaughton shook off his frustration from Stumbo's rebuff as he drove to the city-county building. He arrived at court by mid-morning, and *voir dire* was continuing. Knofel had excused one of the nine jurors who had been seated the previous day, but the questioning was moving at a brisk pace as the lunch hour approached. Indeed, the last of the jurors was seated around eleven-forty-five a.m., forming a panel of eight women and four men, plus two male alternates.

Linden swore them in and then addressed them in her maternal way. "Ladies and gentlemen, the timing is perfect for you to go with the bailiff for lunch. When you return, we'll start with opening arguments. I suggest you eat a light lunch, so that you can be attentive to counsel this afternoon. It's better not to have too many carbohydrates; they make you drowsy. And we need your full attention. Please do not discuss the case with anyone, or even among yourselves, and please do not read anything about the case. Court is recessed until one-thirty p.m." She whisked off the bench and disappeared behind the door to her private office.

McNaughton begged off lunch with the prosecutors, choosing to call Renee to see if she could get away. She was waiting for some calls to be returned, but knew it was unlikely they'd come in during the lunch hour, so they agreed to meet at the King Cole Restaurant for one of its famous salads.

After they had ordered lunch – Renee had the Caesar with grilled chicken, Jack, the Cobb with bleu cheese – he told her about his meeting with Sniffy and about Stumbo's reaction. Renee, usually the first one to lose her temper over something Stumbo had pulled, was uncommonly calm.

"OK, so he's an idiot," she said. "What's new? Why don't you just wire Sniffy up anyway?"

"I thought about that. But you know it would be my job if he found out. They could get me on insubordination. And if I made a case based on Sniffy's meeting, there's no way he and the rest of the world wouldn't find out. Can you imagine how bonkers Stumbo would go?"

She paused a moment. "Yeah, you're right. I guess I'd just play it by the book. Maybe Sniffy'll come through for you and you'll get enough to pursue a case. And maybe save a life."

"Yeah. Obviously the best outcome would be that Sniffy totally misunderstood and Baden has no intentions of killing anybody. Honestly, I think that's dreaming; I think Baden is up to no good. So the second-best outcome would be that we get sufficient info to stop the hit from happening. Let's keep our fingers crossed.

"So how's the salad?" he asked.

"Mmmm. Good!

They ate in silence for a few moments, and then Renee spoke. "It's just scary to think that you might be the only hope some guy has of not getting blown away, and that Doyle's idiocy could thwart you. Does Doyle understand the gravity of the situation?"

"I don't know, babe. I even pointed out to him that somebody's life could be hanging in the balance here, and he didn't flinch. Just said no."

"Nancy Reagan would've loved him."

"Very funny.

The new jurors seemed to take their charge seriously, listening attentively during the opening statements, which were lengthy and repetitive of much of what Bennett and Fortner had said during *voir dire*. Late in the afternoon, Jimmy Davis and Todd Bienick, the first police officers on the scene, testified about their discovery. Jack noted that Bienick, to whom he had never been introduced, looked much healthier than the first time he saw him throwing up his breakfast in the Petersons' front yard. His cheeks bore a healthy glow of rose, a welcomed change from the shade of green McNaughton recalled.

It was horrifying testimony for the jurors to contemplate for the rest of the evening, but when Davis and Bienick were finished, Linden recessed court until the next morning. Jack went into the prosecutor's office and checked his voice mail to see if he had somehow missed Sniffy's call. It was well after four, and the meeting should have been over by now. No messages. He called Sniffy, without success, and left a message.

Bennett was ebullient. "Opening went great, don't you think, McNaughton?"

"Yeah, fine, Terry," Jack answered, but his mind was on Sniffy and that situation. Santini walked in, noticing Jack's distraction, and slapped him on the shoulder. "Wake up, Jack. Don't you think your wife is waiting for you in some skimpy negligee? She doesn't want you all spaced out."

"Yeah, right, Paul. Wouldn't you like to know."

McNaughton turned back to the phone. He alternated between irritation and concern that that Sniffy had not called. There wasn't much Jack could do about that, but it struck him that he could try another avenue. Plucking the number from his brain, McNaughton dialed up the department's intelligence division.

"Intelligence. Kuhn."

"Kuhnie," Jack said. He never used her first name when he addressed her, but he was pleased that his favorite analyst had answered. "It's McNaughton. Can you help me out?"

"Sure, McNaughton," she said. "What's up?"

"I need you to find whatever you can on Baden Baden. He's a defense attorney here in town."

"Yeah, I've heard of him. I've seen his ads on 'Jerry Springer.' Not that I watch that crap very often. Just when I need an occasional dose of inanity. Or insanity."

"I know what you mean," McNaughton said. "Watching those shows is sort of like seeing a really bad car crash and not being able to turn away. Anyway, do you think you can check him out for me?"

"Anything for you, dear. But isn't this taking opposition research pretty far?"

"It's not for a case in which he's the defense attorney, Kuhnie. It's for a case in which he may be a defendant."

"Interesting. Say no more. I'll see what I've got."

"Thanks, kiddo."

"No problem, McNaughton. Any time."

The first witness on Wednesday, the third day of the trial, was the lead technician on the crime scene at the Peterson house, who testified about the methods of gathering evidence and displayed shocking pictures of blood-soaked beds and red spatter patterns. Even more grim was the second witness: Dr. Pravin Shadwani, the county's chief forensic pathologist, who had performed the autopsies on four of the Peterson children and supervised the work of another pathologist on the other two. Much of his testimony was clinical and perfunctory, necessary only because the prosecution had to establish, as the basis of its case, that there are six dead victims. But the jurors shuddered at the blood-covered night clothes Shadwani had removed from the children's bodies and at the photographs he had taken of them. One woman cringed as she barely glanced at each of the six photos passed to her before she pushed it to her left; McNaughton caught a glint of a tear in the eyes of another woman and one of the men.

So it was a relief for the jurors when McNaughton took the stand that afternoon, although his testimony as lead investigator would touch on some of the same gruesome details. But they were mesmerized as McNaughton, his voice soothing and clinical, walked them through the crime, explaining what he witnessed that sunny April morning, and described the ensuing investigation.

Prosecutors had more than once told McNaughton that he was their dream witness. He was clean-cut but not severe, and handsome. His credentials, from his education to his experience, were impeccable. His azure eyes twinkled with intelligence, providing an exclamation mark to the knowledgeable and concise testimony he gave. And he never seemed stiff or nervous; his easy manner exuded confidence in the evidence and in his work and that of his squad.

During cross-examination, however, Fortner deftly turned Jack's expertise back on him. It was a crucial moment for the defense, which had been devastated earlier when McNaughton testified about finding the bloody clothing – the same size as the clothing in Peterson's closet – and the broken mallet. Fortner chose not to shy away from the damage.

"Sergeant McNaughton, you testified earlier that you found a mallet and clothing you believed to be Mr. Peterson's in the basement of the Peterson home. Were they hidden?"

"No, they weren't," Jack answered.

"In plain view, then?"

"Yes, sir."

"Is it your experience that people who are trying to hide their commission of a crime leave items involved in the crime in plain view?"

"Sometimes they do, sometimes they don't."

"Well, sergeant, do your cleverest criminals do that?"

"Objection!" Bennett shouted. "What is the relevance?"

Fortner all but rolled his eyes. "Your honor, if Mr. Bennett would just give me a moment."

"Yes, Mr. Bennett. Let's give him a moment to show the relevance. Go ahead, Mr. Fortner."

"Sergeant?"

"It depends on your definition of 'clever,' Mr. Fortner. Some perpetrators are so clever that they make jurors think they're something they're not."

Score one for the prosecution. But Knofel wasn't deterred.

"Sergeant, I don't believe that was responsive. The cleverest criminals certainly don't leave obvious evidence lying about, do they?"

"Not obvious evidence, I suppose," Jack said.

"And when someone does that – when someone makes no effort to hide commission of a crime – it could be because he's not aware that he has done anything wrong. Is that correct?"

"Perhaps. But sometimes it's a crime of passion, and the perpetrator doesn't think to do anything to cover up his actions. Or sometimes there isn't time."

"And sometimes it could be that the perpetrator is unable to appreciate that what he has done is wrong and therefore has no reason to consider a cover-up, correct?"

"I suppose that's possible," McNaughton answered grimly.

Score one for the defense, he thought.

As far as Jack was concerned, Fortner kept scoring points. After McNaughton testified about finding the wet bar of soap and water-splattered shower, Knofel asked him to speculate on why someone who had just committed a crime would have taken a shower.

Bennett screeched "objection," but Linden bought Fortner's argument that McNaughton's vast investigative experience gave him sufficient basis to draw such a conclusion.

"It seems rather obvious, Mr. Fortner," Jack said flatly, avoiding enunciating the sarcasm that his words implied. "Mr. Peterson was covered with the blood of his children and wanted to wash it off."

"But Sergeant," Knofel said, "isn't it possible that Mr. Peterson came out of his dissociative state upon finding himself covered in blood, and that his shower was a desperate attempt to get away from whatever had happened to him?"

"I wouldn't know. I'm not a psychiatrist," McNaughton answered, but he sucked in his breath with the knowledge that Fortner had again made a point.

McNaughton also had testified on direct about the bloody handprint that had been found on the staircase wall. It tested out as a mixture of two blood types – all of the Peterson children had one or the other – and forensics got a decent impression of two fingers. The others weren't clear because of the texture of the wallpaper, but it didn't matter. The readable ones clearly were Peterson's.

But Fortner didn't challenge that the prints belonged to his client. That only proved what he had already acknowledged – that Peterson did it. He made his point another way.

"Sergeant, from your experience, isn't it true that a confused person sometimes stumbles?"

"I suppose so, Mr. Fortner. Everyone does at one time or another."

"But if someone is dizzy or disoriented or hazy, that condition cause him to stumble all the more, correct?"

"I suppose so, Mr. Fortner," Jack repeated. "I'm not a doctor, so I wouldn't know what causes someone to stumble, or when they're more prone to do so."

"You were a street officer before becoming a homicide detective?"

"Yes."

"And was one of your duties pursuing allegedly drunken drivers?"

"Yes."

"And when you did field sobriety tests – caused them to walk in a straight line, or touch their fingers to their noses – sometimes you witnessed a lack of coordination in the subject. Is that right?"

"Well, certainly. But they were intoxicated on a substance they had ingested. And I wouldn't know if they were dizzy or disoriented, as you said earlier."

"But they might have appeared that way?"

Santini rose quickly. "Objection, your honor. Irrelevant."

Fortner responded: "Your honor, this is not irrelevant. I think Sergeant McNaughton has pertinent information about the physical coordination or lack thereof of a seemingly disoriented person."

"No," Linden said, "I don't think so, Mr. Fortner. There's been no evidence that Mr. Peterson was intoxicated. Let's move on."

"Yes, your honor." Fortner returned to the defense table to peruse his notes, and then went after Jack's testimony that even the family dog had been bludgeoned to death – evidence, McNaughton had said, of the utter brutality of the crime.

"Sergeant, I'm wondering why any sane person would go to such extremes. You didn't find any evidence that Mr. Peterson was angry with the dog, right? Uh, its name was Shottzie, I believe."

"No, sir."

"And there was no evidence that Shottzie bit Mr. Peterson during commission of the acts or that the dog tried in any way to deter him, was there?"

"No, sir."

"So there is no explanation for Mr. Peterson killing the dog, is there, sergeant? That's not a rational act, is it?"

"To me, Mr. Fortner, it seems like an irrational act, but there's a big difference between irrational and legally insane."

"Your honor!" Bennett interrupted. I've got to object to this line of questioning. Sergeant McNaughton is not a psychiatrist, and he shouldn't be asked to render expert opinions."

"First of all, Mr. Bennett," the judge said, with some exasperation in her voice, "your objection isn't timely. The witness has already answered. Second, I've already ruled that Sergeant McNaughton is qualified to render opinions based on his own professional experience."

Bennett sat down dejectedly. The episode caused a momentary lapse in his confidence. A prosecutor for twelve years, Bennett had won a lot of cases, lost a few, but he couldn't conceive of this female-heavy jury letting Peterson off after he admitted committing such a heinous crime. Santini was there to listen to the cross, so Bennett allowed his mind to drift. He thought it wise to show the photographs of the corpses as often as he could get away with it. He decided then and there that, during his closing arguments, he would display the children's blood-soaked night clothing on hangers; no – better yet – on child-sized mannequins. He wasn't going to let those jurors, most of whom were parents, forget the little victims or forgive their gigantic killer.

By the next morning, Sniffy still hadn't called, although McNaughton had left several messages with his cell, office and home phone numbers. It was as if Smith had fallen off the face of the earth. But McNaughton would worry about him later. He returned to the witness stand first thing, and his testimony dragged on all morning. Around ten minutes before noon, Judge Linden interrupted Fortner's cross.

"Mr. Fortner, I'm trying to figure out when we should give these kind people a break for lunch. Shall we break now, and ask Sergeant McNaughton to return to the stand after lunch, or do you expect to conclude your cross-examination soon?"

"Your honor, I believe I'll be finished before twelve-thirty, so I'd like to continue, if it pleases the court," Knofel replied.

"That's fine, Mr. Fortner. Please continue."

Knofel was true to his word, finishing up around twelve-twenty-five p.m. It was a momentous conclusion.

"Sergeant McNaughton, you've been a police officer for how long?"

"Almost fifteen years, sir."

"And you've been a homicide detective for how long?"

"For about ten years," Jack replied.

"And during those ten years, I imagine you've investigated scores of homicides. Would that be correct?"

"Yes, I suppose so. I've never counted."

"OK. But that's a good estimate?"

"Yes."

"Some of those have been pretty horrible, yes?"

"Yes, Mr. Fortner. Quite horrible."

"Sergeant, can you recall any case more horrible than the Peterson homicides?"

Jack thought for a moment. "No, sir, I can't. I can't imagine anything more horrible than a father killing his kids, and in such a brutal way." His voice remained even and unemotional, but the impact was powerful.

"You've investigated some cases in which the defendants were found to be not guilty by reason of insanity, isn't that correct?" Fortner, recovering quickly, was homing in.

"Yes, that's correct," Jack said grimly.

"And were any of those crimes – those in which the perpetrator was found to be insane – were any of them any worse than this crime?"

"No, I wouldn't think so."

"Well, sergeant, can you imagine anybody but a crazy person committing the most horrific crime that you, a veteran homicide detective, have ever investigated?"

"I'm not a psychiatrist," Jack stammered, trying to minimize the damage.

"No, you're not, Sergeant McNaughton. But then a psychiatrist wouldn't have investigated this or any crime."

He turned toward Linden. "That's all I have, your honor."

Over at the Legal Beagle, Jack silently picked at the corned beef-on-rye that lay before him. Bennett and Santini wolfed down fat, greasy cheeseburgers, talking with their mouths full as they strategized about mitigating the damage Fortner's cross-examination had done. They'd have Jack back on the stand for re-direct examination, and they'd erase the image that Fortner had left, Bennett insisted. It was "doable."

Jack hated that word, and especially when Bennett used it to describe something that was eminently undoable. He knew that his testimony was damaging – irreparably so – and that nothing would erase that lasting doubt in the jurors' minds that only a crazy person could do what Peterson had done. From that, it was only a small leap for the jurors to believe that Peterson was legally insane and thus not culpable.

Santini handled the re-direct, and while his questioning was pointed, Jack feared it didn't alter the jurors' impressions. Santini focused primarily on the difference between "crazy" and "legally insane," but he and McNaughton knew that the distinction was often lost on lay people. And Knofel had done an amazing job of blurring it, of reminding the jurors of what they inherently believed from the beginning – that only a crazy person would commit the acts Peterson had admitted. When McNaughton returned to his place at the prosecution's table, his hopes were dashed, his mood deflated.

Only Bennett remained optimistic, and Santini tried to provide the buffer between the extreme emotions of the colleagues that sat on either side of him. Bennett and Santini sharply examined their last witnesses, determined to leave the jurors with visions of battered children in their heads. Father Phillip Renault, the Petersons' priest, testified that he had counseled Mrs. Peterson when she was dismayed about her marriage, but he said she was not specific and, if she had been, he would have been constrained from revealing what had been told him in confidence. Still, the testimony was enough to suggest to the jurors that all was not well in the Peterson household. Mrs. Parsons, the nearly deaf neighbor who lived to the north of the Petersons, could provide no help. Marie LaPierre, the neighbor to the south, reinforced the notion of a troubled marriage when she testified about overhearing an argument – a loud, potentially violent one – between Barbara and John Pius Peterson. The only problem with her testimony was that the argument she overheard was about seven or eight months before the murders, and her testimony provided little more than the suggestion that the Petersons weren't too unlike other couples. Then Luke Linley, the burly bartender at Jake's, testified that Peterson had complained several times about his wife, including his belief that she was having an affair. It was the closest thing the prosecution had to motive, but on cross Knofel elicited from Linley that it was his inference, not anything Peterson had said directly, that made him think Peterson suspected his wife's infidelity.

The most difficult reality for McNaughton to swallow was that Barbara Peterson couldn't testify about the phone conversation she had had with her husband after the murders. Having invoked the spousal privilege, Peterson refused to allow his wife to testify against him – a legal exception to compulsion to testify. Consequently, the jurors heard nothing from her about their phone conversations on the evening of the murders, when he threatened to kill the children, and the morning after, when he informed her that he had done so. They heard nothing about his repeated threats over the years to kill them, his accusations to her about extramarital affairs or his jealous rages.

The jury didn't even learn that the phone calls had been made. While phone records showed that Mrs. Peterson had telephoned home the evening of the murders, the fact of the call alone proved nothing if Mrs. Peterson couldn't testify about its content. And Kit could never find any evidence that Peterson had called his wife the next morning; he must have done so after leaving the house, and she couldn't locate a pay phone where the call had been placed.

So the prosecution closed its case, having proved that horrendous murders had occurred, probably even having proved that Peterson had committed them – and if not, Peterson himself would provide the proof. But Jack couldn't shake the feeling that, in at least one juror's mind – and that was all it would take to hang the jury – the murders were the acts of an insane man.

The defense started its case early Friday morning, day five of the trial. Fortner called Dr. Henry Rosterman, a psychiatrist for twenty-seven years, who had examined Peterson numerous times since his arrest. After the perfunctory – and boring – litany of his credentials, experience, published works and teaching assignments, Rosterman, clearly established in the jurors' eyes as an expert, explained how Peterson had had a "dissociative reaction" and therefore did not know what he was doing when he killed the children. Peterson thought somebody else was doing it, and that he couldn't stop the person, Rosterman testified. And then when Peterson realized that *he* had committed the crimes, he tried to atone by cutting off his right arm – or so he thought. Rosterman also testified that Peterson's unstable personality had begun to manifest itself in his recent and extreme embrace of the Bible.

The testimony took all morning. It was an intriguing mix of clinical terms and explanations and Rosterman's observations of Peterson during their sessions together. One juror, the youngest on the panel, dozed during some of the drier stuff, but most of his colleagues studied the aging man's lined face carefully. McNaughton feared that they came away from their examination trusting him more than the prosecution would like.

Only an aggressive cross-examination could salvage the day. Santini had gotten the nod because he loved to play attack dog, and Bennett, knowing Rosterman had to be undermined, gladly handed him the opportunity. Bennett wanted to save himself for Peterson's cross-examination anyway. Retreating to the Legal Beagle for lunch again, the two prosecutors and McNaughton poured over their notes from Rosterman's testimony and together plotted the strategy for cross-examination.

"Dr. Rosterman," Santini said shortly after court resumed, "you testified earlier that Mr. Peterson began showing signs of psychological instability when he started reading the Bible, uh, *religiously*." A few people in the gallery tittered, and Linden raised her eyebrows to register her disapproval. "Well, doctor, are you suggesting that anyone who regularly reads the Bible is a *nut*?" He clipped off the last word and jerked his head for emphasis.

"No, Mr. Santini, I am not," Rosterman said patiently.

"Well, then, doctor, are you saying that anyone who regularly reads the Bible is capable of beating innocent children into *pulp*?" Same inflection.

"No, Mr. Santini, I am *not*." Rosterman mocked Santini's emphasis, a hint of irritation in his voice.

"Well, doctor, just what are you saying? I think a lot of people out there" – he swept his arm across the jurors and into the gallery – "good-hearted, God-fearing people who believe in the Bible – want to know just what you *are* suggesting about them."

"Mr. Santini, I am not suggesting anything about them. Believing in the Bible is one's prerogative, just as any religious allegiance is. I'm talking specifically about Mr. Peterson, who does not have a healthy relationship with God. He looks to God and to the Bible to place blame for his troubles, not for comfort or solace or inspiration – any of the usual reasons one prays and reads Scripture."

"Oh, so Mr. Peterson has troubles and is trying to find somebody to blame for them. Is that your testimony?"

"Well, yes, Mr. Santini. Mr. Peterson *has* been out of work for some time. He has, uh, had *six* children. He had the usual stresses of a family, a big family, and then lost his job. He's an old-fashioned kind of person, who felt inadequate because his wife had to support the family. That was complicated because he had to learn to be a stay-at-home father, something he was neither used to or comfortable with."

"So Mr. Peterson resented his wife for wearing the pants in the family?"

"No, Mr. Santini. I didn't say that. Everything . . ."

Santini interrupted. "Dr. Rosterman, please just answer the question 'yes' or 'no.'"

"Your honor," Fortner interjected. "Dr. Rosterman was trying to do that when Mr. Santini cut him off."

"Your honor," Santini began.

"Mr. Santini, I think Mr. Fortner is right on this one. Let's give Dr. Rosterman a little latitude to explain his answer," Linden said.

Santini looked perturbed but didn't argue, lest he irritate the judge. "Yes, your honor," he said dejectedly. Then he turned back to Rosterman. "Doctor, you were saying?" he said patronizingly.

"Uh . . " Rosterman had lost his train of thought. "Oh, yes. As I was saying, everything I've heard and seen suggests that Mr. Peterson is grateful to his wife and that he loves her and admires her."

"Oh, really? Well, would it surprise you to learn that a priest counseled Mrs. Peterson about their marriage?"

"Not really. Couples have their troubles. It's natural to talk to one's spiritual adviser in such a situation."

"Doctor, isn't it true that Mr. Peterson thought his wife had been unfaithful to him?" Santini couldn't get Barbara Peterson's testimony in, but he could boost Luke Linley's testimony a bit.

"I'm unaware of that, Mr. Santini," Rosterman said flatly. Neither his answer nor his unfazed demeanor pleased Santini, but at least the prosecutor had planted the seed.

"Uh, Dr. Rosterman, let's shift gears here a little. I imagine that you've examined people charged with crimes before?"

"Yes, many times, Mr. Fortner."

"Ten times? Twenty? Three hundred?"

"I can't say for sure. Perhaps in the low hundreds."

"And you were always paid for this testimony?"

"Well, yes, sir. The usual fee that all expert witnesses receive for their time and trouble."

"Well, doctor, do you recall any crime that was more horrific than this one?" Santini was trying to turn Fortner's tack back on him.

"I really couldn't say, Mr. Fortner. I come into a case after it is well underway. I'm not always privy to all the circumstances."

"C'mon, doctor," Santini said with exasperation. "You saw the pictures, didn't you? And you're telling me that beating six kids into pulp isn't the absolutely worst, most heinous crime with which you've been involved?"

"Yes, I saw the pictures and no doubt this was a horrible crime," Rosterman said. "But I am averse to all violence. It all abhors me. I have difficulty assigning degrees because to do so would diminish the seriousness of crimes that wouldn't rank quite as high on your scale. I can't say that killing a perfect stranger isn't just as horrible."

"You can't?" Santini was incredulous, and his flailing arms illustrated it."You mean to say that you don't think it's more horrible, more heinous, more atrocious to kill your own flesh and blood, six times over, than to kill someone you've never met?" He stabbed at the air with his forefinger.

"Mr. Santini," Rosterman said, his voice still as even as when he described his credentials, "all killing is wrong. If you insist that I rank the Peterson killings against others, all I can say is that they exhibited a greater pathology than some of the others in which I've been involved. That is, the perpetrator was sicker, more disturbed. *Insane*."

McNaughton resisted the urge to groan aloud. Santini had hanged himself.

Chapter 10

"Your honor, I call John Pius Peterson to the stand."

Knofel Fortner's voice was strong and confident at the outset of day six of the trial. It was eight a.m. Monday, and it had been an unendurably long weekend for the trial's principals – for Peterson, whose days in the county jail all seemed the same, and for the others, who struggled with what would come next. Jack had gotten through the weekend by rote, delving into mindless work of straightening the cluttered basement while Renee did the laundry and other chores. Together they cooked up a pot of chili on Saturday evening, a hot, red concoction with chunks of beef and pork, beans and half a bottle of beer, lots of spices and Jack's secret ingredient – a little chocolate. They play-argued over who was head chef, but that mattered little to Angel, who dropped the chocolate kisses into the mixture for her daddy and then pronounced it perfect. McNaughton tried to forget both the trial and his frustration with Stumbo, and his family helped, but it was impossible. He worried that Sniffy still hadn't called and troubled with the last impression the Peterson jury had before adjournment Friday. On Sunday, he, Bennett and Santini met at Bennett's roomy white-brick house on the city's northwest side to go over strategy, plan their cross of Peterson and discuss their rebuttal witnesses. McNaughton smiled slyly, but didn't say anything, when Bennett served up bowls of his homemade chili, announcing that all his friends thought he made the best chili in

Indianapolis. Well, Jack begged to disagree. Bennett, after all, put *spaghetti* in his.

Despite their preparation, the members of the prosecution team were no more emotionally prepared for the moment that Monday morning when Knofel intoned his client's name than anyone else in the courtroom. There seemed a collective gasp – although Jack wasn't sure if he heard it or imagined it – when Peterson was called to the stand. Jack tried to push the thought from his mind, but the truth was, he wondered why Fortner was willing to risk the points he'd already made by letting Peterson testify. No matter what Bennett and Santini said – and they had voiced their confidence often over that bland chili supper – McNaughton feared that Fortner had already established reasonable doubt in the minds of at least one juror – and one was enough to hang the jury. Why tamper with success?

But sometimes defendants insist, and their counsel is bound by the rules of professional responsibility to abide by their wishes, even against their better judgment. Whatever the reason, John Pius Peterson awkwardly pulled himself up from his chair, moving as if he were stiff, and lumbered toward the witness stand. The shackles that had bound his ankles each morning were always removed before the jury filed in; the court didn't want anybody to assume he *had* to be guilty or else he wouldn't be shackled. But Peterson moved almost as if his legs were still connected by a thick eighteen-inch chain.

He started to sit in the witness box when Judge Linden gestured for him to stand. "Mr. Peterson, please place your left hand on the Bible and raise your right hand," she said.

The hulking defendant seemed more gigantic than ever. The witness box was one step up off the courtroom floor, adding eight inches to his huge frame. The bailiff approached tentatively until Linden flashed a disapproving look, here eyebrows forming a deep V, which prompted the bailiff to move more quickly toward Peterson.

Peterson's eyes set upon the plain black Bible in the bailiff's left hand. He seemed mesmerized, McNaughton thought. "Repeat after me," the bailiff said. "I, John Pius Peterson."

Peterson did not speak. His gaze did not leave the holy book.

"Mr. Peterson," Linden said abruptly. She sounded perturbed. "Please repeat after the bailiff."

Peterson literally shook off his trance and looked at the judge quizzically. But still he did not position his hands in anticipation of the oath.

"Your honor," Fortner said, "may I approach the witness?"

"Yes, please do," she replied with exasperation.

Fortner moved close to Peterson. "John," he said sharply, loudly enough to be heard by those sitting near the front of the courtroom. The tone of his voice caused Peterson to turn toward his lawyer, who leaned closer and whispered instructions. Peterson didn't move. Fortner took the big man's left hand and placed it on the Bible, and Peterson slowly moved his right hand into the air.

"I, John Pius Peterson," the bailiff began. Peterson repeated his name so quietly that McNaughton could barely hear him.

"Mr. Fortner, please advise your client to speak up," Linden said.

"Yes, your honor. Mr. Peterson, please follow the judge's instructions, OK?"

Peterson nodded. The bailiff started again, and Peterson repeated the oath in a robotic monotone audible to Judge Linden, the court reporter and Fortner, but few others. Then the huge defendant sat in the witness chair and leaned self-consciously over the microphone.

"Please state your full name and spell your last," Fortner began.

"John Pius Peterson. P-e-t-e-r-s-o-n."

"Where do you reside, Mr. Peterson?"

"3540 North Ellison Street, Indianapolis, Indiana."

"Mr. Peterson, are you employed?"

"No."

"When were you last employed?"

And so it went for nearly an hour, with Knofel asking questions intended to establish John Pius Peterson as a normal working man, a husband, a good father, a church-goer. It was obvious to Jack that Fortner had worked diligently with his client, preparing him as best he could for his testimony. Eventually, though, Fortner would have to broach the subject of Peterson's deeds, and those in the courtroom braced for the moment. Jack could feel the muscles in his neck tighten with each passing minute.

"Mr. Peterson," Fortner finally said, "let me direct your attention to the evening of April twelve. Can you please tell the court what you were doing that evening?"

With that simple question, Knofel had opened the door to the more horrifying statements most of these jurors would ever hear. Peterson, his voice clear but subdued, recounted the horror of that night and early the next day, when he – by his own admission – bludgeoned his own six beautiful children to death. His story, Jack noticed, did not vary from the one he told in the interrogation room seven months earlier. McNaughton had read and reread the transcript from that interview, intent on catching Peterson in a contradiction or some mistake that would prove what Jack felt to be true: That it was premeditated murder, intentionally committed to hurt Barbara Peterson, and not the mad acts of an insane person.

For three hours, Peterson recounted his story. Fortner delved into every detail, asking Peterson questions about his children's deaths that would render most parents into sobbing, hysterical messes. At one point, mucus trickled from his right nostril, astonishing Jack. But just as he had in the interrogation room, Peterson showed emotion only when he talked about "that awful man" whom he had witnessed killing the children.

By the time Knofel had finished, everyone in the courtroom was emotionally drained. Jack was amazed that Peterson's tale could still affect him, after having read it so many times. But his belief that Peterson had concocted the whole thing was unchanged.

Linden had leaned forward in her chair, resting her arms across her bench, throughout the testimony. Now she leaned back, her head against the smooth maroon leather of her high-backed chair. She glanced at her elegant Rado watch. "Gentlemen, it's nearly one p.m., and I imagine everyone is hungry and in serious need of a break. Let's break until two-thirty, when we'll have cross-examination. All right?"

The lawyers mumbled "yes, your honor," in unison and rose for the jurors to be led from the room. Jack studied them, concerned because several of them had wiped their eyes or sniffled during Peterson's descriptions of the children's deaths. Juror number four, a twenty-six-year-old secretary in an insurance office, had openly wept. It was true that the thought of those children dying could bring anyone to tears, McNaughton thought, but he worried that Peterson had engendered sympathy. In his cross-examination, Bennett would have to dispel any notion that Peterson was a sympathetic figure.

"Good afternoon, Mr. Peterson," he said firmly after lunch, as he approached the defendant for the first time. Bennett wanted to establish himself as civilized before he went for Peterson's jugular. It didn't take him long. "You mentioned that you had your boys say their prayers before they went to bed. Did you direct them to pray for their eternal salvation?"

"N-n-no," Peterson stuttered, a sign of nerves rather than any permanent condition. "As I told Mr. Fortner, I had the boys pray for help in developing respect for their elders. The girls prayed for their mother and her salvation."

"Well, if you believe as you say you do, wouldn't it have been more appropriate for the children to pray for their own salvation?"

"I had no way of knowing that my children would die that night, Mr. Bennett," Peterson intoned quietly.

"Oh, you didn't . . .," Bennett said sarcastically. He was about to continue, but Knofel jumped to his feet. "Your honor," he said with exasperation. "He need not badger the witness, nor should he be testifying. The jurors really aren't interested in Mr. Bennett's theories."

Linden, her head cocked, moved nothing but her eyes from Fortner to Bennett. "Mr. Bennett, let's watch it, OK?"

"Yes, your honor." He turned back to Peterson. "Mr. Peterson, you also testified that you didn't read that night. But when you do, what kind of books do you read? Murder mysteries? Whodunnits?"

"No," Peterson replied steadily. "I prefer biographies."

"Not 'In Cold Blood?' Not stories about insane people? About evil men who kill their children and try to get away with it?"

"No, sir," Peterson said evenly before Fortner could object. Knofel rose abruptly, but sat back down after his client handled the inquiry without event.

"Biographies, huh? Whose? Charles Manson's? Theodore Bundy's? O.J. Simpson's?"

"No, sir. I read a lot of historical stuff, about the presidents and other famous men. And I liked Father Hesburgh's book." He was referring to the retired president of Notre Dame University. That angered Bennett, a Notre Dame grad.

"I see," Bennett said. "Do you ever read romances? Love stories? Books about love gone wrong?"

"No, sir. My wife sometimes does. She buys them by the bagful at the used book store."

"Well, Mr. Peterson, if you didn't read fiction about love affairs, exactly how did you concoct the fiction that your wife was having an affair?"

Fortner popped up again, buttoning his jacket as he rose. "Your honor, Mr. Peterson has not testified to that. Mr. Bennett is asking about things that were not the subject of direct examination."

"Mr. Fortner is correct, Mr. Bennett," Linden said. "Let's confine the questions to matters that arose on direct."

Bennett didn't acknowledge the judge. He was too focused on the defendant. "Mr. Peterson, directing your attention to the night of last April twelve. You testified that your wife called home from her business trip. You threatened her, didn't you?"

"No, sir, I didn't."

"You accused her of being a bad wife, did you not?"

"No, sir, I didn't."

"You told her that you were going to kill your children, didn't you?"

"No, sir, I didn't."

"You accused her of having an affair, isn't that correct?"

"No, sir, I didn't."

"You told her that she'd pay for the way she was treating you, the way she was living her life, didn't you?"

"No, sir, I didn't."

"Well, Mr. Peterson, what exactly *did* you discuss? Seems like you've ruled out most topics of conversation." Bennett's voice dripped with sarcasm.

"We talked about the children – mundane things like how much each had eaten for dinner and how they went to bed and how Claire was doing with potty training. Nothing important."

"Did you talk about her trip or her job?"

"A little. I don't remember much."

"You argued about it, didn't you?"

"No."

McNaughton was struck at how calm Peterson remained, even as Bennett was more combative than Jack had ever seen him. There was no question that Bennett was doing everything he could to elicit Peterson's true emotions, but the defendant's voice never betrayed his lies, or what Jack was convinced were lies; he recalled all too well what Barbara Peterson had told him and Kit.

"Directing your attention to later that evening when, according to your testimony, you saw a man on the stairs. Mr. Peterson, you were really looking in the mirror on the landing, weren't you? It was just a moment of startle as you firmed up your plan – and your resolve – to kill your children, wasn't it?"

"No, sir," Peterson said. "Like I said, I saw a man. I don't know what else to tell you."

"And you say he had a mallet in his hand. You owned one just like it, didn't you?"

"Yes, sir, I do."

"When did you purchase that mallet?"

"I don't remember. I've had it an awful long time. Ten, fifteen years at least."

"You didn't just purchase this mallet?" Bennett knew he hadn't; the rubber head was deteriorated, indicating its age. But he was doing everything he could to get under Peterson's skin.

"No, sir. Like I said, I've had it a long time."

"Mr. Peterson, if you were screaming at this man, as you claim . . ."

Knofel was up again. "Your honor, that was Mr. Peterson's testimony. It is not a claim. The jurors must know this."

Linden sighed and paused a moment, mulling the situation. "Ladies and gentlemen of the jury, you'll hear instructions later about the amount of weight you are to assign testimony. And please recall earlier admonitions that the lawyers' questions are not testimony, just questions intended to elicit responses. Mr. Bennett, you may proceed."

"Anyway, Mr. Peterson, if you were screaming at this man, *as you claim*, how is it that you didn't awaken your children?"

"I don't know. I *was* screaming. I would have done anything to stop him."

"But you didn't, did you, Mr. Peterson?" Bennett was moving closer to the witness box, making sure, however, that he didn't block the jurors' view of Peterson's face. "You didn't do anything to stop this man – *you* – from killing your children."

Peterson's head dropped. He paused, took a deep breath through his mouth and shuddered. "No, sir. I couldn't stop it."

"Exactly, Mr. Peterson. You couldn't stop it because, if you had, you wouldn't have exacted your revenge on your wife for the fantasy affair you suggested she was having."

Fortner again, angrily. "Your honor, is that a question?"

Linden didn't speak. She merely looked at Bennett and raised her eyebrows as if to reiterate Knofel's query.

"I'll rephrase," Bennett said in response. "Isn't it a fact, Mr. Peterson, that you couldn't stop it because, if you had, your whole plan would have been thwarted?"

"No, sir," Peterson said, still calm. "I couldn't move my legs fast enough. They felt so heavy, and he was moving so much quicker than me."

"You were quiet as a mouse so that you didn't awaken your children, weren't you, Mr. Peterson?"

"No, sir. I wish they had woke up. Maybe they could have got away."

"Mr. Peterson, in your statement to Sergeant McNaughton, you quoted the Bible to the effect that the Lord stopped after striking down the first born. If that was good enough for the Lord, why didn't you stop after killing Mary Elizabeth? Do you think you know better than God?"

"Oh, no, Mr. Bennett. Scripture tells us 'Humble yourselves under the mighty hand of God.' I would never think I'm better than God. No one is."

"Well, then, why? Why didn't you stop after Mary Elizabeth? Wasn't it enough revenge against your wife to kill her first daughter?"

"I never tried to get revenge. I just tried to stop the man."

Bennett was growing exasperated. He pulled out the big guns.

"What did your children look like, Mr. Peterson, after they were beaten to death?"

"Oh, please," Peterson said, shaking his head slowly. "Don't make me think about that."

"Oh, yes, Mr. Peterson," Bennett said as he walked toward the evidence table and picked up a stack of photographs. He headed toward the witness stand and slapped them down in front of Peterson. Even those in the gallery could glimpse the massive spread of bright red on them.

"Oh, noooo," Peterson said, turning his head away. He closed his eyes and moaned, wrapped his huge arms around his chest and began to sway back and forth.

"Mr. Peterson," Bennett said sharply. "You recall looking at your children in his condition, don't you?"

Peterson continued to moan. "Please," he pleaded. "Please don't make me look."

"Mr. Peterson." Bennett was shouting now. "Look at these photographs and tell us if this is the condition you remember your children to be in."

Fortner had had enough. "Your honor, this is going too far. We know these are photographs of the Peterson children. They've been identified as such by other witnesses. What is the purpose of this, other than to badger my client?"

Bennett responded: "I'd like to hear from your client if he is aware of what he has done."

Linden went deep into thought. After a long moment, she spoke. "I think Mr. Peterson can answer the question without looking at the photographs. Mr. Peterson, please answer."

Peterson was still swaying. "Mr. Peterson?" Linden addressed him as Bennett moved in to retrieve the photos.

"My children, my children," he moaned.

Bennett continued relentlessly. "You said you cut off your arm after you realized that it was you who had killed your children. But obviously you didn't, Mr. Peterson. You chickened out, didn't you? You are a big, tough guy who can beat innocent children but you chicken out when it comes time to following your own biblical belief about an eye for an eye, isn't that correct?"

"I thought I had paid for my deeds," Peterson said. "I thought I did what God would have wanted me to do."

"What? By going to bed? Why *did* you go to bed? Why didn't you call the police and turn yourself in?"

Fortner again. "Your honor," he said with great exasperation. "That's three questions at once. How can my client possibly be expected to answer with Mr. Bennett pummeling him with questions in such a manner?"

"Mr. Fortner is right, Mr. Bennett," the judge said. "Objection sustained. Please ask your questions one at a time."

"I'm sorry, your honor. We wouldn't want to *pummel* Mr. Peterson."

Fortner cringed at his unfortunate choice of verbs, which had handed Bennett that opening. He tried to look nonplussed.

"So, Mr. Peterson," Bennett continued, "why didn't you call the police after you realized what you had done?"

"I don't know. There just wasn't anything I could do to help my children."

"So you went to *bed*?"

"I didn't know what else to do."

"I imagine you were exhausted after what you'd just done."

"I was tired, yes. And I was sickened."

"Mr. Peterson, why didn't you kill yourself? Did you even think about doing to yourself what you had done to your children?"

"No, sir. It's a sin to kill yourself."

"And it's *not* a sin to kill six innocent children?"

"Oh, yes, Mr. Bennett. It's a sin. I'll be paying for that in the afterlife, for the rest of eternity."

"And hopefully that will come quickly," Bennett said quietly, as he turned away from the jurors. They didn't appear to hear him. Linden shot him a fierce glare, but before she could speak, Bennett said, "That's all I have, your honor."

Fortner passed on re-direct, but the day was still spent. Linden had again set court to begin at eight a.m. Tuesday. "Gentlemen," she said, with only a hint of sarcasm, "while I thoroughly enjoy the company of all of you, I'd like to expedite this trial in every way possible – as long as it does not interfere with Mr. Peterson's right to a fair proceeding. In case you haven't looked at the calendar, the day after tomorrow is Thanksgiving. And this morning, I put a twenty-two-pound frozen turkey into the refrigerator to begin to thaw. Now, my daughters and my sons-in-law and my grandchildren are all planning to be at my house Thursday, and while I usually put my girls to work, I really would like to be there to supervise. Do you suppose I'll be wearing my pink robe and making stuffing at six o'clock Thursday morning, or will I be donning my black robe and making overly harsh rulings to all of you?"

"Your honor," Bennett said, rising from the table and buttoning his brown-checked jacket, "I don't see any reason why you won't be pretty in pink." He thought himself clever; Linden did not crack a smile at his insulting remark but decided against reprimanding him.

"Your honor," Fortner said, "I have every reason to think that testimony in this trial will be concluded. Obviously, there's no way to predict how long it will take the jury to deliberate."

"I'm going to guess," Linden said, "that they'd all prefer home-made Thanksgiving dinner to the meal they'd get from us, even if it is free. But please rest assured that I will intervene if I have any reason to think the jurors are moving too quickly, refusing to review the evidence just so they can spend the holiday with their families. Bailiff, please bring the jury in."

"Thank you, your honor," both Bennett and Fortner said, one after the other.

The trial had moved into the rebuttal stage, when the prosecution can call witnesses to refute testimony put on by the defense or elicited from prosecution witnesses during their cross-examinations. Santini took the first two witnesses, Randy Harding and Alex Shoemaker, the uniformed officers who had found Peterson at Jake's. Both testified – almost identically, although Shoemaker, who went second, was not in the courtroom while his partner testified – that Peterson was calm when they approached him at the bar. At the time, there wasn't sufficient evidence to arrest him. Harding, a freckled and stocky guy of about twenty-five, testified that he introduced himself and Shoemaker, and asked Peterson to come down to the stationhouse with them. Santini hit on the same point as McNaughton had the previous April: Did Harding say that the police wanted to discuss the *deaths* of Peterson's children? Harding testified he was sure that he never mentioned their deaths.

"And Mr. Peterson never asked what the matter was about his children?"

"No, sir," Harding testified.

On cross, Fortner pushed the point. "How can you be sure that neither you nor Officer Shoemaker used the word 'deaths,' Officer Harding? Don't people often forget the exact wording of something they say virtually as soon as it comes out of their mouths?"

"I don't know about other people, sir, but I know what I said," Harding replied.

Both Harding and Shoemaker testified that they refrained from engaging Peterson in conversation, their response to a direct order from McNaughton not to talk with him. During the drive, they said, Peterson stared out the window and occasionally recited what sounded to be Bible verses. Shoemaker, a handsome, black, thirty-year-old with short-cropped hair, recalled it from his Baptist Bible school days and could repeat it: "For the Lord is enraged against all the nations, and furious against all their hoards; he has doomed them, has given them over for slaughter."

Bennett was up next. "Your honor, I call Susan Friedmann to the stand."

Friedmann was the state's psychiatrist, who had examined Peterson to determine if he were competent to stand trial. She was tall and slim, probably in her mid-forties but as fit as someone ten years her junior. She wore a stylish, two-piece beige suit that buttoned to the neck and matching beige pumps. Her blonde hair was parted on the side and chin length. She wore roundish wire-rimmed glasses and gold jewelry, but no wedding ring.

After the usual recitation of credentials, Bennett questioned her quickly about Peterson's competency to stand trial. Then he got down to the real reason he called her to testify.

"Dr. Friedmann, during your examination of Mr. Peterson, did you delve into Mr. Peterson's state of mind at the time of the crime?"

"Yes, I did."

"And did you form an opinion about that state of mind?"

"Yes, I did."

"Please tell the court."

"While Mr. Peterson's story was a compelling one, and he certainly exhibited many signs of mental illness, I did not feel that Mr. Peterson was legally insane at the time of the killings. That is, I felt that he knew what he was doing was wrong, but he did it anyway. I determined that his rage was a result of his belief that his wife should be punished, perhaps for some extramarital affair to which he alluded, but never described in detail."

"You say that Mr. Peterson exhibited signs of mental illness. What do you mean?"

"What Mr. Peterson described – *described*, as opposed to exhibited – is a classic example of dissociative reaction. That's a mental condition in which a person has multiple personalities. It's what most laypeople think of as schizophrenia, but that's a more generalized term. Mr. Peterson describes watching another person, only to find out it was himself. He implies at least two personalities. And his demeanor during my interview of him was unusual. That is, he gazed off into space, rarely making eye contact with me. His nose ran, although I did not detect that he was weeping. He spoke in a monotone, registering little distress even when he spoke about his children's deaths."

The nose! McNaughton couldn't believe that Peterson had perfected his ability to make his nose run so well, and was willing to employ it so often.

"Dr. Friedmann," Bennett continued, "under the circumstances that you describe, what led you to believe that Mr. Peterson was *not* mentally ill?"

"Mr. Peterson was capable of registering emotion when he spoke about his wife and her job, and when he insinuated that she had been unfaithful to him. The shifting between a virtually catatonic state and a normal range of emotion was too facile for him. It was *studied*."

"So, Dr. Friedmann, was Mr. Peterson faking?"

"I believe he was. Yes."

Finally. The prosecution had made a point, and a crucial one. Jack studied the jurors' faces. A couple looked skeptical, but most of them looked as if they were disturbed by the testimony. It seemed to have made them consider that Peterson was a remarkably good actor. One of the men, a bookish-looking black man who wore a tie to court every day, shook his head just a bit, barely perceptibly, and looked down in a manner that Jack thought indicated disgust.

"That's all I have," Bennett said, barely closing his mouth before Fortner bounded from his chair, buttoning his jacket as he rose. "Dr. Friedmann," he said before Linden could ask if he wanted to cross, "in all of your very impressive studies, how much was focused on people who allegedly fake mental illness?"

"Well, I don't believe there was ever a course, or part of a course, that focused on faking."

"Then how can you sit here and conclude that Mr. Peterson was faking?" Fortner's voice was more forceful than usual; he was perturbed.

"I base that conclusion on my many years of observing patients, Mr. Fortner," she said.

"But you don't *know*, do you? Mr. Peterson never told you that he was faking, did he?"

"Of course not."

"So it is merely an opinion, one formed by a fallible human being. Correct?"

"Well, of course I'm fallible. But my opinion is a learned one, not just a guess. I've worked in this field for many years, as I mentioned earlier."

"Dr. Friedmann, how many of your other patients were faking?"

"I have no way of knowing that."

"You mean you didn't form an opinion about them?"

"Well, certainly I did. At the time of their examinations. But without studiously reviewing all my case files – and there are hundreds – I'd have no way of even estimating how many had faked."

"How about a guess? I mean, if you're so sure about Mr. Peterson, then certainly you can give this jury a rough idea of how often you see similarly disingenuous patients."

"I don't know. A few dozen. A handful. It doesn't happen often."

"A *handful*? You're basing your opinion in this life-and-death case, one that will determine this man's entire future" – he gestured toward Peterson – "on a *handful* of prior examples?"

"I didn't say that. I'm basing my opinion very specifically on Mr. Peterson's demeanor and answers during my interview with him."

Knofel dropped the issue; he had made his point. He turned and went to the exhibit table, retrieving the color photographs of the children's bodies.

He handed them to Friedmann, who adjusted her glasses, gulped hard and took a deep breath before looking at them. "Have you seen these pictures before, Dr. Friedmann?"

"Yes, I have," she said quietly.

"Look at them again, please." Fortner waited a moment for Friedmann to flip through the six photographs. When she was finished, she looked up at him and tried to hand the photos to him, but Fortner did not let her rid herself of them quite so soon.

"Dr. Friedmann, could a sane person have done this, committed the acts you see depicted in those photos?"

Friedmann blinked hard several times. "Ummm," she stammered, before Knofel interrupted.

"What does your gut tell you?"

"Your honor!" Bennett shouted.

Linden shook her head. "You may answer, Dr. Friedmann."

The psychiatrist gazed up into Fortner's face and said quietly, "No."

"If it pleases the court," Bennett said. "Ladies and gentlemen of the jury. . ."

He had buttoned the middle button of his single-breasted navy suit coat over his flat abdomen. He was confident that his receding brown hair was coifed perfectly, his teeth were gleaming white and his conservative red striped tie was straight, the results of a quick trip to the washroom during the break. Bennett wanted everything perfect.

It was late afternoon, but Linden insisted that closing arguments would be given then and that she'd send the jury to its deliberations. She still held out hope that she'd be head chef on that twenty-two-pound bird, but it was looking less and less likely. Even if a guilty verdict came back quickly, the court would have to go through the death-penalty phase of the trial. But both sides assured her that their testimony would be limited if that phase should occur, and Linden privately thought that it wouldn't be difficult for the jurors to send Peterson to the electric chair if they'd taken the first leap of finding him guilty of such a heinous crime. Not that it would be easy. She had learned that, no matter how heinous the crime, it was never easy for jurors to decide to put someone to death.

She and the attorneys had met for an hour and forty-five minutes after lunch, going over the instructions that she would give the jurors about what they could consider and what they could disregard. But first, they were to hear Bennett and Fortner's summations.

"I want to go over the state's testimony for you, help you to put it all together in a way that makes it comprehensible and meaningful to you," Bennett told the jurors. "But first let me thank you, on behalf of the state of Indiana, for your diligence and patience during this trial. We asked you to perform a very difficult task – to sit in judgment of one of your peers – and we asked you to do it under difficult circumstances – immediately before a major holiday. Please know that we do appreciate what you have done and are about to do.

"Now, let me just walk you through the testimony that you have heard. Please recall the testimony of the first police officers who arrived at the Peterson house, Todd Bienick and Jimmy Davis. They set the scene for you. You will recall Officer Bienick's testimony. Remember that he was the big, strapping kid who testified that he had wanted to be a police officer since he was six? He was embarrassed to admit to you that he vomited after he found the Peterson children. But he told you that, didn't he? Here was this tough police officer, four years on the force, and he was sickened by the sight of those beautiful children butchered in such a horrible way. Just couldn't believe what he saw. He couldn't help but think about the baby his wife is expecting.

"Some of the most compelling testimony of the trial came next, when Sergeant McNaughton" – he gestured toward the prosecution table and Jack nodded toward the jurors – "told you in great detail about the arduous investigation the police undertook. How they looked under every rock, and ruled out the possibility that anybody other than John Peterson could have killed those six beautiful children. Sergeant McNaughton found the clothing Peterson had been wearing, and found the wet bar of soap that Peterson had used to wash his own children's blood down the shower drain. Sergeant McNaughton told you all about all the technical work that his police officers performed. As you could tell, Sergeant McNaughton left nothing undone. He is the consummate investigator, the best in Indianapolis and, for that matter, anywhere, and that is why he has been working in homicide so long.

"Let's not forget the testimony of Officer Harding and Shoemaker, who picked Mr. Peterson up at Jake's. They told you about his calm demeanor, how he did not seem like a man who might be distraught about something. No, ladies and gentlemen, we maintain that Mr. Peterson was perfectly calm because he had just done exactly what he set out to do – level revenge on his wife in a calmly executed plan. Surely each and every one of you has, at one time or another, had some wrong done to you by someone else. And if you were able to do something in kind – get a little revenge – admit it: You felt better, didn't you?" A couple of jurors nodded. McNaughton could tell they were listening intently and that they were relating to what Bennett was saying. "Now, that doesn't make you a bad person. It was just an effort to see that justice was done, right? But Mr. Peterson took that seeking of justice to an extreme. Instead of handling the situation like most people would do – getting marital counseling or getting a divorce – he *killed his children!* Mr. Fortner would have you believe that's the act of an insane man. I suggest to you that Mr. Peterson was thinking clearly, that he knew full well that what he was doing was wrong. But he did it anyway. He wanted too badly to see his wife suffer.

"You heard the testimony of Marie LaPierre, the Petersons' neighbor. She told you about the loud and violent argument she overheard coming from their house. And what about the bartender at Jake's – Luke Linley? Remember that muscular guy?

He told you that Peterson claimed his wife was having an affair. Reason – in Peterson's mind, anyway – to seek revenge. That's motive, ladies and gentlemen. Motive for committing murder, not for acting out during a moment of insanity.

"Dr. Friedmann, a very experienced psychiatrist, told you that in her opinion – a very learned, professional opinion – Mr. Peterson was faking a mental illness. That he wasn't sick at all – just faking. She has examined thousands of patients over the years, and she'd be able to tell when one was faking. Mr. Peterson was a computer expert, not a psychiatrist himself. Nobody who isn't intimately involved with mental patients could know enough about the condition he claims to have had to fool a professional psychiatrist like Dr. Friedmann. She told you so. You must listen to her.

"Peterson *himself* told you he did it. He testified about *beating his own children to death!* In all my days as a prosecutor, I don't think I've ever heard such cold, heartless testimony. And do not forget that even he admitted that he must pay for this crime for the rest of eternity. You must make sure that he begins paying now, while he is still breathing air and enjoying life – something his six beautiful children can no longer do.

"But ladies and gentlemen," Bennett said, raising his voice to speak over the rustle beginning to emanate from the judge's chambers, "there was no testimony more compelling in this trial than that of Dr. Shadwani, the forensic pathologist who examined the six tiny bodies that were removed from two bedrooms in the Peterson house. Taken from the beds that those children thought were their safe havens.

"He told you how they died – a horrible, horrible death. A painful death. A senseless death. An unnecessary death. Six unnecessary deaths. And he introduced these to you." Bennett turned toward the chamber door and nodded. Six law clerks filed out, each rolling a headless mannequin that was affixed to a poll with four roller feet. Four of the mannequins wore bloodied night-gowns of descending size. Two wore the tops of boys' pajamas. Linden, ever cool, was not visibly moved, but virtually everyone else in the courtroom – except McNaughton and Santini, who were expecting the stunt – gasped in unison. The clerks deposited the mannequins in a single line immediately in front of the jury box.

Bennett knew he was taking a risk with the stunt. He waited stoically for Fortner's objection that the night clothes were more prejudicial than probative. He, Santini and McNaughton snuck looks at Fortner, waiting for him to object to the theatrics. But Knofel didn't move, didn't flinch, didn't utter a word. Even as others in the courtroom shifted nervously, Fortner was calm. No objection.

Bennett had borrowed the child-sized mannequins from a local children's clothing store. While Steve Stewart, the display manager and son of the owner, was most cooperative – "I'll do anything I can to help convict anybody who could do such a horrible thing," he told Santini when the deputy asked – he asked that the heads be left off. Stewart's mannequins were distinctive, and Stewart didn't want his store associated with such a horrendous image. Bennett was peeved at first; he wanted badly to put a face to the dead children. But then he thought it most appropriate that the mannequins were faceless, just as the Peterson children had been rendered.

"Ladies and gentlemen, John Pius Peterson did this" – he swept his arm broadly toward the mannequins – "to six innocent children, his own flesh and blood. This was Mary Elizabeth," he said, moving toward the mannequin wearing the largest night-gown. He held up an eleven-by-fourteen school photo of the girl, placing it where the mannequin's head should have been, secured in a bracket specially fashioned by the clerks.

"She was a fourth-grader at St. Ambrose Elementary, just one week away from her tenth birthday. She and her mom had been planning a special shopping trip to buy her a new dress as a present. Matthew," he said, taking out the next photo and positioning it above the bloodied blue pajama top, "was eight, going on nine. A third grader right behind his sister at St. Ambrose. He was very close to his little brother, the only other boy in the family. John Peter. Named after his father. He was six. A first grader." He left the younger boy's photo above his bloodied pajamas.

Bennett, with perspiration breaking out on his bald pate, moved to the next mannequin. "Sarah Ruth had just had her fifth birthday in January," he said as he placed the photo above the deeply reddened pink nightie. It was a fuzzy reproduction of a snapshot her mother had taken at home. "She felt like such a big girl. She was so proud of herself because she was going to start kindergarten in the fall. Claire," he said, moving to the toddler-sized mannequin, "had just turned three. She was a happy, smiling child who brought joy into the life of everyone she encountered." Now he moved to the infant-sized torso. "And Teresa Ann was the light of everyone's life. She was two years, one month old, when her father slaughtered her."

His voice had dropped, and then he startled the courtroom with a burst of voice and emotion: "*Slaughtered her and all of her brothers and sisters!* Good God! How could anyone do this to his own children?" Bennett returned to each mannequin. "Ladies and gentlemen, he beat and killed Mary Elizabeth!" he shouted, ripping down the photo. He repeated the ritual: "And Matthew Mark! And John Peter! Sarah! And Claire! And even little Teresa Ann! You *must* find John Pius Peterson guilty of the murders of his six children. To do less would be to render their young lives meaningless, to say that they didn't count! But I will tell you – they *did* count! And they deserved better than to be the helpless pawns in their father's sick revenge against their mother for reasons he had concocted in his own mind. You must find John Peterson guilty of six counts of murder!"

Bennett was winded and his brow glowed from perspiration, but he was pleased with his performance. He breathed deeply and walked behind the prosecution table where Santini surreptitiously gave him the thumbs' up sign so that the jurors could not see. A long moment of silence passed; finally, Linden said, "Mr. Fortner?"

Fortner stood at the defense table and buttoned his tweed jacket. "Ladies and gentlemen of the jury, Mr. Bennett, Mr. Santini, your honor. I agree with Mr. Bennett: You have done a wonderful service to your community by serving on this jury. Thank you."

He remained behind the table, the fingers of both hands fully extended and planted on the highly varnished wood, rendering his hands into two miniature tents. His head was bent deeply as he inhaled heavily. Then he moved around the table and in front of the jury box, gesturing toward the horrible mannequins as he went.

"I want you to look at these mannequins, to look carefully at the bedclothes that each wears," he said, raising the eyebrows of more than one observer in the gallery. "Ladies and gentlemen, I want you to *study* – yes, study – the crime-scene photographs after you've retired to the jury room to deliberate. And I want you to remember the words of the state's own witness, a trained psychiatrist, Dr. Susan Friedmann, who said that no sane person could commit these acts. Thank you."

He strode back to the defense table and sat down, his demeanor humble but his gut confident. It was over, just that fast. McNaughton admired Knofel's brilliance. What more, after all, had to be said?

"Ladies and gentlemen of the jury," Linden began, and she proceeded with the intricate instructions that they were to follow.

It used to be conventional wisdom that, if a jury brought a verdict back quickly, the defendant was guilty. That's why defense attorneys always looked so grim, despite their best efforts to give moral support to their clients, when they were summoned back to court even before they had had a chance to go home for a quick shower and change. Then the O.J. Simpson jury came back with an acquittal after just four hours, nowhere near long enough to even review the evidence much less thoroughly analyze and discuss it. So these days, attorneys and cops tended to hang around the courthouse – or its immediate environs, such as the Legal Beagle – waiting for a verdict. Jack joined Bennett and Santini for a beer at the Beagle while he waited for Renee to come downtown to meet him. She had asked the neighbor to watch Angel, who would have been a little too spirited for Jack's somber mood this evening. Renee wouldn't be able to wait out the verdict indefinitely, nor would she want to. But she wanted to be there for Jack for just a little while.

Jack checked his phone again to see if Sniffy Smith had called. Nothing. But his spirits lifted as soon as Renee walked into the Beagle. She was still gorgeous to him –deep, dark eyes; full lips; thick mahogany hair swept back from her pronounced cheekbones. She was fuller through the hips than when they had met; all the years, plus motherhood, had taken their toll. It bugged her; she constantly planned diets and promised elaborate exercise plans that, in the press of everyday life, never got done. But it didn't matter to Jack. Sure, he'd have loved if she were as fit as she was when they met. But if anything, her mind had improved, she was more insightful, more capable than she had been. And that, after all, was what attracted him to her in the first place.

"How're you doing, honey?" she asked as she leaned over to peck him on the lips. She didn't wait for an answer before mumbling "Hi, guys," to Bennett and Santini.

"Can you join us?" Terry asked. Renee glanced at Jack to measure his plans. He caught the look and said, "No, guys, I'm hungry and I think we'll go somewhere to get a bite. I don't think I can take another Beagle burger."

"Thanks anyway," Renee said. "And good luck."

"OK, then," Bennett said. "Jack, we'll call you the minute we get word."

"OK. Later."

There weren't many casual places to eat in downtown Indianapolis, although the new mall had helped the situation. Jack had a taste for El Rodeo, which served up wonderful Mexican food that he was pretty sure was authentic. They were greeted enthusiastically by the owner, Rafael, who shook their hands and seated them in a comfortable booth. Ramon, the waiter, brought chips and salsa and took their order: Jack could not resist his favorite burrito loco, despite the irony of its name, and a Dos Equis; Renee asked for chile verde and a frozen lime margarita, unhealthy salt included, please.

As soon as Ramon had left the table, Renee turned her face up toward Jack. "So?"

"Well," he answered, knowing exactly what she wanted despite the brevity of the question, "I think Bennett did a pretty good job with the closing argument. The mannequins were pretty outrageous, but Knofel didn't object. And I think they worked, to some degree anyway. I watched the jurors, and they were pretty horrified. A couple of them looked away. Sort of like you do at the movies." He made the latter remark with a slight lilt in his voice, a good-natured reference for Renee's penchant for hiding her eyes when she could anticipate a particularly violent cinematic moment. She had no love for watching heads explode.

"Unfortunately, they weren't looking at the work of some ketchup-wielding makeup artist," she said flatly. "I can't imagine having to look at that stuff." She broke a chip in two, dunked half of it and then held it as she continued speaking. "You said Knofel didn't go berserk when Bennett tried to bring the mannequins in?"

"No, that's the worst part. He didn't say a word. And then he turned the mannequins to his own advantage. His closing took all of thirty seconds. It was pretty obvious that he discarded what he had planned for his closing after seeing Terry bring in those mannequins. He told the jurors to look closely at them and – get this – the crime-scene photos. And the only witness he mentioned was ours, Friedmann. The psychiatrist. He told the jurors to remember that she admitted somebody would have to be crazy to do what Peterson had done."

"Oh, geez," Renee said, incapable of disguising her worry. "How bad was it?"

"Bad," Jack said matter-of-factly, tugging at the collar of his white shirt. He finally gave in, loosened his tie and unbuttoned the top button of his shirt. "I think we lost it, honey."

"Oh, geez," she repeated quietly.

They sat there, sipping on their drinks and munching on chips and peering around the restaurant, looking for Ramon to bring their entrees. Renee resumed the conversation. "He was probably trying to convey confidence to the jurors. What more could he say, after all? What else could make a difference? But I doubt that Knofel is *really* that confident, Jack. I mean, he can't be. No jury is going to let Peterson off the hook after what he did to his own kids."

"I'm not so sure," Jack said.

Their food arrived, and both ate voraciously. Renee decided to let Jack talk about the case if he wanted to. In between bites, she told him about her day – nothing much happening on the political front. The election, which had kept her busy for months, was two weeks earlier, and the political world pretty much shut down from then through the end of the year. Renee liked it that way; it allowed her to do some of the holiday things at home that her mother used to do.

They finished their food, and sipped the last of their drinks. "I probably ought to get home to our girl, honey," Renee said. She looked at her watch; it was nine-thirty, and she had promised the neighbor she wouldn't be late.

"Yeah, I know. Listen, is it OK if I stick around the courthouse for a while? I want to stay close."

"Of course. Just try to get some rest, OK?"

He nodded. "OK. Give Angel a kiss for me, and call if you need me."

"OK." She leaned to kiss him as they stood.

"I'll walk you to your car, babe," he said gently. He tossed some bills on the table; Renee threw an extra dollar to beef up the tip, and they left.

"Good luck, sweetie," she said as he closed the driver's side door for her. She wound down the window. "Call me. And no matter what, just remember that you did your best." He nodded half-heartedly and gave a little wave as she drove away.

The prosecutor's office was on the fifth floor of the City-County Building. McNaughton decided to take the steps; he knew he'd be out of breath when he got there, but perhaps the effort would take the edge off of that burrito. When he arrived, out of breath, he learned that Bennett and Santini were already ensconced in Terry's big office. Jack knocked once and started in before either answered. Bennett was sitting at his desk, feet precariously propped on the edge; Paul was sprawled out on the Naugahyde couch, a magazine tented over his face. The chairs around the conference table were barrel-shaped and relatively comfortable, and Jack relegated two for himself, slouching in one, propping his feet on the other. They spoke only occasionally as the hours passed. McNaughton read a two-week-old Time magazine, glanced at the colorful graphics and sprightly writing in a copy of USA Today; he had already poured over the Sun that morning. Using a desk phone, Jack called his own cell phone to make sure it was working and that he hadn't missed Sniffy's call because of malfunctioning phone. It worked. He managed to doze, despite the heavy feeling in his stomach, courtesy of that burrito loco and Dos Equis and, most likely, the tension of the moment. He felt as if he had jumped six inches off the chair when a loud buzzer went off; it was Bennett's intercom.

"Yes?" Bennett said sleepily into the antiquated machine. "Terry," a nasal female voice intoned, "the judge's office called. They have a verdict."

"Thanks," Bennett said mindlessly, then seemed to get his brain working again. His eyes darted to McNaughton, then Santini, and he got no reassurance from either. It was two-forty a.m. Wednesday, the morning before Thanksgiving. The jury had had the case for just over six hours, and some of that time had to have been spent over dinner.

"This is good, gentlemen," Bennett said. "Six hours. I think that means we've got us a conviction."

Neither McNaughton nor Santini spoke. "Jack," Bennett implored. "What do you think?"

"I don't know, Terry," McNaughton said quietly as he popped two Tums into his mouth. "We'd better get down there."

They took turns peering into the mirror that Bennett had hung inside a closet door. Santini had dark circles under his eyes; Bennett couldn't get a short lock of hair to lie in place. McNaughton wished he could brush his teeth, but opted instead for a mint that Ramon had brought with the check. They hustled out of the office and down the hall to the world's slowest elevator. "Let's walk," McNaughton suggested, and Bennett and Santini followed him wordlessly into the stairwell. When they arrived on the second floor, reporters who had virtually camped out outside the courtroom had gotten up off the floor (a non-professional trial watcher had squatted on the one wooden bench in the hall) and milled anxiously, waiting for the sheriff's deputies to open the locked courtroom. Each reporter would have to be swept with a hand-held metal detector before he or she could enter, and they were getting concerned that the routine might take too long for them to get to their seats on time. McNaughton, Bennett and Santini entered through the judge's office and took their places at the prosecution's table.

It seemed like an interminable time before sheriff's deputies escorted Peterson to his place at the defense table and unlocked his shackles. Knofel occasionally whispered something in his client's ear, but Peterson was unmoved. Finally, Linden whisked in, looking better than she had a right to at this hour, and gestured to indicate that no one need stand at this late hour. She asked the bailiff if there had been time for all the reporters to get into the courtroom, and he answered affirmatively. Then she turned to the lawyers. "Gentlemen, the jury has sent word that it has reached a verdict. The bailiff has gone to bring the jurors in; it should be any minute now. Are there any matters for us to address before they are brought in?"

"No, your honor," Bennett and Fortner said, almost simultaneously.

And then they waited. Jack's stomach continued to ache. He felt as if his heart was racing; he instinctively reached for his neck and felt his quickened pulse. He peered at the others in the room. Peterson sat stock still. McNaughton wondered how he was able to contain his emotions. Fortner emulated his client, although he was more erect as they sat at the defense table, both with hands folded in front of them. Knofel looked lost in thought. Bennett kept rubbing his palms together, nervously massaging his fingers. He reached up and swiped the perspiration from his forehead. Santini unconsciously tapped his foot.

Finally, the bailiff called out, "All rise," and led the jurors in. Each deftly slipped into the jury box, having had plenty of practice over the previous days. The handsome black guy in the back row, far right seat, who had been so attentive, making frequent eye contact with the prosecution, gazed at the floor in front of him. The eyes of his seat mate, an older white woman who wore flowing gypsy-style clothes and her grey hair long and wild, darted about the courtroom, touching everywhere but the prosecutors' table. The twenty-ish white woman, who always dressed impeccably and cried frequently, dabbed a tissue at her reddened eyes, but did not lift them from the floor. Others followed suit – the black grandmother, the white computer geek, the grungy white kid who wore his clothes too big and his greasy hair too long. Only the middle-aged white guy, the kind of person that populated every seat of every jury in the old days, looked directly at McNaughton. His eyes flashed what Jack took to be an apology.

McNaughton's stomach churned, but not from the food. He had seen too many juries; those who have convicted avert their eyes from the defendant, but glance at, or even nod a greeting to, the prosecution. Jack's heart began to beat so violently that he was sure it was visible through his sports jacket. He could feel the blood rush up through his neck into his pounding head, leaving a mask of crimson across his cheeks. It was the color of embarrassment or anger or, in this case, despair. His ears were deaf to everything but the pounding, so he took his lead from others after Judge Linden invited everyone to be seated.

Jack felt as if he were watching a silent movie running in slow motion. Linden addressing the jurors. The foreman, the attentive black man, responding, passing a slip of paper to the chunky Hispanic man who was Judge Linden's bailiff, and him passing it to the judge. The absolute absence of emotion on Linden's face as she reads the verdict slip and returns it to the bailiff. And then the bailiff announcing the verdict. Fortner and Peterson turning to one another and embracing. Bennett's face sagging, but his body remaining motionless. Santini dropping his head, covering his face with his hands. Barbara Peterson's face erupting in horror, her mouth agape in a silent scream.

McNaughton awoke from his dream state when the gallery gasped. A couple of reporters who still had a chance to make late edition dashed from the courtroom to call in the news.

John Pius Peterson, whose hands bore the blood of his six children, who had committed the vilest crime imaginable, had been found not guilty by reason of insanity.

CHAPTER 11

"Jack."

"*Jack!*" Renee raised her voice to get her husband's attention. He had barely budged from the leather chair in the family room since he returned home before daybreak on Wednesday, the day before Thanksgiving. Later that morning, Renee had hastily called her mother, explaining that she and Jack wouldn't be very good company anyway and asking her forgiveness that they wouldn't be making the three-hour trek to Chicago for the annual feast. She rounded up Angel, who was surly because she wouldn't be seeing her grandparents and cousins, and then struggled to brush the snarled evidence of a wild night from the little girl's lustrous hair. They went off to O'Malia's, their favorite grocery, in hopes of finding a turkey breast that would quickly thaw and thus salvage the holiday for the disappointed child. It was not to be; every last one had been purchased. So Renee reluctantly went to the TV-dinner case and selected four boxes – enough for seconds that way – that promised all white meat, savory stuffing and mashed potatoes with gravy. She bought some fresh green beans and an onion to dress them up, and grabbed a cellophane cone of brightly colored wild flowers to make an impromptu centerpiece.

The next day, Thanksgiving, Renee baked the dinners in the oven instead of the microwave so that they'd all be ready at once. She carefully scooped them from the compartmentalized trays onto the family's best china; she figured it looked more like

Thanksgiving dinner that way. She had clothed the dining-room table with the Battenberg lace cloth her late mother-in-law had given her, a delicacy she had never had the nerve to use before. And then she set the plates of food just so, each equidistant from the glass vase that held the rainbow-colored posies.

Jack had made one of his rare departures from the leather chair for the meal. He smiled wanly and thanked Renee for the effort, and even commented how lovely everything looked. "I guess we should use the dining room more often," he offered. But that was the extent of the dinner conversation, at least Jack's portion of it. Angel was still peeved, and grunted most of her portion. Despite her growing irritation with both members of her family, Renee tried to keep her temper, knowing that a family argument would upset Jack all the more. Finally, she told Angel to follow her to the bathroom, where she quietly lectured Angel that Daddy was upset and tired and begged the little girl to think about him instead of herself. It was pointless; Angel was too little to think of anyone *but* herself. But the break seemed to defuse the situation long enough to get them through the meal.

Then Jack had returned to the recliner to brood. Angelica whined that she wanted to watch a video, but Jack wanted silence. So Renee hauled the girl to the master bedroom, propped up some pillows and left her there to watch "One Hundred and One Dalmatians" for what seemed to Renee to be the thousand first time. Belle, the sweet-faced cat, curled up next to Angel for a mid-afternoon snooze.

And so the family continued for two more days, until Renee, who wasn't into self-pity and who had trouble tolerating it in others, had had enough.

"*Jack!*" she said abruptly, loudly. He sat up and looked at her, the startle on his face. "Enough is enough," she said firmly. "Your brooding isn't going to change the verdict or bring those kids back or help Mrs. Peterson or do anything except drive your family nuts. I'm sorry he was acquitted. I'm just as sure as you are that he killed those kids to punish his wife. And I'm heartsick that he'll never be punished for what he's done. But *you* can't change that."

Judge Linden, who had been unusually pensive during her family's more elaborate and festive Thanksgiving feast, had ordered Peterson to be immediately transported to Jonathan Jennings State Hospital – named after the first Indiana governor – for further mental evaluation and confinement until he could be pronounced sane. That's all she could do. Under the law, she could not specify a sentence, and she, like Jack, had known of people who had been found not guilty of murder by reason of insanity and who had been released in only a few months, ostensibly cured. The release date was up to the second-rate psychiatrists – the only kind of people who would work for the state's low wages – who manned Jennings State; Peterson was no longer the official concern of her court.

And so it was over. Bennett was miserable, worried about what this would do to his career. Santini was wondering if he *wanted* a prosecutorial career, if this is what it meant. And Jack brooded, unwilling to talk to the one person whom he had always taken into his confidence.

"This is making *me* a prime candidate for Jennings State, Jack," Renee said angrily. "If you've got something on your mind, say it. If not to me, then to somebody else. Mitch. Kit. A professional."

"Oh, yeah," he said. "I really want to talk to some psychiatrist. Don't you understand they're the bane of my existence? Their hogwash is why Peterson is going to be on the street in a few months!"

"No, Jack," she replied tersely. Her face was taut as she enunciated her words. "That's not why. It's because of the law, and you know why it was written that way. It's not right to hold an insane person responsible for his actions, no matter how heinous they are."

"He's *not* insane!"

"Well, you don't think so, and I don't think so, but twelve jurors were convinced that he is. And that's all that matters."

"It's a bullshit law," he said angrily. "Indiana is so fucked up. Practically every other state has a 'guilty but mentally ill' verdict that at least would have put Peterson away permanently. But not Indiana. God, why is this state so backward?"

Indiana was one of only a handful of states that did not have a law that allowed a defendant to be found guilty but mentally ill. Under such a law, a jury may express its opinion that a defendant was insane when he or she committed an act, but it still holds the person responsible. The idea was that a person convicted under such a law would first get the psychological help he needed to return to sanity, and then would spend time in prison to pay for the act. Some in the psychiatric community argued that such laws made no sense; why, they asked, should someone be held responsible for doing something when he had absolutely no control over his action? That was the reason the M'Naghten Rule had evolved into the common law in the first place. But proponents of the verdict contended that society demanded that the person be held responsible. There were mixed results in those states that tried it. A few provided the psychological help that was supposed to be the first step, but many more provided nothing of the sort. So prisons across the country were experiencing an influx of certifiably crazy people, who were coming to live with and learn how to commit crimes from plenty of others who were crazy enough, if not certifiable.

Jack thought the laws provided society with a sense of justice. He figured that some acts – such as bludgeoning your kids – were so horrible that one should have to pay, even if he wasn't in absolute control when he committed them. Like the death penalty, which didn't really deter crime but seemed to answer a societal demand for an-eye-for-an-eye justice, the "guilty but insane" verdict was no panacea. But it was one answer.

As usual, Indiana had bided its time, even while other states – even some of the ostensibly more backward Southern states – moved forward to experiment. Taking it slow seemed to suit most Hoosiers just fine. They were a conservative lot, not just in their political choices but in their life choices. They shunned change so much that Indiana for decades refused to adopt daylight savings time when most of the rest of the country switched its clocks. The mindset long baffled Jack, who found individual Hoosiers to be kind, caring, resourceful people. But that personal compassion, as well as any passion to aspire to great things, seemed to evaporate among the masses. Progress was something Hoosiers learned about in history class, not something they lived – or even aspired to experience. But that's how Hoosiers wanted it to be; last place suited them just fine as long as taxes did not rise and government didn't interfere in their lives.

It was a conversation that Jack and Renee had had often. Both would have felt more comfortable with the progressivity of some Eastern states, or that of Renee's home state of Illinois. But Indiana had good qualities that kept them there – relatively low crime and pollution; a low cost-of-living; decent, hard-working and friendly – if conservative – people. It was a good place to raise a child.

"You know, Jack," Renee said, "it seems to me that the time may be ripe to make old slow-poke Indiana catch up with the rest of the union. Hell, a 'guilty but mentally ill' verdict sounds pretty tough on crime, and Lord knows the governor loves anything that allows him to cloak himself with that mantle. Why don't you think about pushing something in the legislature?"

He nodded, but did not speak. Jack liked to make a difference, but he wasn't terribly savvy about the legislative process. So the very suggestion – while enticing – unnerved him. But Renee was intimately familiar with the way ideas became law. He looked at her, squinting his eyes a bit to signal his assent and said, "I don't have a clue how to do that."

He *responded!* Renee squelched the urge to howl out and shake a victorious fist in the air. Instead, she restrained herself, sucked in a breath and calmly said, "It's easy."

The timing, in fact, couldn't have been better. For several months, the people who staffed the legislature had been gearing up for the next year's session, which would begin shortly after the new year. They were so busy preparing bills for the one hundred fifty lawmakers for whom they worked that most could ill-afford to take Thanksgiving off, much less the Friday after it, even though the rest of state government had been shut down for a four-day holiday.

"You'll need to get a legislator to carry the bill," she said, pausing to allow her mind's eye to scroll the list and find the best one.

"Who?" he asked.

She did not speak for another moment. A lot of the legislators that Renee had known when she was in the Statehouse had retired from the General Assembly – some voluntarily, others by command of their constituents. But she still knew some of them, and it didn't take her long to hit on the perfect person.

"Kim Woolums. A senator from New Albany. She's perfect," Renee said. She clapped her hands together. "Perfect. Do you remember me talking about her? She's great – smart, articulate, compassionate but tough. She's a real champion for kids, and I'll betcha she is beside herself over this verdict. You ought to go talk to her. Just call her office at the Statehouse and make an appointment."

"OK. I'll do it." It was just that simple; McNaughton had decided that he would make something good come of the hideous situation after all.

Jack called Woolums' office from home first thing Monday morning, and the senator's legislative assistant, intrigued by his proposal and relatively sure that Woolums would be as well, agreed to give him a fifteen-minute appointment for Wednesday morning, November thirty, when Woolums would be in Indianapolis. The knowledge that he'd be seeing the senator invigorated him, making it possible for him to do a most distasteful thing: Go back to the homicide division, and face Doyle Stumbo.

As horrendous as the Peterson trial had been, it also had been a respite from Doyle and his unreasonable demands, his irrational behavior, his insecure self-importance. "All good things must come to an end," McNaughton mumbled to himself wistfully, a resigned smirk on his face. Carrying a to-go coffee mug from which he had been sipping java since leaving home, he mounted the steps to the stationhouse, taking them a bit more patiently than usual. No sense in rushing back, he thought.

"G' morning, sergeant," the uniform at the desk said absently as McNaughton passed. Jack nodded and smiled slightly before heading up the staircase that would take him back to homicide. He'd been here only a few times, mostly late at night, over the last several weeks, to check messages and watch the stack of things to do grow on his desk. The pile finally succumbed to gravity and teetered over, spreading itself over virtually half of McNaughton's work space. He let out a deep breath when he saw it, set down the coffee mug and started gathering up loose papers even before sitting down.

There were half a dozen new phone messages; he had handled the others on a current basis during breaks in the trial action. A sergeant at eastside homicide needed to discuss an old case, but she said there was no rush. Human resources wanted to check, for the umpteenth time, how many dependents Jack had claimed for insurance coverage. A civilian in personnel had called to remind him that, if he hoped the police board would approve another detective on his squad at its next meeting, his supervisor needed to submit the request, pronto. But nothing from Sniffy Smith.

And then there was the paperwork, the most mundane part of police work. Boring as it was, it was as crucial as the more stimulating investigations. McNaughton knew few cops who didn't complain about doing it – even the burned-out guys who loathed the streets weren't all that happy about doing the very work that could keep them behind their desks. Jack always tried to keep current on his paperwork, doing it in dribs and drabs, a discipline that made it considerably less onerous. He had no such luxury now; there was no way to avoid a pile like this when you spend all day, every day for a couple of weeks in court.

And so went his first morning back. He talked to the homicide sergeant, explained to human resources that he really had only one child and made a mental note to ask Stumbo if he had yet approved the request for another detective. He tried Sniffy again. Kit wandered in, her wild, dark hair still wet from her morning shower. She looked tired, and mumbled something about being out on surveillance *way* too late. "You shouldn't have come in so early," Jack offered.

"Yeah, and if I don't, you know how the paperwork'll get backed up," she said sullenly.

He couldn't argue as he surveyed his own desk, now covered with a number of neat, but nevertheless intimidating, heaps of work. The phone rang; the piles would have to wait a while more.

"McNaughton," Jack said as he put the receiver to his ear.

"Jack? It's Sally Rutherford," the strong voice on the other end said. She was a deputy prosecutor with whom Jack had worked a few times.

"Well, hi, Sally. How're you doing?" Jack had always liked her, particularly her work ethic and appreciation for the job police officers do. It wasn't too difficult to muster a little enthusiasm for her.

"I was OK until I got a call this morning," she said soberly. "Donnie Crawford is out, released from the loony bin."

"Oh, shit." Jack said quietly.

Crawford was the hitchhiker who had strangled the woman who picked him up and repeatedly had sex with her corpse, and then was found not guilty by reason of insanity. The judge had ordered him to a mental institution, where he had stayed less than seven years. It was nowhere near enough to pay for the crime, but that's the way the system worked.

"I can't believe it, but the shrinks say he's fit to live in society," Rutherford said. "You know their word is gospel on this stuff."

"I feel for the first person who picks him up hitchhiking," Jack said.

"Well, yeah, so would I," Sally answered, "except I hope people have gotten wiser to that in the years since he did his deed."

"Yeah, well, let's hope," McNaughton said. Then, in the background, came an awful sound: "McNaughton!"

"Good God, who's bellowing?" Sally asked.

"That's Doyle Stumbo. Remember him?" Jack answered.

"Oh, yeah. Well, Jack, sounds like you've got your hands full. See ya."

"Yeah, see ya, Sally. Thanks for the info."

"Anytime."

McNaughton returned the receiver to the cradle. "McNaughton!" Stumbo was getting more insistent, but apparently he was not eager enough to see Jack to cause him to remove himself from his lopsided, dilapidated chair.

Jack signed, grabbed his coffee mug – its contents quickly cooling – and walked to Stumbo's office. "I was on the phone, Doyle," he said without inflection as he sat in the chair in front of Stumbo's desk.

"I expect you to answer when I call you," Stumbo drawled, a toothpick adhered to his lower lip with a spot of spittle. Jack remained silent, unwilling to take it on. "Anyway, well, let's see. . ."

He bumbled about his desk, pushing papers every which way, clearly not prepared for the conversation he had deemed so urgent. "Ah," he grunted when he found a piece of paper. "You gotta be in Cap'n Hensley's office in internal affairs at ten o'clock tomorrow morning for your interview on the Trueblood complaint."

"Doyle, I've got an appointment with a state senator tomorrow morning to discuss the change in the insanity-defense law. I just got back from two weeks in court. I'm up to my eyeballs in paperwork and phone messages. What is the rush on this?"

"Beats me, Jack," Stumbo replied airily. "I'm just passing on the order."

Jack could feel his face flushing and his pulse beginning to race. The department, it seemed, cared about everything but good police work.

"Fine, Doyle. I'll go to Hensley's goddamn office for the goddamn interview. But don't say one goddamn word to me about goddamn late reports."

"You don't have to get huffy," Stumbo replied. McNaughton walked out, slamming the door behind him.

As he drove home that evening, Jack remembered that, in the rush of activity during the Peterson trial, he had forgotten to tell Renee about the Trueblood I-number.

"Well, I think it's bullshit," Renee said, a little too loudly, when he told her about it that evening. Angel, who never failed to miss a thing her parents were saying – unless it was an order addressed directly to her – was playing with her baby doll in the family room. Jack and Renee were in the kitchen, making a chicken-and-spinach pasta dish together.

Renee gulped down the last sip of wine that had remained in her glass, went to the refrigerator and poured more. She held up the bottle toward Jack, a question mark on her face, and he slid his almost-empty glass so she could pour more for him.

"God, that pisses me off," Renee said angrily. She usually got more incensed about the injustices of the system than Jack did. Or perhaps it was just that she was better about expressing it. In any case, it was one explanation for why Renee was relatively healthy, while Jack frequently had a deep gnawing at his gut that he instinctively knew – but was reluctant to confirm – was the precursor of an ulcer.

"So how are we going to fight it?" Renee, ever the fighter, said. "This is bogus, and they know it. They're just afraid that Trueblood'll go to the papers and give 'em another chance to knock on you guys. But from what you said about him, I have a hard time believing that anybody – even the TV geeks – would buy into that bullshit."

McNaughton sat at the kitchen table, rubbing his forehead with his left hand. "Jack," Renee said as she pulled out a chair to join him. She recognized that her anger, righteous as it was, wasn't helping Jack, and her tone changed. "I'm worried about you, honey. You've got too much going on – with the Peterson verdict and the I-number and just being back at work with that idiot DC-10."

"Oh, yeah. I forgot to tell you about Donnie Crawford." He proceeded to tell the story, one more thing for Renee to worry about. She spoke: "Maybe you ought to talk to somebody, honey. You know, a therapist."

"I'm not crazy, Renee," McNaughton said flatly.

"Jack, you know you don't have to be Donnie Crawford to see a therapist – or to be helped by a therapist. It's just somebody who'll listen."

He stood up and moved behind her chair, leaning over and embracing her from behind. "I've got you to listen to me," he said warmly.

"You know I'll always be here for you, baby," she said, turning to look into his eyes and taking his face into her hands. "But sometimes that's not enough."

Renee groaned when the alarm went off at five-thirty a.m. Wednesday, but Jack knew it would be a good day. Not only would he get his fifteen minutes with Senator Woolums, but it was Angel's fifth birthday. Jack showered while Renee got on the treadmill, walking briskly for thirty minutes. Then she showered and dried her hair before awakening Angel. Jack prepared the girl's breakfast on a tray and brought it upstairs to his and Renee's bedroom. That way, Angel could watch "Sesame Street" and eat breakfast in bed, allowing her parents to get ready for work with some semblance of peace. This morning, he inserted a single candle in the top of her lemon poppy seed muffin and lit it.

"Happy birthday, doll!" he said happily when he spied her on the bed. He held out the tray to present it to her.

"Daddy," Angelica scolded indignantly. "I'm five, not one."

"Well, I'm sure we'll find four more candles to put on your cake this evening, OK?"

She nodded animatedly and hugged her father before being distracted by Grover, the bombastic blue monster who never failed to delight father or daughter.

After he had tied his tie and donned his sports coat, McNaughton called in to remind Stumbo of his early appointment with the senator. The previous day, after cooling off from the confrontation over the Trueblood complaint, Jack had told Stumbo of his plan to meet with her and pursue a change in the insanity-defense law. He loathed having to clear such a thing with Doyle, who did not take well to the notion of change, but he also knew that Stumbo would go berserk if he didn't clear this through channels. Stumbo had seemed distracted when Jack told him of his plans, so McNaughton offered to call the higher-ups to get their clearance. Stumbo agreed, and McNaughton found the captain surprisingly amenable to the idea. "Go for it," Ryan had said. "I'll get Captain Hensley to hold off on the Trueblood I-number for a few days."

"Does that mean I can testify before the legislative committee?" McNaughton asked.

"Absolutely."

So McNaughton was feeling good as he bounded up the Statehouse steps two at a time. Stumbo had been on the phone when he called in, so Jack left word with Carla, one of the division's secretaries, thereby avoiding the inevitable hassle that Stumbo would have created.

After an inordinately slow elevator ride to the third floor, Jack found the Senate chambers and was greeted by an exquisite-looking black woman with close-cropped hair and Kente-cloth garb. The plaque on her desk indicated her name was Wanda Christmas, and the decorations that festooned her environs indicated she took her surname seriously. She called up to Woolums' desk to announce McNaughton's arrival, then turned her gaze back to him: "You can go right up, Sergeant," she said warmly, pointing to the narrow staircase behind her desk.

Jack mounted the stairs, and found himself in a maze of desks and office dividers. Suddenly, an attractive white woman in her mid-fifties and wearing a hot pink business suit appeared. "You must be Sergeant McNaughton," she said, offering her hand. "I'm Kim Woolums."

She shook Jack's hand firmly and then gestured for him to follow her. "My desk is this way," she said, turning to lead him there. Her straight, jet black hair was cut in a side-parted boyish style, with a few loose pieces falling onto her forehead. She had large, dark eyes, a small nose and chin, and just enough lines in her face to prove that she'd been around the block.

When they reached her tiny cubicle – one of a dozen or so that were assigned to senators in this particular room – she pulled out the lone chair that she had for visitors. "Have a seat," she said as she squeezed around the desk and took her own.

"Larry – that's my legislative assistant with whom you spoke – tells me you have an interesting idea about the insanity defense. I had him pull some newspaper clippings about the Peterson case, and I must tell you I'm very disturbed by what transpired. I mean, if the man is insane, he needs help. But it bothers me that he'll never pay for what he's done to those beautiful children."

"Exactly, senator," Jack said. He felt remarkably calm; she had a way about her that immediately put people at ease. "I'm also disturbed, and I don't believe for a minute that John Pius Peterson is insane," he said. "I think that he's as sane as you and I are, that he planned to kill his children to punish his wife and that he's a very clever man who got away with murder."

"Well, let's figure out a way to make sure that never happens again."

Their fifteen-minute meeting stretched to forty-five, with Woolums taking copious notes as McNaughton talked. Although she was not a lawyer – she was, in fact, a high school English teacher when the part-time citizens' legislature wasn't in session – she was familiar with a lot of criminal law, and that made it easier for Jack to explain the situation. Finally, they mapped out what they thought would be the best approach to take.

"Now, you know that the Legislative Services Agency will be drafting the bill, and the staff attorneys there will be able to tell us if what we want to do can be done," the senator said.

"That's fine; I'm not a lawyer either, so obviously I'll defer to their judgment."

"But I think we've made a fine start, Jack," she said.

"Thank you so much, senator," McNaughton said, making moves to begin his departure.

"Jack, if we're going to work together, you'd better call me Kim." Jack nodded and, just then, his cell phone rang.

"I'm so sorry," he said.

"No, that's fine," she said. "Go ahead and answer it."

"Thanks," he said as he looked at the screen. "It's one of my detectives. I'll just be a minute."

Kit Alvear was calling. "Hi. What's up?" he asked.

"We've got another nut case. Two decapitated and dismembered and left out for the trash man at 2180 North Hycliffe Avenue. Victims apparently were residents of the house, a mother and one of her sons. I've got a uniform sitting with the other son, but I think you should be here before we start talking to him. He's talking kind of crazy, but apparently was together enough to tell the garbage man that the bodies were mannequins. Can you come?"

"I'm on my way." He hung up the phone and remained silent for a brief moment. "Senator – uh, Kim – I have to go to the scene of a double homicide. It sounds pretty grisly, but my detective tells me it's an unusual case and I've seen too many of this kind not to suspect that the defendant will end up claiming insanity. I know you're a busy person, but would you want to come out to the scene with me, and hear what this man has to say for himself?"

Woolums looked over her calendar. "Let me get Larry to reschedule another appointment I have. I don't have any committee meetings today – I had just planned to catch up on some paperwork – so I think the rest of the day is clear. Let's go."

Everybody was always up to their eyebrows in paperwork, Jack thought, smiling grimly. He and Woolums headed out, stopping briefly at Larry's desk so she could tell him of her change in plans and then momentarily at Woolums' car, where she doffed her high heels and donned white crew socks and walking shoes.

McNaughton, grateful that a meter-patrol officer hadn't spotted the "violation" flag at his parking spot on New York Street, pulled out cautiously and radioed in that he was back on the air. "Thirty-four, thirty-eight, be advised," the dispatcher said, "we have a double ten-zero at 2180 North Hycliffe Avenue."

"Clear. I'm en route," McNaughton said into the mouthpiece as he turned a smooth, one-handed left turn to head north from downtown. It took fewer than ten minutes to reach the scene, where several uniforms were clustered around what appeared to be the not-yet-collected garbage left outside the small house. A small crowd of gapers gathered on the opposite curb, as close as one of the uniforms would let them get.

Kit was leaning over, poking something among the green-plastic trash bags with a pen when she glanced up and saw McNaughton and Woolums getting out of his car. She stopped and met them as he approached.

"Kit, this is Senator Kim Woolums. Senator, Kit Alvear, my best detective."

The women shook hands and exchanged pleasantries, although their tone was grim. Alvear then turned immediately to Jack.

"We think our dead are Lola Snuff and her son, Hector. Son number two is Homer, who is mostly muttering weird stuff. The neighbor lady over there gave us the names of the residents, but we haven't asked her to ID the heads – we thought that a bit much. My guess is that old Homer got pissed at mom and bro, cut 'em up and put 'em out for the trash."

Woolums flinched and grimaced as she listened, but stayed silent.

"How'd we find them?" Jack asked.

"Well," Kit said, "it seems that there were some body parts here and there – there's no indication that they had been put in trash bags – and several of the neighbors took a gander. A man over there – Hank Newland – lives down the street and passed here on his way to Mass this morning, and then again on his way home. He says he thought they were parts of a broken statue like the ones in front of church."

McNaughton raised his eyebrows and shot a skeptical look at Kit, who returned it. She continued: "You may want to see Alma Folsom, the woman who lives across the street, for yourself."

"OK, let's do that before we see Homer," McNaughton said.

He and Woolums followed as Kit led them to Folsom, a short, round woman with short, poufy white hair. She was dressed in a pink cotton housecoat and dirty white terry-cloth scuffs. Kit made the introductions, and asked Folsom to tell her story to McNaughton.

"Well, I just *never* dreamed they were real people – I mean, the Snuffs," Folsom drawled. "Well, the Snuffs are real, but I didn't realize that was them!" She had a thick southern accent, not unusual in Indianapolis, where many southern emigrants had settled. "I just cannot believe it." She appeared close to tears.

"I realize this is very traumatic, Mrs. Folsom," Jack said, "but it's important that I learn as much about the situation as I can."

After that, the tears vanished and there was no stopping her. "I just happened to be looking out my front winda this morning – I live over there," she said, pointing toward her small Cape Cod – "when I thought I saw somethin' flesh-colored under the Snuffs' garbage bags." Kit tried to hide a smirk; Mrs. Folsom, the quintessential busybody, "just happened" to be peaking out at her neighbors.

She continued, seemingly without taking breaths between sentences. "So I came over. I mean, I didn't want to butt into the Snuffs' bidness, but I thought that Miz Snuff oughta know that there was something flesh-colored in her garbage. I mean, *I'd* want to know. I know that I was glad when the paper boy told me that some animal – a coon or dog or somethin' – had got into my garbage bags some months back. I mean, it made such a mess, and that boy not only told me but helped me clean it up before the garbage men got here. I 'preciated that. So anyways, I came over here but before I went to the door, I wanted to make sure I knew what I was talking about so I just took a look under the bags and saw those mannequins – or I thought they was mannequins. I mean, they just wasn't bloody enough to be dead bodies, I didn't think. But then I got to thinkin', Miz Snuff probably would think I was snoopin' in her garbage, and I didn't want her mad at me. We've always been friends, Miz Snuff and me. Got along real good, exchanging recipes and cups of sugar and that sort of thing. So I went back home. I kept watching for the garbage man, 'cause I wanted to warn him not to be alarmed at those mannequins. And ya know what? I saw at least three cars slow down, real slow-like, in front of the Snuffs' house, with the drivers just a-gaping. And they musta thought they was mannequins too – otherwise they'd a-stopped. Don't ya think?

"So I got to thinkin' maybe Miz Snuff would be unhappy that ever-body was gaping at her dummies. So I changed my mind and went on over there and knocked on the door. And Homer – he's the weird one, ya know – well, he answered the door and I says, 'Homer, why do you have them dummies out there at the curb? Ever-body's gaping, and it's gonna upset your mama.' And he says he put 'em out there 'cause he was mad at her. Said that he had got them for her to use for her sewin' but that she wasn't gonna be doing any more of that. Well, I thought that was odd, 'cause Miz Snuff was pretty handy with the needle. But I didn't want to upset Homer, so I just says 'I think you should put them out in some plastic bags at least.'

"Then I went back home and kept watchin' and do you know that boy never came outside to put them dummies in plastic bags? I guess he really was mad at his mama."

Jack interrupted. "I'm not sure I follow you, Mrs. Folsom."

"Well, I mean, Miz Snuff and Hector are dead, aren't they? And who's not? Why, Homer. And I don't mind telling you that he has been a regular resident of Jonathan Jennings mental hospital, if you know what I mean. Oh, poor Miz Snuff."

Her voice broke, but it did not deter her. She began to speak again, but Jack interrupted. "Mrs. Folsom, do you know how recently Homer was a resident of the hospital?"

"Well, he got out just about a week ago, I believe. And I don't mind telling you that I have heard more than one fight between him and his mama ever since he came back."

"Could you hear specific words? Do you have any idea what they fought over?"

"No, I don't believe I could say. I'd just happen to be lookin' out my front winda, and I'd see Homer stormin' out of the house, his arms just a-flailin' and him turnin' back and yellin' at his mama. It's just been too cold to have the windas open, so I couldn't tell what he was sayin'."

"OK, Mrs. Folsom. Thank you for your help," McNaughton said.

"Well, I didn't mind at all. Ya know, I did feel kind of silly that I thought they was mannequins, but I'm not the only one. When the garbage men finally came – an hour late, I might add; can you tell the mayor 'bout that? Well, anyways, I told them not to worry about them dummies. They didn't seem to be too worried. But I guess that's why you-all were called, wasn't it?"

"Yes, ma'am," Jack said. "Thanks again." He stopped her by turning and ushering the senator with a hand on the back of her arm. Woolums shot McNaughton a look of horror and disbelief; he raised his eyebrows in a silent response. They again followed Alvear, who led them to Roger Renfro, the garbage man who had called the police. He was tall and mahogany-skinned and wore a worn flannel shirt open over an insulated, long-sleeved under-shirt, but no coat. Again, Kit made the introductions and asked Renfro to recount his story.

"Tony was driving and me and Sid were picking up the trash," he began. "When we got to 2180, this little ol' lady came running across the street, shouting at us not to be afraid of the mannequins that had been set out for the trash. I took one look at those things and I didn't think they were no dummies. They looked too real to me. I've seen dead people before – you know, at the funeral home and such – and they looked awful suspicious.

"So I said to Sid, 'Tell Tony to hold on; I'm gonna talk to the people who live here.' I went up to the door and this guy comes out and I asked him about the dummies. He says they were mannequins that he got at the medical school – the med students use them to practice so they gotta look lifelike. Anyway, he got them for a Halloween gag and put ketchup all over them to scare the neighborhood kids. But they got to stinking, so he decided to get rid of them. I said OK, but I still didn't feel real good about this, and neither did Tony and Sid. So we called you guys."

"Thanks, Mr. Renfro. We appreciate it. We'll be back in touch," Jack said as he and Woolums turned away and began walking toward the front door. Kit stayed behind to explain how he'd be needed as a witness and to get his personal information. She soon caught up with McNaughton and Woolums, and the threesome went up to the stoop of the red-brick bungalow.

Jack knocked, and then entered through the arched wooden door.

"Mr. Snuff, this is Sergeant McNaughton, the officer I mentioned to you," Kit said to son number two. The uniform who had been watching him, a pimply-faced, gangly kid who couldn't have more than a year or two on the department, stood and silently departed.

It was a 1940s-style house, with the living room to the immediate right of the tiny foyer. The couch and the matching easy chair were made of floral-patterned green velour, the type you'd see in an old mobile home. On the wall behind the couch hung a large reproduction of Rembrandt's "The Last Supper" on black velvet. A wooden rocker sat opposite the arm chair, and a sewing basket was placed on the floor next to it. A big television – forty-two inches at least, McNaughton guessed – sat atop a credenza, dominating the room. Kit couldn't take her eyes off the "artwork" closest to the arm chair: A garish, black velvet rendition of Elvis Presley, complete with a silver teardrop – or was it sweat? – running down his face.

Homer Snuff was short and bulky, a bullet of a man who appeared to be in his late thirties. Although he remained seated on the couch when they arrived, Jack figured he couldn't have been more than five-foot-six. His greying hair, once black, badly needed a cut. It had a funny wave that ran the full length, front to crown, of his side part, causing the front part to dip down onto his forehead. McNaughton imagined that had been a source of self-esteem problems during Homer's teen years. Snuff's round face, with its full, reddened cheeks, was clean-shaven, almost as if he had prepared for their visit. He sat muttering unintelligible words, holding a conversation with himself, but looked directly at Jack when the police officer spoke.

"Mr. Snuff," Jack began, "I'm Sergeant McNaughton from Metro-Marion Police. Is it all right if we come in?"

"Well, yes, I guess so."

"We'd like to talk with you, Mr. Snuff," Jack said. "Are your mother and brother here?"

"No," he muttered. His hands were folded, prayer-like, in front of him and he leaned his elbows on his knees, which were crossed pretzel-style. He stared at the damaged parquet floor when he spoke.

"Do you know where they are?"

"Well, Mrs. Folsom said that they're dead. I just don't know anything about that."

"You don't? Do you know how their bodies got out there with the trash?"

"No. I wouldn't know anything about that."

"Mr. Snuff, did you have any problems with your mother?"

"No. I love my mother," he said quietly, still staring at the floor.

"Yes, I'm sure you do, Mr. Snuff. But, I mean, here you are, a young man having to live with his mother. I'm sure there had to be tensions."

"Yes, of course. But nothing extraordinary. My mother is very good to me, and I to her."

"C'mon, Mr. Snuff. Surely she did things that irritated you, prevented you from living the kind of life a man of your age would like to live."

"Sometimes she says I have no business going out at night, and she says I'd better not be seeing any women or going to any bars. And sometimes she gets on me for leaving my razor out after I shave." Jack detected just the slightest edge in his voice as he recounted his troubles.

"She complains when I read the newspaper first – says that she's been the one to unfold it for forty-five years, and that's how she intends to keep it. And she doesn't like it if I forget to make my bed. Or if I don't change my towels often enough. Or if I forget to feed the freakin' cat. Or if I don't clear the table after dinner."

He was becoming more exercised, but then stopped abruptly. "But that doesn't mean I don't love her."

"Mr. Snuff," Jack said calmly, "why don't you tell us what happened?"

"I don't know what happened."

"Let me tell you what *I* think happened," McNaughton offered. "I think that your mother had been nagging you and getting on your case and making your life miserable, and this morning she was doing it again. And something she said just really got to you, and you hauled off and slugged her. And she fell, and she hit her head, and you realized that something awful had happened, and you had to do whatever it took to make sure nobody found out. Am I right?"

"Not exactly," Homer said in a near whisper, still staring at the scratches in the hardwood.

"Well, then, you tell me how it really happened."

"She just was nagging me and nagging me and nagging me and I could *not* take one more minute of it!" Homer said, his voice louder now. "But I didn't hit her. I would never hit my mother. All I did was try to make her shut up. I just put my hand over her mouth and told her to shut up. She kept struggling against my hand, and still trying to talk all the while. *Finally*, she shut up, so I let her go, and she fell to the floor. I tried to wake her up, but she wouldn't come to. And then Hector came downstairs and saw Mother, and he got extremely upset. Started shouting at me, 'What have you done? What have you done?' I tried to explain it to him and I tried to calm him down, but he just wouldn't stop screaming at me. So I put my hand over his mouth too. And after he shut up, well, he fell down too."

"Did you realize they were dead?" McNaughton asked.

"After a little while, I did. I knew that wasn't good. I knew that might land me back at Jonathan Jennings and I *hate* that place. So I took them upstairs to the bathroom, so there wouldn't be such a mess to clean up, and I took care of them. Just chopped them up a bit so they wouldn't be so hard to handle."

"Strong little fucker," Kit muttered to herself.

"Mr. Snuff, I think you know we're going to have to arrest you and charge you in this case," Jack said. "I'm going to ask Detective Alvear here to read you your rights and to take you down to the stationhouse. All right?"

"Yes, sir, Sergeant McNaughton. Thank you, sir."

McNaughton stood and signaled for Woolums to join him as he left the home. "Oh, my God, he's *insane*," Woolums said in horror when they got outside and the door was closed behind them.

"Senator – Kim – that's exactly why I wanted you to come along with me. Yes, he's insane – to you, to me, to the average person. We all figure you'd have to be crazy to do the kind of things he just admitted doing. But he's not insane – at least not legally so."

"What do you mean?"

"Oh, I'm sure he'll use the insanity defense, and it may work. He's loonier than anything that lands on the White River, believe me. But you heard how he first denied having anything to do with the deaths. And you heard from the neighbor woman and from the garbage man how he told two different stories about where he had gotten his 'mannequins.' And then you heard him describe how he tried to cover up his actions. That means he knew what he had done was wrong. And if you know the difference between right and wrong, you're legally sane. Homer Snuff is a fruitcake, but he knew what he was doing was wrong. He should be convicted of two counts of murder."

"Do you think he will be?"

"I don't know," Jack said thoughtfully. "I don't predict those things anymore – not after a lot of the cases I've seen and especially not since Peterson. Under the present law, Homer may be going back to Jonathan Jennings for a while, but he may never see the inside of the state prison."

"That's a travesty," Woolums said. She set her jaw, and then spoke with resolve: "Homer Snuff may not be headed for Michigan City, but we're going to make sure that future Homer Snuffs will be."

CHAPTER 12

Jack was fiddling with the fire when Renee came downstairs from putting Angel to bed. The reddish-orange flames licked hungrily against the black iron walls of the fireplace insert, pushing super-heated air out of the vents. That was just the way Renee liked it. She retrieved her glass of wine from the kitchen table, where she had left it to tend to her daughter, and sat on the floor at the hearth.

"How'd she do?" Jack asked, taking a sip of his wine.

"Oh, fine. A little restless, but she and Arielle are fast asleep now." She was referring to Angel's favorite stuffed manatee.

They sat in silence for a while, watching the exotic flames contort themselves behind the glass-windowed door. Renee was perpetually chilled – a trait that prompted plenty of jokes about her being a cold-blooded reporter – and she loved to sit in front of the fireplace to warm herself. It was early January, and frigid winter had settled on Indianapolis. A fire had become a nightly routine at the Somers-McNaughton house since Christmas, after all the hubbub of the holidays had settled down and life returned to normal. Jack and Renee had told Angelica that they had arranged for Santa Claus to come a day early, allowing the little one a whole day to play with the new toys she opened Christmas Eve morning. The adults rose at an obscene hour Christmas morning and packed up Renee's Volvo for the trip to Chicago, where her burgeoning family would gather at her parents' house. Jack carried the sleeping Angel and buckled her into her car seat in the back, and then they were off before sunrise. The strenuous schedule accommodated Renee's love of the pre-dawn drive on Christmas, when the colorful lights reflected on the white sheets of snow that had drifted across Indiana's farm fields and Jack and Renee sang sweet carols to put the drifting Angel back to sleep.

They both had taken a few days off around Christmas, and spent them around the house, reading and puttering, or at The Children's Museum, where Angel never tired of the dinosaurs and Wenuhotep, the mummy. But then the magic of the holiday waned, and it was back to work and day care for the family.

Renee turned from the fire and looked at Jack lovingly. "You're nervous," she said. He pinched his lips and cocked his head, gazing at her through the corners of his eyes. "Yeah, I am."

"Don't be, babe. I know that's easy for me to say, but you've talked in front of a lot of groups. And Kim has arranged everything so that this should be easy."

"I know, honey. I've just never spoken before a bunch of senators."

Renee laughed. "Geez, Jack, you act as if they're people or something."

"C'mon, honey. I'm serious."

"OK. I really do understand. But these people are not really all that intimidating. I mean, Sherman picks his nose."

"Great. Now, every time I look at him, I'm going to expect him to do that."

"Good!" Renee responded enthusiastically. "That's the idea. Remember, just imagine every one of them is sitting there, around the committee table, wearing only underwear. You can imagine Sherman is wearing his underwear *and* picking his nose. And then it won't be so hard to talk."

"No – it'll be impossible 'cause I'll be laughing so hard."

He laughed again and pulled her to him, giving her a long, hard kiss. They stopped long enough to turn and carefully set their wine glasses out of the way, and then resumed their kissing. Jack reached up under Renee's sweatshirt and began to massage her breasts, and she moved to unbutton his jeans. "Oh, great," she whispered in between kisses. "Now you're going to be thinking of *this* tomorrow when you testify."

"I can't think of anything that would relax me more," he murmured, returning to the task at hand.

They made love on the floor in front of the fireplace, stopping only to readjust and get comfortable from time to time. It wasn't like the movies, that was for sure. Bad backs and hard floors and a nosy cat ensured that nothing went quite as smoothly as those passionate scenes on film. But familiarity and love ensured that it was, in fact, better.

When they were spent, they held each other tightly and watched the fire for a while, Renee's head snuggled deep into the bend between Jack's cheek and shoulder. Then they went upstairs to their bed, and their lovemaking served as a relaxant for Jack, putting him fast asleep. Renee read a few pages in the Pat Conroy novel she was reading and, although it was too good to put down, she turned out the light when she considered that it was just five hours until the alarm would sound.

The Senate Judiciary Committee was scheduled to meet at nine a.m. Jack had arranged to meet Senator Woolums at her desk at eight-forty-five. He felt a sting of excitement that he was about to do something good, something that could make a difference. But his stomach betrayed his confidence, and he worried that it might get vocal once he was ensconced in the committee room. He popped a couple of Tums.

Jack listened intently as Woolums explained the committee's procedures and protocol. It was all pretty straight forward, mostly a function of common sense and common courtesy. But he felt more confident if he knew exactly what he was about to face. With less time than Jack would have allowed, he and the senator started their circuitous journey from her cubicle on the half-story above the fourth floor to the basement of the Statehouse, where the committee would be meeting. Surely they'd be inexcusably late, he worried. But when they arrived, only one other senator had taken a seat at the rectangular committee table, although the audience chairs were mostly filled. Woolums noticed Jack's surprise.

"That's legislative time for you," she explained. "Everything runs twenty minutes late."

Her aide, Larry, had come to the committee room early to save front-row seats for the senator and Jack, and he rose as soon as he spotted them. Jack could tell that the people on either side of him and Kim were newspaper reporters; both had those skinny, lined notebooks that only reporters – and cops – carry. And they looked nonchalant, even bored, with what was about to happen; recalling the way Renee had described things, they likely had spent way too many hours waiting for action in the legislature. Two television cameramen had set up their massive equipment near the committee table, making Jack nervous that they might soon be aiming their lenses at him. He tried not to think about that.

The committee chairman, Senator Sam Pushkins, finally arrived and flipped through papers while waiting for a quorum of members to arrive. That eventually happened, but not until about twenty-five minutes past the posted start time. Everybody in the room seemed to be used to this "legislative time" that Kim had talked about, although the reporter to Jack's right impatiently beat out a rhythm with her pen against her notebook and glanced at her watch every five minutes or so.

The committee took up two other bills, obviously less controversial, before Pushkins announced it was time for Senate Bill 358 to be heard. There was a rustling as reporters perked up, lobbyists sat up in their chairs and likely witnesses began straightening their clothes to make their best appearance.

"Senator Woolums? Will you please describe your bill for us?" Pushkins asked. Woolums rose and began.

"Senator Pushkins, fellow senators, ladies and gentlemen. I wish Senate Bill 358 were not needed. Because if it were not, that would mean that justice had prevailed in some of this state's most heinous crimes, that people who had committed horrendous, unspeakable acts would be punished justly for having done so, that we could go to sleep tonight knowing that those who would prey on our most innocent and helpless members of society – our children, our elderly – would not be free to perpetrate their horrors because of some quirk in the law.

"But that is not so, and that is why Senate Bill 358 is needed. Can you imagine the horror of a father killing his six children? Or of a son murdering his loving mother? It's hard to imagine, I know, that there could be such violations of the most basic relationships of our society. That's something I've had to deal with. But these things happen, all too often.

"I'm not suggesting that Senate Bill 358 is the cure-all to stop such heinous crimes from occurring. But I will tell you that, if you pass Senate Bill 358, you can rest assured that people who commit such crimes will be punished. They will not go free to repeat their terrible crimes.

"Under the current law, there's a huge chance that they *will* go free. After all, wouldn't one *have* to be crazy to beat his own children to death? And wouldn't one *have* to be crazy to kill his own mother, the woman who had given her life – now both figuratively and literally – for her son? Well, yes, in the general sense, in the way you and I talk. But these people usually *aren't* insane in the legal sense. They know the difference between right and wrong, and that, in a nutshell, determines if someone is legally insane or not. But that's a difficult concept to grasp. And the good men and women who sit on juries in our state, well-intentioned as they are, sometimes have difficulty differentiating between their layman's definition of crazy and the legal term 'insanity.'

"Consequently, we find that all too many juries are letting those who have committed horrible crimes off the hook. The juries don't want to convict someone who is insane, and thus not responsible for his or her actions. And so they acquit, much more often than they should.

"Senate Bill 358 would change that. It would give Indiana juries another option, just like juries in almost every other state already have. Instead of deciding that a defendant is either sane and thus guilty or insane and thus not guilty, our juries would have a third option: Guilty but mentally ill. It would allow juries to register their firm beliefs that a defendant was not thinking rationally when he or she committed a crime, but to nevertheless hold that defendant responsible for his or her heinous actions.

"In the name of those six innocent children, in the name of that loving mother, I ask you to vote 'yes' on Senate Bill 358. Thank you."

There was silence for a moment, and then Pushkins spoke. "Senator, will you please introduce your witnesses?"

"Certainly, Senator Pushkins. I'd like to introduce Sergeant Jack McNaughton of the Metro-Marion Police Department. Jack?"

McNaughton rose from the hard folding chair and felt his muscles stretch. "Ladies and gentlemen," he began. "I've been a homicide detective or supervisor in that division for about ten years. And in that time, I've seen more miscarriages of justice than I would have thought possible. There are times when police officers know who has committed a crime, but just can't find the evidence to prove it beyond a reasonable doubt. And there are times when it's a close call that you know can go either way. Both of those situations are tough on police officers, who live to put bad guys away.

"But there is nothing worse – *nothing* – than seeing someone you *know* is guilty of a horrible crime – and you have the evidence on him – but he still walks out of a courtroom scot-free because a jury thought he must have been crazy to do such a crazy thing. I've watched that happen too many times.

"Usually, a judge will stick somebody who's been found not guilty by reason of insanity in a mental hospital for a while. But he can't hold him there; as soon as the doctors at the hospital decide the guy is sane, he can walk out. And believe me, that happens a lot sooner than you might imagine. I've seen people who've killed several people get out in less than a year. Just the other day, I learned that a defendant who had stabbed a woman who had picked him up hitchhiking, and – pardon me for this – then repeatedly had sex with her corpse, got out of the mental hospital in less than seven years. Meanwhile, there are other defendants, found guilty of doing about the same thing, who are on death row.

"'Guilty but mentally ill' is a workable, fair verdict. There's a common law concept known as the M'Naghten Rule – yes, not so very far off my name, is it? – that tells us that we don't want to imprison someone who is insane and not responsible for his actions. And an acquittal of someone like that is appropriate, and always will be. But too many defendants are getting off because their crimes – often the worst, most heinous, goriest, most sickening crimes we see – are so horrible that jurors can't imagine the perpetrator wasn't insane. Juries seem to think that a defendant who has shot somebody dead with a gun has committed murder, but one who has sliced up or disfigured or mutilated his victim or victims has acted so horrendously that he can't possibly be responsible for his actions. The upshot is that some of the most heinous crimes are going unpunished. A 'guilty but mentally ill' verdict would give them the option of expressing the belief that the defendant is crazy, for lack of a better term, but still holding him or her responsible.

"In all these years in homicide, I've seen more dead faces than I ever thought imaginable. You never get used to it, but sometimes it's perilously close to becoming routine. Other times, the carnage I witness is unforgettable. I dream about the faces of innocent victims whose lives ended so violently, no needlessly and ultimately, so much in vain. And there's nothing worse than knowing that, in the end, the system let them down. Their killers are walking free as you and me.

"Maybe if you pass Senate Bill 358, that won't happen quite as often. Maybe some of those victims can rest a little easier.

"That's all I have to say, but I'll be happy to answer any questions you may have."

"Thank you, Sergeant McNaughton," Pushkins said. "Questions, anybody?"

The committee members sat in awkward silence; the crowded committee room was eerily quiet. McNaughton had said it all.

After a few moments, Pushkins broke the silence. "Well, thank you, Sergeant McNaughton. I don't think we have any questions, but I hope you'll be available to the committee members should something arise."

"Of course, Senator," Jack said. "Here are some business cards," he added, leaning to place a thin stack on the committee table. "Any of you are welcome to call me for information at any time." Then he turned and sat back in his front-row seat.

Survivors of several victims whose killers had gotten off on insanity pleas testified next, followed by those who opposed the bill. They were primarily people in the mental-health field, who feared that, if the law were changed, genuinely insane people would be held accountable for acts over which they had no control. But their general appeals lacked the emotional punch that first-hand experience and poignant testimony from Jack and the survivors had had. Finally, an hour and forty-five minutes after Woolums first described the bill, Pushkins asked if she wanted to close the discussion.

"Just one thought, Senator," Kim said as she stepped forward toward the committee table. "Please think about the victims, the innocent victims, whose lives are cut short and then are denied justice in death. Please vote 'yes' on Senate Bill 358."

"Do I hear a motion?" Pushkins asked.

"I move Senate Bill 358 do pass," a Hispanic committee member, whose shiny black hair swooped down onto his forehead, said.

"Second," responded a middle-aged, balding white member.

"Discussion?" Pushkins asked. No one spoke.

"Seeing none, take the roll, please," the chairman said to the committee staffer. She began: "Senator Abrams?"

An elderly white man, whose mustache was neatly trimmed above his lip, responded: "Yes."

"Senator Efrem?"

"Yes," said a chunky woman wearing a royal blue suit.

"Senator Gonzalez?"

"Aye." It was the senator who had made the motion.

"Senator Hollings?"

"No," a bespectacled, forties-ish man said.

"Senator Nelson?"

"Yes." He had seconded the motion.

"Senator Ostrowski?"

"No."

"Senator Raphael?"

"Yes."

"Senator Zimmerman?"

"No."

"Chairman Pushkins?"

"Yes."

The staffer leaned close and whispered to Pushkins, who announced the vote. "Six to three. The committee recommends Senate Bill 358 'do pass.' The meeting is adjourned."

Woolums rose and hugged Jack, who bit his lip to stop himself from breaking into a huge smile. "It's only a first step," Woolums said, "but an important one. I'll need you to come back and testify again, at least one more time, when the bill moves over to the House. And I'll need you to be available to talk to individual legislators who are balking at supporting us, OK?"

"Absolutely, Kim," Jack said joyously. "I'll do whatever I can."

"That's all I need to hear," she said, patting him on his shoulder. "You make a marvelous witness."

"Thank my wife for that," he said. Woolums was about to ask for an explanation when a middle-aged man with a notebook approached Jack.

"Hi, Kim," he said, then turned to Jack. "Sergeant McNaughton?" the man asked. He stuck out his hand as he said, "I'm Andy Policinski, a columnist for the Sun. I know Renee."

"Yeah, she's mentioned you," Jack said, turning to shake Policinski's hand. "I'm surprised we've never run into each other before."

"Yeah, I know. Anyway, I'd like to talk with you about SB 358. If you have a few minutes."

"Now?" Jack asked. Policinski nodded. "OK. Where do you want to do this?"

"How about going over to the cafeteria in the state office building? I'll buy you a cup of coffee – or what they purport to be coffee."

"Sounds good," McNaughton said. "Anything with caffeine would be welcomed right now. Kim, do you want to join us?"

"No, Jack. I've got to get to another committee meeting. Andy knows where to reach me if he has to."

"Right, Kim. In fact, I'll call you this afternoon, OK?" Policinski said.

Woolums suggested he call around two-thirty, and McNaughton and the reporter made their way to the state office building, the first of two giant annexes that the state had built when it outgrew the Statehouse. A tunnel allowed them to get there without enduring the elements, no small benefit in Indianapolis in January. Jack could see where water had seeped into the tunnel, staining the wall and the grey carpet that had also been worn in a strip down the middle by thousands of shoe soles.

It was just a little after eleven when they reached the cafeteria, so they beat the lunch crowd. Both Jack and Policinski got cups of black coffee – Policinski bought – and they sat down at a long table that was pushed against the wall. Jack noticed a sticky spot, and he moved one place over before settling in.

Policinski was about the same age as Jack but slightly heavier. He had thick brown hair that showed the slightest grey tinge at the temples, but had not yet begun to turn on top. His nose – a hawk-like beak – was the most prominent feature on his face, unfortunately dominating his kind, brown eyes that drooped on the sides and were outlined by long lashes.

The columnist took copious notes in one of those long, narrow notebooks. His scrawl was every bit as unintelligible as Renee's, a curse of the reporting profession, Jack thought. Policinski looked directly into McNaughton's eyes as they spoke. Jack liked that; it bothered him when people gazed at the floor or at some point in space when they were talking. It always made him wonder what – or from whom – they were trying to hide.

They talked for forty-five minutes, Policinski asking McNaughton how the "guilty but mentally ill" law would work, what the chances were of getting it passed and why he thought it necessary. The columnist seemed genuinely interested, and not the slightest bit bored, as Jack explained some of the more mundane parts of police work. It was obvious to McNaughton that Policinski was good at his job, or at least this part of it.

McNaughton had read his column many times, and found it to be insightful and interesting, if a little conservative for Jack's – and especially Renee's – taste. Sometimes Policinski was compassionate and sometimes, especially in the case of politicians, he was wittily sarcastic. Jack hoped he wouldn't be the victim of the latter, but Policinski's demeanor put him at ease and left him no reason for him to think he'd be burned.

"So when do you expect this'll run?" Jack asked as they stood up simultaneously and each began taking his jacket from the back of his chair.

"Tomorrow," Policinski said. "I write three columns a week, and I've got one due this afternoon."

Jack nodded. A lot of people marveled at how reporters could attend a hearing in the morning and turn it into a story or column that afternoon. But Jack was used to the way Renee worked, so he registered no surprise.

"Great," he said. "I'll look forward to reading it."

"Yeah. Hey, thanks a lot, Jack. Good meeting you."

"Same here."

After he left the Statehouse, McNaughton went through Arby's drive-through for a large roast beef sandwich and a large diet Coke, which he took back to the office. As he waited in line, he had remembered all the paperwork that awaited him, and blanched at the thought.

He deposited the fast-food bag on his desk and went to hang up his coat when it started

"McNaughton!" Stumbo bellowed. "In my office. NOW!"

Jack stood facing the coat rack, his back to Doyle, trying to summon his patience. His eyes closed, and he resolved to maintain his cool. But the acid began to seep into his stomach.

He sighed, and turned to meet his fate. He walked slowly to Stumbo's office and entered.

"What is it, Doyle?" he asked resignedly.

"Sit down, Jack." McNaughton obeyed. "I understand that you testified at the Statehouse this morning. Now, who in the hell do you think you are, doing that? Do you think you represent this department? Do ya?"

For the shortest moment, Jack relished the thought that he had Doyle by the throat.

"Doyle, Captain Ryan knew I was testifying, and was quite enthusiastic about it."

"Well, why didn't I know?" Stumbo demanded.

"You did. I first told you about this at the end of November, when I was going to meet Senator Woolums for the first time. At the time, you wanted me to alert the brass, and Captain Ryan gave me his blessings. I called his office yesterday to tell him I was testifying today. And I wrote a memo to you, and cc'ed it to him. If you check your e-mail, it should be in the system."

"How in the hell do you think I have time to look at that damned e-mail?"

"Doyle, we're under orders to use e-mail to make sure we've got a record of important communications. And honestly, I can't imagine life without it. It makes everything so much easier than how things were before."

"Well, I don't know how the hell that damn thing works. It keeps beeping at me all day."

"It's telling you that you have mail," Jack said patiently. "If you check it immediately, it's easier to keep on top of it. When was the last time you checked your e-mail?"

"I don't know," Stumbo said haltingly. "I guess I never have."

"Good God, Doyle," McNaughton said, unable to mask his surprise. "We've had e-mail for years."

"That's not the point, McNaughton. The point is, you didn't clear this testifying stuff with me. I have a good mind to bring you up on insubordination charges."

"Doyle," Jack said, trying to stay calm. "For your own good, to save yourself from embarrassment, forget it. It's too easy for me to prove that I sent you the e-mail yesterday. I'd be exonerated, and you'd be embarrassed. Can't we just forget this?"

"No, McNaughton, we can't just forget this." His voice dripped with sarcasm. "I don't like your smart-aleck attitude. Get out of my office and let me decide how to handle you."

McNaughton remained motionless for a moment, mulling how to respond. He thought better of speaking and simply rose and strode out of the room.

Jack heard nothing from Stumbo by the time he left the office, and he made a conscious decision to forget about DC-10 for the evening. He, Renee and Angel had a quiet dinner of frozen pizza, salad and cold milk – nobody felt like cooking. Then Jack read to Angel, trying vainly to settle his daughter down.

She would have none of that, and it took every ounce of Jack's patience not to scream at her. Finally, Renee rescued him, dispatching him to the bathroom for a long soak while she lay with Angel until the girl fell asleep.

"We make a good team," he told Renee later, when she joined him in bed. It was nearly midnight; she had fallen asleep in Angel's room and Jack, relaxed by the bath, had quickly fallen asleep with a book on his chest once he got into bed. They kissed, and Renee turned so Jack could spoon her.

McNaughton had forgotten about Policinski's column when he and Renee arose early the next morning; his trip to the paper box was just part of the routine.

But when he performed the next step of that routine – digging the local section out of the paper so he could read that while he visited the bathroom – he saw Policinski's mug peering out from the small black-and-white photo that headed his column, which ran down the left side of the page.

"Indiana needs guilty but mentally ill verdict," the headline read. Under it was a subhead:

"M'Naghten Rule should give way

to newer, better McNaughton Rule"

Jack smiled to himself, then called up the stairs to Renee – quietly enough, he hoped, so Angel wouldn't wake just yet, but loud enough to be heard. She was headed that way anyway, and bounded down the stairs when she saw Jack's face.

"Andy's column?"

"Yeah," he said happily. "I haven't read it yet, but the head's great."

He showed her, before grabbing the paper back so he could read the column. He settled in at the kitchen table, and Renee stood over his shoulder, reading along:

"Jack McNaughton has been a homicide detective for a long, long time. And he's seen some horrific things.

"Kids who've killed their parents, guys who've killed their lovers, women who've killed their husbands. Strangers who've done in strangers. Crimes of passion; crimes of wanton disregard for life.

"The 15-year veteran of the Metro-Marion Police Department has spent two-thirds of those years in homicide, first as a detective and then as a sergeant, supervising other detectives and helping them do their gruesome jobs.

"In all those years, despite all the horror he's witnessed, the worst thing he has seen, McNaughton said in an interview yesterday, is injustice. And he's seen it more times than anybody ought to have to endure.

"One of the worst injustices McNaughton has seen is when people who, it would seem, had to be crazy to commit some horrible crime get off just because they're crazy.

"You think that's crazy? Well, so do I.

"It's true that a normal person wouldn't go around shooting or carving up folks. You've got to have something wrong with you to do that. And I suppose the bleeding hearts have a point when they say a crazy person shouldn't be held responsible for something he did when he was crazy and out of control.

"Actually, McNaughton said the idea that you can't be held responsible for an act you committed while insane is based on an old legal principle that dates to at least the 1600s and took its name – the M'Naghten Rule – from a 1840s British case. The M'Naghten Rule says that you're legally insane if you don't know right from wrong.

"But the modern-day McNaughton, a non-lawyer who's pretty sharp when it comes to knowing the law, points out that there's a difference between being crazy and being legally insane. He agrees that most of the perpetrators he sees are crazy.

"But damn few are legally insane, and according to the law, that's what you're supposed to be to get off scot-free when you've offed somebody.

"The difference is pretty easy to discern. If you know you did something wrong, then you're legally sane. If you whack your next-door neighbor and then walk around carrying his head like a trophy, as if nothing out of the ordinary has happened, then you may be legally insane. But if you try to hide the head, you're sane.

"Still, McNaughton says when juries hear about some horrific crime that they can't imagine happening, they're all too ready to say the perp had to be nuts to do it.

"I'm not talking about some drug killing or a murder that occurs when somebody comes home and surprises a burglar. Juries don't mind convicting those guys, even giving them the death penalty.

"But in a large percentage of homicides, victim and perp know each other. And jurors don't like to think that mama can kill Junior unless she's crazy.

"So, given the choice between finding mama guilty of murder (or some lesser, but still serious, crime) or saying she couldn't have meant it, juries keep acquitting these people.

"Remember the John Pius Peterson trial late last year? Peterson killed his six kids but got off because the jury decided he had to be nuts to pulverize his own flesh and blood.

"Yeah, I think he had to be nuts to do it. I can't think of anything worse. But McNaughton got me thinking – did Peterson really fail to realize that what he was doing was wrong? How could he slaughter all those beautiful kids – and even their pet dog – without having some thought in his mind that this had to be wrong?

"But as I'm sure you remember, Peterson was acquitted and is spending some time in the loony bin, not prison. I expect he'll stay there a while, but not nearly as long as he would spend in prison, and not nearly as long as he ought to.

"McNaughton was the lead investigator on that case, and it was sort of the last straw for him. Now he's pushing for Indiana to come out of the dark ages and to adopt a change in the law that most other states already have.

"He wants to institute a 'guilty but mentally ill' verdict. That way, juries can acknowledge that the perp might have been wacko, but that he's still responsible for the havoc he has wreaked.

"McNaughton has enlisted one of the state's most conscientious lawmakers, Sen. Kimberly Woolums, D-New Albany, to sponsor a

bill in the legislature. It passed out of the Senate Judiciary Committee yesterday and now heads to the full Senate for its consideration.

"Here's hoping the rubes in the state legislature, who seem to want Indiana to be last in everything, see the wisdom of Woolums' bill and pass it, and that the governor signs it posthaste.

"And here's a thought: Lawmakers are always naming their laws. Zachary's Law. Megan's Law. To remember McNaughton, who brought the whole idea to Woolums' attention and ought to get the credit he deserves, I nominate a name for this one:

"The McNaughton Rule."

"It's *wonderful!*" Renee squealed when they'd both reached the end. "I love it!"

Jack sat silently, pinching his lips to squelch a smile. "It *is* nice, isn't it?" he finally said, as he got up to resume his aborted bathroom visit.

"God, Jack, do you think you could be a little excited?" Renee called after him. "Andy did a great job, and you look like the hero of all time. Even the rubes, as Andy called them, can't ignore this. Your bill is all but passed!"

"You think so?" he asked, stopping at the bathroom's threshold. "I mean, you know these guys a helluvalot better than I do. Do you think it's got a chance?"

"Babe, after this column, it's greased!"

Jack tried unsuccessfully to control his smile as he drove to work, humming along with music on the radio. He felt like he was making a difference: He may not have gotten Peterson convicted, but the next time somebody tried something similar, he'd have a rude awakening. Better yet, maybe a change in the law would prevent somebody from making the kinds of plan that Peterson did, because he would know that merely convincing a jury that he was insane no longer would guarantee he would walk.

McNaughton decided he would not let Stumbo irritate him today. True, he hadn't gotten all of the steam out of his system over Jack's testimony at the legislature. And the column, if Stumbo bothered to read the paper, would exacerbate the situation. But this is what police work is all about, McNaughton thought – making a difference in somebody's life.

The euphoria lasted for only a few minutes after Jack reached his desk.

"McNaughton!" It was Stumbo.

Jack got up jauntily and decided to take Stumbo head on.

"Doyle, did you see Policinski's column in the Star this morning?" he asked brightly, knowing full well the blast he was about to endure.

"You know goddamn well I saw it, McNaughton, and I am filing an I-number on you." Stumbo leaned back in his rickety chair and crossed his log-like arms as far across his chest as they would reach. His mouth formed a smirk.

"Doyle," Jack said as calmly as he could, "I don't understand where you're coming from. You and the captain knew about my testimony before the legislative committee. This column emanated directly from that."

"I don't think so, McNaughton," Stumbo replied smugly. "In case you didn't read this shit close enough, it says you told him this 'in an interview.' Now, who in the hell authorized you to give this piece of shit an interview? You know those goddamn newsies just want to dig dirt, and you know that they're supposed to go through the PAO before they talk to any of us."

"Doyle," Jack said, still trying to remain calm, "the proof's in the pudding. This is a fantastic column. He obviously supports the bill, and we couldn't have made a better case for why it's necessary. Why not just accept that and let it pass?"

"Because, McNaughton, you are getting a little too big for your britches. Who do you think you are? I'll remind you that I am commander here, not you. You know, I got rid of your shit-for-brains pal Simons, and it seems like you want to take his place as resident asshole. I've had it up to here with you," he said, motioning toward his fleshly throat.

"Doyle, I've done nothing wrong, and you know it. You're pissed because the column focuses on me. Well, I'm sorry, but I *am* the one who came up with the idea. When you come up with an equally good one, maybe they'll write a story about you." McNaughton's voice was rising now. "But don't try to minimize the idea, and don't fuck with me, Doyle. Mitch Simons is a helluva cop, and it was homicide's loss when he took his expertise and moved to narcotics. Don't bad-mouth him to me. I mean it, Doyle. Don't fuck with me!"

He stormed out, slamming the door. Stumbo pulled on his collar and scratched his neck, trying to look nonchalant.

CHAPTER 13

Carly Wellstone struggled as she tried to use the rearview mirror to touch up her Red Delicious lipstick without blocking the ceiling dome light with her head. Having done her best, she smacked her lips together several times, and ran her tongue over her front teeth, just in case some lipstick had stained them. Then she fluffed up her streaked blonde hair, painstakingly arranging her wispy bangs so that they'd look windblown.

It was after midnight, the first half hour of a frigid Saturday morning. She shivered as she stepped carefully out of her red Cobalt, planting each spike-heeled foot so that she would not lose her balance. It was bone-chillingly cold, but fortunately most of the snow had melted during a freak warm spell several days earlier, making her trek less precarious. After locking the door, she teetered around the front of the car, onto the curb and up the walk in front of the grey clapboard bungalow, adjusting her clothing as she went. By the time she reached the door and lifted a hand to knock on it, everything was just so – her skin-tight, low-riding black jeans, the form-fitting floral sweater that skimmed the top of the jeans, the dark green car coat that topped them.

Her slender knuckles were an inch from the painted wood when Wellstone realized the door was ajar. She frowned, wondering how Mitch could be so careless on so cold a night. She tossed her head as if to say "oh, well," and pushed the door open the rest of the way, stepping over the threshold.

"Mitch," she called. "Mitch, honey, do you know you left your door o. . ." Wellstone stopped speaking and walking, and peered down at the lighted brass lamp that lay on the living room floor. She started to bend to pick it up, but was distracted by the papers – bills and such – that were strewn across the way.

"Mitch?" she said tentatively. She noticed a dark mark on the floor, not far from the lamp. On closer inspection, she realized it was one drop in a series that formed a long curved line of beads, a perverse rosary. She followed it as it led her behind an easy chair, where she saw a small pool, maybe six inches in diameter, of something dark. The only light came from the downed lamp, which lay on the other side of the chair, so she could not tell what she was looking at. She reached to touch the pool, and stopped just before her forefinger was going to break the surface.

"Oh, my God. Oh, my *God!* It's blood! Mitch! Mitch, where are you?"

She turned frantically about, her eyes darting to each corner of the living room, over to the kitchen, separated only by a high counter, and down the hall. It was dark that way, and she felt a stab of fear pierce her throat. She tried to control her breathing, telling herself that Mitch had just cut himself badly while shaving or had a bloody nose or . . .

Or *what?* There was nothing broken on which he could have cut himself. And if he had had merely a nasty shaving accident, where was he? He was a light sleeper, and he should have been awakened by her call if he were in the bedroom. Why was the door ajar? And why was there so much blood? Wellstone stepped backwards toward the door, stumbling but catching herself, pushed it aside with her elbow and ducked out as quickly as she could. She ran as best she could in those high heels down the walk toward her car and around the front. Her hands shook violently as she fumbled with her keys, finally finding the right one and jabbing it into the car lock. Inside, she pushed the lock closed again, started up the engine and fumbled for her cell phone. Using her knuckles, for her maroon-painted fingernails were too long, she punched in nine-one-one.

"Emergency response. What is your emergency?" the operator said calmly.

"Police! I need the police. My boyfriend – he's missing and there's blood. I think something's wrong!"

"Ma'am, can you calm down? You say your friend is missing? How do you know?"

"He was supposed to be home. We had a late date. But he's not there, and his place – it's a mess! And there's blood!"

"OK, ma'am. Stay calm; we'll send a car over. My computer isn't registering an address. Are you using a cellular phone?"

"Yes. I'm at 6453 North Wilmington."

"OK, ma'am. That's six-four-five-three North Wilmington. What's your friend's name?

"Mitch Simons. Mitchell W. Simons. He's a narcotics detective with the Metro-Marion Police."

"OK, ma'am." The operator's voice registered no surprise or concern. "We're on it. Now, just try to stay calm. Is your car door locked?"

"Yes."

"OK. I've got a car on the way. I'll stay on the line with you until the officers arrive, OK?"

"Yes. OK. Thank you."

It seemed like forever for Carly Wellstone, but it was only four minutes until two uniforms pulled up to her car's back bumper and hopped out. Lighted flashlights in hand, the officers shone them into her car, and Wellstone rolled down her window.

She and one of the officers spoke at once.

"Are you . . ."

"I'm the one who called you."

"What's the problem, ma'am?"

"Wait a second," she said, then turned back to her telephone. "The officers are here," she told the operator, who responded: "OK, ma'am. They'll help you. I'm signing off."

Then Wellstone repeated the story for them, and they asked her to wait in her car while they checked out the house. They went in and observed the disarray.

"Look here," the taller cop, a young, light-skinned black man with short-cropped hair, said to his partner. He pointed to the pool of blood, and then touched it to find it still wet. He held is finger up for his partner to see.

"Hmmm," replied the other, a medium-height, medium-weight, medium-brown-haired white man. He nodded, agreeing to an unspoken question put to him by his partner, causing the partner to act.

"Uh, Dispatch, two-twenty-one," he said into the radio that was pinned to the shoulder of his uniform.

"Two-twenty-one, go ahead."

"Request you contact Sergeant Basker and advise him we've got a situation at Detective Simon's house. He'd better Signal eight."

"Clear."

The partners continued to survey the scene for a few minutes. Back at dispatch, the operator, a veteran of sixteen years of calmly handling such situations, telephoned Frank Basker, who headed

Mitch's narcotics squad, to ask him to go to the scene, as the uniform had asked.

"Should I call homicide, sir?" the operator asked.

Basker thought for a minute. While the situation was curious, and Basker was worried about his detective, there was no proof that anything untoward had happened. But Basker was uneasy about the situation. "Yeah, but let's go straight to Sergeant McNaughton, please," he responded. It couldn't hurt, he figured, to have a veteran detective, and one that cared about Mitch, on the scene.

The dispatcher turned back to the radio to alert the beat officers. "Two-twenty-one. He's en route. I'm calling Sergeant McNaughton too."

The uniform acknowledged the information. "Two-twenty-one."

The phone rang about one-forty-five a.m., jolting both Jack and Renee from dead sleep. "Shit," Renee groaned as Jack reached for the receiver. At this hour, it was undoubtedly for him.

"McNaughton," he said. After about eleven p.m., he always answered the phone that way.

"Sergeant McNaughton, sorry to wake you up but Sergeant Basker asked me to call and tell you you're needed at Mitch Simons's house."

"What's going on?" Jack responded. The information shocked him into alertness, and he sat upright in bed.

"Uh, there's some disarray there and apparently Detective Simons can't be found."

"OK," Jack said, his brow furrowing in worry. "I'm on my way."

McNaughton turned to Renee, whose eyes had bolted open as soon as Jack had sat up so abruptly. "What's wrong?" she asked.

"Mitch is missing," he said as he pulled on the jeans he had left across the bottom of the bed. Next came a sweatshirt. "I don't know any details, but Frank Basker asked me to come over to Mitch's house."

"Oh, God," Renee said. "I hope nothing's wrong."

"Me, too, babe."

He leaned to kiss her goodbye. "Get some sleep," he said, but he knew that that would be impossible for Renee now. Mitch was like a younger brother to her.

"Call me the minute you know something. I don't care what time."

"OK."

He had pulled on the socks he'd taken off and dropped at his bedside several hours earlier, and slipped into brown deck shoes. Grabbing a jacket, he dashed to his car and took off on the short jaunt to the Broad Ripple neighborhood when Mitch lived. As he drove, he recalled the other times Mitch had given him, and the department, a start. He didn't know if he should hope that this was one of those times, too, or that it wasn't. Two lab technicians were arriving at the same time McNaughton did. He acknowledged them with a nod and jogged into the house, not waiting for them while they unloaded equipment.

"Frank," McNaughton said breathlessly, "what have we got?"

"I don't know, Jack. But I'm concerned."

McNaughton looked around the house, gingerly stepping to make sure he didn't destroy anything that might be evidence. It did not look good. There obviously had been a struggle. There was more blood than there should have been if Mitch had accidentally sliced himself with a knife, and that still wouldn't explain why the pool of blood was in the living room. What's more, there were smears that made it appear that something – a body? – had been dragged into the kitchen toward the back door. Jack wanted desperately to think that Mitch was preparing something to eat, cut himself badly and driven himself to the emergency room for stitches, but the evidence, and his instincts, told him otherwise.

The technicians were focusing on the blood, taking pictures and collecting samples. Basker was surveying everything in sight and the uniforms stood out of the way, available to assist if needed.

"Has anybody checked to see if his car is here?" McNaughton queried. The technicians shook their heads, as did Basker and the uniforms. Jack, dodging the bloody smears, went toward the back door, then thought better of it; the knob had not yet been dusted for prints. He left through the front door and dashed around the side of the house to the back yard, toward the detached two-car garage, a requirement of Mitch's when he bought the cozy house. More than anything, Mitch had wanted a place to store his department issue as well as his pride and joy, a black Jeep that usually looked like it had just been driven from the dealership's showroom floor. McNaughton used his coat sleeve to wipe off a small window and peered inside the garage. Mitch's grey Mustang, the car he had been assigned when he went undercover for narcotics, was inside, but the Jeep was not. Its absence gave credence to the theory that Mitch had injured himself and gone to the ER, but it was far from proof. McNaughton made a mental note to have someone check with area hospitals as soon as he got his people together.

McNaughton went back to the house, and told Basker what he found. "Frank, I'm going to call my squad in. I'm worried too. At the very least, Mitch may be hurt and in need of our help."

"Let's hope that's all it is, Jack."

Alvear was the first to arrive, followed closely by Allen and Stutz. Kit was visibly shaken, and could not stand still. "God, I wish I had a cigarette," she said as she paced, recalling a habit she'd given up years earlier. She had pulled her shiny long hair into a ponytail, revealing a sculpted face, on which she wore no makeup. She wasn't big on it anyway – usually used just a touch of mascara – and she wasn't about to take the time to apply it under the circumstances. "This is unreal. God; do you realize that last night was Friday the thirteenth?"

"Since when are you superstitious?" Jack said. "Let's keep good thoughts." He turned to the others. "And let's get down to work, folks. First of all, I want to believe the best, even though things don't look so good right now. We put out an 'attempt-to-locate' for Mitch and his Jeep, and with any luck, we'll find him and we'll feel sorry that he cut himself and needed stitches and everybody'll laugh about it tomorrow. Going on the idea that the worst thing that's happened to Mitch is that he'll have an ugly scar on his otherwise perfect body" – Jack tried to lighten the mood with his sarcasm, but failed – "Chris, I want you to check with all the area hospitals to see if he's been to their ERs. Also, the immediate care centers in Broad Ripple, Meridian-Kessler and Butler-Tarkington, at least. Look farther if none of those are open late at night. After you've finished with that, I want you to talk to the neighbors to see if they heard or saw anything out of the ordinary.

"Kit, while I was waiting for you guys, I found Mitch's 'little black book' in his nightstand. There are so many names of women in here, we'll be checking them out for three weeks. But that's just what we've got to do. Let's just be glad he kept the book, because

I haven't been able to find his cell phone. Kit, I need you to start talking to these women, starting with the woman who called us. She said she found the house as you see it now, but we've got to make sure. Her name's Carly Wellstone, and she said she had a date with Mitch after she got off work at midnight. She's waiting in her car out front right now. After her, start checking out other girlfriends. Did they know they weren't exclusive with Mitch? How'd they feel about that? And take it a step farther. Are any of these women married or otherwise attached? Could a jealous husband or boyfriend have decided to protect his woman's honor and confronted Mitch?"

"OK," Kit said. "I'll look through the book and get right on it. I imagine I'll recognize some of the names – at least those of the women he was dating when we still worked together."

"Right," Jack said. "But don't discount any of them, even if you had met them and liked them. Now, I know that'll keep you busy for a long time, but I'll get you help as soon as I can. Specifically, Chris and Joe will help you out after they're done with their assignments. Joe, that brings me to you. I want you to check out people from Mitch's professional past. For example, he and I worked a case back some years ago involving a real sicko named Donnie Crawford. Donnie got out of the loony bin late last year, and maybe he paid Mitch a visit."

"What was he in for?"

"He killed a woman who had picked him up hitchhiking and had sex with her corpse a bunch of times. He was acquitted, but he was furious at Mitch for arresting him in the first place, and he threatened him during the trial."

"OK," Stutz said.

"Jack, if Crawford's involved, you may be a target too," Kit said. "You'd better watch out."

"I'm not worried about me. For one thing, Donnie took a liking to me. It was Mitch he disliked."

McNaughton continued: "Besides, let's stay focused on Mitch. Joe, after you check out Crawford, do the same with anybody else that Mitch pissed off over the years. That list may be almost as long as Kit's. Plug his badge number into the department computer, and you should get a list of the cases he's worked on in the last several years. You may be able to rule out some just by seeing who's still in prison – although that's no guarantee, if the perp felt particularly aggrieved by Mitch. And you can talk to me, Kit and others who've partnered with Mitch on some of the cases."

Jack knew that it would have been easier for Kit to handle that assignment. Because she'd worked with Mitch so much, she'd be able to automatically rule out some people and to include others. But he needed her touch on the more sensitive interviews – the lovers and lovers of lovers. Big, gangly Joe would put some of those people off, he feared.

"I'm going to go through some of Mitch's stuff here. See if I can find his bank statement and credit card bills so we can find out if they're being used." He surveyed the mess around him and sighed. "Unfortunately, it looks like it'll take a while, and we'll have to wait until Monday to get the banks to cough up the records.

"Uh, make that Tuesday, sergeant," Allen said. "Monday is Martin Luther King Day, and the banks'll be closed."

"Damn," McNaughton said. "Well, we've still got plenty to do to keep us busy until Tuesday. Frank," he said, calling Basker over, "can you and your people check on Mitch's recent cases in narcotics?"

"You got it, Jack," Basker said.

McNaughton continued: "I'm going to call the brass in now; I think they need to know what's happening here."

Just then, one of the technicians approached Jack. "Sergeant, we're all through with the blood. We figure, from the amount of drying, it got spilled around eleven last night. We'll get it typed pronto. Do you want us to do DNA analysis on it too?"

"Well," Jack said, breathing out hard and weighing the decision. "If the blood type matches Mitch's, it's a pretty good bet that it's his, unfortunately. I'd hate to miss something by failing to do the DNA stuff, but I don't have anything to compare it with until I have Mitch."

"Uh, Jack," Kit said quietly. "Can I talk to you privately?"

"Sure, Kit. Just a minute, please," he said to the technician. He and Alvear walked down the hall. "Jack, if you think matching DNA is a good idea, I think I've got some of Mitch's DNA."

His eyebrows formed a deep V. "How would you have his DNA?"

"Well, this is sort of embarrassing," she said, her eyes downcast. "But I'll do anything to help Mitch. You know, my biological time clock is ticking away. I'm not getting any younger. And given that I have a talent for picking assholes, I figure it's pretty unlikely I'm ever going to meet the man of my dreams who I want to father my children. So Mitch and I talked about it a lot, and he agreed to do it. I mean, not by *doing it.* I got a turkey baster for that. But I've got some of Mitch's DNA in my freezer, waiting for the day when I decide that I do want to be a mommy."

Jack looked at Kit without speaking. He never realized that having a baby was an issue with Kit, who seemed perfectly contented with her life.

"No, Kit," he said quietly. "I don't think we want to destroy your specimen. But thanks for the thought." He did not speak his biggest fear, that if something horrible had happened to Mitch, the specimen – and thus Kit's dreams – might be irreplaceable.

"No problem," she said, the embarrassment evident in her voice. She still couldn't look Jack in the eye.

Jack walked back to the technician. "Skip the DNA analysis for now," he said, "but keep enough of a sample that we can do it later if necessary."

"Yes, sir."

By seven a.m. that cold Saturday, Wendell McCarthy, deputy chief for operations; William Ryan, captain over homicide; Anthony Caselli, captain over narcotics and vice; and Doyle Stumbo had descended on Simons's tiny house. Kit didn't see the point; she thought they just got in the way and, the way she saw it, Stumbo in particular wasn't needed at all. She figured he got his fat ass out of bed only to impress the other brass.

"Chief," McNaughton said to McCarthy, a white-haired gentleman who postponed retirement when he got his dream job, "it's only a matter of time before the media get wind of this. Do you want me to get Pat Houston out here?"

"That's a good idea, Jack. Thanks for thinking of it."

Soon, the department's public information officer had joined them, and none too soon. The newsies did indeed descend; a missing cop was unusually good fodder on a weekend. Meanwhile, Basker sent one of his detectives back to their squad room to go through Mitch's files. He and McNaughton settled into Mitch's second bedroom, where Simons kept a computer, bookshelves and workout equipment, to look for bank statements, credit card bills and anything else that might shed light on Simons's disappearance. An intimidating stack of CD-ROMs sat next to the computer; the team would have to take a look at them, McNaughton thought.

"Mitch has been doing real well in our unit," Basker said. "Making a lot of cases off some of my old snitches."

"Can you think of any cases in which the defendant would want to harm Mitch, where he'd have so much to lose that getting Mitch out of the picture seemed the easy way out?"

Basker mulled the question. "Right now, I'd say there's only one that fits that description. Luther Grubbs. He's facing 'the bitch' if the case Mitch has on him right now sticks."

"The bitch" was a mandatory additional thirty years in prison given to what Indiana law deemed "habitual offenders" – those convicted of a third felony. The additional time ran consecutive to whatever sentence the perp would get for the underlying offense, so it was a significant punishment.

"Grubbs is in his early fifties, kind of a latter-day hippie if I recall correctly, so another thirty years for him might as well be life without parole," Basker added.

"What's Mitch got him on?" McNaughton asked.

"He bought an ounce of coke off of him, and Grubbs was bragging that there was plenty more where that came from. We didn't care; we had him on a felony, and that's all we needed to put him away for good. The only problem was that Mitch was cowboying; he took Grubbs off and *then* called for backup."

"Which means that Mitch is the only witness against Grubbs. If he's out of the picture, Grubbs walks," McNaughton said soberly. "We've gotta go talk to Mr. Grubbs, Frank."

"Let's go."

They started toward the front door, dodging people as they went. "Sergeant?" It was Chris Allen who, like Stutz, still addressed Jack by title.

"What'd you find out, Chris?"

"I checked every hospital anywhere close to here, and every immediate-care center too. No sign of Mitch. No record of someone by his name or description."

"Shit," Jack said under his breath. "OK, Chris. Thanks. Start with the neighbors now. See if they saw anything strange last evening or late last night. *Anything*. A car. A guy. A bunch of guys. A lot of noise coming from here. One loud noise, like a gunshot. Whatever. OK?"

"Yes, sir."

"Thanks, Chris. Let's go, Frank."

Basker followed McNaughton out to Jack's car, and they headed to the east side, location of the dives that Mitch had mentioned in connection with Grubbs. They tried three all-night bars before they found Grubbs at Millie's, a small, dark place that smelled of body odor and stale beer.

"Luther," Basker began. "I'm Frank Basker from Metro-Marion Police. This is Jack McNaughton. We were wondering what you know about a missing cop."

"I don't know nothing," Grubbs sneered. "Did ya check the Dunkin' Doughnuts?"

"Very funny," Basker said flatly, his mouth a straight line. "But answer the question. You hear anything?"

"I don't know what you're talking about. Leave me alone."

"Well, I understand you know one of my men, Mitch Simons."

"That asshole is missing? Good. He framed me," Grubbs answered. "But don't be looking at me. I don't know nothin' about him. He's probably out dicking around."

"Maybe. But then again, maybe something's happened to him. You're *glad* he's missing?"

"I didn't say that," he said, backtracking. "I couldn't care less about that lying shithead. Whether he's missing or not doesn't mean shit to me. When I get to trial, his ass is grass anyway."

"That's right, Luther. You're innocent, right? You were framed. You didn't sell that cola to Mitch, huh?"

"No, man, I didn't. But I don't have to talk to you, so leave me alone."

"In a minute," McNaughton said. "First, I want to ask you a couple of questions. What were you doing last evening?"

"Working. What's it to you?"

"Where do you work, and what time do you get off?"

"Ford. I work third shift, so I get off at seven in the morning."

"And you worked last night?"

"Yeah, all seven-point-five hours. What's it to you?" he repeated.

"Will we be able to verify that you worked a full shift?" Jack asked.

"I don't give a shit what you do."

It was Basker's turn. "So if I check with personnel at Ford, they'll say you were at work last night?"

"Yeah, but shit, don't be doing that." Grubbs' voice had a plaintive edge to it now. "I don't want the cops bugging my employer, and making them wonder what I'm into. I'm trying to earn an honest living."

"Right, Luther. We'll go gentle."

"Uh, Mr. Grubbs," Jack began. "What did you do for lunch?"

"I brought it, like I always do." He paused a moment. "Now leave me alone; I'm tired of talking to you."

"Did you spend the entire lunch break with other people?"

"Yes, for Christ sake. Now will you leave me alone?"

"Just as soon as you give me the names of the people you ate with."

"Jesus Christ! OK. I'll tell you if you'll leave me alone. Tony Baker, Stan Singleton and Wimpy Monroe. That's Thomas Monroe."

"OK," Jack said as he and Basker rose simultaneously. "Thanks for your time, Mr. Grubbs." McNaughton nodded toward the waitress who was cleaning up in back, and Basker went to talk with her. Jack took the bartender.

"How long has he been here?" he asked.

The bartender, badly in need of a shave and a shampoo, breathed out, revealing that he also was badly in need of brushing his teeth. "He got here a little after seven. Right after he got off work, I guess."

"How do you know that?"

"He comes here almost every morning."

"And you're always open that early?"

"We never close. We like to take care of our third-shift friends."

"OK, then. Thanks."

Basker got the same story from the waitress. "Well," Jack said after they were both back inside the car, "he's got a good alibi. But I think he's dirty. I think we ought to keep looking at him."

"I agree," Basker said as McNaughton pulled out from the curb.

The snow – big, heavy, wet flakes – started about ten that morning, and continued relentlessly until nearly midnight, making it nearly impossible for the detectives to do their work for the rest of Saturday and on Sunday. Every short trek became a tortuous, time-consuming journey. Then, once the snow stopped, the temperatures plummeted, leaving the roads impassable sheets of ice.

But the cause inspired McNaughton and his squad to persevere. And so did the fact that Mitch failed to show up for work on Monday, confirming that he hadn't merely disappeared for a weekend's romantic rendezvous. Simons was not one to skip work like that, so things did not look good.

Records over at narcotics showed that Mitch worked until six-fifteen p.m. the previous Friday. Chris Allen visited the video store where a movie found atop Simons's DVD player had been rented, and computer records there showed that the transaction had occurred at six-fifty-four p.m. He had apparently stopped on the way home from work.

The detectives also knew that Carly Wellstone arrived at Mitch's house around twelve-twenty Saturday morning; that was Carly's best guess, confirmed by the time of her call to nine-one-one. So whatever happened to Mitch had occurred in those five-plus hours.

On Monday, the department lab typed the spilled blood and found it to be A-positive, the same as Mitch.

With those tidbits of information in mind, McNaughton's squad went about its work. Captain Ryan authorized another squad of detectives to assist whenever Jack asked, and Basker's people wanted to help, but for the most part McNaughton preferred to work only with his own people, even if it meant that neither he nor any of his people got much sleep over the following days.

Alvear spent her days and evenings contacting the women in Mitch's phone book. They were usually blonde, Simons's apparent preference, although there were a few brunettes and two African-Americans. And, almost to a person, they were vacuous and, if employed, working in a menial job. Two were exotic dancers. While Mitch had always shown a healthy appreciation for Kit's brains when they worked together, his preference for the women he saw socially was vastly different.

Alvear had started the interviewing with Carly Wellstone, who struck Kit as a well-meaning, sweet, young woman who had been thrust headlong into this horrible situation. She was not particularly deep, but it did not tax Wellstone's limited imagination for her to conjure up horrific thoughts of what might have happened to Mitch. Alvear did not doubt it was Wellstone's imagination, and not any direct knowledge, that was causing the young woman so much discomfort.

"I don't know Mitch very well," Carly said between sobs, "but he's been so nice to me I just pray nothing bad has happened to him."

"How did you meet?"

"I'm a bartender at the Delaware Street Bar and Grill." She wiped her nose on the wrinkled pink tissue she had dug out of her purse. "He comes in there a lot, and he usually sits at the bar so we can talk. He's real nice."

Kit got a mental image of the yuppie fern bar where Wellstone worked. Mitch frequented his share of dives, too, but this was an upscale joint.

"So how many times have you gone out?"

"Just twice before. This was supposed to be our third date. Mitch was going to rent a movie and make popcorn."

"Are you married, Carly?"

"Oh, no. I wouldn't have been seeing Mitch if I was."

"Seeing anybody else?"

"No. I just broke up with my boyfriend."

"Did you break up because of Mitch?"

"No. We broke up before I ever went out with Mitch."

"Does your ex know about Mitch? Is he the jealous type?"

"Well, he wants to get back with me, but I told him that I didn't want to. He seemed to take it OK. But he had seen Mitch sitting at the bar and asked if he were the reason. I said no, but I don't think he believed me."

"What's this guy's name, and where would I find him?"

"Wes Huber. He works for Shireman Construction."

"Thanks, Carly. I'll be in touch."

Joe Stutz, meanwhile, located Donnie Crawford, who had been living in a group home for former mental patients since his release from the institution in late November. Crawford's red-rimmed eyes seemed empty to Joe, who found it impossible to draw him out enough to talk with him. Crawford sat rocking back and forth, mumbling incomprehensively to himself. He was extremely docile, nothing like the person he must have been when he killed the woman. Perhaps he was on medication, Stutz thought, but he still wondered how any psychiatrist had deemed this man capable of living outside an institution. The group home was intended to provide a transition for former patients before they moved into society. That meant that its rules were looser than those at the institution and that Crawford, no longer the subject of a court order, had the ability to come and go as he pleased. But the director of the facility said that Donnie rarely left.

"Friday night? I'm sure that Donnie was in his room all night, starting around eight p.m.," the director, a tall, kind-looking man, said. "He helped with the dinner dishes, watched a little TV and then turned in. That's pretty much what he does every night."

"Is there any way he could have left his room without you seeing him?" Joe asked.

"I don't think so, detective. I was in the living room, reading, until about one-thirty in the morning or so. And the only way out after nine o'clock is the front door; we keep the back door dead-bolted, and I keep the key. There's just no way he could have gotten past me." He paused to think, and then continued:

"You know, I can't think of a single time that Donnie's gone out after dark, except when he was with the group on an outing. He just isn't comfortable doing that yet."

"OK, sir. Thanks for your cooperation."

Joe found no other promising leads among the perps Mitch had put away while in homicide. Almost all were still in prison, and it would take a lot of interviewing to determine if any were still angry enough at Mitch to have orchestrated a hit from the inside. There were no likely prospects among those who were not in prison. They held no particular grudges, and some had moved on to lives in which they wanted to forget their pasts.

Chris Allen had no more luck. None of the neighbors had seen anything. It seemed they were a private lot, who kept to themselves and considered the neighbors' business none of their own. Chris imagined Mitch liked such a neighborhood, where he didn't have nosy neighbors watching his considerable comings and goings. But it was working to his disadvantage now.

Basker's squad members chipped in by working their CIs, hoping to pick up something off the streets, and Ryan ordered a hotline set up to take tips. Over the next few days, two ransom requests came in and another caller suggested the Mexican mafia had kidnapped Simons because of his work against drug dealers. Another caller insisted that Mitch had been assumed into heaven. When Chris Allen, who took the call, repeated back the information to say Simons had ascended into heaven, the caller became angry, insisting that only Jesus could ascend – that is, do it by himself. Everybody else, including the Virgin Mary, had to be *assumed* through an act of God, she said.

There were six more callers, all insisting, in various permutations of the same story, that Mitch had been kidnapped by aliens. Some said he was sure to be the subject of scientific experimentation, most likely a reproductive study. That provided a moment of levity for the squad, who thought Mitch would enjoy that prospect. But that was the extent of the calls; not a single, serious tip – not even after the Fraternal Order of Police offered a five thousand dollar reward for information leading to the arrest and conviction of anyone who had anything to do with Mitch's disappearance. After Jack had manned the phone during one of the alien calls, he threatened to rip the phone out of the wall. Kit, who was working the phones nearby, thought that perhaps – for the first time since she met Jack – he might really do it.

"Jack," she said later, approaching him when they had a moment's privacy near the coffee urn, "the stress is getting to you. Is there anything I can say or do to take some of this off your shoulders?"

"No, Kit," he said somberly. "But thanks. I apologize for letting it get to me. I'm just so fuckin' frustrated! What the hell has happened to him?"

"I wish I knew."

For his part, Jack finally found a bank statement that suggested Mitch had a debit card and he found a credit card bill from a different bank. He requested two prosecutor's subpoenas and served them on the banks Tuesday morning; Monday was Martin Luther King Day, and the banks had been closed. Meanwhile, he continued looking into Mitch's narcotics cases, often going back to Luther Grubbs but unable to find anything that would implicate him in the disappearance. And none of the other cases seemed promising. In the few hours that he actually spent in bed, McNaughton lay awake, going over the cases he'd checked, the information his squad had provided him, the evidence at the house. And he kept coming up with nothing. He was missing something, he knew. But mostly, he was missing Mitch.

CHAPTER 14

Jack took another sip of the spicy zin that Renee had given him for Christmas. "I just wish I could figure something out, babe," he said quietly. It was late Sunday, eight days since Mitch had disappeared, and all of his squad's efforts turned up nothing of value that day – and little of value since the investigation began.

"Of all the frustrations rained on me from the department, and of all of those from the difficult cases I've worked, I've never felt as frustrated as I do now," McNaughton said. "Hard as it is to believe, asshole Stumbo seems almost insignificant compared to Mitch's just vanishing into thin air."

"I know, sweetheart," Renee said lovingly. "I'm so sorry. I miss him too."

They sat silently for a moment, both gazing at and enjoying the warmth of the toasty fire. Angel was happily ensconced in her pink-and-white bedroom, worn out from an eventful day playing with the little girl down the street. Her belly was full with Greek lemon chicken soup that Renee had made, knowing how much Jack would appreciate such comfort food after the day he had had. She fed Angel early, nearly as soon as the soup was ready, and reheated the pot when Jack dragged himself in late.

He had spent the better part of the last week running down charges on Mitch's credit card and ATM withdrawals on his debit card. Whoever was using them kept one step ahead of the good guys. McNaughton had a fuzzy idea of what the perp looked like, thanks to a videotape at an ATM. But that did nothing to lead the cops to him, only to confirm they had a decent suspect when and if they tracked someone down.

Renee had soaked up the last of her soup with some crusty bread when she broke the silence. "Where do you go from here? I mean, what more can you do?"

"Well, we keep following the money trail in hopes that the perp settles down in one place. He's been really squirrelly, never going to the same place twice. A little too smart for my taste. And we've still got some people to check out. We had kind of forgotten about the woman that Mitch was messing around with at the rest stop last spring. Her name wasn't in Mitch's phone book. But we got her name out of the old reports, and Kit's going to talk to her tomorrow. Maybe she'll give us a lead."

"Maybe," Renee said. "I don't mean to pooh-pooh the idea, but it seems rather remote. I mean, it's been almost a year."

"Babe, I'll take whatever I can get," Jack said. He paused for a minute or so, and then spoke again. "You know, the brass is on my ass about this, especially Doyle."

"You must be kidding. I thought he hated Mitch."

"Well, yeah. But that doesn't matter. The editorial pages are criticizing us for not solving the case, and the brass take that personally. Shit. They act as if we don't want to solve it."

"I know you do. Don't let the editorials get you down. They're written by a bunch of ivory-tower types who haven't spent any time on the streets in two decades."

"It's not the editorials that get me. It's the paperwork that's piling up, and the phone messages. And it's Stumbo. Did I tell you that Doyle actually filed that I-number on me? The one about testifying before the Senate committee?"

"You are kidding me! I cannot believe he'd take it that far! I'd like to wring that fat fucker's neck." She stopped, and leveled her voice. "Jack, you've got to fight this one."

"I know, babe. I will. But I just don't have the heart for it right now."

They had been sitting in silence for a few moments when Jack's cell rang. "McNaughton," he said when he answered it.

"Sergeant McNaughton, this is Webster Summerall. I'm chief of the airport police department."

"Yes, Chief Summerall. What can I do for you?"

"Sergeant McNaughton, every Sunday my officers make a log of the vehicles that have been parked in our long-term parking lot for more than a week. We run a check with the Bureau of Motor Vehicles to check for stolen vehicles."

"Uh-huh."

"Well, we ran into a 2003 Jeep today that I understand is the subject of an attempt-to-locate dispatch you put out. Sorry to be calling so late, but we didn't make the connection until just a little while ago, when one of my night guys was comparing the attempts-to-locate with our inventory. And I figured you'd want to know right away."

"You figured right, Chief. Thanks," Jack said excitedly. Renee noticed, and she sat up erectly. "Can you make sure nobody touches that vehicle – seal it off and keep an eye on it? My people and I will be out ASAP."

"Yes, sergeant. I thought that's what you'd say, and I've got my men on it as we speak."

"Thanks, chief. I really appreciate it."

"No problem."

They hung up, and Jack turned to Renee. "We've got Mitch's Jeep. It's at the airport's long-term parking lot. Been there more than a week."

"Honey, is this good news?" Renee asked tentatively.

Jack thought for a moment. "I don't know, babe. At this point, I have to admit I've lost most hope that Mitch is alive. But I've still got to know what happened to him, and who did it to him. And why. I need to know that. And Mitch deserves that."

McNaughton called Kit, who answered on the first ring. "I'm a nervous wreck," she confided in Jack. He said he had called in a crime-scene technician, and asked her to call Stutz and Allen. Everyone was to meet at the airport police office as soon as they could get there. Alvear reached Allen, but had to leave a message for Stutz, who had taken off enough time to make an obligatory appearance at his in-laws' for Sunday dinner. He called her back shortly, and promised to be right along.

McNaughton was the first to arrive at the airport police office, a small, cheap-looking prefabricated building without a smidgeon of charm. It was still frigid outside, and he walked gingerly to avoid the patches of ice that dotted the parking lot. Once inside, he was greeted by Chief Summerall, a tall, slender man with thinning hair and a prominent nose. He invited Jack to sit and offered him a cup of coffee, which turned out to be watery, while they waited for the others. Alvear came first, followed soon thereafter by Allen. Jack approached the young officer who was manning the office.

"I'm expecting one other detective and a team of technicians. I wonder if, when they arrive, you'd please direct them to where we are?"

"Yes, sir, sergeant," he said, a little too enthusiastically, his mouth breaking into a smile.

"Anything to help a fellow officer." Under other circumstances, his eagerness may have been comical. This time, Jack just nodded his head.

McNaughton and Allen drove in Jack's Ford, following Summerall, with whom Alvear rode, as he drove to the Jeep. It was parked far back in the lot, about as far from the airport as one could get, in an area that likely filled up only at particularly busy times. Jack noticed immediately that the car was spotless – not an unusual condition for Simons's car to be in, but perhaps a bit too clean for a stolen vehicle. As Kit and Chris stood shivering, waiting for instructions, Jack approached the driver's side, and lifted his hand to block the security light from casting a strong reflection. He could see that the door was locked, and that nothing lay on the seats or floor. He returned to his own vehicle to retrieve a Slim Jim, with which he could open the door without a key. But first he donned plastic gloves, so as not to leave his own fingerprints anywhere.

McNaughton opened the door and stuck his head inside. He noticed some ice buildup in several places, especially concave areas, suggesting the interior had recently been wetted down. He pulled his head out to address Kit and Chris.

"It looks pretty clean in there, guys. Too clean. That worries me, because somebody had a reason to make it so clean. But it's hardly a detailed cleaning. I can't imagine Mitch would take such a haphazard approach to his vehicle. I . . ."

He was about to suggest their next course of action when he noticed Stutz and the technicians pulling up in two vehicles. He nodded his greeting as they exited. "Joe, I don't know if there's much we can do here. These guys," he said, gesturing toward the techs, "will tell us in a few minutes, I'm sure."

The techs mumbled greetings and got down to work, as the detective squad stood, hands shoved in pockets and clouds of steam streaming from their mouths. Within a few minutes of cursory examination, one technician turned to McNaughton and offered his analysis:

"Sergeant, it looks to me like this vehicle was washed, inside and out, with a high-pressure water hose. I'll be surprised if we find much of anything."

A lump formed in Jack's throat, and he swallowed hard. "OK. Let's take the vehicle back to the garage, where we can at least get out of this cold to go over it."

Jack sent his detectives home to get some rest, telling them to be prepared for a meeting at nine the next morning, when the squad would review its progress and make suggestions for where the investigation should head. He followed as the technicians towed the Jeep to the garage, and then stuck around for about an hour as they combed through the vehicle. They found two hairs and two fibers; under normal circumstances – even as clean as Mitch kept his vehicle – there would have been dozens of each. Assured that those findings would be processed immediately, McNaughton headed home.

It was after midnight when he arrived. Renee was reading in bed with Belle Starr curled up next to her.

"I'm sorry I'm so late," he said. They talked about what had just occurred, then paused for a few moments while Jack undressed and brushed his teeth. He broke the silence. "I haven't said this to the squad yet, but I don't see how Mitch can possibly be alive," he said somberly.

"Oh, babe. Surely there's some hope."

"I don't know where it would come from."

McNaughton spent another restless night, waking periodically and dwelling on what more his squad could do. He was exhausted when the alarm went off at six-thirty a.m., but he was ready for the morning meeting.

McNaughton stopped for doughnuts on the way to the office, pushing from his mind Luther Grubbs' insolence about finding Mitch at the doughnut shop. The truth was, a tiny part of Jack's brain wanted to believe that he would walk into the shop and spot Mitch downing a hot cup of java and a chocolate-frosted long john. Of course, it was not to be. Jack arrived at the squad room before the others; he made a pot of coffee and placed the steaming carafe, small paper cups, the box of doughnuts and paper towels from the washroom in the center of the conference-room table. Just to make sure Stumbo couldn't claim he was failing to communicate, Jack left a handwritten note – he didn't want to mess with e-mail this time – in the front center of Doyle's desk, alerting him to the meeting and inviting him to drop in if he wished. Jack prayed he wouldn't.

The others arrived pretty much on time – Kit, Joe and Chris, Frank Basker and one of his detectives, Ruthie Jackson. Several had dark circles under their eyes, and yawns were frequent occurrences at they spread out around the table and got down to work.

"OK, folks, I think we're all pretty much up to date on what everybody has been doing, so let's not spend any more time reviewing that – unless there are any questions." McNaughton paused to allow them to be asked; there were none, so he continued.

"I'd like to hear what each of you has in mind for today, and then let's brainstorm on what else we need to do. Kit, you first."

"OK," she said wearily. She cautiously took a sip of the steaming brew, swallowed hard and began: "I'm going to talk to Vanessa Goodbody. She's the one Mitch was messing around with at the rest park last spring."

"Tell me that's not her real name," Jackson said incredulously. The newcomer was an attractive black woman in her early thirties who looked wholly different under these circumstances than she looked when out trying to buy dope off pushers. She wore a conservative business suit; her usual work attire was old, grubby castoffs that she had relegated to her house-painting detail before signing on with narcotics.

"I doubt it, Ruthie, but that's how she's listed in the reports from that incident. I understand she's a dancer at The Pussy Cat Lounge. Anybody care to go with me?"

Allen and Stutz both look sheepish, and gazed down at their coffee cups.

"C'mon, Joe. I don't want to go to that kind of joint alone."

"OK," he said reluctantly. "I'll go."

Jack broke in. "What else do you have, Kit?"

"Well, while I've got Joe with me, I think we'll go see one Wes Huber, Carly Wellstone's ex-boyfriend. Remember, she's the one who first realized Mitch was missing. She said that Wes wasn't all that happy about breaking up, and he knew that Mitch had come into the picture. I haven't a clue if Carly meant enough to Mitch for Huber to go after him, but that's what I'm going to find out." She looked around the table, indicating she was finished.

"Good. Joe? How about you?"

"Yessir," Stutz responded. "I plan to go to the Bureau of Motor Vehicles and have them do a run on Mitch's plate, just to see if there was any activity on it from Friday night on. You know, just on the off chance that some police agency ran the plate since Mitch's disappearance. And then I can be available t run down more bank activity if you need me."

"Good," Jack said. "How about you, Chris?"

"It seems to me that it's possible whoever left the Jeep at the airport could have boarded a plane," Allen said. "Why else leave the Jeep there? Now, I know that it probably wasn't Mitch; that doesn't make any sense. But maybe I can go over airlines' manifests to see who went where."

"It's a thought," McNaughton said, "but I don't think you're going to get anywhere. For one thing, how would you narrow it down? There's what? – fifteen or so – airlines flying out of International. We haven't a clue which one the perp would have taken. But even if we come up with anything to point us in a particular direction, the airlines will have thwarted us. They purge their manifests twenty-four hours after a flight has landed safely. There won't be any records of any flights left from ten days ago."

"Shit," Allen said.

"Any other thoughts, Chris?"

"Yeah. I know Joe's checking on bank activity. But what about a gas credit card? Maybe he had one, and he had one from the department too. I'm thinking that the perp could have used it to gas up the Jeep or his own vehicle. If it's just Mitch, there shouldn't be any charges after seven p.m. on Friday the thirteenth. If there are, I'll get out to the station and interview the attendant who was on duty."

"Good thought, Chris. I didn't find any sign of a gas credit card in Mitch's name but you're right; he had a department card. After you check on that, I want you to get a subpoena from the prosecutor to serve on the phone companies for Mitch's land line and his cell phone. With any luck, the perp will have made a call or two from Mitch's phones."

"Yes, sir."

"Frank, Ruthie – anything to add?"

Basker spoke up. "I'm sorry to have to bring this up, but I think you all should know." Everyone at the table turned to peer at Basker, waiting anxiously for his words. "I've got a snitch who says the word on the street is that Mitch got too close to some heavyweight dopers, and that they killed him." He paused, allowing that information to sink in, and then added, "That's the gist of it, anyway. Ruthie and some of the guys are digging for details."

No one spoke for a long moment. Then McNaughton looked up from his notes and, in turn, gazed at each of the people around the table. "Folks, as hard as it is for me to say this, I think we've got to go on the theory that Mitch is dead. Believe me, it pains me to think that. But nobody just disappears as thoroughly as he has unless there's foul play. We know Mitch was doing dangerous work and, if truth be told, we know he could be something of a cowboy. If we accept that he probably is dead, we can do a better job of investigating. For example, we have to figure out why the perp didn't leave Mitch's body at the house. Why would he – or they – take it?"

"That's easy," Kit said, speaking up as if she forgot for a moment that the victim was her close friend. "Perps always think that they can't be charged with murder if there's no body. If Mitch is dead," she continued, gulping hard as she spoke the words, "his body has been well hidden."

"But that won't stop us from charging," Stutz said defiantly.

"No, not as long as we've got enough other evidence," McNaughton reminded him.

The door flew open, and banged loudly against the wall behind it. Stumbo lumbered in. "McNaughton, you could have told me about this meeting," he said.

"I left you a note, Doyle." Jack swallowed back his desire to raise his voice.

"An e-mail?"

"No, Doyle, I wrote you a note and left it on your desk. I'm sure you'll find it there if you look."

"You *know* that little slips of paper get lost. Why the hell can't you use e-mail like the rest of us?"

McNaughton was incredulous, but didn't want to fight a battle in front of all these people, especially Basker and Jackson.

"I will next time," he said through clenched teeth. "Now, do you want to stay?"

"No. I'm too busy," Stumbo said. He turned and slammed the door behind him.

"Fat fucker," Kit said, and then glanced around to make sure she hadn't spoken out of turn.

"Don't worry, Kit," Basker offered. "He's the reason I cut out of here."

"What an asshole," Jackson said. She seemed astonished by Stumbo's behavior.

"Believe me, Ruthie, that was mild," Kit said. "He is one of the biggest fools on the department. And I'm not referring to his girth."

"Anyway," Allen began, trying to return the meeting to its purpose, "the perp probably thought he'd escape prosecution if there's no body. Likewise, he probably thought he was pretty clever to leave the Jeep at the airport. I mean, if he had ditched it on the road or burned it up or something, that would have drawn attention to it. Instead, he probably thought it'd never be found at the airport. There's got to be four or five thousand cars out there in long-term parking. And who would think that the airport police would actually log the plate of every car that comes into the lot, and then check them if they're still there a week later?"

"They've got nothing better to do," Kit said derisively.

"Anyway," Chris continued, "once the Jeep was found, it still wouldn't present much of a problem for the perps. They got rid of any evidence by cleaning it so thoroughly."

"That's true," Jack said, "except for one thing. I'm going to tell the techs to use luminol on the Jeep."

His announcement rendered the group silent again. Luminol, a chemical with ultraviolet properties, would be sprayed onto the interior of the Jeep. If blood had been shed there – even if it had been washed away and was not detectable by the human eye – the luminol, mixed with the iron found in blood, would glow blue when illuminated with a black light. They all knew that, if blood showed up, their worst fears would be all but confirmed.

McNaughton broke the silence. "OK, folks. We've got some other things to consider. Mitch's Jeep was taken. That means one of two things – either there was more than one perp, and one drove their car while the other drove Mitch's, or there was just one, and he got to Mitch's some other way. A cab, for example.

"Joe, while you're waiting on your information from BMV, start checking with cab companies. Unlike the airlines, they keep their manifests for a while. If we get a hit – a fare getting delivered anywhere near Mitch's during the hours in question – let's get a composite drawing from the driver."

"Jack," Kit broke in, "that could be awfully difficult. A lot of people take cabs to the restaurants in Broad Ripple, and that number has to be particularly large during those hours on a Friday night. It's date night."

"True," Jack said, "but most of those guys will have a woman with them, right?"

"Yeah. So who's to say which couple is on a date, and which one wants to kill Mitch?"

"Point taken," McNaughton said. "But it's worth a try. OK, Joe?"

"Yes, sir."

"OK. Chris, as soon as you get Mitch's phone records, get with me. I'll help you review them, and if there's too much for the two of us to handle, we'll get Kit and Joe in on it, too."

"Uh, boss?" Stutz was sheepish as he drew Jack's attention, and that of everyone else at the meeting. "I know this is going to sound stupid, but you said we ought to consider every option for solving this."

"Try me, Joe," McNaughton said. "I'll listen to anything."

"Well, have you considered contacting a psychic?"

"No, I hadn't thought of that. I s'pose we could." McNaughton's voice was non-judgmental.

"What do you have to lose?" Basker said.

Kit's face registered her disapproval. "Only our reputation," she said sarcastically. "C'mon. Since when do we resort to psychics when we've got good, old-fashioned investigative techniques to rely on?"

"Well," Jack said, "maybe when those good, old-fashioned techniques aren't turning up much. I'm willing to try, Joe. Any idea how you find one?"

"The Yellow Pages?" Allen offered.

"Shit, no," Alvear said angrily. "What are you going to look up? 'Nuts?' 'Goofballs?' 'Self-anointed prophets?'"

"You could get an eight hundred number off TV," Allen said. "You know, those psychic hotlines advertise late at night."

"Actually, boss," Stutz said, "I've got this neighbor, a sweet, older lady who lives across the street and always makes chicken soup for Anna and me whenever we get sick. It's kind of weird, because she makes it when there's no way she can *know* we're sick. She just senses it. Anyway, she came over the other day and told me that she had been reading about Mitch's disappearance in the newspaper, and she said she wanted to help. She told me she's used what she calls her 'gift' to work with the police before. She gets these feelings, or these images or something that tell her things. And she thought she might be able to help us. And Kit," he concluded, looking toward his colleague, "she's not a nut. She's real nice, and real sincere."

"Right," Alvear said sarcastically. "So are the tooth fairy and the Easter bunny."

Jack chimed in. "I don't think it can hurt. Joe, why don't you have a talk with her?"

"OK, boss. She said it might help if she could go to Mitch's house. Do you mind?"

"No. Let's arrange something; I'd like to go along. Now, does anybody have anything else?" No one spoke up. "Then let's get to work, folks. Remember, this is for Mitch."

It took a few minutes for the meeting to break up, as the participants paused to speak to one another. Eventually, Kit and Joe went off to find Vanessa Goodbody; Chris started making phone calls from his tidy desk; and Basker and Jackson left to return to their squad's stationhouse.

Jack returned to his desk and tossed his notes atop it. He punched Renee's number into the phone, but reached only her voice mail. "Just me, babe. Just called to say I love you. Later."

He hung up, and headed for Stumbo's office. He did not knock, but opened the door and glared at Stumbo until the big man hung up his telephone. Doyle did not have a chance to speak.

"Don't you *ever* do that to me again! *Ever!* You do *not* undermine me with my people, and with Basker's people! Do you understand me?"

"McNaughton," he drawled, "I suggest you take that back, and do it fast!"

"No, Doyle," he said, then louder: "Fuck you, Doyle! I left you a note about the damned meeting. It's your problem if you couldn't find it. Don't blame it on me, and don't try to embarrass me in front of my squad. And since when are you a convert to e-mail?"

"You know the department wants us to use e-mail to improve communications."

"Fuck that, Doyle. A week ago, you'd never read a single e-mail message. I'm warning you, Doyle. I've had it up to here with you," he said, gesturing toward his Adam's apple. "Don't fuck with me!"

"McNaughton, *I'm* warning *you*. Keep this shit up, and I'll have you on department charges of insubordination."

"Try it, Doyle. I really don't give a shit. Just file another I-number on me. I'm collecting them – trying to break the record for how many one cop can get in a year. You know, as far as I'm concerned, *you're* responsible for Mitch's disappearance. If you didn't drive everybody who works here crazy, he'd never have left homicide, and we wouldn't be investigating his murder. One of my best friends in the world, one of the best cops I've ever met, is dead, and it's *your* fault. So do anything you want to me. You can't hurt me anymore than you have."

"That's it, McNaughton. Consider yourself suspended. I am not going to let you blame me for Simons's stupidity. You can't talk to me that way."

"Oh, no, Doyle? What are you going to tell Captain Ryan? That the lead investigator on a missing-cop case has been suspended because he hurt your feelings? Grow up, Doyle. You know, and I know, you're in over your head. Just try to run this investigation without me."

"Well," Stumbo drawled, "perhaps I spoke too hastily. I know you're just upset because Simons is missing. I won't suspend you, but I expect you to show more respect to your superiors."

"You're damned right I'm upset, Doyle. I have a right to be. And let me tell you something: You may outrank me, but you are *not* my superior. And I'll show you respect when you earn it."

"Let me remind you, McNaughton, that I have attained a higher rank that you. That makes me your superior. One more outburst, and I'll reconsider my willingness to overlook this little incident. Just try me."

"No, Doyle, I won't try you. I've got a job to do; I want to do better by Mitch than you ever did. So stay off my ass, Doyle. I'm not kidding you." He started turned toward the door, stopped, and turned back. "And don't you *ever* suggest again that Mitch was stupid."

He jerked the door open and flew out, denying Stumbo the opportunity to say anything more.

McNaughton returned to his work station, breathing hard and willing his hear to stop beating so furiously. He sat on the edge of the desk, pushing some papers aside, and dialed the number for the garage.

"Tony, it's Jack McNaughton. What do you say if I were to come over now, and we run a luminol test on Mitch's Jeep? I really want to be there for it."

"Sure, sergeant. When do you think you can get here?"

"I'm on my way."

It took only ten minutes to make the trek. What was about to happen was so ominous that McNaughton began to forget about the episode with Stumbo.

When he arrived, the tech had secured the Jeep in a windowless bay at the garage, and he had prepared the mixture that would be sprayed on the interior of the Jeep with a gardening spray bottle. It took only a few minutes to wet down the entire interior. The tech grabbed the portable black light, then turned off the overhead fluorescents. For a moment, he and Jack were in cast in blackness, but it was a moment McNaughton would savor. A split second later, he knew more than he really wanted to know about Mitch's fate.

There, on the heavy-rubber mat in the cargo area, glowed an eighteen-inch-diameter, ragged circle of bright blue. Blood. It would take tests, of course, to make sure that it was human. But Mitch was not a hunter, and there would be no explanation for having a spill of this size in his vehicle. Except, of course, the explanation that Jack feared the most.

Jack sat on the edge of the brown plaid sofa, his elbows planted on his knees and his head in his hands. His eyes brimmed with tears, but they would not fall; he would not let them. It was the first time that he had allowed himself even this much display of emotion over Mitch's disappearance, and even now he permitted himself to feel the loss only because he was alone.

He had sought a refuge from Stumbo, and found it in Simons's quiet house. He heard the house sigh as it settled in the winter's cold, and he marveled at how different the virtual silence was from every other time he had been here. There had been the parties, including a bachelor's party for another homicide detective that ended up getting both Simons and McNaughton in trouble. They hadn't invited Stumbo, who didn't like the groom anyway, but he fussed that he should have been included. And then he filed an I-number against Jack for fraternizing with his subordinates.

There had been Jack's visits, when the stereo was always blasting Bob Seger or the Eagles and the phone rang incessantly. Usually women.

And there was the nightmare of Friday the thirteenth – actually, the early morning hours of Saturday, the fourteenth – when all the noisy activity at the house symbolized not the effervescent hub of Mitch Simons's life but, almost assuredly, his death.

"God, Mitch," Jack said aloud. He kept seeing the horror of that glowing blue circle in his mind's eye. And he couldn't forget Stumbo's suggestion that Mitch's own stupidity had caused his death. How could he have slipped up so horribly, so fatally? How couldn't he have been more on his toes?

"His gun." Jack said those words aloud too. Mitch's department issue, a nine-millimeter Sig Sauer, hadn't been found in the house, nor had any other weapon, and McNaughton was sure that Simons had a smaller pistol that he wore in an ankle holster for backup.

Could the guns' absence mean Mitch was alive, that he had intentionally disappeared out of self-preservation? Could the blood in the Jeep be someone else's? McNaughton let himself mull the possibility for a few moments. It would have to mean that Mitch was in serious trouble, that he had seriously hurt, or even killed, someone and had tried to conceal it. But then Jack's eyes fell upon the splotch of Type A-positive blood that had dried hard behind Mitch's recliner. And he knew that, as horrible as that scenario would be, an even worse one was more likely.

What are we missing? He thought. *Surely there's something – there has to be; there's no such thing as the perfect crime. Especially not one committed by a doper.* But he could not fathom any stone the squad had not yet turned, or did not plan to. He made a mental note to have one of his people check on the types of guns used in crimes and seized since the disappearance; the Sig Sauer's serial number would be available in departmental records, and perhaps Jack could find information on the other pistol in Mitch's personal records.

He stood wearily, his knees stiff, and started to walk to the bedroom, where he would rifle through Mitch's dresser drawers just in case he had missed something the other times he had done so. The phone rang, startling Jack in the silence. *What the hell?* He thought. It rang again, and he moved to answer it.

"Hello?"

"Yes, sir," it was a woman's voice, spoken almost robotically. At first Jack wondered if this were a computerized solicitation. "This is Western Union. We have an order to send two thousand dollars cash to Room 214 at the Good Times Inn in Indianapolis, and we want to verify your address and your bank account number. Will that be all right, sir?"

"Um, run that by me again, please?"

The woman repeated what she had said the first time.

"Who put in the order?" Jack asked.

"Well, you did, Mr. Simons. You *are* Mr. Simons, are you not?"

"No, ma'am, as a matter of fact, I'm not. I'm Sergeant Jack McNaughton of the Metro-Marion Police Department, and I'm at Mr. Simons's house to investigate a crime. I wonder if you can put a hold on that order until further notice."

"Well, I don't know, sergeant. Perhaps if I can have some way of verifying that you really are who you say you are."

"I'll come immediately to your Indianapolis office, if that will help. This is important in solving a very serious crime, ma'am. Now, can I count on your cooperation?"

"Well, I guess so, sergeant. We certainly like to cooperate with the law."

"What's your name? And are you in Indianapolis?"

"Yes, sir, I am. My name is Audrey Little."

"OK, Ms. Little. Now, please, do not contact the party that put in the request for the money transfer. That's very important. OK?"

"Yes. OK," she said.

"Great. I'm on my way. Where's your office?"

She told him, and they signed off. He grabbed his jacket, checked the front door to make sure it was locked and dashed to his car. The excitement of the call pushed the horror of the luminol test out of his mind. He started up the engine and pulled out swiftly, barely glancing behind to ensure he didn't crash. Then he picked up his cell phone to call Kit.

Her phone rang once. "Alvear," she answered.

"Kit," Jack said excited, "I think we've finally got a break."

Chapter 15

Alvear and Stutz had spent the afternoon talking with Vanessa Goodbody, who seemed innocent enough – at least when it came to any involvement with Mitch's disappearance. Miss Goodbody's name befitted her appearance, which was reminiscent of Marilyn Monroe. Recalling the incident in which Vanessa had come to the department's attention, Kit nearly laughed out loud as she imagined poor Orval Crumpacker, the town marshal of French Lick, and his eleven-year-old son, Ernie, as they beheld Miss Goodbody's round behind. The seriousness of the situation made any laughter seem inappropriate, but Alvear longed for something – anything – that might bring a smile to her face again. Goodbody's information was not it. Although she was used to showing her attributes to admiring customers at the Pussy Cat, Vanessa was so angry at Mitch for making her the butt of cops' jokes at the Lebanon rest park that she had not seen him or talked with him since that day. She had had no husband or boyfriend at the time, nor did she now, and she was unaware of anyone in her life who had jealous designs on her. Indeed, when Kit first approached her, she still seemed angry at Simons, but that faded when she learned of his fate. When the interview had concluded, her eyes were misty, and her face wore a mournful expression that suggested she was wondering what, under different circumstances, might have been.

Alvear and Stutz next visited Wes Huber, Carly Wellstone's ex-boyfriend. They found him at a house-construction site, drinking coffee and smoking a cigarette during a break from his job as a drywall finisher for Shireman Construction Co. He was wearing a formerly white uniform that bore the mark of an expressionistic painter. Huber had an excellent alibi: He had been visiting his mother in Ohio on Friday evening, staying over until Sunday. Mom would verify it, he assured the detectives in a calm fashion. Kit sensed immediately that Huber had nothing to do with Mitch's disappearance; he seemed distressed that something like that would happen to anybody, but his upset was not so great as to suggest he was feeling guilty. Alvear made a mental note to call his mother, whose name and number she got from Huber, but she felt confident it would be a fruitless avenue.

So when Jack's call came, Alvear and Stutz were ready to do his bidding. They were only ten minutes away from the Good Times Inn, and they agreed to meet there. McNaughton was ahead of them by a few minutes, and made the trip quicker by using his lights and siren until he was just a few blocks away. After hanging up with Kit, he called for a district patrol car to meet him at the inn. He told the uniforms to make sure that nobody left, and to detain anybody who tried. Then he called Chris Allen, who he found at his desk at the stationhouse.

"Boss, I'm glad you called. I've got some good news. I went to BMV for Joe, and they ran the check and found out that Beech Grove police stopped Mitch's Jeep in the early morning hours of Sunday, the fifteenth of January. A woman – a Lisa Myers – M-like mother-Y-E-R-S – was driving. They got her for going sixty in a thirty-five. I've got an address on her in Speedway, and I went there, but no sign of her. I'll check again."

"Good work, Chris. Talk to Stumbo right away and get some people out there to surveil her house so we don't miss her. What else do you have?

"I've got nothing else at the moment, but have you talked to Joe? He got a cabbie who remembers taking a fare to Mitch's neighborhood – the residential part, not the restaurant district. He doesn't remember a whole lot about what the guy looked like – said he wasn't that memorable except that he was dirty – but a sketch artist will get with him first thing in the morning. I'm not sure yet whether Joe or I will go."

"Great. What about the phone records?"

"Nothing yet. I should have them for both land line and cell tomorrow."

"Good work. Now, I need you to go to Western Union for me." He explained the situation and asked Chris to assure Audrey Little that they weren't playing games.

"Right away, boss," Allen said, happy to be involved in what could become the break in the case.

McNaughton ended the call just as he was pulling into the Good Times Inn's parking lot. The motel was a dingy, two-story affair located on a stretch of Shadeland Avenue where virtually everything was dingy. And the overcast sky on this cold winter day didn't help the scene much; Jack had the distinct sensation that snow was on the way. He parked outside the front office, marked by a faulty neon sign. Another sign informed those who cared that the establishment offered free adult movies.

Jack jogged over to talk with the uniforms, who got out of their car to go with him into the office. Then Kit and Joe pulled up. "I wonder how many people spend the whole night here," Alvear said sarcastically when she rolled down her window to greet McNaughton.

"Damn few, I'm sure," he retorted.

She parked, and she and Joe joined McNaughton and the uniforms. "I had the woman at Western Union hold up on transferring the money, so I'm afraid our perp may get a little hinky when his money doesn't come fast enough. We've going to move on him immediately," he said to his entourage.

Jack pushed open the aluminum storm door with the torn screen, and let Kit enter before him. Joe and the uniforms hung back while Jack and Kit approached the front desk together. The five of them nearly filled up the entire room.

"Hello," McNaughton said to the grizzled man lounging behind the desk, his feet propped up. "I'm Sergeant McNaughton of Metro-Marion Police and this is Detective Alvear."

The introduction caused the man, who looked as if he had had no sleep in the three days it had taken to grow the stubble across his chin, to swing his legs down and rise. Only then did he see the uniforms, and he startled slightly. Clearly, Jack's introduction had taken a moment to sink in. The man was of medium height, and thin, with stooped shoulders and the telltale ruddy complexion of someone who had stopped enjoying his liquor but needed it to make it through the day. He wore a sleeveless undershirt, blue work pants and cheap black running shoes on inordinately small feet. His greasy grey hair pointed in various directions, including straight up. It was cool in the office, but Kit figured he had ingested something to keep his toasty.

"Yeah. Whaddya want?"

His tone was that of a defeated man. Jack sensed that he wouldn't be much trouble. "Can you tell me who is in Room 214?"

The man looked a bit put out, but did not hesitate before swinging the old-fashioned sign-in register around so he could see it. There was no computer in sight. "Two fourteen. Uh. . .," he paused as he looked. "That's, uh, that's Mitch Simons."

Jack felt his heart jump, and for the briefest of moments he let himself believe that it really was Mitch who had registered at this dive. And whatever the reason, whatever trouble he was in, whatever bender he was on, McNaughton wouldn't have cared. But reason took over, and he knew that the guest was an imposter who was just using Mitch's name and bank account.

Jack turned the register back to face him and found Mitch's name. The signature was unfamiliar.

"How did Mr. Simons pay for the room?"

"Let me look here. Uh, I took an impression of his VISA. Ya wanna see it?"

"Yes, please," McNaughton said.

Again, the name was Mitch's, the signature was not.

"When did he register?" Alvear asked.

"Uh, he came in night before last, so he's on his third day," the man answered. Then he offered: "That's longer than most of our guests stay."

"I should say so," Alvear mumbled under her breath. McNaughton gave her a look to quiet her.

"Is Mr. Simons alone?" McNaughton asked.

"He checked in alone, but I've seen him come and go with a woman. But I don't ask no questions. The rate's the same, one or two people in the room."

"Did they have luggage?" Alvear asked.

"I can't say, ma'am. Didn't notice."

"Is there a phone in the room?" Jack asked.

"Oh, yeah."

"Sir, would you please prepare a list of the phone calls Mr. Simons had made since he checked in? These officers," he said, gesturing toward the uniforms, "will stay here with you. You can give it to them. Detective Alvear, Detective Stutz and I are going to pay a visit to Mr. Simons. I'd appreciate if you didn't call him to let him know." Kit shot a look at the uniforms, signaling that they should ensure he didn't. They got it; one nodded his ascent.

"Which way to Room 214?" Jack asked.

"When you go out here, hang a right, and then another quick right. Take the stairs to the second floor, and it's about halfway down."

"Fine. Please stay here behind the desk, all right?"

"Right, sure."

"OK. Thanks for your help."

"Yessir. I keep an honest establishment here. I always want to cooperate with the law." He stretched out the word "cooperate" as if he were trying it out for the first time.

Alvear and Stutz stood with their backs to the wall on either side of the door of Room 214. Their guns were drawn, as was McNaughton's. His back was to Alvear as he stood off-center from the door and knocked.

"What?" responded a perturbed voice from the other side.

"Maintenance. Gotta fix the heater," Jack said, just loud enough to be heard by the occupant but, he hoped, not by other guests.

"It's about time," the occupant mumbled. Jack could hear him tramping toward the door. As he got closer, and as the threesome watched the door handle turn, they all braced, their bodies taut, their minds sharp.

The man who had registered as Mitch Simons wore only a towel, holding onto it with his left hand as he opened the door with his right. And then he wore a look of surprise, as Jack, in one swift move, grabbed his arm, twisting it slightly and forced the man, face first, against the door. The towel floated to the floor.

"Police," McNaughton said firmly. He holstered his gun as soon as he saw that the man wasn't armed and, given his state of undress, couldn't be hiding a weapon. He pulled his leather badge case from his pocket and held it in front of the man's face.

"*Shit!*" the man responded. "What the hell do you want?"

Alvear and Stutz swooped in behind McNaughton, sweeping the room with their eyes. Both sets landed on a woman who had sat up abruptly in bed, making no effort to cover her naked torso.

"Some hotshot you are," the woman mumbled as she began to rise from the bed, scouting for clothing.

"Just a minute, ma'am," Kit said. She approached the woman, picking up clothing as she moved, as Stutz averted his eyes. The detectives kept their weapons drawn, but at their sides, waiting to take direction from their boss.

"Do you have identification, sir?" Jack asked the would-be Simons.

"If you let go of me, I'll get it," he spit. McNaughton did just that, although his eyes never left the man.

He was in his mid- to late twenties, a skinny guy whose build resembled that of the desk clerk. His shoulder-length brown hair was filthy and in disarray. He had bloodshot eyes and a couple days' growth of beard. It struck Jack that this could be the guy he had seen in the fuzzy bank videos.

The man moved toward the television set, on which lay a wallet, some loose change and a few haphazardly folded bills. Kit and Joe raised their guns and kept them trained on him as he grasped the wallet and thrust it at McNaughton, who took it and opened it.

The Indiana driver's license identified the scrawny man as Rodney Jenkins of Indianapolis, DOB 7-6-82.

"Well, Mr. Jenkins, can you tell me why you're registered at the front desk as Mitch Simons?" McNaughton asked. Before Jenkins could answer, the woman responded, "What the fuck? You ain't Mitch?"

"Shut up, bitch!" Jenkins shouted, and then to McNaughton: "I ain't talking to you without a lawyer."

McNaughton tried another tack. "We'd like permission to search your room, Mr. Jenkins."

"I said no! I want a lawyer!"

"Fine," McNaughton said sternly. "We're impounding this room until we can secure a search warrant, which should be no trouble, Mr. Jenkins. You're under arrest for theft and credit card fraud." He recited the Miranda rights to him and asked if he understood. Jenkins didn't answer, so Jack asked again, his voice firmer. This time, Jenkins muttered a belligerent "yeah."

"Get dressed," McNaughton ordered. He grasped his hand-held radio, which had been hooked on his belt, and radioed for the department's detention van to come pick Jenkins up. While Joe watched Jenkins dress, Jack turned his attention to the woman, who by now was clothed and fixing her disheveled hair.

"What's your name, ma'am?"

"Lisa Myers." McNaughton's heart jumped; it was the name of the woman stopped in Mitch's Jeep by the Beech Grove police.

"Kit, can you go get a key for another room from the front desk, and tell the uniforms to come back here?" Jack asked. Then he turned to Myers. "Ms. Myers, Detective Alvear will take you to another room where the two of you can talk about your relationship with Mr. Jenkins."

"I barely know him. He said his name was Mitch."

"That's one of the things we'd like to hear about, OK?"

"Sure. I ain't got nothin' to hide."

Kit was already out the door by the time the conversation concluded, and she was back within minutes, with a key and the two uniforms. She took Myers to a room two doors down.

Lisa Myers was about five-foot-five, a hundred ten pounds, with particularly long legs for her height. She accentuated them with platform-soled sandals that she wore beneath her skin-tight jeans that were wearing thin at the knees. She wore a form-fitting white lace shell that was discolored and speckled with what appeared to be spaghetti sauce.

After Alvear unlocked the door, Myers loped into the hotel room with long, awkward strides, the kind that one has to take when wearing such ridiculously high and unyielding platforms. She plopped into one of the burnt orange chairs at the far end of the room, slouching down with her long legs crossed at the knee in front of her. Her leg kicked lazily, indicating her boredom with the situation. She pulled a nearly defunct package of Virginia Slims from her purse and lit up.

Kit sat in the stained matching chair opposite Myers and placed a digital voice recorder on the octagonal table between them. The table's laminate top had not protected it from chipping along the edges. Alvear pushed the "record" button and began reciting the usual introduction to all recorded sessions. That concluded, she turned to Myers.

"Ms. Myers, I want to ask you a few questions about you and Mr. Jenkins. Is Lisa Myers your full legal name?"

Myers nodded. Then, thinking about the recorder, she leaned toward it and answered: "Yes, it is."

"That's OK, Ms. Myers. The recorder will pick you up from where you're sitting. What's your date of birth?"

"December twenty-first, nineteen eighty-one," she said.

"Where do you live?"

"3475 West Highland Avenue, apartment three-C, Speedway."

Alvear nodded her knowledge of the area. "How long have you known Mr. Jenkins?"

"Well, I didn't even know his name *was* Jenkins until you guys came in. He said his name was Mitch Simons."

"OK. When did you meet him?"

"Uh, well, shit, it's got to be a little more than a week ago. Um, I think it was a week ago Saturday."

"So that would have made it Saturday, the fourteenth?"

"Yeah, I guess so."

"Where'd you meet?"

"At work. The Suck-It-To-Me Lounge over there in Speedway. I'm a waitress there."

"A waitress. Uh-huh."

"No, really. I am. I don't really want to dance there. Like, the dancers make good tips, but mine are pretty good too. And, I mean, the uniform's skimpy and all, but I don't have to tolerate all those hands all over me all the time."

"OK. So, you're waitressing at the, uh, Suck-It . . . the, uh, lounge, and he's a customer and he picks you up?"

"Well, sort of. Only it was the end of my shift. Like, we're not supposed to date the customers, but I needed a ride home."

"OK, tell me the story."

"Well, he offers to give me a ride home. I don't live that far from the club; I mean, I walk to work. But it was, like, really late, and I was tired, so I said, OK. When I got out into his Jeep, he asked if I liked having a good time. I said, sure, but that depended what he meant. He said he'd come into some money, and that he was ready to party, to go out on the town. So we went some place on the south side – I don't remember the name – and we danced some. And then we went downtown to another place and danced and drank some more. I guess it must have been about three in the morning when he asked me if I wanted to shack up for the night. I thought, what the hell. I mean, he seemed nice enough. So we went to some motel on the south side; I forget the name. We partied there a day or so, then moved to some other place, then here."

"So you met a little more than a week ago."

"Yeah, I know. He was kinda weird, but I liked him enough. He was fun. Liked to spend a lot of money. So we had a good time."

"How much did he pay you?"

"It wasn't like that. I don't do that shit. Like, I just wanted to have some fun."

"And he had enough money to make sure you did."

"Yeah."

"So did he take you to work throughout the week?"

"Nah. I was pretty sick of that place, so I just skipped going. Shit, they're always looking for somebody so I'm sure I can go back if I wanna. I guess maybe I will."

"What did you do all week?"

"Well, you know. The usual."

"No. What's 'the usual?'"

"OK. I don't want to get in no trouble here. Like, I'm being straight with you. We went out to a few clubs, did a little blow, a little reefer. Mostly just beer, though. And, well, we fucked a lot. He's not bad for a little guy."

Alvear ignored the last remark. "You said that, on the night you met, the two of you went out to his Jeep. Right?"

"Yeah."

"Can you describe it?"

"I'm not so good with cars. Like, I don't know the year or nothin'. But I know it was, like, a Jeep, 'cause I remember seeing the name on the back. It was black – or maybe dark blue; it was hard to tell."

"Did he let you drive it?"

"Well, sort of. He didn't really want me to, but he was so drunk on that first night that I had to take the keys away from him. He was pretty scary, and I knew I didn't want to end up in no mangled mess on the front page of the paper for my mama to see."

"Uh-huh. Any trouble with the law?"

"Well, yeah. I got a ticket for speeding. Really, I didn't know I was going that fast. I was just tired and wanted to get home. Well, not home, really. Like I said, we stayed someplace on the south side. I had quit drinking a lot earlier – I really don't drink that much – and the cop said he was glad that it was me driving, and not my friend. Mitch – um, *Mr. Jenkins* – was really shit-faced. What'd you say his real first name is?"

"Rodney."

"Oh. Dorky name."

"Had he told you his name was Mitch?"

"No. I noticed it on his credit card when we went to get cash from the ATM."

"Where was that?"

"At the First National branch right across the street from the Suck-It-To-Me. He needed cash after we decided to go out partying."

"How much did he get out?"

"I think it was two hundred."

"And do you remember which police department stopped you?"

"Um." She paused to think. "Beech Grove, I think."

"OK. Anyway," Kit continued, "where's the Jeep now? I didn't see any dark-colored Jeep in the lot."

"Well, that was the one thing he did that made me a little hinky. On Sunday, the day after we met, we slept in. He really needed to, believe me. Anyway, after we got up, it was like noon or somethin', and he said he had to take the Jeep to the airport and leave it there for a friend. I thought that was kind of weird, but I guess it made sense."

"So what'd you do?"

"We went to the long-term parking place and parked. That was about it."

"Did you wash the car before doing that?"

"Oh, yeah. I forgot. First we went to this do-it-yourself joint, and he hosed down like the whole Jeep, even the insides, with this high-pressure hose. Said his friend liked his car spick-and-span. He wouldn't even let me touch anything inside after that. We just dried off the leather seats so we wouldn't get our clothes wet, and then I had to, like, sit there with my hands in my lap the whole way to the airport. He yelled at me when I went to change the station on the radio."

"Didn't that strike you as odd?"

"A little, maybe. But, different strokes for different folks, right? I guess I thought it was a little weird when he even wiped down the steering wheel and the door handle when we left. Like, they were already dry."

"Did it occur to you he was getting rid of fingerprints?"

"Shit. I didn't think of that."

Alvear marveled at the woman's vacuity. "OK. So you drop off the Jeep at the airport. How'd you get back here?"

"We took a cab. That's how we've gotten around all week. Mitch didn't seem to be too worried about the money. Rodney Jenkins, I mean."

"Did he visit other ATMs?"

"Oh, sure. Several."

"Did he always pay cash when you went out?"

"Oh, yeah. He always had a big roll. Said he didn't trust them credit cards. He even paid with cash at the motels, but they made him give a credit card for security."

"Lisa, you said earlier that you thought Rodney was a little weird. How come?"

"Well, some of the things he'd say. One night, we were, um, *making love*" – she enunciated the euphemism slowly and coyly – "and he was showing off and asked if I had ever fucked a guy who had killed somebody. I said no, and I didn't plan to. He said, 'Too late. You're doing it right now.' I said, 'I don't believe you.' And he said that he could use a gun as good as he used his cock. And he came real quick then, like what he was saying excited him, and he got up and showed me this big, ol' gun. I didn't believe him, though. I thought he was full of shit. God, if I'd of thought he really killed somebody, I would have been out of there so fast . . ."

She paused, then continued. "Did he kill somebody?"

"That's what we're trying to find out."

"Oh, shit. Tell me it wasn't a woman."

"No. It was a man. A police officer. I don't think you were in any danger. Besides, it's all over now."

"Shit. Yeah. Like, it's all over."

McNaughton was relieved that the detention van had come promptly, because he was quickly losing his patience with Rodney Jenkins. Jack had dealt with plenty of wiseasses over the years, but Jenkins was particularly grating; Jack could not forget that he likely was looking at the man who had killed Mitch. What's more, Jenkins smelled of beer and body odor and sex, and the hotel room, with its one, sealed-shut window, was stifling. That, combined with the empty gnawing in his gut, was enough to make McNaughton feel like vomiting.

He felt better when Jenkins, newly attired in jail clothing, was whisked away to the county lockup, where he would be charged with as many theft and credit card offenses as Jack could think of. That way, they could hold him until the squad had something more. Jenkins' absence did not let McNaughton forget what the man probably had done; Mitch was never far from Jack's mind. But the demands of a homicide case required him to set his emotions aside, and before long, McNaughton was functioning as if the victim had been, like all the others, just another stranger.

He left Kit in charge and told Stutz to assist her if she needed help or to handle whatever else might come up. Meanwhile, McNaughton went to secure a search warrant for the hotel room.

The uniforms remained, standing guard of the room in case Stutz had other things to attend to. McNaughton used his lights and siren to speed to the stationhouse, where he parked illegally but covered himself by dropping a laminated "Official Business" card on the dash. He took the stairs two at a time to the squad room. Even before he sat down at his desk, he picked up the phone to call the clerk's office to see if any judges were working late; it was already after six p.m. and, unless they had a trial, most of them would have been long gone.

"Judge Mullen is still in his chambers; let me check how long he'll be there," she said. McNaughton thanked her and listened to obnoxious music as he waited on hold.

He shut his eyes to sort out his thoughts so that he might make the best case for seeking a search warrant, then began typing while he waited for the clerk.

"Uh, hello?"

"Yes, I'm here," McNaughton responded.

"Judge Mullen said he'd wait for you, if you think you can make it over in a half-hour."

"I'll be there."

McNaughton was pleased to hear it was Mullen who was in late tonight. He was regarded as a cop's judge, and generally agreed to search warrants if they had any kind of reasonable basis. Some other judges were a lot pickier. Jack knocked out the warrant in fifteen minutes, spelling out specifically what he was looking for – debit or credit cards and other personal effects of Mitch Simons – and his reasons for thinking such items could be found in Room 214 of the Good Times Inn. He printed it out and then speeded over to the City-County Building.

He badged his way through security, then tapped his hand against his leg impatiently as he waited for the ancient elevator to pick him up. He mulled whether it would be quicker to run up the eight flights or to wait for the antiquated thing. Its arrival made the decision for him, and it deposited McNaughton just outside the outer office of Judge Charlie Mullen's chambers. Jack was greeted by a lovely, dark-haired woman of Asian Indian heritage.

"Hi, Jack," she said; McNaughton had been in the chambers on previous cases. "The judge is waiting for you."

"Thanks, Kamla," he said as he passed behind her desk, knocking on it with his knuckles for emphasis.

It took little to persuade the aging, pop-eyed judge with frantic grey fringe for hair that the cops ought to be able to search Jenkins' hotel room. He scanned the warrant that Jack had prepared, signed it and handed it back. The whole process took less than five minutes.

"Good luck, son," he said.

"Thank you, your honor."

It would be a quick search, Jack knew. One bureau, two nightstands, the mattresses, the few nooks and crannies that could be found in a standard hotel room. Still, he enlisted Stutz's assistance when he returned, and together they foraged through the stinky room.

Stutz started in the bathroom, and found a small plastic bag of what he figured could be cocaine suspended on the bulb above the water in the toilet tank. McNaughton took the bedroom, looking first in the long bureau that contained a Gideon's Bible.

"Bingo," he said, as he moved a T-shirt aside and spotted a .45-caliber Colt. Next to the huge handgun were three of Mitch's credit cards, an ATM bank card, forty-five dollars in cash, some change, one of Mitch's business cards with a four-digit number written on it and a fake diamond man's ring that Jack knew Simons used on some undercover assignments.

"Look at this," McNaughton said, handing the business card to Joe. "I'll betcha that's Mitch's PIN. That's how Rodney's been using it to get cash from ATMs for the past week and a half."

"Yup."

Neither McNaughton nor Stutz found anything else of significance. The trash can held a party's worth of empty beer cans, an empty baggy that Stutz thought might contain cocaine residue and several used condoms; clearly the Good Times didn't offer daily maid service. He saved both drug bags for testing, just in case they needed to file a drug charge to keep Jenkins in jail a little longer while they worked the homicide. McNaughton also bagged Jenkins' clothing for the laboratory to test; Jenkins didn't appear to be terribly fastidious, so there was a chance that there still might be residue of gun powder or Mitch's blood left on it from ten days earlier.

When they were satisfied that they had checked everything, they alerted the desk clerk that he could have his room back.

"Do you s'pose he'll change the sheets before he starts renting it out by the hour?" Stutz asked.

Stutz hooked back up with Alvear to take Lisa Myers home. McNaughton told them they could head home themselves after that; it was unlikely they could do much more that day. But he decided he'd take one more pass at Rodney Jenkins to see if he'd changed his mind about talking.

Jack headed to the jail, which was a block south of the City-County Building in a complex that was all city-owned. He got clearance to go back to Jenkins' cell, which Rodney shared with a large man whose snore virtually shook the metal bars. Sleeping off a good drunk, Jack figured.

"Get the fuck out of here!" Rodney screeched when he saw McNaughton.

"Rodney, I came to see if you've changed your mind. Do you want to talk?"

"I said get outta here! I want a lawyer, asshole."

"OK, Rodney. I was trying to make it easier on you. But fine; you can get your lawyer. See you in court tomorrow."

Jenkins shot a furious look at McNaughton and then turned his back on the cop.

Chapter 16

Jenkins' initial hearing was scheduled for nine the next morning in the courtroom of Judge Graham Hunter, a relative newcomer to the bench who was, therefore, a mystery to most courtroom participants. Jack didn't care; the initial hearing was perfunctory: Under Indiana law, the judge would automatically enter a plea of not guilty for the defendant and likely would appoint a public defender to represent Jenkins after he assured the judge, in his most sincere voice, that he had no money with which to obtain counsel. If the prosecution deemed Hunter too much of an unknown – or too favorable to defendants – there was plenty of time to move for a new judge, a request that was usually granted.

But it was too early to worry about such matters. McNaughton just wanted to ensure that Jenkins would be kept in jail long enough for the squad to gather evidence for a murder charge. He had called Terry Bennett, the county prosecutor, the night before, to apprise him of the circumstances. They decided together that Jenkins would be charged with possession of cocaine and several counts each of credit card fraud, theft and possession of stolen property. They also would cite Jenkins' prior offenses and explain to the judge that the defendant was being investigated in connection with a police officer's murder. That, Bennett said, should be enough to persuade any judge in the county to set a high bond.

Bennett also planned to appear at the initial hearing to emphasize the gravity of the case. Usually, a low-level deputy prosecutor would handle such charges; Bennett handled only the most serious – and newsworthy – cases. What's more, Bennett had assigned his chief deputy for homicides, Sylvia Ambrogi, to be lead prosecutor for the case, also an indication to the judge that there was much more to the case than a few property crimes.

The two prosecutors agreed to meet McNaughton twenty minutes before court was due to start to review the facts of the case. The threesome knew they'd have Judge Hunter's courtroom to themselves almost until the hearing began because most reporters wouldn't have yet caught on that this was an important case. Jack had called Myra Spricker to tell her to attend the hearing; that's all he would say, but he assured her that she wouldn't be wasting her time – and he knew that was enough to spur her attendance.

McNaughton arrived at the courtroom first, followed within moments by the two prosecutors. He reviewed the case for them, including his reasoning for thinking that Jenkins had killed Mitch and his assurance that it was only a matter of time – probably that very day – before there was sufficient evidence to prove it. Indeed, murder had been charged with less evidence. But McNaughton wanted to ensure that nothing could possibly go wrong, so he wanted to withhold the serious charges until the case was sewn up.

Bennett listened in silence, satisfied with the information provided by a cop he'd known for years. Ambrogi, also familiar with McNaughton's work, nonetheless asked some questions just to ensure she was thoroughly versed before addressing the judge; one thing that was known about Hunter was that he could not abide a lack of preparation.

"All rise," the bailiff said without enthusiasm. "The court of the Honorable Graham D. Hunter is now in session."

"You may be seated," Hunter said as he sat in his black leather swivel chair. He was a handsome man in his mid-fifties, still possessing a full head of lush blondish hair that he wore longish, not unlike that of the actor Robert Redford. Hunter listened attentively as public defender Nat Kingsley, whose name had been first on the roster and thus was temporarily assigned to represent Jenkins, explained his client's indigence and asked that counsel be permanently appointed. Ambrogi did not object.

But the chief deputy prosecutor argued vociferously against the low bond requested by the young public defender, who appeared to be a recent law school graduate. Ambrogi was about the same age as the judge, and had been prosecuting for her entire career. She had a runner's taut body and wore her short, dark hair in loose curls around her forehead and behind her ears. Her dark, intelligent eyes were deep set; she hid them behind half-glasses when she peered at documents. She had a thin mouth, prominent cheekbones and a narrow nose that ended in a sharp point.

"Your honor, may we approach?" Ambrogi asked. Hunter gestured for her and Kingsley to come to the bench, where they could quietly discuss the bond out of earshot of the gallery. Myra Spricker scooted up in her seat to try to hear, but to no avail; she figured she'd get the story from Bennett after court.

"Your honor," the prosecutor said, "we have reason to believe that Mr. Jenkins is involved in a much more serious crime, the killing of police officer. Facing such a serious prosecution and, indeed, a possible death penalty, Mr. Jenkins may be prone to flee this jurisdiction. We ask that you hold Mr. Jenkins without bond so that he will have no choice but to stay."

Hunter turned to Kingsley. "Your honor," the defense attorney said, his voice revealing the apprehension he felt, "if the prosecution has enough evidence to charge Mr. Jenkins, then it should charge him. Otherwise, bond should be set at an amount appropriate for the crimes with which he's charged."

"Ms. Ambrogi," Hunter said, "Mr. Kingsley has a point. Why don't you just charge Mr. Jenkins?"

"We are quite close to doing so, your honor," she replied. "Perhaps even today. But your honor, you know how sensitive such cases are, how apt they are to draw attention from the news media. We'd like to make sure all our 'i's' are dotted and our 't's' are crossed before we file."

Hunter thought for a moment. "OK, Ms. Ambrogi. I'm not crazy about doing this, but I also don't want to give Mr. Jenkins a chance to flee in case he is involved in the police officer's death. I'll set his bond at five hundred thousand dollars, or ten percent cash."

"Your honor," both attorneys said in unison; the decision pleased neither. Hunter held up his hand to stop them. "We'll leave it at that. Get me more evidence, Ms. Ambrogi, and you'll get a higher bond. But if I don't see more evidence in here within forty-eight hours, I'll summon you all back here and we'll set one more appropriate to the charges that Mr. Jenkins actually faces."

"Thank you, your honor," both again said simultaneously, dejectedly.

The rest of the hearing was perfunctory. Afterward, Spricker cornered Bennett, who was pleased to be. He prattled on about Jenkins and his possible involvement in the disappearance of Officer Simons, and Spricker had her story. She winked at Jack to signal her gratitude; the TV stations and the Star would be playing catch-up on this one.

McNaughton had to suppress a smile when he walked into the squad room and saw his small team of detectives handling the work of a group twice its size. Allen had already met with the cabbie and the sketch artist, and together they came up with a drawing of a thin-faced man with shoulder-length hair. Could be Jenkins, Jack thought. Alvear had performed a field test on the two plastic bags that Stutz had found in the hotel room; they tested positive for cocaine, so drug-possession charges would stick – all the better to keep Jenkins in jail a while longer.

Alvear met again with Lisa Myers and got details about where she and Jenkins had gone – lounges, bars, ATMs and motels. Using Mitch's bank records like the clues to a treasure map, she and Stutz drove Myers around town to locate places when she couldn't remember their names.

"Does this look like the place?" Kit asked as she pulled up to Greg's Lounge, knowing full well that there was a charge of fifty-one dollars from Greg's Lounge on Mitch's debit card. They repeated the scene over and over until they had pieced together virtually every place Rodney Jenkins had gone since picking up Lisa Myers at the Suck-It-To-Me Lounge.

Allen, meanwhile, finally got Mitch's phone records for both his land line and his cell. Everything seemed to be in order; there were several calls, on January one and eight, placed to a number in Kokomo. Chris knew Mitch's mother lived there, and it appeared the dutiful son called his mother weekly. He'd check records, rather than bother the grieving mother, to be sure. Chris called a number that was listed as being in Fort Lauderdale, Fla., and found it to be a Holiday Inn; the reservation clerk said a Mr. Mitchell Simons had reservations for the third week in March; that coincided with Kit's recollection that Mitch had been contemplating a spring vacation.

As he went over the list one more time, Chris noticed a one-minute call to the 502 area code in Louisville, Ky., made at eleven-thirty-two p.m. January thirteen. "Jack, look at this," he called out, prompting McNaughton to get up and walk to Allen's desk.

"That's a curious time," McNaughton said after looking at the number. "Call it. Let's see who Mitch was calling so late the night he disappeared."

Allen punched in a "nine" for an outside line, and then the ten numbers listed on the bill.

"This is the Army Corps of Engineers information line," a recorded voice responded. "Water levels for area lakes are as follows . . ."

Allen listened as the recording ticked off numerous lakes in Kentucky and Indiana, including several in the Indianapolis area. Then he hung up.

"This is weird, Jack," he said. "That was information about water levels at the lakes around here, like Morse and Shafer. Why would Mitch be calling about that so late at night? Seems a strange time of year to be planning a day or fishing or skiing, anyway."

McNaughton paused. "Maybe *Mitch* wasn't. Maybe it was somebody else – like the person who killed him."

They waited in silence another moment, then Jack called Kit and Joe over to explain Chris' finding. "I'm thinking that the perp – Jenkins – wanted to know what the water level was at a local lake to determine if he could dispose of a body there," McNaughton said.

"Shit," Alvear responded. "That makes sense, but it means he could be anywhere."

"Yeah, but let's call the dive team and find out if they can run some ultrasound for us at a few of the area lakes to see if there's anything unusually big under there – something bigger than a bass, at any rate," McNaughton said. "Ask them where they'd like to start."

"OK, Jack. Right away."

The dive team agreed to meet McNaughton and his crew at Lake Shafer at two that afternoon. While he was eager to begin the ultrasound search, Jack thought the timing was fine; it gave him and Joe the time to meet with Bertie O'Toole, Joe's psychic neighbor in Southport, south of Indianapolis.

Stutz went through the drive-through at McDonald's for a Big Mac on his way to pick the woman up at her home, a small and tidy ranch on a narrow and tidy street. She asked if she could be taken to Mitch's house to heighten the images she hoped would come to her. On the way through downtown, Stutz stopped at the stationhouse to pick up McNaughton; O'Toole got into the back seat while Stutz went in the stationhouse to get Jack.

McNaughton was immediately taken by the tiny woman. Her hair was dyed a flat black that didn't match the fine lines that were forming around her happy green eyes, but her round, open face softened the look.

"We're very grateful to you for helping us out, Mrs. O'Toole," McNaughton said as he turned around from the front seat to address her.

"I just hope it is a help, dear. I want to do whatever I can," she replied. Then, a short moment later, she said: "Your grandfather had a bad left leg."

Jack blinked hard. "Yes. You're right. He was injured on the job and couldn't work to support my mother's family for years. But my gosh – he's been dead for more than thirty years, and I haven't thought about him in ages. How did you know?"

"I don't know how I know these things," she said. "It's just a feeling."

They drove in silence for a few minutes, and Jack could not contain his curiosity. "Mrs. O'Toole, I hope you don't mind me asking, but what exactly do you do to summon up these feelings?"

"Nothing," she said. "I don't know what does it. I've been like this since I was a kid."

"Can you turn it off?" Joe asked.

"You can turn it off to a degree just by telling yourself you have earthly matters to attend to. But sometimes it's too strong. Sometimes you can't."

Several minutes of silence passed, and then she continued. "Some people think I can read their minds; that's just silly. And some think I put hexes on them. That hurts my feelings. I'm Catholic; I'm not a witch. I don't know why I have the powers. They're just there. I didn't do anything to learn them. And sometimes I wish I didn't have them. These images come to me – things I don't want to know about people.

"Joe, dear," she said without missing a beat, "you shouldn't have eaten that lettuce for lunch. You know your colon can't take it."

Stutz raised his eyebrows. "How in the. . ." He stopped; he knew.

They reached Mitch's bungalow around noon, and O'Toole again became silent as Jack tore back the "crime scene" yellow tape and unlocked the front door. He held it open for O'Toole as she stepped in tentatively. Jack and Joe exchanged glances, unsure if they should speak or follow her lead. So they did the latter, and walked several steps behind as she surveyed the living room, including the blood spot behind the recliner.

She finally spoke. "It's not good, dear," she said. "I'm very sorry, but I'm getting a strong feeling that your friend is dead."

"Could it be someone else?" Joe asked hopefully. "I mean – sure – that blood indicates somebody was seriously hurt. But are you sure it was Mitch?"

"I'm afraid so. Yes. I feel he has been shot," she said, hesitating a moment. "Once. In the back. I don't think he suffered much, though, dear. I think he died quite quickly."

"Mrs. O'Toole," Jack began, "as much as I had hoped you could tell us otherwise, what you're saying is not a surprise. But can you tell us anything that would help us find the body?"

"Well, dear, I get a strong impression of water. Do you have a map of the area?"

"I've got one in the car," Joe said. He left the house and sprinted to his LTD, returning a moment later with a map of the Indianapolis metropolitan area.

As Stutz unfolded the map and spread it on the kitchen table, O'Toole unlatched the crystal pendant that hung around her neck. "It gives me energy," she said in response to Jack's questioning, raised eyebrows. She held the chain with two fingers, suspending the crystal about three inches above the surface and slowly passing it over the terrain. When she reached northern Hamilton County, the county immediately north of Marion County, she moved even more slowly. McNaughton and Stutz watched in amazement as the chain started moving in small circles and then, like a leash with an invisible dog at the end of it, stopped stock still at a thirty-degree angle above the map.

"He's here," she said somberly, pointing with the forefinger of her left hand. She indicated a specific spot on the north side of Morse Lake. "You'll find him here."

"Joe, call Max Gill right away and tell him to forget Lake Shafer and to get his team to the north side of Morse. We'll still meet him there at two."

"Right, boss."

While Stutz made the call, McNaughton turned to O'Toole, whose face had taken on a wistful look.

"Thank you very much, Mrs. O'Toole. You've been an enormous help."

"I just wish I could have given you better news, dear."

Max Gill was so self-assured that he struck most people as cocky, but Jack appreciated the sergeant's self-confidence. It made McNaughton feel satisfied that the job would be done right. Gill's team of four – three men and a woman – had assembled at a boat launch on the north side of Morse Lake and prepared for the possibility of a dive. It was an unpleasant task – diving for a putrefied body – in the best weather conditions, and the January cold made it even worse. But as soon as McNaughton arrived with Kit in his Ford, followed by Joe Stutz and Chris Allen in Joe's LTD, Jack noticed that Gill's team was upbeat; as divers in landlocked Indiana, they didn't have as many opportunities to ply their trade as their counterparts in other states did. And this case, if they helped solve it, would be particularly gratifying: Solving the murder of a fellow police officer. McNaughton noticed that the divers did not seem to dwell on Mitch's death; that was fact to them. Instead, they focused on what they could do to bring to justice the person who had made it so.

Gill's face broke into a wide smile and he swung his right hand from his side to grasp Jack's as McNaughton approached. "Jack," Gill said, stretching out the syllable. "Good to see you, bud. Just sorry about the circumstances."

"Yeah," McNaughton responded. "Thanks for getting here – especially given the change of plans."

"We're here to please," Gill said. "Here to please." He greeted the rest of Jack's team, and then turned back to his own, who continued to prepare for their task. Jack looked up and saw something he wished he could blink away. Waddling toward them were Stumbo and Ryan, frick and frack, Mutt and Jeff. McNaughton hadn't given it any earlier thought, but of course there was no keeping the brass away from the scene if there was the possibility that a cop's body might be found. "Shit," Jack said under his breath, realizing that he was about to get an earful for failing to notify the brass.

"Shit," Alvear said louder and more vehemently. "Why did those pricks have to show up?"

The grief started before McNaughton could answer. "McNaughton," Stumbo began when he was within ten feet of Jack, "it would have been nice to be informed about this detail. You know, Simons worked for me."

"Right, Doyle. Only he was working for Frank Basker most recently." McNaughton left out the fact that he also had failed to notify Basker. "I didn't think you'd care about this detail," he said, the sarcasm a little too obvious as far as Stutz was concerned.

Stumbo's mouth opened as if he were going to speak, but Ryan cut him off. "Jack, you know supervisors should be here, if for no other reason than to keep decorum and provide the proper atmosphere of dignity for a fallen officer."

"Yes, sir, captain," McNaughton said. "But I think my people and Max's have the right attitude. We all know the gravity of the situation. We're not just looking for another cop; we're looking for a friend."

"Uh, yes, Jack," Ryan continued. "I'd really prefer not to argue about this."

"Yes, sir," McNaughton mumbled.

Officers Liz Pretoria and Tom Wesley, both members of the dive team, were decked out in black wetsuits. They had climbed into a small motorboat while the conversation had been going on, and would handle the ultrasound depth-finders. Their colleagues, Gordon Krance and Nick Fallows, next in the boat, would be the first to dive if Pretoria and Wesley indicated they'd found anything promising.

McNaughton retrieved his black leather gloves from his car and turned his jacket collar up. Alvear found herself wishing she'd brought a hat, and she yanked her scarf up around her ears. Stutz, who never seemed to get cold, stood bareheaded and barehanded. And Allen paced so relentlessly that it was doubtful he'd feel the chill.

"God, it's cold," Alvear whined.

"Yeah," added Joe. "If Mitch were here, he'd say it's cold as a witch's tit." He let out a halfhearted chuckle.

"You know, Joe," Kit said, "Mitch *may* be here. But I don't think he'll be commenting on the weather."

"I know, Kit. I know."

McNaughton watched the dive team, whose boat had already moved a hundred yards from shore. He tried to wiggle his toes inside his wingtips, but realized they were numbing up. He stomped his feet, one at a time, to try to restore some circulation. While he and the others waited, a Marion County medical examiner's van pulled up, and Hans Bierbich, a forensic pathologist and deputy coroner, sprung out.

"I'm sorry I'm late," Bierbich said to McNaughton as they reached simultaneously to shake hands. "It takes longer to get up here than I expected."

"That's OK," Jack said.

"Jack, I contacted the Hamilton County coroner, and he was supposed to send somebody too, since this is their jurisdiction. Have you seen anybody yet?"

"No. But we haven't been here all that long."

Bierbich joined the silent entourage, as did the Hamilton County technician when he arrived ten minutes later. Stutz guessed that the air temperature hadn't even dropped to freezing and it still felt uncomfortably cold; he couldn't imagine how chilled the divers must feel.

Gill's radio squawked. "Max, we've got something here," Pretoria said from the boat. They'd been out for about forty-five minutes, methodically sweeping the lake in search of an unusual underwater shape.

"Does it look good enough for a dive?" Gill radioed back.

"Yeah. Gordon and Nicky are going down."

Fallows and Krance pulled on their masks and adjusted their mouth pieces and then, in unison, each swung one leg, then the other, over the side of the boat. They pushed off simultaneously and disappeared quickly below the choppy grey surface.

The wait seemed interminable, but was probably only five minutes or so. McNaughton saw a black hood surface, and a diver pulled the mouthpiece out. A moment later, Pretoria radioed again. "They think they got him," she said somberly. "He may be anchored down, so it may take a little effort.

"Ten-four," Gill responded.

No one else on shore spoke. They watched as the diver fixed his mask and submerged again, and then nothing happened for what again seemed an impossibly long time. Finally, something bobbed up; it looked like an inner tube. Then one black hood, and another, surfaced. Krance and Fallows retrieved whatever object had been casting a large and irregular vertical shape on the ultrasound machine and, with Pretoria and Wesley's help, they began hoisting it over the boat's side.

"Oh, shit," Allen said, covering his mouth with his hand and turning away from the lakefront. Alvear's head sunk low; there was no doubt that, whether or not this was Mitch, the dive team had located a body.

Again, the wait was agonizing. The misshapen, bloated body was difficult to maneuver; the sodden clothing made it particularly heavy and the body's submersion made it particularly slippery. Fallows could feel the skin slide unnaturally under his grasp, but he was no longer spooked by the horrid sensation; he'd retrieved far too many corpses to have this one strike him as any different. Finally, the dive team got the body into the boat, and Fallows and Krance followed. Wesley gassed the engine, and the boat headed straight toward the launch.

Those onshore used handkerchiefs or gloved hands to cover their noses and mouths as they moved toward the boat to view the fetid corpse. Everyone there had worked plenty of homicide scenes, and they knew the unmistakable odor of death – a stench to which one could never become accustomed. And they knew that a body that had been submerged, maybe for more than a week, would be even more rank.

The corpse, which had dark brown, shoulder-length hair, wore cheap blue jeans and a dark green hooded sweatshirt zipped all the way up. It was barefoot. The body was not as bloated as it might have been had it been summer; the water's frigid temperatures had kept the gases in check. But the fish and turtles had had their way, feasting on the soft tissues and rendering the corpse faceless.

"It's not Mitch," Kit said. She wasn't sure if she were alarmed or relieved. "He's too small."

"Yeah," Joe agreed. "Simons wouldn't have been caught dead in those clothes." He blanched when he realized what he had said.

McNaughton remained silent, studying the body that lay in front of them. He crouched and grasped the sweatshirt zipper, giving it a tug. It stuck, having been rusted by the water. He pulled harder, and it finally gave way. He pushed open the sides, revealing a large bullet wound, the edges of which had been gnawed by lake creatures. The hole, on the left side of the chest, was just below a tattoo of a skull with a dagger and a red rose through the eye socket. On the corpse's other breast was a heart with an illegible inscription.

"God," McNaughton said, almost whispering. "I think this is my snitch. I think it's Sniffy Smith."

"Shit," Alvear said, turning her back and walking away from the group.

"Folks," Gill said, "let's get back out there and keep looking for Mitch." His team went back to their boat to resume their search. The Hamilton County technician assisted Bierbich, who – by agreement with the Hamilton coroner – would be handling the findings here. They had not, however, discussed what to do if more than one body turned up.

McNaughton did not speak for a long time as he watched the dive team. He couldn't figure this – how did Sniffy get mixed up in Mitch's disappearance? Or was he? Could this be a horrible, sick coincidence? It was just all too bizarre to fathom.

Forty minutes after the first body was found, the radio squawked again. "We've got another hit," Pretoria said. "Tommy and I are going down this time."

It took even longer this time for the twosome to bring the object to the surface. Alvear, again teetering between emotions, was the first to observe, "They've got another body, guys."

As it had the first time, the group fell silent, preparing for another hideous sight. The lake life had feasted on the second corpse, just as it had with the first, making the face unrecognizable. The body was dressed in designer blue jeans, a long-sleeved denim shirt, athletic socks and Nike gym shoes. It appeared that the sleeves of the shirt had been rolled up; one still was partially in place and the other cuff hung open, revealing a tattoo. The skin on the neck and hands were a ghostly white, and strands of green algae snarled what appeared to be golden blond hair.

Alvear saw the rolled-up sleeves, the tattoo, the 7 For All Mankind jeans. She felt a sharp pain under her breast bone, and grasped her stomach. "Aw, Mitch," she said quietly.

CHAPTER 17

McNaughton was relieved that Hans Bierbich was the pathologist on duty when the bodies were pulled from Morse Lake. For one thing, Jack did not want to deal with the elected coroner, a pediatrician and politician who knew little about death and even less about forensic pathology. Bierbich, on the other hand, was a trained and experienced forensic pathologist and one of the best people on staff at the county coroner's office. What's more, he and McNaughton went way back, so Jack did not hesitate to ask Bierbich, shortly after he arrived on the scene, to do the cut on the lake corpses ahead of schedule. The pathologists generally handled autopsies as bodies came in, but if they were taken in order, these autopsies might be three days away. When Bierbich heard that one of the victims might be Mitch Simons, the pathologist immediately agreed to Jack's request.

And so it was just after six a.m. Wednesday morning, about twelve hours after the bodies had been brought in to the county morgue, when Bierbich was ready to begin his examination of the body McNaughton thought was Mitch.

"I worked with Simons several times when he was still in your squad," Bierbich said as he stood over the navy blue plastic body bag and reached for the zipper. "He was a nice guy. Flirted relentlessly with the receptionist, though."

"Yeah, that was Mitch," McNaughton said wistfully. He caught himself using a past-tense verb; he realized that there was little doubt in his mind that it was Mitch lying inside the thick plastic.

Chris Allen stood next to McNaughton. His face drooped, and he was already questioning his request that he be allowed to witness the autopsy along with Jack. It would be Allen's first, never a pleasant experience for rookie cops and one made even less so because the subject was a friend. His eyes darted as he briefly contemplated bolting from the room, but he knew he would never live it down – even if the only witnesses were McNaughton and Bierbich.

Bierbich adjusted the overhead microphone so that it was level with his mouth. He would dictate each of his findings as he made them, rather than waiting until the autopsy was completed and trying to remember details. It made for a much more complete record, which sometimes meant the difference between conviction and acquittal.

"Chris, make sure you keep your mask on," Bierbich reminded Allen. The odor from a body long immersed in water could be overpowering, and Bierbich had put tincture of benzoin on his and the cops' surgical masks to try to tame it. One of the morgue technicians had, at Bierbich's direction, placed the bodies in deep freeze the previous evening, another technique used to overcome the odor before it took you over.

"Chris," Bierbich began again, clearly pleased he had a student, "you may already know this, but the fingertips won't be in good enough shape to get us any useable prints," Bierbich continued. "I mentioned that to Alvear last evening, and she's getting dental records from Simons's dentist. We haven't a clue if the other guy ever visited a dentist; from the looks of his mouth, he hadn't recently. Our tech took X-rays of both of their mouths last evening, when the bodies first arrived."

Allen nodded; he pinched his lips tightly.

"Oh, and guys," the pathologist said, turning to McNaughton and Allen. Their eyes, all that was visible on each face, met. "This isn't going to be pretty. I know you saw the body at the lake, but it'll look even worse here, under these bright lights. As always, you're welcome to stay; you're welcome to observe. But I suggest you hang back a little bit. I know what Mitch meant to you."

McNaughton nodded. Even on run-of-the mill cases, he generally stayed back from the autopsy table, and he had no intention of changing his routine on this one. He looked at Allen. "Do you want out, Chris?"

"No, sarge," Allen said hesitantly. "I'll be OK."

"OK then," Bierbich said. He turned to the overhead mike and flipped a switch. "In the matter of Case Number zero-five-fifty-five," he began. Jack winced. Mitch had been reduced to a number.

It took about seventy-five minutes for Jack's friend to be rendered into a bunch of specimens. McNaughton had never before thought of an autopsy that way, but this one was different. He was able to watch only because it was hard to believe that what lay on the stainless steel table had been Mitch. The exterior of the body was in bad shape, having fallen victim to the water and its inhabitants, but it was not bloated. The water was too cold to allow many gases to build up. The internal organs, meanwhile, were well preserved, the result of submersion in the cold lake.

There was little unexpected. The body was seventy-four inches long, Mitch's height. It had longish, auburn hair. And what appeared to be a tattoo of Tweety Bird was still discernible on his right forearm, giving still another bit of confirmation to everyone's strong hunch that this was Mitch. McNaughton had always chuckled at the goofy little tattoo that a macho guy like Simons had submitted to, and Mitch had consistently refused to explain what had possessed him to mar his nearly perfect body with such a strange picture. After Bierbich dictated his findings about the tattoo, Jack let his mind wander to one of the many times he had teased Mitch about the Tweety, and he nearly smiled at the thought.

Bierbich concluded that death was caused by a single gunshot wound in the back from a large-caliber handgun. It was fired from at least several feet away, as there was no evidence of soot around the wound, which would indicate a close range.

"Looks like Mitch may have been trying to get away when he was shot," the pathologist observed to McNaughton and Allen.

"Geez," he continued, covering the microphone with a gloved hand. "Somebody really wanted him dead. Look at the size of this slug." He held up a misshapen missile that he had pried from the body's breastbone, its resting place after ripping a destructive path through Mitch's right lung and heart.

"Looks like a hollow-point," Bierbich said. "In pretty bad shape. A comparison's going to be a bitch." But having the slug to attempt the comparison was better than not finding it at all.

He turned back to the microphone and dictated. "Entrance wound in center of back at T-six with a small beveling, indicating a slight head-to-foot path. The bullet did not exit the front of the body because it splintered the vertebrae, T-seven and T-eight. Bone fragments were found in the lung. Lacerations of the aorta and heart suggest a tumbling of the bullet, which then stopped and imbedded in the sternum."

He held his hand in front of the microphone and turned to the officers. "I figure Mitch had about a minute to contemplate his fate before he ran out of blood to the brain."

Bierbich let the observers mull that notion as he continued his work. He had been right; there were no fingerprints to be had, so positive identification would have to wait until the dental comparison was completed.

Alvear retrieved the dental records and brought them to the morgue late that morning, after Bierbich had moved on to the body suspected to be Sniffy Smith. The pathologist broke away from that autopsy to peer at the dental X rays. A forensic dentist would have to confirm his findings, but Bierbich had done plenty of autopsies and the limited dental work on the corpse was so identifiable that he had no trouble drawing his own conclusion: This was Mitch Simons.

By late afternoon, the forensic dentist signed off on Bierbich's findings, and Hans called Jack with the news. "Thanks, Hans," McNaughton said. "I'll notify next of kin. When do you think they can have the body?"

"Tomorrow, I'd think. Shouldn't be any reason not to turn it over," he responded. "I'm still working on the other body. Do you know any next of kin?"

"No," Jack said. "But I'll see what I can come up with."

"Uh, Jack?"

"Yeah?"

"I'm really sorry about Mitch. About Sniffy too."

"Yeah. Me too."

McNaughton's decimated squad had been hanging around the squad room, waiting for the news they didn't want to hear. Each watched Jack's face as he took the call, and they knew what the news was from his demeanor.

"Folks, let's go into the conference room," McNaughton said. "We've got to talk."

They filed in – Alvear first, then Stutz, and Allen and McNaughton. Jack closed the door behind him and remained standing, even as the others took seats around the table.

"I don't think this'll surprise anybody. The ID's been confirmed. It was Mitch."

"Shit," Stutz said. The others were silent.

"I'm going to call his mom and his sister after we're done here," McNaughton continued. "I know we'll all want to help them out as much as possible, and attend the wake and the funeral and all. But let's not forget we've got a murder investigation going on here. I want the son of a bitch who did this to Mitch. I don't believe for a minute that that two-bit loser Jenkins was acting alone. What would a punk like him want with Mitch?"

"I agree," Alvear said. "I cannot believe this was home invasion or burglary. I mean, why would somebody bother with a little house like Mitch's when they could head up to some of the multi-zillionaires' houses in Carmel?"

Allen chimed in. "Do you s'pose Jenkins knew Mitch was a narc and thought he might have a stash at home?"

"It's worth considering," Jack said. "But that would suggest he was working alone, acting on his own behalf. I still think he was too much of a punk to take on a cop."

"Jack," Stutz began, "don't you think we've got enough to charge Jenkins now? I mean, what difference does it make *why* Jenkins did it, as long as we can prove that he did?"

"I think we're almost there. It'll help if ballistics can match the slug with the forty-five we got in Jenkins' hotel room. But with a body and all the circumstantial evidence, and with Lisa Myers' testimony, it's pretty solid. But let's make it airtight, folks. What haven't we covered?"

"Shit," Joe said. "I forgot to tell you about the phone records from the hotel."

"What about them?" McNaughton said.

"Well, this morning, while you were at the morgue, I was checking the places Jenkins had called. Nothing too exciting – Domino's Pizza delivery, the liquor store, an adult video and book store. But he made a couple of calls to a local attorney – um," he hesitated, looking at the notes he had made – "a Baden Baden. Ever hear of him?"

"Sure," Alvear said. "He's a defense attorney. Takes a lot of low-lifes' cases. Maybe Jenkins knew he was in deep shit and wanted to line up an attorney, just in case."

McNaughton pulled out the chair at the head of the table and sat down. His squad members could tell he was deep in thought, and they fell silent, waiting for him to speak. Finally, Alvear had had enough.

"What, Jack?" she asked, the irritation evident in her voice. "Do you know something about this goofball Baden Baden that we oughta know?"

"Back during the Peterson trial, Sniffy called me and told me that Baden Baden was looking for a hit man. Sniffy was gonna get wired up and go see him for me, but that fucking Stumbo . . ."

"What does Stumbo have to do with it?" Stutz asked.

"That's what I'm gonna find out."

McNaughton drove furiously to the jail, a four-story building that lay a block south of the boring City-County Building and was equally nondescript. That put it about a mile from the downtown homicide squad room. Jack had declined Alvear's pushy suggestion that she accompany him; he wanted Rodney Jenkins to himself. Kit, frustrated at Jack's decision, decided to drive to Kokomo to inform and console Mitch's family; Stutz asked to tag along.

The lights seemed to be against him, and McNaughton pounded on the steering wheel at every red one. The ten-minute drive turned into an irritating fifteen, and then he spent another three or four minutes looking for a spot in the ever-crowded police-parking lot. Finally ensconced in a place that could not have been farther from the jailhouse entrance, Jack jogged to the front door and badged the attending officer.

The uniform nodded at him and pressed the buzzer that automatically unlocked the door. McNaughton nodded back, in no mood for pleasantries. He walked quickly past the elevator bank and took the stairs, two at a time, to the second floor. The smell of disinfectant was nauseating; McNaughton wondered how anyone could work, let alone live, here. At the front desk, he again flashed his badge.

"I wanna see Rodney Jenkins," he said curtly. Again, no pleasantries. This officer nodded too, and pushed an intercom button to alert the uniform who'd bring Jenkins to an interview room.

It was an antiquated process that was irritating in the best of times, and this was far from it. McNaughton paced, unable to calm himself enough to sit in one of the hard wooden chairs that had been placed in the waiting area for officers in his exact situation. This sometimes took five minutes, sometimes twenty, and there was no predicting when or why it would become protracted. Jack peered at his watch repeatedly, watching the minutes – five, then seven, then nine – tick away. He had just looked again, registering that it was now eleven minutes since his request, when a new uniform poked his head out of a steel door.

"Sergeant McNaughton?"

Jack nodded.

"We've got Jenkins for you. He's in interview room A."

"Thanks," McNaughton mumbled. He passed through the door and past the officer, heading for a room that he'd visited many times over the years.

Jenkins was digging in his nose and standing with his back to the door when McNaughton entered.

"Quit picking your nose and sit down," McNaughton ordered sternly.

Jenkins quickly pushed his hand into his pocket but remained standing.

"I said sit down," McNaughton repeated, this time pushing Jenkins on his scrawny shoulders for emphasis.

Jenkins stared back defiantly. "I ain't got to talk to you. I got me a lawyer."

"Yeah, so I noticed in court, asshole," McNaughton answered. "I don't give a shit. I'm not interested in what you have to say; I'm here to do the talking."

"Well, I don't give a shit what *you* have to say," Jenkins retorted. "Why don't you just leave me alone?"

"You know, you're awfully rude for somebody who's being paid a courtesy visit. I'm a busy person. I'm taking time out of my busy schedule to do you a favor."

Jenkins did his best to hide his curiosity. McNaughton ignored the effort and continued.

"I'm just here to let you know, asshole, that you're going to fry," Jack said, leaving out that Indiana used lethal injection, not the electric chair, to dispatch its condemned prisoners. "We found Mitch Simons's body in Morse Lake where you dumped him. Sniffy Smith's too." He was nearly spitting the words at Jenkins, whose eyes widened upon hearing the news. "I watched Mitch get autopsied this morning. Now it's just a matter of time before

I can watch the pathologist do the same thing to your stinking body, fresh from the electric chair."

"Just leave me alone," Jenkins growled. "I got nothin' to say to you."

"I don't care what you have to say or not say, you son of a bitch. Our case against you is so solid that I'm already planning which suit I'm going to wear to your execution. You don't ever have to open your mouth, and I've got you cold."

"Go tell it to my lawyer."

"Your lawyer? That snot-nosed P.D.? Hell, he can't even find his own ass with both hands. The good news for you, though, is that I expect you'll be getting a more experienced lawyer any day now. The bad news, asshole, is that's because you're about to be charged with a capital offense – murder of a police officer. And it's only a matter of time before we pin Sniffy's murder on you too. So the court will appoint somebody with experience in death-penalty cases. As far as I can tell, all that means is that it'll be somebody who's watched flames shooting out of the ears of several of his clients."

Jenkins flinched, but stared defiantly at the marred, carved-up table in front of him, trying hard not to let McNaughton see that he was rattled.

McNaughton balled up his fists and planted them on the table, leaning over at the waist to do so. His face was no more than a foot from Jenkins'. He continued: "And what makes you think that your precious P.D. could give a shit about you anyway? Oh, he'll go through the motions, whatever it takes to collect his guaranteed hundred bucks an hour for trial work. Then after we convict your ass, some other lawyer with *experience*" – the word dripped with sarcasm – "will bill the state for twenty grand for your appeal, which means he'll copy a bunch of briefs that other lawyers have written for other scumbags who killed other people and ended up in the electric chair too.

"All the while, he'll be screwing his wife at night and his girlfriend over the lunch hour, while you're playing with yourself – if you're lucky – or you're taking it in the ass from your new prison boyfriend. And ten years from now, you're *still* going to have your head shaved and your leg shaved and you're *still* going to make that last walk to Old Smoky up in Michigan City, and they're *still* going to fry your ass. And that lawyer? He'll make sure he earns his twenty grand by shedding a tear or two for the TV cameras as he explains what a crime against humanity this all is and how the state has no right to take your fucking life, as sorry a fucking life as it is."

McNaughton poked his forefinger toward Jenkins for emphasis. "But you know what? It won't make a bit of difference, because his last official act will be to watch as they send twenty-three-hundred volts of electricity through your brain and you piss and shit all over yourself and jerk and twitch till you're dead."

"You're crazy, man! Why don't you shut the fuck up?" Jenkins shouted, his voice quivering almost imperceptibly.

"No, fuckhead. I'm not crazy. Too bad I'm not, because that'd give me a good excuse for wringing your fucking scrawny neck, and then some jury would let me off because I couldn't help myself. No – I'm not crazy. I'm just telling you like it is."

McNaughton stood upright again and began to pace. He continued his narrative: "After it's all over and the coroner's got you on his cold steel table and your lawyer's been crying all over the tube, well, then he'll go off for a drink to drown his sorrows over his poor, pitiful client. While the doc is hosing you down, 'cause he can't stand your stink, your lawyer is going to be downing his third scotch-and-water, and he'll be wondering if the cameras got his best side. Then, while the doc is carving this big, ol' Y into your chest" – he traced the letter over his own body – "your lawyer'll be on his fourth drink, and he'll be admitting to his buddies that, as bad as the death penalty is, well, at least that's one more scumbag who can't kill anybody else. And then, while the doc is peeling back your face, that lawyer of yours – on drink number six by now – will be peeling a jumbo shrimp and dunking it in cocktail sauce, and he'll comment on how, if truth be told, you looked kinda comical the way you were twitching and jerking and how it kinda reminded him of his cousin doing the funky chicken. And all his lawyer buddies'll laugh. And then, while the doc is using a Stryker saw to cut open your skull – and while he's pulling out your frazzled, charred brain – your devoted lawyer will be on his tenth scotch, and will be feeling kind of sappy and he'll offer up a toast to the dearly departed Rodney Jenkins. And maybe he and his lawyer friends will sing a little Irish wake song for you.

"The next morning, when your precious lawyer wakes up with a helluva hangover, he'll decide that you've caused him a lot of stress and that he really needs a vacation. So he'll have his secretary book him a long weekend in the Bahamas, and maybe he'll take the wife, or maybe the girlfriend, or maybe he'll just go so he can ogle the girls with asses and tits hanging out of little threads of material that pass for bikinis. And while he's soaking up the sun and sipping pina coladas, you, Rodney – your pitiful, fried, pieced-back-together body – will be getting lowered into the ground, six feet under. And your mama will be crying big tears right on top of you."

McNaughton stopped pacing and leaned into Jenkins' face. "So don't tell me to go talk to your lawyer, Rodney. 'Cause your lawyer doesn't give a rat's ass about you or any other scumbag he represents – not as long as the state's paying the way."

He fell silent, and pulled a chair out from under the table. He plopped into it, exhausted, and sat directly across from Jenkins, who was still staring at the table. A few moments of silence passed.

"*Fuck it!*" Jenkins said abruptly. "I am not going down for any scumbag lawyer. I didn't *know* he was a cop," he said plaintively. "I swear to you: I didn't know."

"Tell it to your lawyer, Rodney," McNaughton said unsympathetically.

"No! I want to tell you! Shit – my lawyer won't even take my calls!"

"Kingsley won't take your calls?" McNaughton's voice betrayed a smidgeon of concern.

"No, man. Not the P.D. *My* lawyer – Baden Baden. He said he'd be my lawyer. He said he'd get me off. Hell, he said I'd never get caught. And now he won't even take my calls."

Jack glared silently, unsympathetically, at Jenkins, who felt pressured to continue.

"It was Baden, man. He hired me to do the guy. He didn't tell me it was a cop; he just said he had this important client who had to get somebody out of the way – that this rival was causing him trouble. I didn't know he was a cop. You gotta believe me."

McNaughton still did not speak.

"You *gotta* believe me. Baden said I'd get ten grand for doing it – two up front and eight when the job was done. And then after I did Simons, he says I've gotta off Sniffy to get the other eight. Said that Sniffy was getting too nosy. That cocksucker said he'd take care of things if the heat came down – that his important client knew all the right people. But he never came through with my money."

"Who's the client?"

"I don't know, man. All I know is he's supposed to be some big-time dealer. You gotta believe me. I did *not* know Simons was a cop!"

McNaughton opened the door to the interview room and stuck his head out. "Officer," he called, "I'm about through in here." He turned back to Jenkins.

"Rodney," he said, "you'd better be telling the truth about not knowing who the client is." Then his voice softened; there was no emotion in it. "You need to contact your P.D. and tell him what you've told me and tell him you're willing to make an official statement in exchange for the state not seeking the death penalty. He can approach the prosecutor with the deal."

"Will the prosecutor agree? Will you put in a good word for me?"

McNaughton peered at the man who'd taken the lives of two friends and said nothing. He let the uniformed officer lead Jenkins away.

The red lights did not irritate Jack on the way back; he simply ignored them. Having flipped on his flashing grill lights and siren, he made the return trip as quickly as the car could carry him, flying over bumps and causing traffic to stop dead still as he passed without care. It was dusk now, making it more difficult for McNaughton to see other cars and for his to be seen, even with the flashing lights. Thoughts flew through his brain, and he began to put it all together. Sniffy and Stumbo and Jenkins and Mitch and . . .

It was too much to comprehend. It couldn't be. But the evidence was there: Just as surely as Jenkins had pulled the trigger, Stumbo had made it possible for him to do so. Jack's heart ached as he negotiated the last turn and pulled haphazardly up to the curb in front of the stationhouse.

Stumbo's red Mustang was in the parking lot; for once, he had not snuck out early. McNaughton didn't know what he would do; he didn't care.

He bounded from the Ford, forgetting to lock it – or not caring what some supervisor from a department that would let his friend die had to say about something so ultimately insignificant. He dashed into the stationhouse, ignoring the mindless greeting of the bored uniform manning the front desk, and took the stairs as if his feet had wings. The squad room was empty, thank God. Stumbo was in his office, playing with paper clips or with himself or God knew what.

"Doyle, you asshole," Jack said, his voice more filled with passion than anger. "How could you do it?"

"What the fuck are you talking about, McNaughton?" Stumbo replied, looking up from a fat book he had laying before him. He was chewing on a toothpick, which he pulled from his mouth and studied. He returned it there and ingested the bit of food he had harvested from his teeth. Then, trying to be nonchalant, he lifted some papers from his desk and laid them across the open pages. McNaughton noticed the furtive move.

"It'd be nice if you knocked."

"Shut up, Doyle," McNaughton said, pacing a step or two in front of the desk. "Don't you know what you've done? You've killed Mitch. And Sniffy Smith."

"Are you nuts, McNaughton?" Stumbo said angrily. "Simons got hisself in trouble. He was sloppy. If you want to blame anybody but the triggerman, blame your pal. And who the hell is Sniffy Smith?"

"You don't get it, do you? You son of a bitch. You and your bombastic pronouncements about the way we'll do things around here. You and your utter ignorance of the law. You and your steadfast refusal to acknowledge that anybody might know more than you." McNaughton was pointing at Stumbo now, poking the air with vehemence. "*You* got Mitch killed. If you had just listened to me when I told you about the hit that Sniffy suspected. But, no. You were so sure in your ignorance that we'd be violating attorney-client privilege if we moved on our tip. It had nothing to do with attorney-client privilege, you fool. It had to do with *murder*. And now Mitch is dead and Sniffy is dead and you're to blame.

"But that doesn't matter to you, does it? You don't even have the decency to feel badly about this. Hell, you don't have the decency to remember the name of the snitch you got killed. It just doesn't matter to you. All that matters to you and this entire fucking department is getting the paperwork done. Or cutting costs. Solving crimes? Hell, who cares about that? Saving lives? So what? Investigations cost money, and God forbid that we spend any taxpayers' money for fear that the mayor may not get re-elected. Let's get more patrolmen out writing tickets, because that brings in money and makes the mayor happy. And investigations are messy; everything's not cut and dried and nice and neat and tied up in a little package with a little bow. They involve people who have to take risks and make decisions and use their discretion, and that just goes against every fiber in your ridiculous body."

Stumbo's eyes were frozen in a defiant gaze, his lips pinched hard around a toothpick. Yet he flinched as McNaughton raged. "You wouldn't know how to be a real cop if your life depended on it, Doyle. All you care about is what makes you look good with the brass or what covers your oversized ass. Whatever's easy. Whatever won't cause you the least bit of consternation. Only you fucked up on this one. It was easier, or so you thought, to stop me dead in my tracks and deny me the use of a body transmitter, even when I told you it might be a matter of life and death. You idiot! It *was* a matter of life and death. Your easy, incompetent, obstinate way backfired! You got two dead bodies out of it, a dead cop to boot."

Stumbo broke in. "I've had about enough of you, McNaughton. Get out of here before I get pissed off."

"What, Doyle, and draw an I-number on me? Don't bore me. Every time anybody in the department puts his neck on the line and tries to do the right thing, you and the rest of the brass cut it off at your first chance. You and your stupid I-numbers. Do you think I give a flying fuck if you write me up? For God's sake, it's become a joke: A murderous drunk pisses all over himself, and they draw an I-number on you. Fail to file one of your all-important reports by a day – even if you're in the middle of a major investigation that has you working forty-eight hours straight – and they draw an I-number on you. Hell, work forty-eight hours straight, without an OK written in your blood, and they draw an I-number on you. Fart in the office, and they'll draw an I-number on you. Don't you see how ridiculous you all are?"

He paused for a moment, and then continued. "In a way, Mitch is the lucky one. He's gone; he no longer has to decide if he can stand another minute of this absurd charade, of this game where we're playing at being police officers. But I'm stuck: I have to decide if I can endure another minute of this, if trying to fight the good fight means that much to me, or if you've finally gone too far. All the frustrations and the shame of being associated with this department have built up so much over the years, and now this. Now I find out this department – *you*, Doyle – have killed my friend. Two friends."

"McNaughton, you've gone and lost your mind. You're babbling," Stumbo said, then allowed his voice to soften. "But I understand; you're upset about your friend getting hisself killed.

That's OK. I'll overlook this insubordination because I expect you'll think better of it in the morning."

"What, Doyle? You think this'll all go away if you can just get me to calm down? I know you'd be all too happy to file insubordination charges against me if you weren't afraid that your role in these deaths would come to light as a result. You're wrong, Doyle. I will *not* feel better in the morning. I will feel worse, because it will have been another day gone without my friend, a cop whose talents you can only dream about. And it'll be another day on which I've got to deal with the fact that you and this department killed him."

Stumbo sneered, and his voice turned hard again. "Get over it, McNaughton. Simons is dead, and I'm getting a little tired of hearing all these tributes to him. You know, he was a fuck-up in life, and he fucked up and got hisself dead. And your goddamn snitch. He was probably hopped up on coke ninety percent of the time. Some loss to society. So leave me alone. Go cry in a beer – if you haven't already had a half dozen."

"You really don't get it, do you, Doyle? Rodney Jenkins talked. He admitted Baden Baden hired him to kill Mitch and Sniffy. Does that name sound familiar? Baden Baden? In case you've forgotten, in November I came to you to tell you that Sniffy thought Baden Baden was trying to put a contract out on somebody. He was my most reliable snitch, and I heard the signals Baden was sending to Sniffy. But you wouldn't let me act on it, and now Mitch and Sniffy are both dead. You killed them, Doyle. Simple as that."

"Get out of my office, McNaughton. I'm busy. I'm studying for the promotions exam so I can get away from the likes of you and all the fools who work for you. Fuck you all."

"You? Promoted? I don't think lightning strikes twice in the same place, Doyle. The brass has got to be on to you by now; even those idiots can't have missed how stupid you are. And just in case there is any doubt, I'll tell everybody from the mayor to the news media about this royal fuck-up. You piece of shit."

"I said, get out of my office! I'm busy!"

"What are you reading, anyway, Doyle?" McNaughton pulled the thick book out from under Stumbo's hands, as Stumbo tried too late to grab it and stop him.

McNaughton scanned the page, of which passages were highlighted in bright yellow. "What the hell does 'dissociative reaction' have to do with the promotions exam, Doyle?"

Stumbo hesitated. "I just got sidetracked. I was about to get back to my studying." His voice had the guilty quality of a teenager who'd been caught with a Playboy tucked inside his geography book.

"Where'd you get this book?"

Stumbo did not answer.

"I said, where'd you get this?" Again, Stumbo remained silent. McNaughton closed the book and saw that it was a text: "Abnormal Psychology." Then he noticed the edge of a light blue booklet peering out from the pages of the book. He flipped to the booklet, the ubiquitous college-exam blue book.

The blank lines on the front had been filled in: *John P. Peterson. Psych 305. Abnormal Psychology.*

"Peterson? This is John Pius Peterson's book?" McNaughton was incredulous. "What the hell are you doing with Peterson's book?"

"Well, I, uh. . . "

"*Answer* me, Doyle! Where did you get this book?"

"Well, I borrowed it." Again, the same guilty nervousness.

"You *borrowed* it? From where?"

"I didn't think it'd make any difference." He was defensive now. "I thought it'd help me on the promotions exam."

"Doyle, *answer* me!" McNaughton roared. "Where did you get this book?"

"From a bookcase in the Peterson house!" Stumbo shouted back defiantly. "What the hell difference does it make?"

"You stupid, fucking idiot! It makes all the difference in the world! It makes the difference between John Pius Peterson paying for butchering six little kids or walking the streets a free man! Don't you see what you've done? We could have proved he concocted his insanity if we had had this book! Obviously, this is where he got the information he needed to fake his insanity – to concoct that perfect act of his, one that a jury believed. You idiot!"

Stumbo began sputtering, unable to form words. McNaughton's eyes bugged out; the muscles in his neck tightened. His throat closed, and he could not swallow. He spit out his words: "You *fool*! Peterson got away with murdering six little kids, and Mitch is dead – all because of you!"

McNaughton's mind shut down; his body acted on its own as he dove over Stumbo's desk and slapped his hands around the huge neck. Papers and paper clips flew off the desk as McNaughton squeezed and squeezed, and Stumbo's arms and legs flailed.

"You fucking idiot!" McNaughton screamed again and again, as he squeezed harder and harder. Stumbo's eyes grew wide and protruded from his skull; his flaccid skin turned deep red. He struggled to pry McNaughton's fingers from his neck, pulling them backwards as hard as he could, trying to inflict enough pain for McNaughton's grip to loosen. But it was futile. McNaughton instincts had taken over; he could not stop.

And then, as the sun sunk below the horizon and darkness fell over the city, it was over. Jack, breathing hard, used both hands to push himself off Stumbo's chest. He sat on the desk for a moment, gulping air, feeling his heart beating wildly in his chest. He swung his legs around and stood, then peered at Stumbo's lifeless face, its eyes protruding, its mouth agape. Reality crashed into his brain.

"Oh, my God," McNaughton said quietly. "Oh, my God."

Chapter 18

"Are you out of your mind, Jack?" Renee screamed at him.

"No, Renee," he said calmly. "That's just the point."

"Don't you dare be so self-righteous with me! Don't you dare be so condescending!" She tramped heavily around the sparsely furnished room, her arms crossed tightly across her chest.

Jack, wearing jailhouse orange scrubs, was seated in one of the two chairs at the gray steel table. He turned in his chair to follow her with his eyes.

"I want you to come home and think about what you're saying," she said. "Angel needs you. I need you. I cannot hold down a job and be a single mother and keep the house and do everything that we're supposed to do together. How can you even contemplate such a stupid thing?"

"Renee," he said, his voice even, "I've thought about this, and you can't changed my mind. Don't you think I've thought about you and Angel? Don't you think I've considered how hard it would be on both of you for me to be away? Don't you think I've thought about how damaging this could be to my relationship with Angel – and to my relationship with you?"

"No, I don't, Jack. If you'd thought this through, you'd never even consider it." The anger faded; her voice became plaintive. "If you won't change your mind for us, then think about your career.

Are you willing to throw away all your hard work over all these years?"

"Forget about the career," he said soberly. "It's over anyway. And I'm not particularly sorry about that part of this whole mess."

A hollow-sounding knock interrupted them. A jailer opened the steel door and stood aside to usher Knofel Fortner in.

"Jack. Renee," Fortner said by way of greeting them. He grasped the back of the second chair and looked to Renee in a silent offer of it. She shook her head sharply and continued to pace; Knofel took the chair. "Have the two of you had the chance to discuss Jack's wishes?"

"No," Renee said angrily. She gestured animatedly. "He won't discuss it. He says he's made up his mind."

Knofel looked to Jack and raised an eyebrow.

"She's right," McNaughton said. "I know how I want to handle this, and that's it. No discussion needed."

"Knofel," Renee said, "can you at least explain our options?"

Fortner turned to Jack. "OK?"

"Yeah, sure," McNaughton said, running a hand through his graying hair. "But don't expect me to change my mind."

Knofel began: "I don't think there should be any problem persuading the judge to set a low bond at this morning's hearing, and you should be able to go home pending trial. As you both know, my recommendation is that we go to trial and that Jack pleads 'not guilty by reason of insanity.' Jack, we can make a solid case that you suffered from temporary insanity brought on my excessive stress. We can put the entire police department on trial. Show the pressure Stumbo and the rest of them constantly put on you. Show how Mitch's death tore away more of your composure. Show how Sniffy Smith's death added to the burden. And make a case that the relentless pressure, brought to a climax when you learned of Stumbo's culpability in two deaths and the Peterson acquittal, rendered you temporarily insane.

"You're a lawyer's dream client, Jack. Your record is clean – exemplary, really. You've never so much as stolen a candy bar from the dime store. Your whole career has been spent putting away the bad guys. You're smart. You're articulate. You're good-looking. You're sincere. I think a jury would have an easy time sympathizing with you."

McNaughton sat with his head down, slowly shaking his dissent. "That's not what I want to do," he said quietly.

Renee spoke up. "Knofel, give it to us straight. What if the jury doesn't buy the insanity plea?"

"Well," Fortner began, "first off, I think we have a reasonable chance of persuading the prosecutor to reduce the charge to manslaughter. We're not sure who that's going to be, though. Obviously, Terry Bennett needs to recuse himself, and really his people have to do the same. I would think he'd move to have a special prosecutor appointed. Even if we get some grandstanding political type who refuses to entertain a lesser charge, I'm sure any judge in Indiana would be willing to include manslaughter as a lesser included offense when he instructs the jury."

"So what would that mean if the jury convicted Jack of manslaughter?" Renee asked.

"Voluntary manslaughter is a Class B felony, which carries five to twenty. As you know, he'd serve half of whatever the judge gave him, earning the other half off his sentence because of good behavior. I'd think any reasonable judge would go for the minimum, given Jack's history and the circumstances, but I can't guarantee it. Judges run for reelection too."

Renee thought for a moment. "And what's the worst-case scenario, Knofel?" she asked. "Death penalty?"

"No," Fortner said. "It's not even an option. Worst-case scenario, I believe is that the state won't budge on the murder charge, Jack will be found guilty and he'll get forty years, out in twenty. There are no aggravating circumstances, so there's no reason for the judge to enhance the sentence. But I gotta tell you, I just don't see this happening. I think voluntary manslaughter is much more reasonable – and an acquittal even more so. I cannot imagine he'd be found guilty of murder."

"I can't take the chance," Jack said. "You know and I know that, if that happened, there's a chance I could get life without the possibility of parole. I might as well hang myself right now. But even with twenty, Angel would be an adult when I got out. I'd lose her forever." His blue eyes peered at Renee. "I'd lose *you* forever."

They all remained silent for a few moments.

"Besides," he continued, "I cannot go into that courtroom and say I'm not guilty because I was insane. I'm *not* insane. I know the difference between right and wrong. I *chose* to kill Stumbo. I have to take responsibility for that decision."

"Jack," Renee said, "you were pushed into this. If ever there was a case when somebody just snapped, this is it."

"Yes, I snapped. OK? I don't deny that a lot of things came to a head. I was frustrated with the department's massive incompetence and wrongheadedness about serving the bureaucracy. I was grieving over Mitch and even Sniffy. I was sick to death of I-numbers and internal investigations and Stumbo's intransigence over everything my team and I wanted to do in the name of good law enforcement. But none of that excused what I did. I was wrong.

"Anyway, think about what you're asking me to do. Renee, honey, how many times have I railed to you about the people who got off with the insanity defense? Knofel, do you have any idea how much I hated you for helping Peterson get off with that defense? When is *somebody* going to take responsibility for his actions?"

"Jack, I don't see why you should be the scapegoat for some political cause," Renee said.

"Listen. I was out front on that issue. The legislature is sure to pass the 'guilty but mentally ill' verdict before the session ends in April. If I try to take advantage of the current law – the very law I've railed against in such a public way – how will that look? Let John Pius Peterson be the poster child for why we need the new law – not me.

"Can you imagine the field day the newspapers and the politicians would have if I tried to get off by saying I was nuts? Can you imagine the headline: 'Cop wants law toughened for everybody but him.' Or 'Cop says he's insane but nobody else is.' I can't let that happen."

"I don't care what anybody else thinks, Jack," Renee said. "This is our lives you're talking about, not a political cause. Anyway, you never objected to the insanity defense being used when the person was truly insane. And you heard Knofel say that he thinks we can make a pretty good case that you were – at least temporarily."

"Was I?" Jack asked. "I don't know what I was at the very moment that I chose to lay my hands on Doyle's neck. I don't think it matters. The fact is, I knew the difference between right and wrong. I was furious with Doyle, and I took his punishment into my own hands. I admit I wasn't thinking about all the ramifications of my actions at that very moment. But it was my choice. My decision. I'm guilty. And I think I should plead guilty. If I don't, and if somehow I get off, I'm not sure I can live with myself."

He looked at Renee, whose face was mournful. "But Jack, I don't know if we can live *without* you."

McNaughton leaned back in the uncomfortable, grey fabric chair, a too-small barrel with an unnaturally straight back, and stretched his legs in front of him. He locked his fingers and cupped his hands around the crown of his head, bony elbows splayed outward and upward. He closed his eyes and sighed.

"That's it, doc," he said, as he lay his hands back on his thighs. "That's the story."

"Well, not quite, Jack," Bernstein replied. He was a narrow and soft-spoken man who sat with his shoulders curved inward. His small eyes were black slits behind black-framed glasses, and his thin lips were deeply cracked. "I'm curious about a few more things. Did the police ever solve the murders of Mitch and Sniffy?"

"Baden Baden was such a wuss. My squad arrested him, based on Jenkins' testimony, and Baden was so scared that, after he cleaned himself up for shitting in his pants, he immediately implicated the guy who hired him. Luther Grubbs. We'd been right all along; we just couldn't prove it."

Bernstein took a tube of Chapstick from his breast pocket and applied it to his lips as Jack continued.

"My squad did a great job. Grubbs got convicted for both Mitch and Sniffy's murders and got the death penalty. He had several aggravators – killing a cop, multiple murders, murder for hire. Jenkins cooperated, so he got life without parole. Baden got sixty years.

"Last I heard, John Peterson was still in the loony bin. I hear that, if he ever gets out, they want to try him for perjury for lying under oath about his involvement in his children's deaths. Not much of a charge, but they can't go after him for murder again because of double jeopardy. I keep hoping the feds will get involved and charge him with depriving the kids of their civil rights, but I guess they've got better things to do than go after a perfectly sane guy who's in the nuthouse."

"You already know that I pleaded guilty to voluntary manslaughter – intentionally causing a death in the heat of passion. It seemed to me it fit. Up until the moment I did it, I didn't want Doyle dead. Hell, I tried to save his life on the basketball court.

"Anyway, I got ten years. I've been a model prisoner for five; you say the word, and I'm outta here."

"Uh huh." Bernstein was noncommittal. "Has Renee come to accept your decision?"

"She had no choice. She was plenty pissed for a while – a long time, really. But she's a smart person, and she eventually understood why I had to plead guilty. She also came around to realizing that five years – and I'm assuming you're going to make it just five years, doc – is better than what I would have gotten if I'd been convicted of murder. She and Knofel kept telling me that the jury would empathize with me. But I kept telling them that you can't predict what a jury will do. God, we all learned that with the Peterson verdict.

"But it's been hard. I miss Renee and Angel *so* much. They visit, of course, and I get to hug them and kiss them in a private interview room, since I'm in solitary. You know, they can't mix me with the general population – I've put too many of my fellow inmates in here."

His voice became wistful. "I think I miss the mornings most, when I used to go into Angel's room to wake her, and she smelled of sleep – you know, that sweet smell that children have because they haven't been tainted by coffee and cigarettes and spicy foods and stuff. And I'd nestle down next to her in her warm bed for a few minutes before Renee would call us for breakfast, and we'd cuddle and just lie there, not speaking. Yeah, I miss that, and I'm afraid she won't have any interest in that now, because she's grown up so much."

"Everything I've seen and heard, Jack, leads me to believe you're ready to get out of here," Bernstein said. He rubbed his lips together to spread the Chapstick. "I understand the parole board has already given its OK, pending mine. But before I sign you out of here, let me ask you: Do you think you're ready to get out?"

"Yeah, I'm ready. I know things will be tough, especially at first. Among other things," he said, his voice lightening, "I have no way to make a living. Who wants a broken down ex-cop who has a manslaughter conviction on his record?"

Bernstein nearly smiled. "I'm sure you'll find ways to contribute to society again, Jack. I have a lot of faith in you."

"More than I have in myself, I fear," McNaughton said, turning serious again. "The one thing I still haven't come to terms with is how I could let one irrational moment ruin my whole life – render everything I've done meaningless."

"Is that true? Has your act against Doyle Stumbo erased all the good you did as a police officer? Did it erase the happy marriage that you and Renee put together? Did it erase the good job you and Renee have done with Angelica?"

"Maybe. I guess I'll find out more about Renee and Angel after I get out of here."

"You should continue with counseling, as a family and individually. Do you think you're ready to face frustrations again?"

"If you're asking me if I plan to kill another boss, the answer is no. I suppose that the mere possibility will limit my employability." He smirked. "I shouldn't speak ill of the dead – and please understand that I'm not blaming him for his own death – but Doyle Stumbo represented what is wrong with too many police departments and, for that matter, what is wrong with too many employers, even in the private sector. Everybody is out to cover their own ass, not do the job. Everybody is out to advance themselves – through promotions or getting rich or whatever – but not concerned about doing what's right. I knew that then, but I had lost sight of it – blinded, really, by Mitch's death and the Peterson verdict. I resorted to the very thing I most abhor – violence. But now, having spent time in here and talking with you so often, I've regained that insight and I can confidently say that I will never resort to violence again."

"You had high expectations for humanity, Jack. Unrealistically high expectations," Bernstein said. "You expected Stumbo to be a good boss, not an insecure, pitiful person who was frightened that his incompetence would be exposed. You expected the department to be free of backstabbing and pettiness and bureaucracy and the criminal justice system to administer justice. It'd be nice, but life doesn't work that way."

"I know."

Bernstein continued. "Your high expectations didn't stop there. You expected Renee to accept your decision about pleading guilty without questioning it and without thinking about the effect it would have on her and Angel."

"That's true."

"And," the psychiatrist said, "you have unrealistic expectations of yourself. You set yourself up as supercop. You expected yourself to always be strong. You expected yourself to solve every case that comes your way. You expected that all the people who dare to commit a crime on your watch to be convicted. You expected jurors to always believe you. And you thought that you should be able to prevent people who work with you – Mitch, Sniffy – from getting hurt.

"I think you've made great strides by coming to realize that others can't always live up to your high expectations – that they shouldn't necessarily have to. Realizing that will save you from great disappointments in the future. But when are you going to place more realistic expectations on yourself? You, and only you, can decide to do that."

McNaughton leaned forward, resting his elbows on his knees. He placed his palms together, his hands touching as if in prayer. He pressed his fingers to his lips, and then moved them again to speak.

"I guess it's time I do that."

He leaned back and closed his misty eyes, then pinched the bridge of his nose, trying to hold back tears that he had not allowed to fall since that day in Mitch's house.

But there was no stopping them now.

THE END

AUTHORS' NOTE

This book is a work of fiction. Resemblances of the police officers and peripheral characters to real people are coincidental. However, we took inspiration from our real-life experiences as newspaper reporter and police officer, so a few of the bad guys share characteristics with some of the convicted criminals with whom we've crossed paths over the years. Mary has had the unenviable experience of covering two cases in which fathers killed all of their children. As a police officer and as a lawyer, Tim has witnessed the many stressors that police officers face, some of which have to do with the incredibly bureaucratic structure of large police departments.

LaVergne, TN USA
28 August 2009
156267LV00004B/1/P

9 781449 014469